Ars Poetica

A Postmodern Parable

Also by Clay Reynolds:

Fiction:

The Vigil
Agatite
Franklin's Crossing
Players
Monuments
The Tentmaker
Threading the Needle

Nonfiction:

Taking Stock: A Larry McMurtry Casebook
The Plays of Jack London
Stage Left: The Development of the American Social Drama

Ars Poetica

A Postmodern Parable

Clay Reynolds

Texas Review Press
Huntsville, Texas

FIRST EDITION, 2003

Requests for permission to reproduce material from this work should be
sent to:

Permissions
Texas Review Press
English Department
Sam Houston State University
Huntsville, TX 77341-2146

*Author's Note: Names, places, incidents and characters are a
product of the author's imagination or are used fictionally, and
any resemblance to actual persons, living or dead, business
establishments, institutions, organizations, or locales is
entirely coincidental. This especially applies to the main
character: no one, living or dead, has ever been that lucky.*

Cover design by Kellye Sanford

Library of Congress Cataloging-in-Publication Data

Reynolds, Clay, 1949-
Ars poetica : a postmodern parable / Clay Reynolds.—
1st ed.
    p. cm.
ISBN 1-881515-48-6 (alk. paper)
1. Poets—Fiction. 2. Texas, West—Fiction. I. Title.
PS3568.E8874 A84 2003
813'.54—dc21

2002014498

For Sam—thanks for the song

&

For Dennis—thanks for the gig

When in disgrace with fortune and men's eyes,

I all alone beweep my outcast state,

And trouble deaf heaven with my bootless cries,

And look upon myself, and curse my fate . . .

— **Shakespeare**

I

"Poetry is the record of the best and happiest moments of the best and happiest minds."
— Shelley

In a way, I think it was always my destiny to be a poet. In a way, it was my curse. I knew it from further back than I can really remember. When I was very young, poems came to me in the night. Not like ghosts or dreams, more like visions. No, that's the wrong word. Images. *That's better, but it's still not exact. Not the* mot juste, *as they say. They really were just glimpses. Of things, of people, of scenes and ideas. After my mother tucked me in, I would lie in bed, close my eyes and whisper my prayer, and then I'd turn over.*

I always turned over. The way a dog has to turn around three times before it lies down. I'd have to turn over just like that. Then they'd come. They would appear just like that. You probably get some crazy idea that they were like medieval monks: hooded figures with skulls for faces, or like Coleridge's "viper thoughts that coiled around my mind." They weren't like that. And they weren't like Emerson's Brahmans or Blake's crazy visions, either. They didn't have that much definition. They were just there. Later, when I read Macbeth, *I thought of that parade of ghosts Banquo conjures. Same thing happens, sort of, in* Richard III. *And there're all those queued up philosophers in Wilder's* The Skin of Our Teeth. *But it really wasn't like that, either. They weren't scary or portentous. They just came.*

Then again, maybe after all they were *portentous. I just didn't think of them that way, then.*

Anyway, out of the darkness behind my eyes, I could see them, sense them. Sometimes they even had odors, smells, tastes, and sometimes I could touch them. I could always feel *them. And I could hear them. They didn't say anything, not words. But they had rhythms, forms, shapes of sound: They were metrical. I didn't think* of them as poems, not then, not for a long time. I mean, I went to school, I read *poetry*. I read all the great *poets*. Then I went to college, and I read poetry there, too. But I didn't like it much. Or I didn't like all of it. Poetry was for sissies, for all those guys who had three names. You know: Henry Wadsworth *Longfellow*, Percy Bysshe *Shelley*, Thomas Sterns *Eliot*, Edgar Allan *Poe*, Samuel Taylor *Coleridge*, William Cullen *Bryant*, John Greenleaf *Whittier*. Can you imagine naming some kid Greenleaf, or Sterns, or Bysshe? "Hey, Greenleaf, you want to come out and play some ball? We got Sterns pitching and Wadsworth catching, and with Bysshe's fast ball, we can't lose!"

See what I mean? No wonder they became poets. They probably got the hell beat out of them every time they went out to recess. Sidney *Lanier, too. What the hell kind of name is* Sidney? It's a wuss name. A geek name. Most of the poets I had to read in college had geeks' names. So, I figured most poets were geeks—or they were gay: QED.

I never much cared for the two-named fellows, either: William Wordsworth, Walt Whitman, and so forth. But I liked Byron. George Gordon Lord Byron. I was twenty-two and in graduate school before I realized that the Lord part was a title. But even without it, George and Gordon were manly names. And he got a lot of tail, too. He kept his wick wet so much and bedded so many beautiful women that people actually thought his lame foot was cloven. There was no question about his testosterone count. And, of course, there was that Don Juan thing. No falling "on the thorns of life" or "a thing of beauty is a joy forever" for him: He knew what getting laid was all about.

But that's not the point. The point is poetry.

I must have been in college when I realized that I could make them come at will. Just sit back, close my eyes, and there they were. And then I got to the point when I didn't have to have my eyes shut. They came in broad daylight, whenever I wanted them, whenever boredom threatened to kill me with pure ennui. That's about all that got me through economics and political science, I can tell you. I didn't know it, but that's what had been getting me through sermons for years. It got me through a lot of graduate seminars later on, too. It was a talent, or that's what I came to think when I found out that not everybody could do it, that I was unique, that they were poems.

Actually, that was Joy's doing. She was the first woman I actually slept with. I mean, I had screwed around. Lost the old cherry

2

before I got out of high school. But I had never slept *with a woman all night, with her next to me in a bed like a satin doll, snuggled into my arms, her breathing softly in rhythm to their rhythms. I found out then that they were connected to her—not to* her *specifically, but to women, to having one there next to me. They were connected to our making love, sleeping together, sharing our breath and our warmth after what I was certain was a mingling of our souls. I told her about them, tried to make her see them, but she never could. She thought I was on drugs. And I had to do something to convince her, so I did something I had never thought of doing.*

I got up, right out of bed—it was the middle of the night—and I wrote one of them down. Just captured it on paper. I think I knew I could do it all along. I just never tried before. It was a villanelle. Can you believe that? A goddamn villanelle. I still have it. It's pastoral, of course, and not as good as Dylan Thomas's famous one, but it's still pretty good. I've kept it all these years, refused to publish it, even when I had the chance. Hung onto it even when everything else got thrown away. It was called "Ode to Joy," a kind of play on Beethoven—or really Schiller—sure, and I know now that a villanelle can't be an ode, but it was certainly to Joy. She loved it! And she loved me for it. And, I guess I owe her. She showed me I was a poet. And she showed me it wasn't anything to be ashamed of, or to feel silly about. Or geeky or queer. It didn't make me any less of a man. She proved that right away, right there in the same bed, that same night. We'd proved it already, of course, in the same bed. But after she saw the poem, heard me read it, read it aloud herself, everything was different. Better. What I mistook for a mingling of our souls turned out to be little more than a jamming together of our innate carnality, maybe, but things certainly changed. She was a different woman, and I was a different man: "rhyme's sturdy cripple" for sure.

Thinking back on it, though, maybe I'm wrong: Maybe poetry isn't the point after all.

The First Reading

He was too old for this shit. And he was late. He huffed up the four broad flights of stairs to the top of the student union building and shook off the rainwater that plastered his clothes to his body. His shoes squeaked from their sousing. The door to the room where the readings were going on was shut, but—Thank God, he thought—

a pale undergraduate sat at a long table. She looked bored out of common sense.

"I'm late," he wheezed, reaching inside his coat for a cigarette. The package was still dry, though his clothes were soaked through. He shook one out. She stared at him with a dead expression. Not unattractive, he thought. A little thin, sallow cheeks, but nice hazel eyes. "I'm very fond of handsome eyes," he quipped. Her expression didn't change. He wondered if she had ever smiled in her life.

There was a metal box full of money in front of her. Chapbooks and flyers cluttered the table. While he lit the smoke, he glanced over them. His book wasn't there. He nodded toward a shoebox, one-quarter filled with small envelopes, said his name, and she fingered through until she came to his. She had nice hands, he thought. Slender fingers, light brown hair on her forearms. She confirmed his name, pulled it out and handed it to him. No smile, no interest. He shrugged.

He shifted his doused umbrella to his left hand and fumbled with the envelope's contents. A cheap, stick-on nametag fell out. He peeled away the backing and slapped it on his sport coat. The material was damp, and the adhesive curled away from it.

"Raining like hell out there," he said, puffing his smoke, feeling his heart dropping back to its normal rate. "I had the very deuce finding a place to park. Why don't they hold these things where people can park?" He offered a smile, hoped for sympathy.

She cast her eyes up and down his water-logged frame, inspected his umbrella, narrow briefcase, then turned her gaze down to a chipped fingernail.

"No smoking in this building," she said.

"What?"

She pointed the broken nail to a large red sign on the opposite wall: **NO SMOKING**.

He looked for an ashtray. None was visible. He cupped the cigarette in his hand to catch the ash. She had returned to reading a flyer in front of her.

"I don't see my book. Do you have *Free Falling, Free Flying?*"

She glanced at the stacks of chapboooks on the table. "Did you send some in?"

"The bookstore was supposed to order it. From the publisher. Melton House. They said they would handle it. Mrs. Ma— Ma-something said they would order it."

"You'll have to talk to her." She returned to her reading.

He looked at the heavy doors. No sound emerged. "How long's it been going on?"

4

"It *started* at seven," she said mechanically. Her eyes stayed down. "They were waiting for you, but they started on time."

He shoved his wrist out of his coat and looked at his watch: 7:40. "I'm late." He tried another smile. Ash dripped into his palm, and he looked up and down the hall again. "Where can I put this out?"

"Don't ask me," she said, then added flatly, "there's a restroom downstairs."

The hallway was deserted. He glared at her, dropped the half-smoked butt onto the tile and ground it out. If she paid any attention to his action, he didn't see it. He pulled open the door and entered.

The room was overly warm. Steam rose from his clothes as he pushed his way through the narrow rows of filled folding chairs to a vacant seat against the wall. There were a hundred, hundred-fifty people jammed into what was apparently some kind of classroom. A tall, blond, youngish man was droning from the lectern and didn't miss a beat as the crowd turned and watched the latecomer squeeze into his seat, stack his umbrella and briefcase beneath him, and cast apologetic smiles toward those he had disturbed.

The room was brightly lit, and almost everyone was well-dressed. A few scruffily clad individuals sat along the back row. Graduate students, he thought. Wouldn't put on a decent suit or sport coat if they owned one. Needed to make a statement. He smiled, reminded of the shade of his younger self, reminded of his own students.

He pulled the registration envelope from his coat pocket and unfolded a program. The cheap, green single-fold of paper hung limp in his fingers. It had been badly typed and then photocopied. IBM Selectric II, he identified the typewriter as one he coveted to replace his antique Remington. A weak and anonymous attempt at art graced the top of each page and the front of the fold. Five poets were listed with a brief paragraph about each following their names. They were not really heavy-hitters, but for this kind of gig, they were good facsimiles of the big time in American poetry, on a regional level at least.

Eustice Carrol had been the first reader: NEA fellow, poet-in-residence at a half-dozen private schools, three chapbooks, and over a hundred poems in little magazines: Small-timer, he thought. He looked up at the front row. Backs of heads greeted him, and he couldn't figure out which one she might be. Probably the one with the Indian braids, he thought. He vaguely recalled that she wrote "Native American Poetry," although her ancestry was Dutch-Irish. She was supposed to be pretty, but he didn't regret missing her reading.

Dolores Goldbalm had been next. Jewish poet, he recalled: heavy-duty feminist. Had been a fellow at Stanford, Iowa, and Princeton. Her poems were angry, pseudo-Ginsburg with a militant female twist: lots of "fucks" and "shits" worked in for effect, no attempt at rhyme or meter. When he reviewed her work, he said she was the only poet who could use "clitoris" as a verb. He remembered she had lectured at SMU a couple of years ago when he was there for an academic conference. Her claim then was that "modernist verse" was both anti-Semitic and misogynistic. "Oppressively political," was her watchword. She was always good for a laugh. He regretted missing her reading, though. Watching the blue-haired patrons squirm at her sexual and scatological imagery would have been worthwhile.

There were a lot of blue-hairs in the audience, too, he noticed, and genuine fur coats, mostly minks, lots of diamonds: no shortage of money. The second through fourth rows had ribbons on them: reserved seating for the reserved patrons. The college was trying to launch its own magazine, which was the occasion for this reading, to attract a donor or two from the local dowagers and wealthy widows. It was an ambitious project for a small urban college, especially one with no English program to speak of. *Oak Creek: A Journal of Urban Poetry* was the touted title. He glanced down again at the cheap program. He hoped they planned to do a better job of printing the magazine.

Bob Cottle was next in the lineup, and he, apparently, was the reader of the moment. Guggenheim, NEA, Ford Foundation, and the Prix de Rome, Yale Younger Poet two years ago: not bad. But he wasn't listed as being from anywhere, no university, no job. Professional poet, he thought with a shake of his head: grant chaser. Not much money in that, and there are only so many grants. Still, Cottle had the reputation of being a "nice guy." He worked well with young poets, and he was a must for any regional reading in the state.

He looked around the room one more time. His clothes were continuing to steam, and the audience's attention was again focused on the reader. Cottle read in a monotone that was broken only when he went up at the end of each line. Must be reading his "epic," he thought. Cottle had published it himself when no one else would touch it: probably used the Gugge money. One-hundred twenty-five pages of continuous-stanza free verse about life in San Francisco in the late sixties as experienced by a deaf-blind, paraplegic, Vietnam-veteran homosexual: *The Day the Circus Left.*

He had been asked to review it for *The American Poetry Review*, but he kept losing interest after the fifth or sixth page. Other reviews told him that there were characters, even a plot, a true modern epic in twelve books. He never could find it. He sent the volume back to the editor after two months with a long letter of apology. They hadn't asked him to review anything else.

Cottle turned a page. Some lifted their hands to applaud, and the crowd visibly shifted in expectation of a finish. He didn't notice but plunged ahead in his singular tone and gait. He wondered if Cottle was going to read the whole damned thing.

The next reader was another woman. Mary Sue Winesong. If that was her real name, he'd eat the five chapbooks listed to her name. She was credited with being a junior college teacher who also edited technical writing manuals "when I don't hear the Muse speaking." She'd also written three plays. Poetic drama. Her blurb said she was attempting to "revive the form." He couldn't spot her for sure, but he noticed that a short blonde woman with a funny haircut was squirming noticeably on the front row. C'mon, Bob, he silently urged, either die or get off the stage and give us something worth looking at.

Bob read on. It was amazing, but he could drone without a breath for two, two-and-a-half pages, and since every fifth or sixth line ended in a conjunction, it was hard to stop him.

His own name appeared last. His one book was all that was listed and the title was smudged, hard to read. No mention of the fact that it was a *real* book, real New York press: no contest, no association backing, just a plain, straight, over-the-transom submission. And they took it. He got a fat advance, and it was still in print. No mention of his Ph.D., his critical book, two dozen articles on modern poetry and theory. No mention at all of his status as a major critic of modern poetry. In fact, none of the other p.r. stuff he sent made the program, but the typing went right down to the bottom of the paper. It might have been cut off by the photocopier.

The opposite fold was full of general praise for the poets who had agreed to read in support of the founding of the magazine. "From the Far Corners of the Country," the headline read. He'd only come forty miles. That wasn't that far, and to his way of thinking, this place was more of a corner than the smaller town where he lived. In truth, it was a hole in the middle of a huge city, an urban-located tech school trying to establish liberal arts credentials against the odds.

His watch read 8:04 when Cottle made the mistake of pausing for a sip of water, and a well-manicured woman with huge breasts strapped under a pink doubleknit suit jacket arose and seized the lectern. She spotted him and he raised his eyebrows in apology. She frowned and suggested a fifteen-minute intermission would be in order.

He picked up his briefcase and umbrella and pushed his way past grateful patrons scurrying for the exit.

"Sorry I'm late." He reached automatically for a cigarette. "It was pouring out there. Couldn't find a parking place."

"We began promptly at seven," she said. "I'm Mrs. Mahaffety: Director of Programs here at the university." He almost smiled. They had had university status for precisely four years. So soon they learn the jargon.

"Yeah, I know. I received your letter. I had a class until five, then I had to go shower and change." He lit the smoke. "Guess I could have skipped the shower." He smiled. She frowned. It was too bad. She was well into her forties, but she had nice legs, a pretty face. The scowl made her ugly.

"There's no smoking in this building," she said. "No smoking anywhere on campus."

"Oh." He looked around. "I forgot." Again, he cupped the burning butt in his palm.

"We didn't know what had happened to you," she said. "We called, and your wife said you were supposed to be here. So, to fill out the program, we asked Gabriela Washington to come over."

"Gabe?" His eyebrows shot up. He hated Gabe: self-righteous bitch. Four books of poems published, poet-in-residence at the most prestigious university in the region, a sixty-grand-a-year-plus-tenure position that required her to do nothing more than boff horny undergraduates and write poems about it. He looked around.

"I heard she was on tour."

"She's in town. Her flight was cancelled. It was really a stroke of luck for us."

He looked down at the program. "She's not listed?"

"We found out she gave a reading across town this afternoon. She was on her way to St. Louis, but the weather has closed the airport there. Someone told her what we were doing, and she called up and graciously offered to fill in for you." She frowned again. "We *couldn't* just leave a gap in the program. We're *trying* to raise money, you know. It was a terrible imposition on her, but she did agree to come on short notice."

I'll bet, he thought. Gabe would read to a gaggle of drooling cretins in a wheat field if there was a hundred bucks in it.

"She's not here, yet," Mrs. Mahaffety said, looking around. "She didn't call until six forty-five. We waited for you as long as we could. You were expected to be here by six for the reception. When it appeared you were standing us up . . . ." She waved her fingers in a dismissive gesture.

He bit down hard on his anger and tried to sound calm. "I told

Lois Whatshername I had a class until five. I didn't count on the weather. The traffic was awful. Two wrecks, and construction—"

"Mrs. Johnson was most specific," Mrs. Mahaffety said, studying something over his shoulder. "She said you agreed to be here by six. It's in the confirmation letter."

"Hey, I called and told her I would be late. I wasn't standing you up. I was out there circling the parking lot in the flood looking for a place to park for half an hour."

"I believe Mrs. Johnson stipulated that you could park in C-Lot, right outside the building. That was in the letter, as well." She was cold, he thought. Ice-maiden. And she was embarrassed. He noticed the huge rock on her ring finger. Good-looking as she was, he felt sorry for her husband. She probably wrote out nightly instructions for copulation and mailed them to him.

He dropped his polite tone and sucked on the cigarette. "Lot C, or whatever, was under water. Flooded. There were barricades up. I parked across the street."

"That's student parking," she said and turned away. "You'll have to move your car. They'll tow it."

"They'll need a tug boat. I'm not sure I can even get back to it."

"Well, perhaps. Anyway, Ms. Washington promised to be here by eight, and that will have to be the program."

Anger gripped him all at once. "Hey, look. I didn't have to come sailing down here. You're not even paying me for this gig. I'll bet you're cutting a fair-sized expense check for the others. And I know Gabe wouldn't read for less than a hundred, even if it was in her hotel room and she didn't charge for the sex." She cocked an eyebrow in ironic reaction. "I agreed to take *time* out from my schedule for this. I could be home: writing."

She turned back and looked at him. "I'm sorry," she said. "You'll have to speak to Mrs. Johnson about the honoraria. That's not my department." She softened momentarily. "I don't mean to appear ungrateful. But we didn't know what had happened to you, so we have more or less filled the program. Ms. Washington will be here in a few minutes, and—"

"And so, I'm out on my butt," he said. His voice was loud, and he felt himself perspiring. "God! You people—"

"There is no reason to cause a scene," Mrs. Mahaffety hissed. Several of those who had not gone outside turned to look at them. She put her hands out in front of her and pushed at the air between them as if to press his anger back inside him. "I *guess* there will be time for your reading. Right after Ms. Washington."

"After—oh, just forget it," he said. He was damned if he'd follow Gabe. "I'll just hang around and listen."

"There is no reason to be petulant." She looked at him as if he were an errant freshman. *Petulant?* Had she really called him that?

"Just forget it," he said. "For-get-it." He dropped the cigarette, ground it out and went out into the hall.

People milled about the table, purchasing books from the pale undergraduate. She was now all smiles, pretty, taking money from the liver-spotted, gem-studded hands of the patrons. The graduate students huddled together over in a corner. He could see wisps of cigarette smoke rising from their knot, and he walked over and joined them.

"What do you all think of the reading?" He lit up again.

A chubby woman shrugged. "It's okay." She shielded a cigarette in her hand and pushed a strand of hair away from her face. "Mostly bullshit, you know."

"Are you students here?"

One of the men, a skinny stick with a badly developed beard, nodded. "Yeah. Sort of. I'm in education. They don't have a graduate English program."

He nodded. "But you like poetry."

"Nancy here writes a little," the young man said, indicating the chubby woman. "We just came along with her."

Nancy smiled. "Are you a poet?"

"Yeah." He took a drag. He sensed an ally in the making. "I was supposed to read. But—"

"Is one of your books over there?" She nodded toward the table.

"I don't see it. I don't think they got them in. They had to come from New York," he added nonchalantly. "*Free Falling, Free Flying*," he muttered in faux modesty. "Melton Press."

Her expression was flat. "Oh," she said. Her interest was gone.

"Reading aloud is bullshit, you know," a short heavy man with a cherubic face next to her said. "If it doesn't read on the page, it's not poetry."

He decided to be humble but assertive, smiled, and looked down at his shoe tops. "My poetry reads on the page. I've never read it aloud."

"So why are you here?" Nancy asked.

"Uh . . . they asked me to read . . . ." He trailed off, feeling stupid, and they looked uncomfortably at each other. He crushed out the smoke under his shoe and walked back to the crowd.

Chat among the patrons was amiable, but it seemed everyone

was staring at him, accusing him of being where he shouldn't. He shifted his briefcase and umbrella from hand to hand, looked for a familiar face. Lois was engrossed in something Bob Cottle was saying. She was an angular woman with skinny calves in black stockings. She looked hard, and her hair was teased and piled high on her head—way out of fashion. She looked like an extra from a beach party movie. Cottle signed copies of his books as he talked, barely giving those who brought them to him a nod. He apparently could talk without breathing as well.

The other poets were all engaged with the patrons. He felt odd, out of place, accused, tried, and found guilty of spoiling their evening, of making them feel guilty for doing the right thing.

A burn of disappointment flickered somewhere inside him, then flamed and spread rapidly. He wanted to read, goddamnit! He wanted to showcase his work. He had no reputation like the others—not as a poet. His only reputation was as a critic, a scholar. But now he was a poet as well. A *real* poet, not just published, but *well* published. He wanted them to know that, to respect that.

He started to move toward Lois Johnson, but all heads suddenly turned toward the landing, as if some silent cue had called their attention at the same time. Gabe Washington had arrived. She came up the stairs followed by a handsome young man who carried a golf umbrella and a briefcase. Her clothing was white and billowing, her long black hair perfect. It was as if she had just crossed a wind-swept quad instead of a rain-soaked parking lot. The young man beside her was flushed, and as she reached the landing, she took a pose, put one lacquered fingernail on her escort's shoulder, and smiled broadly.

"Well," she said in a theatrical tone, "I'm here! Where is Mrs. Mahaffety?"

The graduate students encircled her, and she greeted each one with a light handshake. He saw Lois Johnson push her way through and take Gabe's hand. Mrs. Mahaffety followed close on her heels.

"We seem to be parked in a red zone," Gabe trilled. "There just was *no* other place!"

"That's fine!" Mrs. Mahaffety assured her loudly. "*You* can park anywhere you like!" She failed to meet his furious glance. The women formed a knot and spoke briefly, and she was ushered into the room. He thought to grab Lois's arm when she passed, but his hands were full of umbrella and briefcase, so he just stood aside and steamed.

Mrs. Mahaffety called everyone back in, and within moments, he was standing alone in front of the table with the bored undergraduate again.

"Not going in?" she asked him after a moment. This time she gave him a smile, but it was full of irony, as if she had known what the deal was all along. She probably had.

He lit another cigarette. "No," he said. "Tell them I left. In fact, tell them to go fuck themselves." He unfurled his umbrella and slung water on the stacks of flyers and chapbooks and stormed back out into the rain.

II

"Until I labor, I in labor lie . . . ."
— Donne

I was selling insurance when I decided to become a college professor. I had no idea in the world what the decision meant. I mean, there I was: degree in English, which was worth its weight in used condoms, a four-year-old Plymouth with bad valves and bald tires, and a collection of ties I got from my father after he died. And I was dying in the insurance business. I could have gone in the army, I guess. Lots of guys were doing that after college, then. Vietnam wasn't a big deal, you know, not yet. But I started having these nightmares. Woke up screaming. It was a problem, and when I told them about it, they stamped me 1-Y, which was kind of a sixties version of 4-F, and sent me on my way. Then the nightmares stopped. Just like that. I thought about going back to a different recruiter. They didn't have all the fancy computers in those days, were sloppier in their records. If they checked me out and found out I was 4-F, 1-Y, someplace else, then they might throw me out, but by that time, they'd have six months, maybe a year invested in me. But I didn't join up. I didn't have it in me to follow orders. "Resents authority," was the way it was usually filled in on those recommendation forms. In a way, that's always been a big part of my problem. Funny thing, though, as soon as the nightmares went away, the poems came back.

You see what I mean? Destiny.

So there I was, small town boy selling insurance in the big city. Part of our business was to sell policies to college kids. They were real suckers for the five-buck-a-week debit accounts. Some thought they were putting money away for a rainy day, but half the time, they'd sign up just to get rid of you, you know? Make you quit bugging them and taking up their time. It was like "protection money," sort of legal extortion: "Pay up each week, or I'll come

13

'round an' lean on youse." I was new to that end of the business, though. They sent me over to this big-deal private university to make a call on a co-ed named Christi. She'd sent back a card asking for further information, and I was the one they sent. They liked to send the young guys over to the campuses when the prospect was a female. They knew what they were doing.

She was cool: good-looking, and smart and wasn't into the flower child thing, which was all pretty new at the time. She lived in a sorority house over on the row. I met her in the living room, laid out the program. Turns out her father and mother had both been killed in a car wreck the summer before. They weren't real wealthy, but they'd left her with a trust fund for her education but that was about it. Still, she started thinking about her kid brother, who was living with their grandparents. She wanted a policy in case something happened to her. I signed her right off: twenty-grand policy with options for increase when she hit twenty-one. Then I took her out to dinner. Then I took her to bed.

I know how that sounds: sleazy as hell, right? But that's what happened. I mean, I didn't come on to her as a macho man or anything. I've never had to do that. I just talked about what I knew, and what I knew was poetry. She was an English major, of course—it wouldn't have worked otherwise—and I was a college graduate. Sure, I didn't go to a fancy private college. The school I went to didn't have fraternal organizations. They were lucky to have buildings and professors. But I'd learned a lot, and, thanks to Joy and a handful of other girls, I'd learned I was a poet, too, and the poetry connected to the girls. I couldn't help it. Christi thought that was the coolest thing she'd ever heard, and when we got back to my place, I only had to read two or three—sonnets, of course, what Rossetti called "a moment's measure," a "memorial from the Soul's eternity"—and she was putty in my hands.

That's trite, I know. But that's the way it was.

So anyway, she was a freshman and she had early closing hours, a curfew, you know. And after I dropped her off and promised to call and stuff, I parked the car and just got out and walked around the campus. I saw all the dorms, with lights on and students studying, people going and coming from the library. It was spring, and it felt good, you know? It was like somewhere I belonged. I walked around until all the lights were out and it was really late, and when I was going back to my car, I stopped right in the middle of this big quad. Something clicked in my head, and I knew for sure, right then. This was where I belonged, not in some bullshit insurance office where the major idea of literature was Playboy's *"Party Jokes." I went in and quit the next morning. I had some savings, and in the summer, I enrolled in graduate school. I had made up my mind. I knew where I needed to be, even though I didn't know what it would mean to be there.*

But in spite of Joy, in spite of Christi, in spite of everything, I really didn't believe I was a poet. Not yet. That wouldn't come for a while. For now, it was just a way of getting girls into bed. And in a way, I guess that was the most important part of it from the very beginning.

The Major Reading

He spotted her on the front row as he left his chair following his introduction. It wasn't the first time he had noticed her, but she was the only one in the room not applauding him up to the lectern. She stood out, but she wasn't really outstanding, not compared to some of the softer, younger women in the room. But she was tall, red-headed, and chesty, and when he first saw her come into the room, he had done more than glance at her, pegged her as a sophisticate. Now, studying her through the first two readers' presentations—both student poets, contest winners—he changed his mind. She was older than average for a student: sexy, sort of earthy, a little trashy in some unspecified way. She seemed to be sneaking looks at him whenever he glanced her way, furtive looks that seemed to hide meaning. He wondered if he knew her, had met her someplace, but then he decided if that was the case, he would remember her. She had bright brown eyes, and if she reminded him of anyone, it was Ann Margaret: a low-rent Ann Margaret.

He couldn't believe how nervous he was as he mounted the podium and walked to the lectern. For a person who spent the majority of his professional life standing and talking to classrooms full of people, lecturing at learned conferences and associations, such a reaction was totally uncalled for. It didn't make sense. But it struck him every time he had to read his poetry. He wondered if he would ever come to a point when he was as comfortable with it as he was with his scholarship.

He'd better, he told himself. This was what he intended to do. He was done with scholarship.

It was good to be here, on his own, a solo performance. The honorarium was paltry, but they had paid expenses: provided a plane ticket, set him up in a Hilton, bought him two decent meals. He was at last being treated like a star. And he wanted to feel like one.

When he opened the manila folder containing the poems he planned to read, his hands shook a bit. He willed them to be still. He could use a drink, he thought, although it wasn't yet noon. The urge surprised him. He never drank that early in the day, not until five, maybe four-thirty on the weekends. He cleared his throat, surprised to hear how soft his voice sounded in the room. Normally, he used an old public speaking technique to get around this. He would pick one or two people from different places in the room and concentrate on them, pretend that he was speaking directly to them. It made the presentation more personal, less like a performance. He usually tried to find faces that were receptive, but this time, he picked hers, and when she responded to his light smile and pointed stare with an ironic grin, he felt something sharp strike him in the chest. Was she there to make fun of him?

There had been too long a period of silence since he arrived behind the lectern, he realized. "Graces Amazed," he announced, and with only the briefest nod toward her, he began reading.

The room was only half full, but everyone there was interested in poetry, specifically in *his* poetry, and there was a visible relaxation in response to his plunging into the verse without a lot of introductory nonsense. Smiles and nods started from the first line. She kept her head steady, the same inscrutable light grin at the corners of her mouth. He had the feeling she was about to burst out laughing, even though the poem was about four different ways of dying. It was anything but funny.

He was a big draw, for once. After two years of messing around and being second-billed with chapbook scribblers and grant chasers, it was, he thought, a fitting pleasure to be at last a headliner, or sort of. The reading was part of the Major Poets Series, which was an annual event on the campus, but this time, it was tied in with the school's centennial anniversary celebration. Every day of the week had several "Main Events," so called because the first building on the campus, "Old Main," had just been reopened after extensive restoration and remodeling. In conjunction with his reading, there were lectures, concerts, and all sorts of other presentations in the building. Classes had been let out for the entire week to make sure there was a sufficient audience for everyone, and he was pleased to see the forty or so mostly student souls trooping in to hear him instead of the recital that was going on in the basement.

At other readings during the past two years, he had followed such bad acts that he was often embarrassed to prolong the audience's misery with his own work. This time, there were only the students. Their poetry was pretty awful, but he had judged the contest, selected the least onerous—and the shortest—of the submitted verse and was prepared to enjoy himself for a change. It was nice to see posters all over the campus announcing his name and book title in bright red letters. It was even nicer to see a huge display of his books for sale out on the lawn where the luncheon would be.

Even moderate sales here would guarantee a second printing. Felix, his editor at Melton, would be thrilled.

He found his voice settling into the verse's rhythms, but he couldn't quite relax, and in spite of the poem's darker turns, the smiles continued, especially hers. A light laugh came from somewhere, and several turned slightly to see who had chuckled in the wrong place. But she kept her brown eyes on him, as if she feared he might escape if she looked away. Her mouth maintained its satiric smile, and he glanced down to his trousers to check his fly, wondering if something was terribly wrong that he couldn't figure out. He finished the poem and felt the embarrassing crush of silence that usually rose between selections hurrying him on.

"The next one is lighter," he promised to more smiles and even one or two toothy grins from several others on the front row. Her expression didn't change. "Pool Talk," he said, and plunged in.

He was proud of this one. It was a dramatic narrative in heroic couplets about an unhandsome man meeting a beautiful woman at a public pool. Filled with anatomical references, it had caused him a great deal of trouble with consistency and terminology. He thought he would never come up with any rhyme for "pelvis" other than "Elvis," which he regarded as trite. Besides it didn't fit. Finally he settled for a slant-rhyme, "selfless," and it worked well for the context, but then he had more trouble with words such as "pubic" and "crotch" which fit the narrative's character but, somehow, weren't poetic. It took nearly a week to get it all right, and for the first time, he had consulted a rhyming dictionary, but now it was finished, and he was pleased.

There was more laughter now as he swung into the second stanza. They were getting it. He took confidence from that and became more animated. The redhead looked down at her hands quickly and immediately resumed her bemused stare.

It was all new stuff, the first really new poems he had completed since the *New Yorker* took two of his pieces the previous summer. It was odd, he thought. No one at school had commented much about his book, but everyone seemed to be pleased about the magazine acceptance. The truth was, of course, that it meant nothing. Magazine publications like that were worth little to a poet except that they exposed his name. But in spite of how well *Free Falling* had done in the reviews, he couldn't shake the nagging sensation that the only reason he was here at this reading, the only reason this school had flown him half way across the country, was because of those two skinny little sonnets—both love poems—for which he hadn't made even one percent of what he was earning from the book. He tried not to think of it as he brought the "Pool Talk" to a gratifyingly hilarious close and allowed his narrator's belly to relax when the beautiful woman turned and walked away.

There was loud laughter and applause, and he shuffled his papers unnecessarily and beamed at them. He felt good, accepted, appreciated. He noticed, though, that the redhead only put her hands together softly a couple of times before folding them across a thin envelope on her thighs and staring at him with the same, mocking appraisal.

It was as if she knew him and was sharing some secret and embarrassing thought with him.

The next three poems were, again, darker, but their forms kept them alive in the audience's eyes. He was pleased to be able to avoid the sing-song oral tones of so many poets. Most tended to go up at each end-stop in what he often believed was a way of saying, "Get it?" He believed such poor reading ability falsified the poem. He practiced with a tape recorder. He read each sentence as a grammatical completion, even when it wasn't, thereby allowing the meter and rhyme to communicate the irony, humor, pointed message, emotional power, and permitting the metaphors and internal rhymes to raise the images to poetic meanings and drive them home. He focused on caesura rather than end-stops, and he was slightly shocked to discover an even sharper wit than he thought he had being revealed in places where he had sometimes felt restricted by the closed form to which he was devoted.

Delight registered across the room when he looked up at the end of a stanza, and he was thrilled that, unlike the usual pattern readings took, he was now receiving heavy applause at the end of each selection from everyone but the redhead. She remained still, only occasionally patting her hands together or crossing one high-heeled boot over the other.

She was bothering him too much, and he promised that he would not look at her again. But he did. He couldn't take his eyes off her.

There was a magnetism, a familiarity in her eyes he couldn't keep from watching. But it was tempered with something else, something dangerous. She looked at him as if he were naked, assessing his worth, not even listening to the words he read. Just looking, staring.

It's only ego talking, he told himself, a "strange fit of passion" he would love to know. They're all looking at you. It's just that she's—what? Not pretty, although she was. There were plenty of prettier women in the room, though. And not just that tinge of cheapness, of an easiness of will that he sensed in spite of the fact that he doubted such a thing could be perceived, especially from mere sight. Undeniably, though, she was somehow electric, vibrant. He imagined he could smell her perfume.

He forced his mind away from her and wished his wife was there to see him in action. That might change her mind about his work, his poetry, something that was becoming a wall between them. She had never heard him read a word of it in public, always had an excuse not to come. Sometimes, he thought she was afraid to see how people were reacting to his verse, afraid that it would somehow validate what he was doing and encourage him to do more of it. She was right about that, anyway.

This time their daughter was sick, though, plus she would have had to miss two of her own classes. Or, at least, that was the excuse she gave, that, and the entirely too true point that they couldn't afford the extra plane tickets. He felt fortunate that she agreed that his being a headliner was worth the cost of extra babysitting. Lately, her tolerance for his newfound fame as a poet was diminishing, if it had ever been there in the first place. He remembered her reaction to the news that *Free Falling* had been placed. He received the letter from Melton House when he was at school, cut his afternoon class just to race home and tell her in person. He was calculating the balance of credit left on their Bank Americard, thinking dinner, drinks, dancing. It was the most major *event* of his professional life.

She was napping when he came bursting in, and he held the news until she got up, went to the bathroom, then came into the kitchen and found something to drink in the refrigerator. "That's great, honey," she said, when he read her Felix's letter of acceptance. "Did you go by the dry cleaners on your way home?" Then she looked at the clock. "Why are you home so early, anyway?" They ate left-overs that night. He didn't bring up the book over dinner.

Since then, since he had begun writing in earnest and with a definite purpose in mind, she seemed to regard it as a hobby, or maybe a second career. She worried that it endangered the stability of his teaching position, although, if things continued to work out right, it could enhance it, gain him an actual sinecure, the dream of every poet. She had not yet found anything to do for herself aside from enrolling in graduate school in psychology—"the field for those who can't decide on a field," he always said as soon as she told anyone about it—and she resented his taking off on a new tack before she had found something she called "her direction." The poetry was taking a lot of time on top of his teaching and critical writing load, and she also asserted that it took time away from her and their daughter.

"All you do is write," she yelled at him one Saturday morning when he announced that he was going to the office to get away from the house and—although he didn't admit it, even to himself—her.

"It's just a rough patch," he assured her. "We'll get through it. I need to be working on a second book."

"You already have a second book. Or I should say, you already have a *real* book. What you should be doing is going to the library, doing some research. That's what everyone else is doing. If you don't want to work on something that matters, why don't you mow the lawn?"

"A book of poetry matters," he bristled. "And that book is as real as the other. One hell of a lot more people read that than read dry scholarship."

"'Dry scholarship' will get you promoted," she pointed out, "whether anyone reads it or not. And *nobody* reads poetry, either. You ought to know that. You've said so yourself a thousand times. You may not have noticed, but we're living month to month. If you could make associate next year, we might be able to get out of the hole. Scholarship'll do that. 'Publish or Perish.' You've told me that a thousand times, too."

"So will this," he said with less certainty. The university administration was still not sure whether a book of poetry was worth as much as a researched scholarly work, he knew. He had also heard from a friend on the college committee that his verse was regarded with a narrow view.

"Anybody can write a poem," Leon Gershoy, the head of the chemistry department, declared.

But Marion Dunphy, his own department head, and several others stuck up for him, and now they were leaning toward approving it, particularly since the book was published in New York. That, Gershoy was forced to admit, was something that not just "anybody" could do. Gershoy certainly hadn't. Wasn't likely to, either.

"I'm telling you," he built his argument with his wife, "if I can get another book or a major grant like an NEA or a Gugge, then we'll have it made."

"*We* won't," she said. "*You* will. Then, where will *I* be? Next thing I know, you'll be running around with some little co-ed with big tits and a Farrah Fawcett hairdo, and I'll be back to waiting tables." She broke down at that point, started crying and feeling sorry for herself. It was an old ploy, one she had regularly used with stunning effect since they married.

So he laughed about it, made fun of his own work, and, finally, she laughed back. But she filled his weekends, made him take them to the park, the zoo, the beach, and he knew that beneath all of it, she was seriously distressed. She was reaching that age when a lot of wives began to worry about their husbands and beautiful, adoring young co-eds. He had noticed she was cold to him on the phone if he called to say he had to stay late on campus to meet a student and didn't deliberately identify the youngster as a *he*. He deliberately failed to mention any *shes* to her at all, students or colleagues.

He hated lying to her, but there wasn't much choice. It was that or be frozen out when he came home. Besides, he argued, he was guilty of nothing more than excessive illeism, which was safer by far than committing too much *elle*ism in her hearing.

She was good at that, he thought as he read a section of "Housewifery," a poem dealing with a woman who held back sex from her husband of thirty years in exchange for household appliances and who ultimately committed suicide when he gave up on her and took a male lover. He and his wife hadn't had a good sexual relationship since their daughter was born, since they learned that one child was all there was going to be of the "large family" she had planned since the day they met. That wasn't his fault, but he got blamed for it. He began deliberately trying to be a better husband— sex or no sex—and a better father, but it wasn't working. His heart wasn't in it. His heart was in his poetry, and he felt a desperation about writing it.

The poems came to him all the time now. He couldn't take a shower, eat a meal, watch a television program without one kicking its way to the front of his mind. Sometimes they were more insistent than a racing engine on the starting line. The house was littered with scraps of paper on which he had scrawled his ideas, half-formed verses, metaphors or quick, sudden similes, hastily written when they appeared in his head and then put aside to return to. If one was missing from where he left it by the phone, the toilet, even his workbench in the garage, he became frantic. His wife was never sympathetic, and she seemed to go out of her way to make him feel guilty. He also suspected that she threw them away whenever she found them.

The worst incident had taken place only two nights before. It was their anniversary. Their daughter was with her mother, and she prepared a wonderful meal. Then, at her insistence, they took a chilly walk under a brilliantly clear winter sky. The poems seemed to stalk them like muggers, and he could hardly wait to get back to the house, fly to his desk and begin setting them down. She called him from the living room almost as soon as he sat down, but he pretended not to hear, hoping that she would recognize that he was concentrating and then go on about her evening's business: She usually retired alone when he was working.

"Solstice" came to him in a whole piece, shaped itself into terza rima almost automatically. He was thrilled with it, certain that it would need only a little revision, which he set about completing immediately. Then, two hours later, the idea for a sequence that formed itself into a roumant he called "Moonhouse" appeared. He worked three more hours before his eyes began to burn from the cigarette smoke, and he gave up for the night. It was late, after three. He found her fully dressed, asleep on the sofa, an Irish coffee—colder than the north wind—and a slice of melting cheesecake—her specialty—waiting on him in front of a dead fireplace. His anniversary gift was also there, still wrapped, an Xavier fountain pen, the kind he had told her Robert Penn Warren always used when he wrote his best verse. That was something he made up. But he had lusted after one of the expensive pens from the time he first saw one. He could tell from the streaks of mascara running down her freckled cheeks that she had cried herself to sleep. His gift to her was in the closet, forgotten.

It made him feel terrible, but all his resolutions about making it up to her were frozen away when she refused to speak to him all the next day. She had barely found words to say goodbye when she drove him to the airport to leave for this reading. But she had packed for him. There was still hope.

He had a terrible sense of regret, of guilt, but the poems were good, maybe the best he had ever written. He segued into the "Moonhouse" sequence and was gratified by the continued rapt attention of the audience. It was as fine as he imagined it would be, and everyone leaned forward to catch every word, every nuance. Everyone but the redhead, who folded her arms across her yellow sweater and continued to watch him with a mordant expression.

The only time he had completely free to write was on weekends, and his wife always had something planned for him then. If shopping trips or ticketed events in the city weren't cropping up, she insisted that he spend "quality time" with their little girl. Their daughter became a weapon for her to use against the poetry, and she wielded it without mercy. He took the child to theater matinees that were far too mature for her to appreciate while his wife stayed home to do her own studying, to have what she called "quiet time" to herself.

"I'm home five days a week with her," she lectured him. It wasn't precisely true, since she had classes one afternoon and two nights a week, and the child was in daycare on Mondays and Wednesdays. But he didn't argue. He knew she needed time to herself, needed him and their daughter out of the house. But he taught five days a week. Saturdays and Sundays were his "quiet time," too, and he felt cheated.

Yet he had a sense of justice about it. After all, she *had* waited tables to put him through graduate school, had spent most of what she called her "best years" pushing him through his degree so they could start a family. Finding out that they could have but one child hadn't helped things, but he convinced himself that they were satisfied. And when the poetry started, he discovered that he was more satisfied than he ever imagined that he could be. She, however, was not, and she wasn't about to permit him to forget it.

Another kind of guilt also gnawed at him. As full weekend followed full weekend and the poems continued to come, he began taking his daughter with him to the office on Saturdays and Sunday afternoons, parking her at a secretary's desk with a pile of crayons and paper while he hunched over his desk and drafted poems as rapidly as he could.

"It's our little secret," he told her when he bought her ice cream or some toy or other to bribe her into silence, but he suspected that she had told his wife all about it. Actually, he was certain she had. She was so bored at the office that she almost cried every time he turned their rusty Datsun into the parking lot and pulled a new box of crayons from under the seat. And her whines in response to his assurances that they would leave "in just a few more minutes, sweetie," assured him that she would use their "little secret" against him whenever she was unhappy with him about something. But he didn't care. The poems were coming, and he felt he must get them down or lose them forever.

More to the point, he *couldn't* ignore them. They wouldn't let him.

His wife was only part of the problem, though. Twice, he dismissed a class and raced back to his university office just to put down lines that occurred to him while he was lecturing. He was far behind on deadlines for promised articles, and he had failed to prepare lectures for two conferences because he spent his time revising, ridding poems of problems when the solutions became suddenly almost painfully clear to him. Twice he had driven miles past freeway exits when his mind filled with them and distracted his attention completely. There was a mania about his writing, and he worried about his mental state. But he kept writing.

"The proof of a poet," he reminded himself of Whitman's words, "is that his country absorbs him as affectionately as he has absorbed it." But "country" was Whitman's metaphor, not his. He wanted to absorb life, to be absorbed by it. It was more than an obsession. It was, he assured himself, his *raison d'etre*, his only excuse for getting up in the morning. Certainly, he thought with an ironic, inward chuckle, it was the only reason for going to bed at night.

He finished the last poem of the program and stood up straight to accept the applause. He was always surprised to be so relieved and at the same time disappointed when he completed a reading. This time disappointment overbalanced relief, though, since it was the first time he alone had been the whole program. Usually, he had to share the dais with a half-dozen "tepid versifiers and pitiful poetizers," or so he had anonymously characterized them in an essay in *Poetry*. That piece had outraged hundreds of poets if the nasty letters appearing in his mailbox were any indication. Two of the complainants suggested that he be publicly executed. Three had called for his castration—as a poet, if not physically. More than half suggested that he burn everything he ever wrote as a service to contemporary letters.

This time, though, aside from the simpering student contest winners, the whole hour was his, and he wished he had it back to enjoy the triumph once more: again and again, really. All his former nervousness fell away. He was euphoric.

He glanced again at the redhead while the clapping died out, but aside from crossing her legs beneath her skirt once more, she didn't move. The satiric little smile remained fixed, though, and he wondered suddenly if she wasn't disfigured in some way, perhaps as the result of some horrid accident that forced her mouth into a permanently ironic, pouting grin. If so, it didn't reduce her prettiness. She was damned attractive.

"I'm sure there will be questions," Dr. Lorene Stephenson

announced as she rose. At sixty-three, she had been the poet-in-residence here for nearly twenty years, although she had published next to nothing aside from small, privately printed volumes that she distributed to her friends and local libraries. She seemed genuinely thrilled for him to be on their campus, favoring them with his talent: She was a born cheerleader.

Two or three hands shot up, and he fielded the queries about his work habits with the usual lies. He didn't have a routine that was regular enough to mention. But to say to the anxious young folk who wanted to hear some secret of success revealed to them that all it took for him to write poetry was to see one in his head wouldn't work. Even if he spoke of the revisions, the fine-tuning and shaping of verse, the truth was that the images, the ideas, the connections between phrases and thoughts came automatically, they would think he was just bragging, seeking to feed his ego.

A year before at another reading when he was just one of four on the program, he had tried to deflect the question by quoting Wordsworth:

For oft, when on my couch I lie
In vacant thought or in pensive mood,
They flash upon that inward eye
Which is the bliss of solitude.

Miriam Counter, the headliner that night, waited until he was through, examined the nodding smiles of delight in the audience, then scoffed, "Well, it doesn't come that easily for all of us." She went on to say flat-out that he was less of a poet than she because she worked so hard at each line, each word. "For the rest of us," she sniffed, "writing a poem is like pulling a tooth. And it's usually more painful."

He would fix Miriam, he thought at the time. He had just received her new collection—*The World from a Volkswagen Window*—to review. He had planned to give it tepid praise. Now he would slaughter it. He would teach her something about the pain of poetry.

But poetry wasn't painful for him. It just was. He didn't know how to explain it otherwise. Neither did his wife.

"You can't go out and water the yard without coming in and writing about it," she accused him. "Every goddamn thing you do winds up in a poem. I'm surprised you don't write about bowel movements. About our sex life."

"What sex life?" he yelled back at her. "It's such a goddamn *event* in our lives that it probably *is* worth a poem. Hell, it's probably worth a fucking novel." He laughed at the pun.

She didn't. "If you wrote it, it would be fucked!"

"Well, somebody around here should be, and it's sure not likely to be me."

Things got nasty after that.

He had to admit that the diminished frequency of their sexual union was as much his fault as hers. The demands of his teaching schedule, his critical writing, his attempts to spend that "quality time" with his daughter, and his other paternal duties were more than enough to exhaust him. But he still spent twelve-to-twenty hours a week doing nothing but writing. And when she encroached on his weekend time, he wound up doing it late at night, sometimes all night. He had put his head down on his desk and slept through more than one departmental meeting, and finally the Dunphy relieved him of all but the most necessary committee work. "Your snoring keeps everyone else awake," he laughed without humor. He was too tired for sex most of the time, but then, he consoled himself, so was she.

And her interest wasn't there. He wished he could accuse her of sleeping with someone else, but he knew she wasn't, wouldn't. Her religion wouldn't stand it, and he was convinced that she took a perverse pleasure in the breakdown of love making in their marriage. She had recently taken to undressing and dressing in the bathroom, out of his sight, and since the baby was born, she wore loose-fitting flannel nightgowns and huge, ugly fuzzy slippers that discouraged him even more.

He took three more questions, hoping a little that the redhead would say something, ask something, but she didn't. She continued to stare at him with the same sardonic mask, and he sat down. He wondered how old she was. She looked like a student, somehow, but she seemed older, and she was much better looking than he had first thought, but the tawdriness of her manner was still present.

Dr. Stephenson announced that they had been exceptionally lucky with the weather, so there would be a reception on the lawn outside—"a barbeque luncheon buffet"—and people rose and began to file out.

He wanted a cigarette, but even though there was no posted ban, he was acutely aware that the building was practically a museum piece itself, and no one was smoking around him. He hesitated and hoped to be able to duck outside quickly. Instead, he was immediately surrounded by several students who had been too shy to ask their questions aloud. Most wanted him to look at their work, even though he suspected that in the course of judging the contest, he had already seen most of it, if not the worst of it. He nodded and accepted a fat handful of envelopes and assured them he would comment on their efforts and mail them back to them. He had no idea how he would find the time, but this was the sort of thing he had seen too many of his fellow poets doing. He felt obligated. As a result, over the past year, he had collected over two hundred similar packets. They accused him of unfulfilled promises every time he came into his office.

He finally lit a cigarette and stepped out into the hall, trailing a few stragglers who continued to ask him who his favorite poets were, a question he always found hard to answer. He retreated to his "professorial mode" and held forth about the general emptiness of contemporary poetry, something they did not want to hear about their personal heroes. One or two walked away, shaking their heads, but he didn't care. If they didn't want his opinion, they shouldn't ask.

Suddenly he was confronted by the redhead. She was leaning against the wall in the hallway, listening to him with the same, knowing and slightly amused expression on her face, and as soon as the crowd began to flow into the reception room, she stood up and approached him and put out her hand.

"Connie Fulbright," she said in a husky voice. "Did you ever teach at Claremore College?"

He was surprised to find that she was taller than he unless he stood up straight. Her figure was mostly hidden by the long skirt and boots she wore, but her breasts were large and seemed to push hard against her sweater. There were light lines under the makeup around her mouth. She was no kid, he thought, but she was young. The satire was gone from her face, but there was something behind her eyes that suggested she was still laughing at him.

"Uh, no," he said. "I've never been to, uh . . . where?"

"Claremore College. It's in Oklahoma. Near Tulsa."

"I've been to Oklahoma," he said. "But not to Claremore. Why?"

"I enjoyed your reading," she said, changing the subject. She removed a cigarette from her purse, and he lit it.

"It was hard to tell," he replied. "You were . . . well, you just had a funny look on your face."

"Do you have a brother?"

"Uh, yeah . . . that is, I did. He's dead."

Her eyes brightened even more. "Really? When did he die?"

"Seventy-one," he said. "Vietnam."

Disappointment. "Oh. I see. I'm sorry. I thought maybe I knew him."

"Why are you asking?"

"You just remind me of someone." She moved closer to him. There was barely room between them for her folded arms. "It's silly, I guess. His name was Barry. Barry Newton. I took him for English, though. Sometimes people change their names when they publish. You know: take a pseudonym."

"Not me," he said. "I use my real name."

"It's weird how much you resemble him, though. Spooky. I really thought you were him."

"Sorry," he said. He was distinctly uncomfortable. "Guess I wish I was, maybe." *Stupid* thing to say, he thought. But she seemed not to notice.

She moved closer and peered into his eyes. "I just wondered what kind of man writes poetry like that," she said.

"Like what?"

"Oh, I don't know. Like you write. I kept thinking that the poems didn't seem to say much about you. Now that I can see you up close, I can see that they do. I also see you're not Barry. He could have written poetry like that, but I thought he was unique. It's a little shocking to see that he wasn't."

She stood even closer to him and spoke softly. He felt himself growing uncomfortably warm inside. She had long fingers and well-manicured nails. There was no doubt that she was attractive: very attractive, and eager. The word "animal" came to him. She exuded a sense, almost an odor, which made him want to back away and at the same time touch her. It seemed she was coming on to him, but it was hard to tell for sure. It had been a long time since anyone other than one of his students had shown him much in the way of open flirting.

"Sometimes," he said pedantically, "poetry reveals something deeper than surface appearances."

"I know," she said, and the small grin reappeared. "I can tell *that* from reading your work." She crossed one arm across her breasts over her envelope and rested her right elbow on it. The cigarette pointed up, and her brown eyes studied him, appraised him. Bright as they were, they were seamless, as if she had no irises, just solid brown pupils. "You really remind me of him." Her eyes seemed to be devouring his face.

"I've been told that I remind people of other people before," he lied.

"He was a professor I had at Claremore College. Five or six years ago. I was a freshman."

"I see." He didn't.

"He fucked my brains out," she said impassively. She might as well have said that he'd given her an A on an essay.

"I, uh . . . see." He swallowed hard. His chest was so tight it felt ropes were pulled across it. There was an acidic fire in his stomach. She swayed slightly and dropped her arms. Her breasts brushed against his side.

"I'd like to get to know you better," she said. "Deeper."

He found himself panicked all at once, as if he were falling and could find nothing to grab hold of. It was stupid, he told himself, completely unbelievable. But this woman *was* coming on to him, not just flirting with him, openly and almost shamelessly, but propositioning him, flatly and obscenely. He couldn't tell if she was lying about her old professor or not. It didn't matter. She was saying what she was saying. That couldn't be mistaken.

"Ah . . . well," he stammered. What does one say to a blatant sexual offer, he wondered: how much? The thought almost made him laugh, then he saw Dr. Stephenson coming back inside. She spotted him talking to Connie, frowned, let her eyes move toward the door to the garden area where the buffet was being served.

"Are you a student here?" he asked, wanting to move on but at the same time transfixed.

"Uh-huh, graduate student," Connie said in a tone that said what she did or was wasn't important. Her eyes held his. "You read some of my poems. For the contest."

"Oh," he blushed a bit. "Well, it was a blind reading. No names."

"Bullshit," she said evenly and without anger. She was right. All the students' names were on each page, but he had no recollection of anything she might have written. "You shouldn't lie to me. I *know* you."

"Well," he tried a smile, "I just don't remember yours."

"*That* was clear from those you picked," she said. "I've never heard such simpering romantic pap in my life."

"Now, just a minute," he protested. "I read all the poems. And I—"

"I'm afraid we're just going to have to steal him away," Dr. Stephenson sang as she approached. "He's one of the guests of honor, and they're waiting for him to start the food line." She gave Connie a cold smile, then turned to him as she took his arm. "There are a number of people with books waiting for you to sign them." She beamed at him, shot Connie another nasty look, then took his arm and started to lead him away. "We've had a lot of trouble with that one," she whispered so low he wasn't sure he heard it. Connie waited for a beat, then followed, slapping her envelope against her skirt.

He moved about the lawn, sipped an iced-tea, wanted a beer, and balanced a flimsy plate of tough barbeque and watery cold slaw. He hungered to talk to Connie again. She made him deliciously uncomfortable, and he wondered precisely how far she would go and what, exactly, he might say. It was exquisitely dangerous, and it intrigued him and seemed to give him a distracting bounce as he walked around and made small talk with the crush of people from the recital and a history lecture, who had come out to join them.

As the only poet among two pianists and a couple of lecturers being touted at the Thursday barbeque, he was in almost as much demand as the musicians. Students flocked around him and asked him to sign their books, and a number of alumni were also present. Dr. Stephenson steered him from one group to the other, and he finally put aside his food and the bundle of envelopes he had been given and threw himself into the celebrity routine. This was what he had wanted, of course, he told himself, but she had spoiled it, put the whole thing into a different perspective, dimmed the light around the moment and focused it on something else entirely, something marvelously inviting. He found himself regretting for the first time that he was alone on the poetry program and trying to maneuver himself so he could keep her constantly in sight.

Connie placed herself in a chair by a brick wall and watched him with the same slight smile she had given him throughout the reading. Now, though, it seemed sharper, as if she could read his thoughts. He continued to sign books for one or two faculty members who had come by to be supportive and polite, shook hands with the dean, a red-faced portly man named Hancock who apologized for missing the reading, and then he was accosted by an acerbic woman in a man's suit, complete with button-down shirt and club tie. She had a hawkish nose and wore tennis shoes. Her nametag announced that she was "Ms. Wiseman," as opposed to the others which all were labeled either "Dr." or "Professor." Taking his arm in a firm grip and directing him off to one side, she asked him if he thought there was any market for a book of poetry based on women's athletics. He was barely listening to her when he said there wasn't, and she looked crushed and a little angry when she abruptly dropped his arm and walked away.

Regret struck him. They were *paying* him for this gig, he reminded himself, and he needed to be nicer. He suddenly realized that he was desperate to come back another time—soon—and he started to go after Ms. Wiseman to apologize, but Connie caught his eye again.

This time she rose and walked back into the building. She paused briefly in the doorway and gave him a brief, dark look, then entered.

He didn't hesitate. He went directly to Dr. Stephenson. "Where's the men's room?" She directed him indoors—up the stairs and to his right—and he almost raced inside. Let her think he was ill, he thought. The sauce was sweet enough he could blame it on that. He was breathing hard when he hit the top step of the second-floor landing.

Connie was waiting on him, smoking a cigarette and leaning on the wall next to the men's room. "What happens after this?" she asked. She waved the envelope she carried out toward the barbeque and mingling crowd.

His heart was pounding, but he had taken the steps three at a time. He had trouble keeping his voice steady. "Well, I'm pretty much on my own until I leave for the airport," he said, then added, "My plane's at four-thirty."

She glanced at her watch. "That gives us two hours," she said.

"Us?" He stepped up beside her. It was as if he was someone else, like he was standing outside himself and watching another man move.

"I thought you might like to see some of the campus." She smiled at him again, more broadly this time, and crushed her cigarette beneath her boot toe. In a deft move, her long fingers grabbed his crotch firmly. He was instantly hard. "I have an apartment that overlooks the whole east side," she almost hissed at him.

"I've sort of had the tour." He glanced nervously at the staircase. He could imagine Mrs. Stephenson marching up to check on him, make sure he wasn't seriously ill, and finding him standing there with one of the students' hands between his legs.

"I want to hear more of your poetry, find out what makes you write the way you do," she breathed rather than said.

"I think we need to discuss this in private," he said.

He moved and she stepped back, pushing the door to the men's room open and pulling him inside after her. He pushed toward her gently, and her hand returned to its former position. He kissed her hard.

It was the first woman other than his wife he had kissed since he had been married. Nearly ten years. But his wife had never kissed him like that, not ever. There was something nasty about it, something forbidden and crude. Her tongue filled his mouth, and then quickly withdrew and she sucked his own tongue inside her teeth with such violence that it hurt.

The urinals were vacant, and the newly remodeled interior of the room gleamed with hospital sparkle. She dropped her envelope on the counter, unzipped his trousers and ran her hands up under his shirt, raking his back with her nails. "Someone might come in," he gasped, breaking away. She said nothing but opened a stall door and stepped inside. He almost leaped in after her and pushed the door to behind them.

Her hand was inside his trousers now, and he allowed his own fingers to wander. His right hand slipped behind her and pulled her skirt up. His palm filled with a flabby hip.

"No buns." She pulled away for the brief warning. She then took his left hand and thrust it under her sweater where he found her breasts and began massaging them through a heavy bra. "That's where my assets are," she gasped between kisses. "There and here," she squeezed his erection, and he feared he would lose control. His pants pooled around his ankles. Her mouth was all over his face.

"I want to make love to you," he whispered. "I want you."

She stared at him with wide eyes. "You'd make love to a woman you don't even know?" Her grip on him remained firm, and he slipped his right fingers into the waistband of her pantyhose. "You know I wouldn't be thinking of you. I'd be thinking of Barry. Wouldn't that bother you?"

In response he kissed her again, moved his fingers between her hips, probing downward, finding her wetness. He worked his other hand under her bra and gently tweaked her nipples. Their kisses were deeper, nearly painful. Her breath was becoming more rapid. He pushed her against the stall's metal partition and felt her right leg climbing his left, grasping him to her.

He refused to think of what was happening to him, of what he was doing. He put all his concentration on his hands, his mouth, on the sensations her fingers were creating. He could smell her perfume—it was cheap, cloying—feel her hair, stiff with spray, on the sides of his face, taste the bitter pancake makeup she wore. God, he thought, he wanted this woman worse than anything in the world. He jerked her skirt high and began pushing downward on the waistband of her pantyhose.

Someone called his name. They separated and froze.

"Are you quite all right?" Dr. Stephenson was yelling from outside of the men's restroom door. "We're getting worried about you. Should I find someone?"

He stepped back against the metal wall and pulled up his trousers. Sweat broke out on his face and his fingers wouldn't work.

Connie stood away and smiled her same, sarcastic smile and watched him with her arms folded in front of her.

"What're you afraid of?" she asked him.

"I'm married, for Chrissake," he whispered. "Be quiet! You're a student here."

"None of that seals any holes I'm aware of," she said. One finger came up and played with a strand of her rumpled hair. Her other hand traced the outline of the zipper on his fly.

"Quiet!" he hissed.

He heard Dr. Stephenson walking away, back toward the stairs. She was hurrying, probably to fetch some man to go inside and check on him.

"Listen, I'll go out first, and you follow after I've had time to get back outside."

"What about that tour?" She smiled, refused to fix her disheveled clothing. Her skirt was still bunched up behind her. "I thought we were going to talk poetry."

"I can't. You know I can't."

"I don't know anything," she said. Her voice was low and husky. "I'm just here."

He came out of the stall, stopped and splashed water on his face, careful not to wet her envelope next to the sink. In the mirror he saw himself as if he were someone else. Behind his reflection, she continued her mocking pose.

He met Dr. Stephenson as she climbed the stairs and towed a pale young man in a cheap tweed suit. He looked familiar, and when they came together at the center of the staircase, he recognized him as Clint Harrison, a former graduate student, now an instructor in the music school here. He assured Harrison and Dr. Stephenson he was fine and denied hearing her calling him, and they started down. Connie didn't come out.

"God, I'm sorry I missed your reading," Harrison said. "I was in charge of the recital, and then I had to take my wife home. She's pregnant," he added with a sly smile and then complained, "I didn't even get to eat."

He was both relieved and aggravated by Harrison's presence and barely heard him. He remembered him as a serious-minded young man who was taking a master's in English as well as an MFA in music. Harrison announced several times how pleased and astounded he was to find his old professor—they might have been five years apart in age—was now a published poet and how excited he was to have him there for the series.

"I've got your book. Those *New Yorker* poems, too. You're fantastic!" Harrison assured him. "I was the one who told Dr. Stephenson to call you."

"You?" he asked. Disappointment fell on him. He had believed that Stephenson had chosen him on her own after reading his work.

"Sure. I remember your classes. You're great. I hated like hell to miss it."

They strolled over to the buffet table that was now a ruin of cold food and dirty paper plates. Harrison drew them both a fresh iced-tea. He felt he had never wanted a highball so bad in his life.

It was as if the past few minutes had been some sort of macabre dream. The rush of pleasure he had felt now was overshadowed by a terrible burden of relief that vied with the disappointment of Harrison's revelation. He felt as if he had just narrowly averted his car away from a fatal accident, only to realize that he was the one who nearly caused it. While Harrison babbled compliments and interspersed information about his own developing career, he took stock of his pulse and respiratory rate and tried to will himself to calm down. Unaccountably, the tip of his penis burned, and his tongue hurt at the roots. He couldn't shake the feeling that her moisture had stained his fingers somehow, and every time he brought his cigarette up to his lips, he could smell her musky scent on them. He kept his distance from Harrison. He was sweating and felt awash with guilt.

"So how's your wife, little girl. It *is* a girl, isn't it?" Harrison asked, clearly fishing for queries about his own wife and situation.

"Uh . . ." he had to *think*. "Yes," he offered a false laugh. "Of course. Little girl." He spoke her name, the name of his wife. "They're fine. Really great. Hate it when I'm gone," he added. Why had he said that? If anything, his wife probably celebrated his being away.

Harrison continued babbling, recalling mutual acquaintances, friends, old classmates. Connie emerged from the building.

If she looked at him, he didn't see it. She went over to a group of people on the edge of the lawn and began chatting in an animated style, nothing like the serious, sarcastic woman she had been.

"She's tough looking," Harrison agreed with a deep frown when he saw the direction of his gaze. He started. He realized his head had actually swiveled as he followed Connie's progress across the lawn. "But I'll tell you something," he added softly. He looked quickly around. "She's a tramp. Round-heeled whore. She's fucked half the faculty and most of the graduate students," he said. Then he caught himself and grinned. "If what I hear is right," he added with a blush.

He forced a smile. With no look at him, she drifted quickly over and placed her envelope on top of the stack, then went back to the group. He didn't want to watch her, but he couldn't help it. He was hard again, and he turned away.

"I hear she gives tremendous head, too," Harrison said, clearly uncomfortable in the presence of such obvious attraction. "But you shouldn't put her in *your* mouth. You don't know where she's been."

He laughed too loud at the joke, and Harrison smiled, relieved to have his complete attention again.

"Say," he said to the younger man, "could you give me a lift to the airport? My plane's not for a couple of hours, but I have some, uh . . . papers to look over." He spotted the stack of envelopes next to the group where Connie continued to talk and ignore him. *Student* poetry, you know?"

"Oh, yeah," he agreed with a knowing wink. "I guess they never leave you alone."

He made his manners to Dr. Stephenson, and with a thudding heart, he circled the crowd speaking to one or two people who had been especially solicitous, and made a point of making his manners with Ms. Wiseman, who only returned a cold adieu. Then Harrison put him in his Civic and took him to the terminal.

He went immediately to the men's room and washed his hands again, then soaped them and washed them once more. The sweet odor of her perfume would not go away. It even penetrated the sticky lather when he lifted his fingers up and sniffed them. He looked at his reflection in the mirror and was instantly reminded of the scene in Old Main men's room.

"'Look in the glass, and tell the face thou viewest \ Now is the time that face should form another,'" he quoted to his reflection. Then he shook his head hard, "You are an *idiot*," he scolded himself. "A fool and an idiot. You almost blew it. In a goddamn john in the middle of a goddamn luncheon reception. My God, what a fucking jerk!"

As he dried his hands, he had a familiar flash of regret. He had not admitted its nature before, but when it came to him this time, he knew what it was. He realized that he would never make love to any woman other than his wife again. Not ever. The dangerous and delicious excitement Connie aroused in him was more vital than the sex they spoke of. He desperately wanted that again, but he didn't want the guilt that hung on his shoulders and threatened to pull him down into the sink. He shook his head. Bad thoughts. Evil thoughts.

He left the men's room and went to the bar where he ordered and drank two doubles, one right after the other. The liquor burned into him and calmed him. He brightened on the third drink: There might be a poem there. He would have to consider it.

He also vowed that things were going to be different at home. A kiosk stand of fresh flowers was across the terminal, and he left the bar and tacked toward it, selected the most expensive bouquet he could find, and immediately felt contrition give way to a sense of firm resolve: He was going to be the devoted husband hereafter. What he had allowed himself to do was risky, stupidity that defied definition. He was not going to get caught in that trap again. He promised himself. He also made the same promise to his wife and mentally sent it to her.

There *was* a poem here, he thought: an envoy.

He felt suddenly relieved. He was sure he would not think of Connie again. He moved away from the bar and to a table where he drew up the stack of envelopes the students gave him. He was a *married* man, he reminded himself, a father *and* a husband, and he was going to be a good one. He was also a *responsible* professional, and he had no business boffing students, especially students of colleges that were nice enough to invite him to read and then pay him for the pleasure. He needed to explore these emotions intellectually, not physically. That way madness lies, he told himself.

No, he told himself, he would *not* repeat today's mistake. "Don't shit where you eat," he lectured himself in a whisper. Then he stacked the student poetry on the table and looked down at the first one. The bright red scrawl across the front mocked him just as she had. It told him he was a liar even to himself. Byron's words made his chest tighten and sweat break out on his forehead.

Men have all these resources, we but one,
To love again, and be again undone.

It was signed, "You'd have been better than Barry. Connie."

A sick feeling of loss spread across his heart, and something inside him broke open. He knew suddenly how hard it was going to be to keep his new resolution. He ordered another drink, sat back, closed his eyes, and was not at all surprised to find his poems there waiting for him.

III

"Ah, what shall I be at fifty
Should Nature keep me alive,
If I find the world so bitter
When I am but twenty-five"
— Tennyson

I *didn't write any poetry in graduate school: I didn't have time. When they came to me, I shoved them back, kept them out of sight, out of my senses. Mentally, I yelled, "Get outta here! I got* work *to do!" I had to succeed in scholarship, and graduate school was tough: mean. It has to be if you do it right.*

The truth is that if it wasn't for my wife, I probably wouldn't have made it. "Making it" was everything, you know? I didn't screw around. Not in any sense of the word. It sort of "made me what I am today." I published every damn paper I wrote, though. Every one: Master's and Ph.D. both. Every seminar paper, every bullshit reading-report paper, everything. I didn't type up a thing I didn't rework and submit and publish, sometimes before I got it back with a grade on it. It was a cold world in academics. Then. The "job crunch" was on. To make it, you needed something on your vita other than the names of the girls you took to bed, which in my case would have been none.

I didn't have time for that, either.

I was all over the board the first several years. No focus. I had papers on Chaucer, Shakespeare, Dante, Hawthorne, Hemingway, and Swift all come out in the same year. And they were in Class-A literary journals, too. Well, B+ anyhow. I mean, when I went to MLA to look for a job, I had the credentials. Getting on a faculty with a first-rate institution was no problem for me. I had six offers when other guys didn't get shit. And a lot of them were better than I ever hoped to be. Most of them were, to tell you the truth.

My Ph.D. program was the biggest bunch of competitive crap you ever saw or heard of. And a heart-break. Lots of guys didn't "make it." Shades of the past: I can tell you about them, my friends, my peers, my classmates. We were a kind of group, a kind of literary elite. We were self-defined, and we all knew we all would "make it." But we were wrong. Almost none of them *"made it."*

I remember one night when it all became clear to me, like a goddamn epiphany, the Fourth of July during the second year of my Ph.D. work. I'll never forget it, even though, to be honest, nothing remarkable happened. Except for it being the Fourth, it was just like any other summer night. But that was the moment I saw it all. All at once, I realized where everything was going, where I was going, and what it was going to take for me to get there. You see, I saw right then that I was going to "make it" and they weren't. It came to me in sort of a star burst, which was appropriate for the season. Like a big boom. Destiny, again, although I wouldn't have used such a banal word then. I thought of it more as determination.

And it didn't have one goddamn thing to do with poetry.

As I said, there wasn't anything remarkable about that evening. It started like hundreds of others, except because it was the Fourth, we all had agreed to go down on the river and watch the fireworks. It wasn't dark yet, so we were sitting around in a cockroach-overrun duplex where Tommy, my best friend and one of the brightest and most able people I've ever met, sipped Dr Pepper laced with cheap bourbon. That's disgusting, I know, but that's what he drank. Candy, his wife, drank even cheaper red wine, and my wife and I slurped up the remains of a case of Jax another friend, Delmar, had brought us back from a recent trip he made to his hometown, Jackson, Mississippi.

Oh yeah, I was married then. Two years into it and solid. We were all married then, one way or another. It wouldn't last, though. Not for any of us. Truly, it had already started falling apart.

The Beatles were playing on Tommy's Aiwa reel to reel, and the heat of the midwestern summer filtered through the dust motes that swirled from shades that hadn't been removed and cleaned since they were installed sometime during the Great Depression.

How's that for poetry? I really thought like that, then. But I didn't think it was poetry. I just thought it was graduate school.

No one talked too much. It was too hot. We all had reading to do, papers to write. But it was the Fourth of July. On summer nights, we liked to get together, listen to a little music, talk things out. You see, it didn't take us long to realize that the stuff they were giving us in the seminars was bullshit. The real *literary discussions went* on in the coffeeshops and bars, and in our living rooms. We were the intellectual elite. We knew how things ought to be, and we decided them among ourselves. Fuck everyone else.

The subject for the evening was the relative value of James Joyce vs. Shakespeare vs. John Lennon as an influence on modern culture, but that had faded as we then fell into gossip concerning H. E. Hamby, a fat Shakespearean who hated both Lennon and Joyce. Just a week before he cracked up during his written comps and puked all over his answers as they lay on the desk in front of him. He raced down to the restroom in front of a number of startled students and the proctor, finished his retching, and then marched across campus after bundling up the vomit-laden pages—two hours work completed, the second of three days of exams—and blundered into the graduate dean's office and dumped the whole smelly mess on his desk. "If I have to even say the name Henry James once more in my life, I'll kill myself," he screamed. And then he left campus and didn't even return to clean out his desk in the grad fellows' office.

He didn't have it, you see. He never did. He couldn't "make it."

The Beatles gave way to Roy Orbison, and the darkness gathered more resolutely around us. Paul, who Tommy didn't like, came by along with Delmar, who Tommy really hated. Delmar brought more Jax and a couple of joints, and we drifted into Daniel's story. He had completed sixty hours of Ph.D. course work while commuting back to Texas, every other weekend. Fifteen hundred miles. His wife made fairly good money teaching school there. They had a baby boy he'd spent exactly thirty days with in the two years of his life, if you counted waking hours only. He passed his comps the same time H. E. cracked up, and then he threw one hell of a party. About two o'clock in the morning, he got in his twelve-year-old Rambler and took off for home, for Texas. It was a crazy idea, since he was stumbling drunk, but he said he was too homesick to stay there another minute. He wanted to see his family, eat a decent bowl of chili. No, he didn't have a wreck, or even get a ticket. But he never got home. Not in the way he intended. He got there the next night—drove straight through, like he always did— and walked in and caught his wife in bed with a boyfriend. In flagrante delicto, as the saying goes. I heard from him about a year later. He was working as a baggage handler for American Airlines in Dallas. His wife divorced him, his dissertation never did get written, and I have no idea what became of him after that. But that night in the midwest, none of us knew where he might be. We just knew that he wouldn't "make it" either, and we were feeling really righteous as Roy Orbison faded off and was replaced by the new Bob Dylan album, the one that precursed the country music craze. Tommy could get one hell of a lot of music on a single reel.

Then Paul said he was thinking about dropping out and applying for law school, and Megan, his wife, gave him a Bronx Cheer. She was a New York Jew, dark and sultry with one of the best sets of legs I've ever seen, and by then, she was thoroughly stoned—and they were in trouble. He shut up and sipped his wine. We slandered William, an ex-Green Beret with the personality of a box of Rice Crispies, who Tommy said would never "make it." We all agreed, but we all knew better, even Tommy. Megan fuzzily recollected from her dope-booze haze that William's wife, Lady—that was her real name, I swear—had said she would leave him the same day he graduated, even though they'd married right out of high school: girl next door and all that. It was supposed to be a secret—that she was planning to dump him—but it didn't matter who she told. No one would warn him. He was "liked, but not well-liked," as Willy Loman said. He had the "right stuff," as Tom Wolfe would later say, but we figured if Lady left him, it was over. Next to me, he was the most married guy in the whole program, and the most naïve. "Tis pity learned virgins ever wed/ With persons of no sort of education." Right?

Delmar was sensitive on that topic. Jean Ann had walked out on him around Easter, and it took me, Vance, Tommy, and a half dozen others to talk Delmar out of cutting his wrists with a butcher knife. He was dating one of his former students now, Katie, and was heavy into drugs—and not just pot—while waiting on the divorce to become final. He never brought Katie around, and we all knew why: He was banging Candy every time Tommy was out of the house. It was actually sort of comical. Candy had been "Miss Oregon" back in the mid-sixties, and she still looked pretty good, although her complexion had gone to hell, and her thighs had to be five or six times the size they were when she was a high school senior. I mean, they were more like old William Carlos's "appletrees/Whose blossoms touch the sky" than anything Dr. Bill ever imagined, bark and all. She was a militant feminist now and had really let herself go to prove that she wasn't a sex object. Advancing cellulite probably has more to do with political conviction than people give it credit for.

Delmar had a red afro that sat atop his head like lightning in a sand storm. He was horribly near-sighted and wore bottle-bottom glasses that he looked over the top of when he needed to see anything more than six feet away. He was almost six feet tall, weighed about ninety pounds soaking wet and, when he had time, played keyboard for a rock-and-roll band. He had more time than most of us because he had a photographic memory—no shit, total recall—loved Joyce and Proust, and he was working on a dissertation on John Barth. The thought of his stick-figure frame crawling up between Candy's generous breasts was funny to almost anyone who thought about it. Except Tommy, I guess. He didn't weigh ten pounds more than Delmar, and his teeth were rotten, his hair kind of greenish-blond from some kind of disease-treatment he had as a kid. He was just plain ugly, but like Delmar, he was smart. Together, they represented the intelligentsia of our group. We all said that they would "make it." No question: They had the stuff.

Tommy walked in on them twice. It must be hell to find your wife humping some guy who was supposed to be your friend, but they claimed to have an "open marriage," which meant that Candy could fuck anyone she damn well wanted to, and poor old Tommy just jerked off. He pretended that it didn't bother him, but it was eating him up like a cancer. She was a ball-cutting bitch, and her hatred of men oozed almost as much as did the pimples she couldn't seem to shake, although she'd never see twenty-five again.

Paul was from New Hampshire and hated everything he'd seen since he crossed the Hudson. Megan, his wife and our token Semite, was a faculty instructor, which gave them a status that few of us enjoyed: faculty club membership, Class-A parking sticker, and a better income. They also got invited to faculty parties. Most of us were jealous. Megan did a lot of dope, but she got pissed off if Paul did. No explanation about that. I think she did the dope so we would accept her, forget she was a Jewish girl from the Bronx who had "married up." It didn't work. She was the only one everyone openly had contempt for. Most of us liked Paul, and we felt sorry for him. He knew he didn't have the stuff, not even for Megan.

Tommy hated both Paul and Megan. Their stock wasn't very high with Candy, either. Tommy claimed that Megan was a latent dyke because she stared at Candy's tits all the time. I would have agreed, except that Candy had the ugliest tits in the world. It was hard not to stare at them. They were big, but they were plain funny-looking. They each came to a point. She pretended to like me because Tommy and I were close, but I knew she was faking it. Except for Delmar, I think she hated everybody, and she may have hated him, too. I never was sure why, except that we were men. She liked to make men uncomfortable any way she could. One afternoon right after we all met, I dropped by to borrow a book, and she came to the door stark naked. She didn't cover up a thing. She just sat on the sofa, Indian-style, legs crossed beneath her, and let me look through Tommy's shelves for the book. I was sweating hard, really embarrassed, but I pretended that nothing was going on, found the book I wanted, and left.

I found out later she did this to all the guys every chance she got. She just wanted to see what they would do, I guess. God help them if they ever did anything.

Or that could be wrong. That could be how she and Delmar got together in the first place. He was always borrowing books from Tommy.

Actually, former Miss Oregon or not, with those funny-looking mammaries, I could hardly look at Candy without laughing. I have to admit that when it was cold and her nipples tightened up, she tended to round out, and except for her wrinkled thighs, she wasn't bad looking, acne and all.

I think, though, that she didn't like me because she knew I told Tommy that if I were he, I'd knock her teeth out for fucking Delmar right in their own bed, right in front of him. He said that once when he walked in on them, they finished up, rolled a skinny, put on a record, then sat around and talked, all three of them, Candy and Delmar, naked as the day they were born, and "reeking from the rut," as some poet said, and poor old Tommy: trying to hold up his end of the "open marriage," which I figure is about like trying to hold up the end of a stream of hot water. I wondered if they climbed back into bed and went at it again while he was sitting there—it was a two-room apartment and there wasn't a bedroom worth the name, just a mattress on the floor of the dining room where the table would have gone had they had one. He never said, though, and I thought too much of him to ask. Then.

The winter before, my wife and I had a party. That was the night when Jean Ann and Delmar began to split up—at least, that was the night when it became public. She got sick on vodka and 7-Up, and I think she was stoned too, and she went into the bedroom to lie down. She and my wife were pretty tight, and I went to check on her. Jean Ann didn't wear bras, either, and even though she was uneducated—I mean, she didn't even finish high school—she was smart and pretty hip. You had to be to live with Delmar, I guess, even for a while, and they'd been married for almost five years. She had a nice figure, though, and a tight little butt, and I headed down the hall to see if she was all right, telling myself that no matter what

42

she said or did, I was going to stay straight. All the time trying to talk myself out of the boner I was growing with every step toward the door. I mean, like I say, I was really into marriage then. I lost the boner when I caught Denison, this creative writer—a poet, ain't that a kick?—coming out of the room, though, and it was clear to me he hadn't been in there giving her clues to the secrets of anapests. He was grinning and he winked at me. He had been banging her all along, I guess, and poor Delmar wore the horns, too. I didn't know about Delmar and Candy then, though, or maybe it hadn't started yet. That part's a little fuzzy.

Denison, by the way, owned a piece of a bar and was taking an MFA in creative writing. Most all of us thought he was a shitheel, but he gave us free beer at the bar, so we all associated with him. He was never part of our group, though. He was also married, to Kathy—real socialite: gorgeous, and lots of money, which is how he bought into the bar—but he claimed he was infertile, so they adopted a kid. The adoption started that spring, and they separated a month later. They had to get back together from time to time when the social worker came around to check on the kid's home environment, and I guess they really tried to get back together, since Kathy turned up pregnant by fall. They went back to court to get the adoption finalized a week before they went to court to get the divorce. It was supposed to be one of those "amicable" divorces, you know: I get this, you get that. It wasn't. On his way into court, she told him that she knew he'd been skimming the bar profits for years, and if he opened his mouth to protest one thing she asked for, she'd fuck him over by turning him in to the IRS.

He went to the john and was so distracted, he pissed down his leg. Then, in court, who should preside over the hearing but the same damned lady judge who had finalized the adoption a week before. Kathy accused him of every vile act she could think of, and then she asked for $1,000 a month in child support, a trust fund to be set up and maintained by him for both kids' college, no visitation for him for either kid, and the house, car, and a healthy settlement. He stood there with pissed-on khakis next to a wife who was eight months pregnant and the mother of an adopted two-year-old and couldn't say a fucking word. Kathy got everything she asked for.

I didn't learn a thing from that. I should have, though.

Most of us felt that it couldn't have happened to a nicer guy, since he was an asshole who talked all the time about his poetry and never published a thing. I read a lot of it: I thought it was crap. Derivative and facile, mostly about the kinds of surface emotions that form the plots of musical comedy. He dropped out of the program the next year and went to medical school and is now an ob-gyn in Oklahoma City. I know what you're thinking: William Carlos Williams was a doctor, too—but Denison never did publish any poetry. He just had a thing for pelvic exams.

Dylan's set ended, and Simon and Garfunkle replaced it, over Delmar's complaints that no one there ever listened to the Stones. We talked of Jerry Kilmon who had been working on a Joyce dissertation for four years and faced the termination of his last extension this summer. He stood about six-feet tall and wore his hair shoulder length and a full beard and was thin, almost emaciated. He looked like Renaissance paintings of Jesus. We remembered Paul Halloway, who had left ABD and taken the job as department chairman with a j.c. in western Kansas, where he was now tenured. He had just failed his exams for the third and last time and didn't know what he was going to do. He had just had a second child and bought a house. And there was "Paul the Elder," who was attending school full time, although he had one child with heart disease and who required constant surgery it seemed. He was trying to figure out why he failed his exams the first time around.

The truth was that he wasn't going "to make it"—none of them would.

We did a slanderous catalogue of other colleagues absent. We didn't think of them as "colleagues," of course, but as rivals, as losers, as those who didn't have a thing going for them and who would fail. Some of them were poets and writers, or they were trying to be. We all had contempt for the creative writing people—the MFA poetry types, including Denison—because we said they were fakes and frauds and couldn't write a word of scholarship if their lives depended on it. Couldn't write poetry either. "How can you write a quatrain," Delmar liked to ask us, "when you can't define one?" We all drank to that. Then the tape ran out, and so did the dope, and so did the liquor. But the talk went on.

We soon got to "Dondi." That wasn't her name, of course, but that's what we called her. She sort of looked like that old comic strip character: short black hair, dark eyes, and kind of chubby-cheeked. And sweet: like saccharin. I coined the nickname. She wanted to be a part of our group, but there was something about her that gave us all the willies. It fell to me to destroy her, though. It was in our British Poetry class. She got up to read her paper on Yeats, and she started by saying: "My thesis is that W. B. Yeats was never a political poet." I started thumbing through my Collected

Yeats *immediately, looking up references to rebut when she finished. She stopped dead, stared at me, and yelled, "You keep your mouth shut! You're out to get me!" She was right. I was. She was so tentative after that, the paper was a mess. But I waited until she finished, and then I raised my hand.*

"You know," I said, "I've listened very carefully to everything you said, and I'll be damned if I have any kind of an idea what you're talking about." The professor nodded in agreement. She burst into tears. She got a C. She dropped out of the program a week later. The story was always good for a laugh.

Then there was "The Toad," a squirrelly little guy with big birth marks on his cheeks that made him look like a frog. I got him only a week later, coming out of our Samuel Johnson seminar. He saw that I had several volumes of Johnson's work in my hands. "Are you going to read all that?" he asked.

"Sure," I said. "But I don't know how I'm going to find time to read The Dictionary.*"*

"You're going to read The Dictionary*?"*

"Of course," I said. "Everyone is. It's always a hidden agenda in a Johnson seminar. It'll be on the final."

And he bought it. He dropped not only the seminar, but out. Tommy said it was I who did it. He was right. I'm telling you, we were mean, ruthless. Only a handful of us were going to get top recommendations, and we all knew it. Eliminate the competition, that was the watchword. And I was better at it than anyone, and they all knew that, I think. But they trusted me. Trust: not a good thing in a competitive world.

So there we were. Out of beer and booze, out of dope, out of conversation. It was July Fourth, and we all knew that Independence Day for all of us was coming soon whether we went to see the fireworks or not. Soon, we would all be competing with each other, and when the smoke cleared, there wouldn't be but one or two of us standing. We didn't talk about that, though. Instead, we acted like we would all be standing, that we were all going to "make it." We speculated on our futures, felt good about ourselves. We were all scared to death.

All but me, that is. Because right then was when it hit me. Sitting there in the dark, listening to the gossip, the false confidence, I knew that I was going to "make it," whether they did or not. Survival. That was it. It was too Darwinian not to see. Others were smarter than I, and probably more talented, some of them might even have had poems inside them. But I was the fittest. They

wouldn't beat me because I knew I had what it would take to beat
them. I made up my mind to that right then on that Fourth of July.

I figured it this way: In spite of the fact that we were fucking
each other and breaking each others' hearts, we were really good
people. We hated one another, were suspicious of one another, but
we were friends. That sounds like a paradox, but that's the way it
was. We needed one another—even Candy—and in spite of
everything, I loved them one and all. And I think they loved me, too.
But none of them would "make it." Not one. They would all fail,
because none of them knew what it would take to "make it." I
couldn't have said what "it" was then. I'm not sure I could now. But
it wasn't there. It wasn't in their faces. It wasn't in their hearts.

What was in their hearts was what Lawrence called
"Intellectual disgrace," and you could see it, just as you could see
"the seas of pity lie/ Locked and frozen in each eye."

*You see, they wanted rules—*rules*—they wanted things to be*
honorable, fair, right. They believed in some kind of ideal
community of scholars and that just because they liked—even
loved—one another, that was enough. But it was a long way from
being enough. Hell, it wasn't even a down payment on enough.

But I already knew—instinctively, I guess—that there were no
rules, no honor, that life wasn't fair. I knew that years before Jimmy
Carter said it right out loud, but it wasn't until later that I learned
that Thomas Hardy said it first, lying upon "the leaze" and
watching the sky and considering the importance of tradition. Even
a good old Baptist like Carter wasn't above a bit of illicit
appropriation of material if it suited his purpose.

Three years later, I would be teaching in a pretty decent school,
tenure-track, forty solid publications to my credit, and a first book
on the way. All of the people in that room would be dead:
professionally dead. And I killed them. All of them. I picked them
off one at a time. The same way I picked off "Dondi" and "The
Toad." I didn't play fair. I played with their heads, undermined
their confidence, and if that didn't work, I beat them at their own
game: scholarship. But I was good at it, you know. And I was
determined. And even now, I think I was right.

Like the song reminds us, it's not hard to be hard.

Delmar married his student, completed his exams, and strug-
gled to start his dissertation, only to give it up and join a religious
group as an organist while he worked day jobs re-striping parking
lots. Tommy passed his exams, completed a dissertation on
Finnegan's Wake, *then fell apart when Candy ran off with a Hell's*

Angel who was passing through on his way back to LA. He tried to stay straight. He remarried twice within the next eighteen months, both times to twenty-year-old students, divorced each of them, lost everything he had, which never was much. I last saw him at a conference maybe thirty years ago. He was in the bar, trying to kill the shakes by knocking back double bourbons at 11:00 a.m. He had a job as a book rep for one of those companies that publishes foreign language workbooks that nobody in his right mind ever wants. His liver was dying, but the rest of him died a long time ago.

Megan divorced Paul, married a Negro dean who became president of one of the SUNY schools and then dumped her for a Swedish airline stewardess with a pair of 44-Ds and a ski lodge in Switzerland. The day the divorce came through, she loaded up on acid and took a header off her old building in the Bronx, or so they said. Paul went to law school and moved to Boston with a guy named Kurt. He failed the bar three times and they opened an antique store in the Combat Zone, of all places.

Most of the others fell out of my memory, except William. Lady did leave him six months after he finished, and he hooked a hose to the exhaust pipe of his running car and went to permanent sleep in his garage the same day they called to offer him a tenure-track job at Rutgers.

The irony of that, of course, is that he might have "made it."

But that night, so long ago, that Fourth of July, in that "schoolboy spot," I was the only one who could see all that coming—not the details, of course, just the trends. I wasn't a poet then. I was a scholar. And a teacher. But I knew that to make it, I had to climb over all the bullshit, conquer it, put it behind me. I had to be more than just good, I had to be mean. I had to rely on myself, not on others, and I couldn't depend on anyone but me to make sure my voice was heard, and every one of them had to fall by the way.

There's a slogan that everyone in graduate school should memorize: "Success is not enough: others must fail."

But that night changed me. Right then. With all the dope, the booze, the music, the talk. It changed me. I sat back and closed my eyes, and the poems came while the celebration went on. I shut them out then, though, postponed them. I had other business that was more urgent than poetry, more urgent than fireworks, more urgent than friendship. And that was the hardest part. Knowing what I would have to do to people I truly loved. They were the smartest bunch of people I ever knew, and they loved me. We loved each other. And I was a part of them. But they were all going to fail, and

I couldn't let myself care, not if I wanted to "make it." That's why, I think, they were the best friends I ever had.

The First Tour

It was too good to be true. He hadn't felt like this since he was a sex-crazed sophomore. Even then the expectations had not been so great. He could hardly move around the motel room because every time he stopped to think about what was about to happen, he got a hard-on. Then he felt guilty and lost it, and then he got it again. He felt like a sexual yo-yo.

"Nothing is going to happen," he assured himself aloud. "It's going to be like before. Lots of hope, but no dice." But he pulled a fresh shirt from the suitcase and buttoned it on carefully while inspecting his face in the motel room's mirror. He still looked young, he thought: What was left of his hair was shaggy but not totally unkempt as it raced away behind the steady advance of his forehead. Still, there was just the right touch of gray at the temples, just the right hint of a beard: the unshaven look, the Bohemian look. He splashed aftershave on anyway: subtle.

This was his fourth school on the tour. And they had worked his ass off. He arrived at seven a.m., red-eye out of Chicago after dinner with the editors from *Dissonant Voices*, a new review that was already causing a major stir across the country. He had a regular column, now. For money. It was going to be exhausting.

"Lots of bad poetry out there," he assured the quartet of young men and women who were starting the magazine, "and a lot of it needs killing off before it hurts somebody." They all laughed. They called him "the gunslinger," said that he would keep the integrity of the review high.

"You're the most astounding poetic voice to emerge in the past decade," Kari, the assistant editor assured him. She was about twenty-five, long-waisted, with delicate features and a cascade of dark brunette hair that fell in a silky fall across the shoulders of her "all-business" suit. She wore no makeup, though. Didn't need it. She reminded him of a hippie-girl he used to know in college, one of those ultra-serious types who read philosophy and political theory over a bowl of bean sprouts in the student union and drove everyone crazy when they tried to imagine her naked. "But we can't afford to publish both your poetry and your criticism. That would leave us liable in an artistic sense."

He nodded wisely. "That's fine," he said. She had nice lips, he thought, full and kissable. "I don't think you could afford my poetry anyway." They smiled. "The critical work will be fine. And it will be welcome. I need an outlet for that."

They all agreed, but as he left, Kari took his arm in a tight grip. Her touch was fire. "We're not hiring you to puff bad poetry," she said. "Keep that in mind, especially if you're handling a friend's book. No conflicts of interest."

"No problem," he assured her. "I'm sharpening my pen already. 'In criticks hands, beware thou dost not come,'" he quipped, hoping for a response to the distaff allusion if not to the double entendre. She only looked at him with a blank expression. He coughed slightly. "Critics have no friends," he said.

She smiled, and he noticed that her front teeth were slightly pointed. "You're going to be great," she assured him. "You're going to make this magazine happen." Her grip tightened, and he was instantly erect.

"Just keep the checks coming," he said. And I'll see you later, he thought. But he hadn't: no guts.

It had been a fruitful intermission in the tour's schedule, but now he was back on track. He met with the writing faculty at nine: two poets, no serious publications, three prose writers, one with a failed novel, the others pushing short fiction where they could. *Towers of Glass* was just out, and he was thrilled with the job Felix had done on it. The faculty writers ogled both books right in front of him, made him feel important, asked him to sign them. Then there was lunch with the dean, and following that, he had to stay awake while he read eighteen poems and met with the six student poets who wrote them in workshop. That's where the labor came in.

Poring over the student verse, he had almost lost control, almost yielded to a tendency to slash and cut through them, point out their borrowings from Dickinson, Yeats, Whitman, even Donne, for God's sake. He had to keep reminding himself that they were *students*, not practicing poets, not even the sort of dilettantes he would be handling in the magazine reviews. Still, most of it was pretty awful, that which wasn't was almost blatantly plagiarized by the oversexed little androids searching for something resembling adult emotions. Nothing real, nothing original, nothing that goddamn rhymed or had rhythm for the most part. That's what he should have said.

But he didn't: no guts there either. Instead, he led them through three hours of careful, critical explication. He pointed out—tactfully—their flaws, their clichés, their complete ignorance of strained, trite, dead, and mixed metaphor. All the while he studied them and put his voice on automatic. Had they had *no* courses in poetic theory? Had they read *no* poetry at all? Only three of them were in closed form, only a handful even *looked* like poems.

But there was one there, a woman—girl, really—and he desperately hoped that the sonnets were hers. Of all the poetry, only the three sonnets made any sense, held forth any hopes. Leggy and high-breasted, her yellow hair draped down over her long neck and told her Nordic ancestry. As he studied her sleek, graceful fingers, he had trouble keeping anapest and iamb straight in his talk.

Alas, the sonnets belonged to a sagging brunette, one-seventy-five if she was an ounce, with bad teeth, stringy hair, and onions spilling out with her breath when she leaned over and thanked him for the critique. The blonde—Jenny was her name—*Jenny*, he repeated, ideal!—had offered three simpering attempts at blank verse nature poems that combined the worst imitations of Dickinson and Frost. Pathetic fallacy flowed through each line, and when she came to the end of a thought, she always used a dash. There wasn't a decent metaphor in any of them.

But then, following the dinner and reading, after he wowed them with his own work, she came up to the autograph table and put her lovely hand on his.

"You know, that stuff in the workshop this afternoon. Well, it's not my best work."

He knew that. It couldn't be *anybody's* best work. He looked into her eyes. They were bluer than skim-ice. He fell through them.

"Well, you really should hand in your best work," he choked out. His voice wouldn't work. She had a wonderfully delicate nose, flanked by the barest hint of freckles. Her front teeth overlapped slightly. She was lovely.

"I'm . . . embarrassed to have it shown in public." She cast her eyes down and blushed. "It's so . . . sensual, so personal."

"Poetry should be sensual," he remarked. He was deliberately casual. "And personal. In a way that's a definition of poetry." He was embarrassed. He wondered if raw lust was flashing like a neon sign on his forehead. God, she was attractive, young, fresh. People were in line behind her, waiting to have his name scrawled on their title pages. Money in the bank, but he didn't care. Nothing mattered but her continuing to stand there, continuing to stare at him. "The words should reflect what you feel, communicate that to the reader. Remember: 'Coyness' is not a crime." He squeezed her fingers.

She looked bewildered for a moment, then smiled. "It's still, well, revealing," she said. "Based on personal experience. I'm only a sophomore, but I'm older than I look. More experienced, too." She smiled. Her teeth were white, clean, and framed by full lips.

"I'll bet you are." He smiled back and hoped it wasn't too lecherous. He had a hard-on just thinking about her, about that mouth on his. "I mean, poets usually are. That's why they're poets."

She shrugged. "I was wondering . . . could you, I mean, *would* you look at some of my other poems sometime? Tell me if what I'm doing is okay? Maybe if any of it's publishable?"

He felt himself flush, redden. He released her fingers and played with his pen a moment. His heart was deafening him. "Well, sure. I mean, *all* poetry is publishable. It's really just a matter of finding the right place to submit it. I'd like to look at your work. Your other work. I might be able to recommend something. I mean somewhere to send it." He felt he had stepped outside himself, that he was playing a part. "I have to be in Indiana tomorrow night though. I leave here in the morning."

"I could mail them to you."

His mind raced. A familiar hot, hollow feeling grew in his stomach. Danger lights flashed, but he ignored them and sped on. He placed his right hand over his left, concealing the ring. "Oh, well, sure. You could. But you know, I'm on tour for this whole term. Won't have much time to look at anything for a while." Words spilled out of him. They sounded so rehearsed he was shocked, like he was reading from a script. "I won't even see my regular mail until Christmas." He smiled, opened his palms. "You know how it is. The price of fame." *Price of fame!* Did he really say that?

"Oh," she said. Her blue eyes saddened. She licked her lips. "I understand. You're a *real* poet."

"You know, it's still early," he said, speaking too loudly, too quickly. "I'm at the Holiday Inn. There's nothing scheduled after this. Why don't you . . . I mean, if you want . . . ." He couldn't believe himself. He was really doing this! He didn't think he had that much courage. "Well, I mean, if you like, I could look over some of them tonight."

She brightened, and his heart beat out a regular tempo.

"Well, sure! I mean, if you aren't too tired or anything. I have them at home. I mean, I could go get them."

"Uh, sure," he said, suddenly uncertain. His palms were awash in perspiration. "Yeah. If you want. I mean, I can't do much more than what I did this afternoon, but . . . ."

"That's fine. It'd mean so much. I can't show them to just

anybody. But I think *you'd* understand." The crowd behind her was diminishing, drifting off. People were tiring of standing in line, putting his books back on the stack.

"Tell you what: I'm going to be stuck here another hour, hour-and-a-half. Why don't you go get them, drop them off at the desk, then call. Discuss them."

"Great! I'll do it," she said, turning and swinging her delicious blonde hair behind her. His eyes were fixed on her hips, rising and falling beneath a pleated skirt until she was gone and the book buyers lined up again.

He brushed off the departmental prose writer who wanted to go for a drink and asked to be taken back to the motel.

"Got a headache," he said. "I need to get to bed early." He chewed on the irony of the excuse in his mind. The prose writer was sympathetic, even relieved, he thought. He said he would pick him up at six sharp for the airport. He waited until the car pulled away, then smoked a slow cigarette to make certain that the prose writer wouldn't suddenly remember something and come back. Then he raced to the desk where a purple folder bound with paperclips awaited him. A piece of pink stationery with bright hearts embossed on it covered the stack.

"These are my best," she wrote. "Be brutal with me." *Brutal*, he thought.

The poems were terrible. No two lines went together, and half the words were either spelled wrong or misused, two thirds of the phrases borrowed from popular song lyrics or other poems. She had no sense of metaphoric language, and half the similes were from the same level of experience, forcing meaningless comparisons.

But they were sexy, almost purely erotic.

His breath was short from the first line as he read and imagined her honeyed voice describing orgasms and the sizes of penises she had encountered, the feel of them between her breasts, on her nipples, parting her "wings," slipping inside her, coming. He read each of them five times, getting more excited with each explicitly suggestive stanza. They were all done in her flowery cursive hand with tiny hearts drawn for dots of i's, j's, and periods. The paper was lime green and smelled of rose perfume. He imagined that she had gone home from his reading, hastily written them especially for him. It was like reading an almanac of sexual encounter. Each poem discussed physical sensations that he had only read of in hard-core pornography. She was experienced, all right, he said to himself, or she had a vivid imagination. Either alternative was just fine with him.

The phone rang just as he finished the fifth poem.

"Did you get a chance to look at any of them?" Her voice came through the receiver like quick-silver.

His mouth was so dry, he could barely form words. "I think you've got a real talent. Flair for description."

"You think they're publishable, then?"

"Oh, most definitely," he started. Then he caught himself, and the dank hollow feeling emerged in his stomach once more. A band of tension formed across his chest, made his breath short. "That is, with work. A few changes. Things you ought to consider."

Disappointment: "Like what? I've worked on them so hard. They're all so personal, so deeply a part of myself, my experiences."

"Well, there are specific places . . . ." His mind raced. He couldn't recall a single line verbatim and looked in vain across the room where they lay on his bed, on his pillow. "I think we should go over it, line-at-a-time in places. There are some expressions you need to study. Figurative language. Metonymy. Things like that." He held his breath. Hoped.

"Met-what?"

Bingo: "Metonymy. A figure of speech. Like synecdoche or litotes."

"I don't think I know what those are."

"That's why I think we should . . . uh, talk about them. With the manuscript in front of us. Together." Again, he held his breath. He wondered if she could hear his heart beating in the ear he pressed against the phone. "There are also some . . . gaps here, distances between your abstract descriptions and concrete experiences." What a line, he thought: transparent as thin air. But he hoped. "It's sometimes hard to tell exactly what you mean. There's a need for . . . uh, detachment and recreation. We really should get together and talk about it."

No response. He could hear her breathing. "Well, I guess so. I mean, there's so much in them that confuses me. My feelings. You know? I don't know why, but I think I can share them with you. After hearing you read your work, I think you're someone who can understand, help me get in touch with the way to express these things. These experiences. I have trouble remembering everything when I write it out. Inspiration keeps getting in my way. It overwhelms me. I lose control when I'm writing it down. I lose control just thinking about it."

Was he imagining, or was her breathing becoming heavier, more rapid? "Why not come over?"

"Now?"

"Sure, why not. We can work on them." He glanced at his watch: 10:20. He had a flight to Urbana at seven, then a drive to the campus. Lecture at ten. "I'm wide awake. I've got a bottle of pretty good bourbon." And condoms are for sale in the lobby gift shop, he silently added—"Let's talk all this out. Try to 'get in touch' with what you're feeling, what you're trying to say. Recreate the experiences, so to speak. Work it all out together. Study impersonal detachment. Sometimes," he hesitated, "sometimes it's possible to create the poem while you're actually having the experience that inspired it." He swallowed hard. "I mean, if you're game to try, I am."

"Well, sure!" Her voice sounded excited. "I just thought it might be too late."

"Naw, never too late to talk poetry, to explore possibilities," he chortled, feeling idiotically relieved that she hadn't hung up in his ear. It was the closest thing he could imagine to an obscene phone call.

"Be there in ten minutes."

"'Oh, my America! My new-found land!'" he shouted to the ceiling.

He raced down to the lobby's gift shop and bought the rubbers, returned and filled the ice bucket, brushed his teeth, stripped off his shirt and sponged his underarms, wishing he had time for a shower. He piled his suitcase on one of the chairs in the room, spread manuscripts and books on the other: make it appear he was working all the time, give her no place to sit, he coached himself. He laid out her poems on the bed, smoothed out the pillows, placed two iced drinks, one on either end table. Then he stood back and looked. He saw them reclining there, shoulder to shoulder against the headboard, backs supported by pillows, her poetry on their laps.

Then he shook his head and lit a cigarette. This was crazy! He hadn't stopped to think it out. For the first time in hours, he remembered his wife, his daughter. It was Wednesday. He promised to call every Wednesday, and he hadn't. It wasn't a hard-fast rule, but he had intended to keep it anyway. It would matter to her. It would give her something to hold over him if he failed. In more than fifteen years he hadn't . . . not once, not even though the co-eds who came on to him, particularly after *Free Falling* came out, gave him every chance in the world.

"Don't shit where you eat," he had lectured a colleague who was contemplating an affair with one of his students. He repeated it to his reflection, "Don't . . . ." He cut himself off, bit his lip with the memory of the first time he had used the phrase to lecture himself in a mirror.

"Don't be stupid," he assured his reflection. "Nothing's happened. Nothing's going to. This is silly. You're feeling guilty and nothing's happened. Nothing ever does. It's just what you're supposed to do: help student writers, encourage young poets." He looked at himself in the mirror. Behind him he saw the bed, the poems, the bottle and the glasses in position. He felt like a bad imitation of Maurice Chevalier, like a lecher. She was five—more like fifteen— years younger than he. What the hell was he thinking?

He rose to clear the chairs, made up his mind to get out of it, not to go through it. Then he looked again at the bed, and this time he saw them under the sheets, her riding him high and sensuously. Her wide shoulders thrown back, breasts jutting out, small hard nipples at their tips, her long, firm thighs gripping his hips, her fingers racing across his chest, her mouth, her tongue . . . . The hollowness in his gut, the tightness around his chest returned, and he sat on the edge of the bed and lit another smoke, although the first one still burned in the ashtray.

"You're twelve-hundred miles from home," he said to himself in the mirror. "Who the hell's going to know or care?"

The knock at the door startled him. He rose heavily. His stomach felt solid now, cold and sick. He swallowed hard and told himself he would deal with the guilt when it came. He was too old, had passed up too much to allow this to slip by him. It was the sort of thing that only happened to others. Not him. It was magic: too good to be true. He checked himself in the mirror once more, ground out the butts, waved his hands to clear the air. He breathed into his cupped hands to make sure the mouthwash was still working.

"Jenny?" he said as he opened the door.

"Hi," she smiled. His stomach melted again. In jeans and a bulky sweater, she was even prettier than he remembered or had seen her in his fantasies. "I'm really grateful that you're going to help me get published." She pushed past him and he stepped back. The condoms were still on the nightstand where he dropped them. He crab-walked quickly over and swept them up in his hand while he gestured to the bed. He dropped them on the floor and kicked them under a chair.

"My pleasure," he said expansively. "Have a seat. Sorry about the mess. It all goes with the terri—"

The door opened wider behind her and a tall, clean-cut young man followed her inside. He also was blond, handsome, well-built, and about her age. He had on a college sweatshirt and offered a large grin while he held up a six-pack.

"Oh, this is Jeff," Jenny said, her silvery voice curling about her companion with greater possessiveness than if she had put an arm around him. "We live together. He's sort of my inspiration. Jeff, this is the poet I was telling you about. He's going to help get me published."

"Sorry I missed your reading," Jeff said. He offered a firm handshake, smiled and moved across the room. He pushed the poems aside and flopped down on the bed, making it bounce. Peeling off a beer and settling a pillow behind his head, he pulled a folded *Sports Illustrated* from his hip pocket. Jenny glided down beside him and draped her long fingers into the crook of his knee. "I had a late practice," he said absently. "You want a beer?"

He shook his head, sighed, gave the condoms another kick, pushed the suitcase off the chair, and sat down heavily.

"I think it's great you're helping Jenny out with her poems. Thought I'd come along and listen. Learn something maybe. I've never been too good in English." He opened the magazine. It was the swimsuit issue.

"Jeff's a business major," Jenny said. She settled back, pulled a pillow out and propped herself next to him. "He was the inspiration for a lot of my work. Since he was part of the experiences, I thought it would be good to have him here. In case you had any questions or wanted to know anything." She took his hand. "We're going to get married as soon as my divorce is final. You know, the biggest mistake I ever made was getting married right out of high school." She accepted a beer from Jeff, opened it, and then turned her eyes on him and wrinkled her forehead in concern. "Now, what's all this stuff you were telling me? It sounds interesting."

He sighed, pulled a cigarette from his pocket and lit it. She pushed her shoes off and folded her long legs beneath her, and put her blue stare on him. She was all ears. Jeff popped the pages of the magazine as he turned them. "You get cable TV here?" he asked. "The Bulls are on after while."

She swatted his knee to shush him, then focused her wonderful eyes on him. "Go, on," she said. "*I'm* listening."

He tented his hands, took a cleansing breath, and began. "Well, first of all, metonymy is similar to synecdoche, but there's a difference . . . ."

IV

"What the hammer? What the chain?
In what furnace was thy brain?
What the anvil? What dread grasp
Dare its deadly terrors clasp?"
                                    — Blake

You know, the first time I walked into a classroom as an instructor I was twenty-two: twenty-two. The girls—they were all freshmen, or freshwomen—were on average about eighteen or nine-teen. And I was twenty-two. That gives you something to think about.

I read someplace that a man hits his highest sexual potential between nineteen and twenty-two. So there I was, on the downside of my manly prowess, and I was the objet fixe of ten or fifteen buxom young co-eds two times a day, three times a week. Talk about your kid in the candystore situations.

You see, it's a kind of power trip. When you have the power of the grade over them, and when they're already about halfway disposed to idol worship in the first place, it's really not hard to take advantage of the situation. Some of them are begging to be seduced, dying to have a major sexual experience with the "man of the world" who stands behind the lectern. Some of them wouldn't have gotten out of high school without it.

But I was cool. So were most of my friends in grad school. We had ethics, we said, integrity. We talked about it a lot. I mean, in those days, nobody talked about "sexual harassment" or anything like that. Lots of girls slept with instructors—even full professors— for grades, but we were Children of the Sixties. *We had a sense of pride in what we were doing. You know: Ethics, and all that shit.*

We were also scared to fucking death of getting caught.

This isn't some sort of macho thing. Men didn't have a lock on it. It was a problem for our female colleagues, as well. More than once I heard about some football boy in one of those fishnet jock shirts, muscles rippling, little bitty butt in tight Levi's, sidling up to the desk with a wink and a grin to ask why he got his usual D, offering to take her out for a beer "or somethin', you know?" to talk it over. But the women handled it better than the men. Once they'd been hit on, they could let contempt for the dumb shit who did it override any libidinous urges. It was all out on the open, then, and they could deal with it. From the male point of view, it rarely got past the fantasy phase, which made the whole situation seem like a festering sore that not only wouldn't heal, but also got worse every day. We didn't get that much opportunity to resist the temptation, because the temptation hardly ever became concrete. Or at least it didn't to me. Not at first.

I guess it was because I didn't ask for it. I mean, there were times when I sort of sensed that if I made the first move, some sweet young thing would spread her legs for an A, maybe even for a B, but I didn't do it. I suppose I was partly afraid of getting caught, as I said. But I was also afraid of rejection. Some men may think they're the superior gender, but brother, I can tell you, so long as we live in a society where the men have to do the asking and the women hold the option of saying no, there ain't going to be no equality between the sexes. Eliot was right-on about that, for sure. No man wants to be "pinned and wriggling on the wall," you know? I mean, consider the risks: Here you are, the biggest cheese most of these little gumsnappers have ever seen, the upperest of all upperclassmen, a graduate teaching fellow, and you ask, and she settles the old metaphoric pillow behind her head and says, "Oh, that's not it at all. That's not what I meant at all." That could cause a guy to hurt himself, particularly if he thought he was sure enough of her to ask in the first place.

Nope: So long as women can say "no," or even just "maybe," they have the upper hand. And you can take that to the goddamn bank.

And you know the irony of the whole thing. Even when the women were aggressive, I mean, when they came on strong and left no doubt in your mind at all, you still wouldn't do it. I figure half the guys in the world sit around day-dreaming about some woman hitting on them, putting it right out on the line: no bullshit. But when and if it ever happens, most every one of them would run: scared shitless. Not from marriage, not even from a commitment or a relationship. They'd just run. It's a kind of balance, you know. Something that keeps things on an even keel in sexual combat.

But there was something else, too. If you slept with a student *in your class, then you decided that you want to sleep with someone else in the same class or even in a different class, all kinds of problems could come up. There's built-in safety factors about it, I guess: fear of getting caught, fear of rejection, fear of a knock-down drag-out over you in English 101, MWF, 9:00. Fear: It's the tie that binds.*

There's also guilt, but that's just fear of a different sort. Anyway, I didn't fool around with my students, even though I always wanted to believe I could.

Besides, I was married, which would have made it even more dangerous if I had done anything. And I didn't want to. Or at least I told myself I didn't want to. We all told each other that, but it didn't stop the jokes, the comments, everything else about it that meant, really, any one of us would have done it if we could figure out how to diffuse the fear or at least get around it. Of course, some guys didn't care. Some guys don't fear anything.

There was this one guy in our doctoral program. Lynn Rosen. He was tall, curly-headed, athletic, and smart as a fucking whip. And he was one popular teacher, I can tell you. Everyone admired him. He always went to class in a tee-shirt that showed his physique. The rest of us were wearing coats and ties. But the rest of us weren't scoring. Lynn was scoring. We hated his guts. He must have bedded half the women in every class he taught.

This wasn't something we knew because he said so. He never said a word about it. Wouldn't even join in our erotic banter when we all got into it after a couple of beers. Lynn's boffing of his students was an unassailable fact. Everyone knew about it, and he didn't seem to care.

He would show up in the student union cafeteria with one of his students carrying his damned tray, and they'd get a table off by themselves and talk and hold hands and make eyes at each other a while. Then they'd walk off hand-in-hand, and you knew they weren't going down by the duck pond to skip stones. That really wasn't so bad, you know. I mean, there wasn't a rule against screwing your students or anything, so long as no one complained about grading favors or something. What was bad was that he was with a different girl every time, and always one from his classes. Our freshmen sections had twenty, maybe twenty-five students in each one, and we all had two classes to teach. That meant an average of thirty, thirty-five new girls per term. Subtract those who were really married or too ugly or something, that still meant that he had to make a new girl every week. It would have taken me most of the semester just to work up the courage to suggest such a thing to only one. Maybe that's why I never did.

Rosen was a master at it, though, and for the first two years, nobody complained, not even his wife, Sissy, a legal secretary who worked downtown.

I guess we were all jealous of him, and I guess that's why we hated what he was doing and getting away with so easily. But none of us would admit that. "An intellectual hatred is the worst," Yeats says. And besides, we had ethics, remember? We believed in what we were doing. Right.

In his third year, I guess he went too far. He was with a girl named Daphne, who had this twin named Dianne. Dianne was engaged to a jock who was the school's starting quarterback. The story was that Rosen had both girls in bed at the same time when the quarterback showed up with a bunch of his football buddies, and they beat the living shit out of him. All we knew for sure was that he was in the hospital, and the rumors about his being struck by a hit-and-run driver weren't selling. He had four broken ribs and was still in a body cast when he defended his dissertation. Sissy left him, too.

We all swore we took a lesson from that. But some took it better than others. I didn't take it at all.

When I finished school and started teaching for real, I was too afraid of being fired to mess around. Probably no one would have cared—except my wife, and me, of course—but I imagined that everyone would know the second I slipped into bed beside a student. Even an older student who knew which side of the bed her grade might lie on. So I stayed clean. But the opportunity was there, I can tell you, women's lib and all. You see, there's a difference between liberation and libido, and you don't need a major in psychology to know what it is. In some ways, my own fear made it easier on me. But the longer I taught, the harder it was to avoid the temptation. Sometimes, it seemed they were stalking me, taking bets on what it would take to move me across the line. Maybe they were, but anybody who bet against me—in those early days at least— would have lost. I was straight, and, like I said, I was afraid.

Odd logic, I know, but, hey, I didn't write the rules.

One summer right after I started I had this ultra-small class. It was an added section put on the schedule to catch the overflow, and for some reason, it was filled with these gorgeous women, twelve, fourteen of them, and not one less than Head Cheerleader perfect. There was only one man, some poor hard-lick who nearly fainted when he realized how deep the clover was going to be in that room every afternoon. And it was summer. I don't know when I've seen so much good-looking, deeply tanned thigh muscle outside a chorus line. It was really hard to concentrate for a while, I can tell you. I mean, these women bounced into class with their tits hanging out of halter tops, their hips barely hidden by these little gym shorts, and they would sit there and flash their eyes at me and give me these wonderful, worshipful looks for seventy-five minutes. They didn't have a pound of gray matter, all put together. It was the dumbest bunch of people I ever taught.

My poor wife. I nearly wore her out every night that summer. And that was when I started writing poetry, again. Every day.

I never touched one of them, though. Ethics, remember? And fear. I'm not sure I could have made up my mind who to hit on first, anyway. For the time being, I was content with my fantasies, and with the poetry. Let me tell you, the poetry came in sheets that summer. Reams of it, and most of it was pretty good.

A couple of years later, after I got tenure, I was still afraid. Then I was up for promotion, and I stayed clean. My male colleagues and I talked about it, though. How could you not talk about it? You were confronted with it every day. It was like starving for water on a desert island, surrounded by the illusion of something to drink, but unable to take even so much as a taste without terrible risk. I never understood the myth of Tantalus until then, only, unlike that poor tortured soul, I wouldn't dip my head down to take a sip. I just watched it and wondered. And I suffered.

Dante got that part right for sure.

The older and balder I got, the younger and more anxious the girls in my classes seemed to be. The worse my sex life at home became, the more tempting they became. Every morning began a sexual roller-coaster ride that probably would have killed me— suicide by self-abuse—if it hadn't been for Nelson Brand.

He was young, brand new Ph.D., and I was glad to see him. I mean, I'd been "new kid on the block" for three years, and it was about time for me to have some seniority over somebody, somebody to kick around.

He wasn't very kickable, though. That was clear from the moment I met him. He was such an asshole that putting him in his place or talking down to him wasn't any fun. He was his own worst enemy from the moment he opened his mouth. He looked a little like Robert Redford, but he was taller, better built, and he drove an old Triumph Spitfire, which he kept in mint condition. His first question

*to me after we met was where he could go to "troll for chicks." Can
you believe that? "Troll for chicks." The guy was yuppie—
although we didn't have that term, then—right down to his deck
shoes—first pair I ever saw—and L.L. Bean shirts. And he thought
he was God's gift to women, particularly to women students. And
that was his downfall.*

*By the end of his first year, he'd dated more than half his
students. And I mean* dated, *too. He took them to dinner, movies,
dancing, and even brought them to faculty parties. When the
department head suggested that his bringing this busty red-headed
freshman to a faculty reception was, maybe, inappropriate, Nelson
suggested right in front of the graduate dean's wife that the
department head should "mind his own fucking business." The guy
had no shame at all. He also didn't seem to give a goddamn about
tenure.*

*See what I mean? I didn't have to fuck him over. He was doing
fine on his own.*

*He had nerve, if he didn't have style. I'll give him that. "Pity
he loved adventurous life's variety," but to tell you the truth, he was
absolutely not "so great a loss to good society."*

*What finally tore it with me was when he kept bugging me to
introduce him to some of the women in my classes. When I refused,
he got pissed off. He told me if I was screwing some of them, I could
point them out and he'd leave them alone. He just wanted to choose
from any I didn't want. You'd think we were in a supermarket
picking out watermelons or something.*

*They fired him after his second year. He hit on the president's
daughter, had her right in his office, right on his desk, and she
claimed* against her will. *She was an arch-feminist—Erica Jong
variety—and she blew the whistle. She didn't have much choice.
Two maintenance men opened the door on them, came to change the
light bulbs and caught them bare-assed and going at it hammer and
tong on top of a stack of freshman papers. Nelson left without even
so much as a recommendation, but no charges were filed.*

*I have to admit that the whole time he was "trolling" the
college's hallways, though, I was envious. Not of him: He had no
class, no technique. He just told them that if they wanted a good
grade, all they had to do was put out for him. I couldn't believe that
so many of them fell for it. But I guess they did. I hear he left four
fatherless children behind. But if anybody sued, I never heard about
it. Some guys are just born lucky.*

I was envious of how easy it was for him. Everybody was, even the females on the faculty, I think. Their hatred of him was never as vile as it should have been, you know? I mean, here he was, making a mockery out of equal rights for women, treating any woman with decent legs, big tits, and a pretty face like a sex object, and all the women in the department could work up against him was a half-hearted tsk-tsk. Robert Gorman, the associate head of department—Dunphy's right-hand man and one of my worst enemies, to tell you the truth—may have been right when he said that half of them wanted to get into the sack with him themselves. He might have been more than half right about that. I would guess that more than a couple of them had. The married ones, too.

I took a lesson from Nelson's experience, though. I learned that if you're going to shit where you eat, you'd better be careful when you come to the table. And I learned not to hit on an administrator's daughter, at least not one who might tell. I hung in there with that one for years.

I'd probably been teaching ten, eleven years before I fell from the pedestal of ethics I believed I stood on. Her name was Yvonne, and she was liquid dynamite. My marriage was well on its way to the shitter by then, so I guess it wasn't really cheating. We were both seeing other people during our separations. I wasn't like Lynn or Nelson, though. I kept it quiet, and I stayed with Yvonne and didn't play the field, and I was discreet. We moved in together after seeing each other secretly for about six weeks. I guess ethics still ate at me. I wanted it out in the open.

But it didn't last. I recognized my main weakness was for women by then, and I finally understood that without them, there wouldn't be any poetry. After Yvonne, there was Janey, an "older" freshman just back from the Peace Corps, then Sally, a junior with a Corvette. After that there was a steady stream. It flowed better when I was separated from my wife, almost quit when we got back together. Finally, I just said, "Fuck it," and quit trying to resist. Women got to be like peanuts. Have one, and I was gone.

Sally was a major event, though, a try at something more lasting than a quickie in a parked car or a fast roll before a roommate showed up. She was a pert, bosomy little thing, kind of chubby but pretty with nice hair and dark brown eyes. She was good for a whole series of poems about water: lakes, rivers, even creeks. But after living together, the whole thing dried up, if you know what I mean. She wanted to see guys her own age, and I couldn't be like Tommy, I couldn't handle it. The truth was, though, that I was already seeing Millicent, a gray-eyed sophomore, on the *sly. Afternoons in her apartment got my third book out while the only album she owned,* Frampton Comes Alive, *played over and over. Then, there were Tracy, Lynda, and Karla and book number four, eventually, anyway.*

In the next four years, I lived with a dozen different women, some for a month or two, some just for a week or ten days. I don't even remember most of their names anymore. But from time to time, I still get a Christmas card from several of them forwarded to me from my publisher. They remembered me—fondly, they said—and I remembered them, every one of them, for a while at least. They were never notches on my prick, you see, never hash marks of sexual accomplishment. Their images are permanently imprinted on my poems, and that's the way I rationalized it. Still do. You see, once I stepped off the ethical path, I was lost. It was hard to get back, especially since my poetry depended on my staying lost. It never occurred to me that when the poems stopped, there wouldn't be any way back at all.

The Conference

He sat down heavily after his reading and began mopping his brow with a paper towel he pocketed when he left the men's room. Son-of-a-bitch, he thought, what had he come to?

Sixteen poets reading in a four-hour period, all for the entertainment of a bunch of academic assholes who were more than half-asleep. He looked at his watch: 9:45. At least he had stayed in his time slot. The first four had gone over by five to seven minutes each, and not one of them had read anything he would compliment by calling poetry. But they were proud of their work. They averaged ten-minute introductions for six lines of doggerel. And it was a tough audience.

"New American Poetry for the New World Decade" was the rubric, and the marathon reading was the bright idea of the state's newly organized "Alliance for Poetic Expression," a group of college professors who wanted to revive interest in teaching contemporary poetry and establishing creative writing programs. This was a way to showcase the best poets of this generation, they claimed at every opportunity. He wondered how the poets were picked. He knew how *he* was picked. They knew he'd come for the minimum honorarium and expenses. That was enough.

The program was wrinkled from folding and unfolding. It had been a long, hot day, and the room was oppressive. He had stayed up late the night before, trying to complete a new cycle of poems, trying to finish the next book. There was pressure from New York. Felix wanted the manuscript three months ago, but the poetry was getting harder and harder to write. The poems just wouldn't come to him as clearly as they once had. And he had about decided that without some inspiration coming from somewhere, they wouldn't ever come again.

"The strongest part of our religion today," he reminded himself of Arnold's words, "is unconscious poetry." But conscious or unconscious, he seemed to have lost his faith. At the very least, it was getting harder and harder to sustain.

"It's like performing surgery on myself," he had told his wife. He didn't know why he had told her. She never understood or cared. Their divorce was six months old, then, and they only spoke to argue about her custody of their daughter.

"All you think about is poetry and sex," she told him when she walked out the last time, took their little girl with her. "And not sex with me, either."

He said nothing. The girl he had been with the night before, Abby, the one his wife now knew he had been spending practically every afternoon with for the past two weeks, said the same thing when he rolled out of bed and began trying out some of his new verse on her.

"They're one and the same," he told Abby, quoting, "'A poet in verse or prose must have a sensuous eye.'" And they laughed. Then they made love again.

He doubted if Emerson would approve: Abby was twenty-two, small-breasted, but firm as a ripe peach. His wife was thirty-five and there wasn't a square inch of solid tissue anywhere on her: Except between her ears, he thought with a wry chuckle.

"Go on," she screamed at him. "Laugh. When you get tired of balling every little bimbo who thinks you're something special, you'll sit up and look around. But I won't be there, asshole. I *won't* be."

His daughter looked at him like he was a leper every time they left. That part hurt, mostly because he knew he deserved it. The rest was just an ugly memory that declined into a series of raunchy flings, sometimes with two or three women before he got some decent poems out of it. Then he would call and talk her into coming back. There had been four major fights, four major separations, all over his screwing students, at least ostensibly. The truth was that it was all over his poetry.

Each time she came back, he promised he would quit, but he

couldn't. He found it too easy. It was an addiction, a habit, and it linked him with his poems. When he was with a strange woman—usually a girl half his age—he was inspired. He could write. He couldn't help it. The poems came in armies, rose like the Ancient Mariner's dead crew and wouldn't leave him alone until he committed them to paper. With his wife, everything went dead. His mind became a desert, and he couldn't even conjure a haiku. They stayed married—for their daughter's sake, they promised themselves—but they hadn't made love in two years, not once. He wondered if she had ever had an orgasm with him. Or with anyone. He wondered if she had that much depth.

He opened the program and allowed a drop of sweat to fall on his name. Four more readers to go, and they were way over time. People had gotten up and left and others had come in to take their place all evening. The room smelled like a bus station in a swamp. It was also full, and the hotel must have had the heaters up full blast. If it was under 100 degrees, it was only because somebody died and lowered his body temperature.

He stuffed the sheaf of poems he had read into his coat pocket: All from the new stuff, and he thought it went over pretty well. It was the first time he had been able to rely on new material in over two years. Touring was hard on him, kept him from writing, kept him from thinking. It didn't keep him from fucking, he thought with a silly smile. God, he thought, if he had known that the quickest way into a young girl's bed was through an iambic triplet, teaching would have been a whole lot more fun from the start.

Even back in college, when the girls he dated were often intrigued by his verse, he had believed what little success he had was a fluke. Even then and later, he thought sports and money and a good body—things he could never have—were the ticket. But poetry? Who would have thought?

His reading had gone well. They had liked it, he insisted to himself. It was hard to say, though, he thought with a sideways glance around. These people had heard so much verse—if that's what most of it was—that night, that they were probably numb. He had only read four poems and had cut one of those in half. Time. Last time he would go in for a cattle call, he promised himself. He vowed long ago never to *bore* people. Too many poets hadn't learned that lesson, so high were they on the sound of their own voices. They'd take ten minutes to introduce a six-line smattering of free verse dribble. He was never guilty of that. His reputation stood or fell strictly on the value of his verse.

A petite, older woman was introduced by E.L. Sorens, the somewhat more-than-attractive young moderator. Sorens was a militant feminist by reputation, but the tight knit dress she wore suggested that she might be receptive to a suggestion or two about her beauty, her sexual potential. No one dressed like that and didn't expect to be looked at, to be flattered. She had clearly enjoyed his reading, clapped much louder than she had to, and her smile toward him when she returned to the lectern made him warmer even than the stifling humidity in the room. Definitely potential there, he told himself. If he could only figure out how to exploit it.

The petite woman walked up to the lectern and unfolded a large ream of computer printout. She wore a funny hairpiece that didn't match her natural color, exposed as it was underneath the partial wig. Her nose was pointed, her eyes small and mean. His mind had been more on E.L. Soren's body than on her words, and he had missed the poet's name. He checked his program. Catherine Downing, it said. He didn't recognize her name, and her blurb was conspicuously vague.

"I want to read from some work in progress," she said.

"What she means is half-baked." The comment came from a man's low voice from the back of the room.

The Heckler, he thought, excited, glancing around. He had always wanted to meet The Heckler. Every poet in the country did. Half of them wanted to shoot him on sight.

No one was sure who The Heckler was, but he had been turning up frequently at meetings in the past couple of years. He picked crowded, dark rooms, sat in the back, and then made *sotto voce* comments that carried across the room. Sometimes they were funny. Sometimes they were cruel. More than one poet had been stymied, reduced to tears, humiliated by his caustic remarks in response to a set of introductions and poems. The Heckler was personal, vicious, and apparently didn't care.

He had been wanting a look at him, even so. Thus far, he hadn't been victimized, but he figured his time was coming. The Heckler showed no mercy or proclivity for sex, race, or age. He apparently hated everything he heard, and he was anxious to let people know about it.

He felt a kinship with The Heckler. His own written reviews had almost the same reputation in print as the vocal critic had achieved in person, so to speak. He detested two-thirds of the poetry he read for review, was careful to point out the flaws and errors of his fellow poets, often recommended that they give up the Muse forever, maybe take up graffiti writing or sign painting. He was also mean, and he was tacky. His column in *Dissonant Voices* was widely quoted and had made him a critical force to be reckoned with, more so because he was also a poet himself, a published, practicing poet whose books continued to come out of Melton House in New York, continued to be nominated for major prizes, although they never seemed to win. He felt a special vulnerability, and it gave him a license to be an arbiter of taste.

It cost him a lot of readings, removed him from the list of available poets for tour when he slaughtered too many books by writers who ran programs on the same circuit. But that was all right. They weren't real poets or they could stand the heat. But he hated it that they had so much power.

He wondered if The Heckler was also a poet. It wasn't likely: He was a *maestro* of nastiness, a virtuoso of the well-aimed barb, "the mildest mannered man/That ever scuttled a ship or cut a throat."

He turned his head, but there was no obvious candidate visible, no one looking embarrassed because he or she was seated next to The Heckler. But they all knew he was there, and Catherine was visibly nervous. He figured The Heckler would start in on her in earnest soon enough. He was especially vicious when the poets lacked modesty about their work, and Catherine was prime. She exuded ego while she read, spoke about her poems as if they were people she knew. It seemed that she had personally discovered bad poetry and was dedicated to its exposition.

He sought to remember the title of the collection she kept referring to, which E.L. surely must have mentioned. He couldn't, and he didn't recall ever hearing her read before, although her name seemed uncommonly familiar. The program notes were no help. It didn't matter. He put his mind on automatic and kept an ear open to see if it really was The Heckler and what he would do.

At a meeting in Philadelphia three months before, The Heckler had almost started a riot. It was one of those ultra-serious gatherings of ultra-serious poets. Gary Snyder and James Merrill were there. So were Elizabeth Bishop and Denise Levertov. The headliner, though, was Erica Jong, who no one ever thought of as a poet, although that's the way she began. Half the name poets in the country came, and it seemed that all of them read, and read, and read. It was more like a marathon than a conference.

It was in the feminist poetry section that The Heckler made his move.

He was there mostly to hear two former students read. Both were young women he had taught the previous semester, and both had published and were beginning to make names for themselves. They were also pretty good, both as poets and in bed. One, Rae Ann, and he had just split up when she suddenly transferred a thousand miles away, even though it meant she would lose almost half her credits. He suspected she was going to have a child by him, but if so, she wasn't blaming him—openly—and it was mostly a rumor. Still, he observed, she was unmarried and quite attractive. Tall and thin, her blondish hair and gray-green eyes had captivated him sufficiently for him to give her verse far more praise than it deserved. The other girl, Veronica, was the better poet, far more likely to succeed in spite of her pronounced feminist politics in every poem.

Part of his hope was that he could keep the two women apart, stop them from comparing notes. If Rae Ann found out he had been sleeping with her sister-in-verse at the same time, she might change her mind and unliberate her attitude. His lawyer told him that one more scrap of dirt could sink him financially and forever if his wife went ahead with the divorce, which once more was pending. This time, it looked like she might go through with it. He might never see his daughter again. His soon-to-be-ex had already convinced everyone they knew that he had bedded half the co-eds at the university, probably some of the men, too. But that was a lie.

"Everyone knows poets are homosexuals," she told him when he spoke to her last. "The only reason you sleep with so many women is to evoke a natural defense mechanism of self-denial of your truer, suppressed latent tendencies, of your actual nature. It's nothing more than a sexually gratifying attempt to establish yourself as a 'Pan figure' and prove your prowess to make up for your personality deficiencies and deeply rooted male-hormonal shortcomings." She had finished her Ph.D. in psychology the previous summer. "She is a fucking expert," he told several of the guys at the bar where he hung out, "but not an expert in fucking."

His two former students and lovers read back-to-back, finished, and acquitted themselves well. He gave them each a warm smile, but not at the same time. They filed out of the room, but he decided to stay for one more reading by a woman he vaguely knew. Her name was Bunny Fry, and she was supposedly the sexiest feminist poet writing—not a grand distinction among a collection of flabby-bunned, black-dressed, white-stockinged, sensibly-shod dykes, he thought—and her poetry sucked. He had reviewed her last two chapbooks and found both wanting for anything resembling poetic sensibility, anything indicating that she had so much as a nodding acquaintance with poetic forms. In his last review, he suggested that she might take up Hallmark card writing. Even so, she was supposed to be one of the brightest lights on the reading circuits, and he wanted to see if her personal reputation was earned.

It was. She was a frowzy blonde with a skin-tight sweater mini-dress on over high-heeled boots that had little designer spurs on them. Good legs, great tush, nice tits, salon fingernails, and smoky eyes that said "Fuck me." She had a look about her that suggested that she just rolled out of somebody's bed: rumpled, sheet-hot, sweat-steamy. She started reading from a new book of poetry about her much-touted hitchhiking tour of the United States—funded by the NEA, no less—which she had unashamedly named *Doing It in the Road: A Woman Poet's Perspective of Naked Male America*. After the first three selections—none over a dozen lines long, he decided it was the same old shit—five to seven lines of quasi-erotic sentence fragments and euphemistic innuendo—and he regretted that he hadn't taken a seat at the rear of the room so he could slip out before she finished.

She began each poem with a dedication: "This is for Buzz, who picked me up just outside Salt Lake. We had a wonderful weekend at his place in the mountains." She paused as if waiting for an outraged comment, allowed her fingers to play with a wild strand of hair. Hearing none, she plunged into a more or less metaphorical description of multiple orgasm. "This is for Hank," she segued into the next selection. "He was a long-haul trucker." She emphasized *long* and licked her lips into a snarl to kill any laughter that might respond. "He *hauled* me from Reno to Seattle." Another ten-line depiction of fantastic impalings on an oversized and somehow always throbbing phallus followed a pause that permitted her to pretend to straighten non-existent wrinkles on the front of her dress. The movement placed her false fingernails around and then just under her breasts. Her nipples were hard buttons beneath the thin, double-knit fabric.

"This is for Carter. I met him on the Jersey turnpike. He represented a vineyard and rode me all the way to New York." She took the usual pause and smoothed down the skirt portion over her thighs, but this time, the voice from the back of the room filled the gap.

"Hell," a deep drawl speculated, "I wonder if she needs a lift to El Pasooo."

Laughter sparked, then took flame and exploded. A few people stood up and glared toward the rear of the room, but no one was obviously taking credit for the line. Bunny's eyes fired lasers of death at everyone, and she was screaming something, but he was laughing too hard to hear it. So, he noticed, were most of the women in the room. He finally rose and fled the female anger that was quickly rising to boil away the tears of mirth.

In the hallway, his Rae Ann and Veronica were chatting. They gave him knowing, angry looks, and he felt something fall inside him, like a stone down a mineshaft. He detoured abruptly toward the bar.

The divorce papers were filed when he returned home. Rae Ann's paternity suit was settled out of court a month after the divorce was final. He didn't try to fight either case but took what he was given. He received no visitation rights in either verdict, only a combined child-support bill that took three-quarters of his university paycheck.

The second time he encountered The Heckler was in Oklahoma City only three weeks ago. It was another conference, he recalled, much like this one, only this time the poets were worse, or at least not as well known. This time the audience wasn't filled with a bunch of emasculating feminists, though. This was more the gray-haired, grandparental crowd, who had come to admire the readings. The first reader wasn't a day under seventy, he decided, though he looked older. He was frail and stooped. Thin strands of hair were swept over a pink pate, and his fingers were twisted with arthritis. He had been named Poet Laureate of Seminole, Oklahoma, and he was serious about "my little verses," as he named them. He introduced each of the first dozen poems with lengthy explanations of his family and its relationships, attitudes, and various philosophies.

"My father was a farmer," he began another selection, "and he came to Oklahoma after the War—the *First* World War—to settle down and raise cotton." He went on to detail his father's life, his physique, a mole on his cheek, two or three major operations and a half-dozen devastating disappointments—mostly in his sister, who, it seemed, died of "sugar diabetes"—none of which diminished what was apparently an unflagging optimism. It was his seventh story about this woebegone family member, and everyone was growing weary of her map of misfortunes, none of which had any apparent connection to the poems that followed.

"She always said that every day was like an opportunity knocking on the door," he moaned. "She said that all the time, even though it seemed that something painful was coming up the walk more often than not."

"Should've posted her property, seems to me." The Heckler's voice swelled quietly from the back row, and everyone in the room froze. The old poet's eyes blazed, but he couldn't figure out who said it. He recomposed himself and began reading, but the poem that followed offered a misplaced modifier that rendered it ironic, and there were more patronizing smiles than tears at the end. He began his next introduction with the redundant note that his father had always been a positive man, never dwelling on his troubles and always encouraging others when they were down.

"I'm a product of his factory of philosophy," he announced proudly.

"Seems to me a recall's in order," The Heckler said. That did it: The "Seminole Poet" stood as if struck in the face, his rheumy blue eyes blinking rapidly, his gnarled fingers brushing quickly across his mouth as if he were removing crumbs. His face was pale and his hands were trembling.

"I don't have to take this," he muttered. He moved unsteadily to a chair and sat down without reading further. Everyone looked around with angry, accusing expressions, but whoever had spoken was still anonymous. He must have been sitting next to someone, but no one said anything. No one could persuade the "Seminole Poet" to continue his reading, either. The session was over.

He couldn't decide at the time whether they wanted to punish the Heckler or thank him for interrupting the Seminole's "little verses."

In the world of poetry conferences, The Heckler had developed into a kind of legend: a sort of "masked man" of tacky criticism that could reduce a serious reading to pandemonium. Lately, no gathering of poets was complete without someone claiming to know who he was but being sworn to secrecy. He thought that most who made such remarks wanted to be known as The Heckler themselves, but he doubted that any had the courage to say the sorts of things he said right out loud, or the pure gall to keep a straight face when anger and approbation turned against him.

The Heckler apparently made the majority of poetry readings all over the country. He had been reported in conferences as distant as Colorado and New York, sometimes within the same weekend. He got around, if it was the same guy, and no poet ever stood to read without fearing that he would strike.

"I'm particularly proud of these poems," Catherine, the petite reader, continued. He looked at his watch. She had been reading for twenty minutes, and each poem was introduced by a rambling series of remarks that encompassed no fewer than a dozen personal and contradictory theories of "my ort," as her pronounced Southwestern accent insisted on calling it.

Why do poets feel they have to give long, boring explanations for every poem they read? he wondered. He had long ago developed the habit of simply giving the title and then reading the poem. He found that he could get more poetry in that way, and it confirmed his theory that if the poem doesn't say enough to communicate his meaning, it failed. Still, so many of these clowns love an audience for their crackpot theories and personal revelations. It was like a cross between true confessions and public psychotherapy. Sort of gestalt exhibitionism. This particular woman was one of the worst he had ever encountered.

"I like to think of each of my poems as a *singular* work of ort," she said to the nodding, half-asleep audience. It was hotter than ever in the room, but she seemed cool, unbothered by her listeners' discomfort. Her smile was filled with pompous pride. "I sometimes frame them, put them on the wall of our ranch house." She then read a two-part ode to sunrise predictably called "Dawn on the Plains."

"This one graces the wall of my hallway," she said after sipping a drink of water and holding forth on her generous attitude toward unwanted company. "We live so far out of town, we don't get many callers out on the ranch." It was her fifth or sixth reference to her status as a rancher, and he was reminded of the Seminole poet. He wondered if she was a clone. "I call it 'Guest Unawares.'" Her debt to the Bible bordered on scandal if not blasphemy, he thought.

She seemed to sense the impatience of the audience with her lengthy introductions after the fifth selection, and made a seamless transition into the sixth without benefit of opening remarks. But once finished, she couldn't resist the temptation to hold forth once more. "I hung this one right next to my mama and daddy's picture over my desk," she said, holding up the carefully typed sheet of verse.

"I'd say hanging's too good for that'un," The Heckler's voice announced.

He spun around to identify the secret speaker once and for all. Laughter was general and unsuccessfully squelched. It started from a low snicker and quickly grew to outright belly laughs as the remark was repeated over and over.

"Who the hell said that?" Catherine demanded from the lectern. She seemed to grow, to take on another foot of stature. The grandmotherly facade dropped away, and a hard-bitten ranch woman appeared. "I want to know just who the *hell* said that!"

The snickering died, and an embarrassed silence filled the room. People looked at each other from behind ill-hidden smiles and poorly suppressed laughter and shrugged.

"*You* said it," Catherine said suddenly, and all heads snapped around to see where she was looking. He glanced quickly behind him, anxious to spot The Heckler, defend him if need be. They were kindred spirits, he felt, brothers under the skin, defenders of good poetry from the likes of Catherine's hangable verse. No one looked abashed, however, no one looked defiant or embarrassed or even singled out. He scanned the back row. All women, no male in sight. Where was he?

"I *know* you did it, so you can just quit the goddamn pretending," Catherine squawked. "We all know how you feel about other people's work. You're jealous, and you're a mean and vindictive son of a bitch."

He searched the room behind him once more. Where *was* he? Why couldn't he see the guy? He must be visibly squirming, sweating. He's been revealed at last. Where the hell was he?

He slowly realized that everyone in the room was staring at *him*.

"What? Me?" He jerked around and saw that Catherine was glaring at him. Her fist struck the lectern and upset the water glass.

"You are an egocentric *pig*! That's well known!" she screeched. Her poems had drifted off the lectern onto the floor. "You have no respect for women's work. For anybody's work!"

"Me?" He stood. "You're crazy. I didn't say a thing."

"I *saw* you. I saw you *smirking* when I was reading. I heard you the first time, but I couldn't *believe* you'd say something else. Not right to my face!"

"I didn't say a thing. I swear it." He sensed how much like a liar he sounded. He couldn't believe this was happening. "You've got the wrong man. Person," he corrected.

"I know you! I've read your reviews of my work. I've read *all* your reviews. You don't like anything that's personal, anything by a woman. Sex, sex, sex. That's all you think about. You're filthy-minded." Her hair-piece was askew and falling, revealing a sickeningly bald scalp beneath. She looked like a year's-dead corpse. Her dentures were slipping, and drool ran down her chin.

He racked his brain, tried to remember. *Had* he reviewed her work? He did forty, fifty reviews and roundups of chapbooks and collections each year. *Dissonant Voices* had an insatiable appetite for his vitriol, and they were paying him well. Seventy-five or a hundred dollars a column: good money, important money for a man who was supporting two children he couldn't even see. He tried to recall Catherine's last name. The program was on the floor. Catherine, Catherine Something.

"Look, Catherine," he started. "I didn't—"

"Don't you 'Catherine' me, you prick!" All smiles vanished, and a shock wave rippled through the room. She was livid, screaming, weaving and out of control, near faint with pure rage. Several people on the front row started toward her. Her finger, like a gun barrel, pointed directly at his chest. She was trembling. He shrank.

"You're a self-righteous son of a bitch who thinks that just because you're published in New Goddamn York your shit don't stink. Well, I'm here to say—" She swayed dangerously, gripped the lectern, and started gasping for air.

E.L. Soren reached her and pushed her down into a chair behind the lectern, fanned her, fed her water. Others gathered around her.

He was sweating nails. He pulled out the soggy paper towel, mopped his face, and started babbling. "Look, I didn't say a *thing*. I mean I *heard* it. We *all* heard it. But I didn't *say* it." He looked at the woman sitting next to him. "C'mon. You were sitting *right here*. Did *I* say anything?" She glared at him briefly, then turned her face away. He appealed to the room at large. "It came from back there somewhere. Didn't it? *Didn't* it?" He opened his hands in appeal, but every face was turned against him. He sat down in his chair. "I didn't say a goddamn thing." He sulked.

"You said it," Catherine Something gasped. She fought to her feet and leaned on the lectern. "I heard you. We all heard you. We've read your reviews of my work, of everyone's work. You hate women, you hate poetry, and *you said it*." Her voice was croaking. The other poets were looking at each other and nodding.

"I don't hate poetry," he said. "That's not true. Poetry is my life." He didn't hate women either, he silently added, but this was not the time or place to advance that notion.

"You *hate* it," she insisted. "You've never read a poem by anyone but *you* you liked. You think you're the only poet in the world. And when nobody agrees with you, you try to ruin others. You're hateful and self-centered. I want you to know that. We all think that."

The room was now nodding together, in unison, like she was a preacher and they were all offering "Amens" in agreement to her sermon. He was the devil incarnate. He didn't have an ally in the room. He was sunk. He couldn't prove his innocence by merely protesting it. He felt like he was nine years old, caught playing doctor with the girl next door. Sweat poured out of him, and his face felt feverish.

Catherine had regained her strength, her composure. She straightened her hairpiece, pointed a finger at him again, and spoke in a deep voice. "You've been doing this kind of childish thing for years, just to disrupt others' readings. You're a jealous, mean man, and I'm thrilled that I'm the one who exposed you. You cowardly prick!"

There was nothing else to do. Sweat drenched him. He rose, gathered his papers and left the room. Several others followed him, but they had other reasons for going: He found no sympathy in their faces. None spoke to him. When the door shut behind them, he heard Catherine being encouraged by E.L. to go on with her reading.

He stumbled over to the lobby and lit a cigarette with shaking hands. Those who came out of the room behind him glared at him, and one or two smiled, not in friendship, but with a sense of ironic justice behind their eyes. He hadn't said it, he wanted to yell at them. He couldn't believe what had just happened. His stomach was pure acid and his heart was pounding.

A tall, lanky cowboy with a snap-buttoned, yoke shirt meandered up to him. He had on a high-crowned straw hat and fancy boots. There was a smile behind the toothpick. He was flanked by two plump but attractive young girls. Each had a hand looped in one of his arms, and both had bright, giggly eyes that seemed to be in on some sort of grand joke at his expense.

"'For I have sworn thee fair, and thought thee bright,/ Who art black as hell, as dark as night,'" he quoted. "Gideon," he said, sticking out a weathered hand. "Frank Gideon."

He accepted the shake. Gideon took a half-step back and grinned at him. "Frank Gideon," he took a drag off his cigarette. "Not *the* Frank Gideon. Not the *New York Review of Books* Frank Gideon."

"One an' the same," he drawled. "Guilty on all counts."

Frank Gideon was one of them most respected poetry critics in the country. His review columns were the blessing or, conversely, the kiss of death for any publishing poet. He wrote for *NYRB, Poetry, Transatlantic Review*, the *Paris Review*, even the *Times Literary Supplement*. He was one of the few critics who actually made his living completely from writing reviews and columns. Gideon was never mean, never petty, but he could be hard on bad poetry. He had savaged more than one major poet, and he had made several unknowns into national figures.

"But you're . . . uh, I mean, you're not . . ."

Gideon grinned. "Not a Yankee. Nope. Born in San Goddamn Angelo, Tex-goddamn-as," he imitated Catherine Somebody's tone. "Live in Wimberly, now. Up in the Hill Country. Run some horses. Like horses. Don't got a ranch house, though." He chuckled.

"But you write for the *New York Times*. I mean, how . . ."

"Hell, you can do anything with 'lectronics, these days. Shit, there's FedEx when the wind knocks down the power lines. Don't got to live in New York to write in New York. London, either. Thought you'd know that as well as anybody."

"What are you doing here? I mean, this isn't the . . . I mean this is bush league."

"Never know when you're goin' to run up on some good verse. I found some of the best poetry comes out of the bullshit you hear 'round these little bitty ol' conferences. You can hear the big-name readers all the time. I like to see what I can find, maybe make a major discovery. Like you."

He remembered that Gideon had been in the room before the outburst. The girls sat on his either side on the back row. They disappeared during Catherine's outburst. He had wondered at the time what a cowboy was doing at a poetry conference. He pulled out another cigarette and one of the girls reached out and lit it. The lighter appeared and disappeared in her hand like magic.

"These are my cousins," Gideon nodded to the two women who stood so close to him they appeared to be holding him up. "I got cousins everywhere." He winked. "Kissin' cousins."

He looked at Gideon narrowly, then muttered. "You've reviewed my work. You were the first one to write about *Free Falling*, in fact. *Towers of Glass*, too. Both in *Poetry*. Six years ago. You liked them, actually praised them. Thanks."

"Yep. Loved the shit out of you. You got a way of making words sing. You put an idea in my head 'fore I know it's there. Makes it seem like I thought of it, but in your own language. I read your work, then walk away from it and remember it. Just like you wrote it. But half the time, I think it's me thinking it. That's what poetry's supposed to do. And you read your shit good, too. Don't clutter it up with a lot of pseudo-psychology bullshit and confessional claptrap. Don't go on and on about your mama and daddy and dog and pet rabbit and shit. You get the poem out front. Let it work for you. That's the way. You got what Ben Jonson called 'The Mighty Line.'"

"I think he was talking about Shakespeare."

"I thought it was Marlowe. Don't matter. You're a goddamn good poet. Should have had the Pulitzer. Twice."

He dropped his cigarette into an ashtray, folded his program and stuck it into a coat pocket. "The committee didn't agree with you. Unfortunately. They're in good company. NAL, Guggenheim, nobody with any money thinks my stuff is worth a shit."

"Melton does."

"They're a good press."

"I mean ol' Claude Melton himself. Know him personally. Good ol' boy. Knew him when we was at Columbia. Wanted to be a poet himself, back when he started out. But he didn't have the stuff. Didn't have the voice or the vision. He did have the good sense not to try after he saw that. So he publishes good stuff. Your stuff."

"Well, thanks." He glanced back toward the room. "I needed somebody to say that."

"So what are you working on now? New book for Claude?"

"Yeah. Sort of. It's not coming like it used to."

Gideon winked at one of the girls. "It never does," he said. She giggled.

"I've been reviewing a lot."

"Noticed that. I read you a lot. You're an iron-assed son of a bitch, aren't you?"

"I call it like I see it," he said. He felt defensive all over again.

"Takes a set of balls to do that," Gideon said and picked at his teeth. The girl giggled again and rolled her eyes toward her companion. Neither blushed. "Bet you don't have a friend in the world."

"None who are poets," he admitted.

"Me neither, son. That's the price of criticism. 'Vanity, saith the preacher, vanity!' Hard to ride around that. But you're a goddamn good poet, and that's a fact."

"Thanks again," he said. He glanced once more down the hall toward the room where Catherine Somebody was doubtlessly describing the poems she hung in the bathroom of her ranch house. Now, at last, he remembered her. He had described her verse as "a spontaneous overflow of neurosis, recalled in agitation." He had suggested that with every poem she published, she set modern verse back fifty years. No wonder she was so angry. She had been waiting for her chance to take revenge on him, and he gave it to her. Boy, did he give it to her.

He took another long drag on his smoke, shook his head and looked up. A few people he recognized from the room still glared at him. Villain, their eyes said.

"Aw, hell, son, don't let 'em get your goat," Gideon said. "That bitch is so dried up, it'd take a tub of Vaseline to grease her so she wouldn't squeak."

The other girl giggled, and he suddenly flashed on a recent memory, the sound of a quick, stifled giggle following a remark.

He smiled, suddenly certain. "*You're* The Heckler, aren't you?"

Gideon's grin didn't move. He shifted the toothpick from one side of his mouth to the other and winked. "C'mon, son," he said. He took his right arm, and one of the girls stepped over and snuggled into his left. "You look like a man who could use a drink, and I'm buyin'."

V

"No poems can please for long or live
that are written by water drinkers."
—Horace

*My parents were Deep Water Baptists, which meant that
there was no drinking in our house: I mean no drinking. We lived
right in the middle of five dry counties, and I can tell you, whatever
boozing was going on in our community—and there was a con-
siderable amount, no matter what—was kept strictly out of sight.*

*My mother's father "drank himself to death." That was
something that she was fond of telling me. I never really saw—I
don't see now—how a person can do that. I mean, I understand
about cirrhosis of the liver and all, about heart attacks, ulcers,
other things—the kinds of things that killed the Brontës' brother
and Dylan Thomas and other writers and poets, and I can assure
you I understand about the D.T.s, about how drinking can really
fuck up your life. But it's hard "to drink yourself to death." If it
were easy, I would have done it long ago.*

*Well, I might take that back. I saw this kid in college drink
himself nearly to death. His name was Freeman Something, and he
was a jerk: One of those rich kids for whom everything, particularly
being a real person, was a challenge. Always out to prove
something to his parents who just gave him money and didn't give
a shit about him otherwise. We were at this party out on a lake, and
we'd been sucking down beer all day. Then he pulls out a bottle of
Everclear, you know, grain alcohol, and he takes about five deep
swigs from it. He was really hammered after that. Sloppy and falling
down drunk. Didn't throw up, though. That would have meant that
he was as big a pussy as everybody thought he was. He passed out
after he finished off the Everclear, and nothing would wake him up.
They even took him down to the water and doused him. Nada. He
was gone. After about an hour, we drove him into town and took*

him to the emergency room. They said if we'd waited any longer, he would have died. But at the time, we thought that was bullshit. The doctors all knew we were underage, and I think they were just trying to scare us. The same way my mother always tried to scare me.

In a way, I guess, I was no better than Freeman. I spent half my youth trying out stuff my mother told me would hurt me. I sometimes wonder how differently I would have turned out if she had told me that drinking and sex were good for me. I probably wouldn't have done either to excess. Or maybe even at all. The other half of my life, it sometimes seems, I spent avoiding doing almost everything my mother told me was good for me.

But my folks were strict about it: liquor, I mean. I mean we didn't have a bottle of cooking sherry in the house. Not even that cough syrup that had alcohol in it. I was sort of surprised later that she kept rubbing alcohol around or let my father use Aqua Velva. You know, during World War II, soldiers made hootch out of that. Maybe she didn't know about that. Or maybe she didn't think I knew. But I knew. I knew more about drinking than she did before I ever had a drink. That's what comes from telling kids that something's bad for them. First thing they'll do is run out and try it.

I had this aunt and uncle, Matilda and Marty. I was never sure which one was really related to me. My father hated them, but then, he hated all our relatives, didn't matter which side of the family they were on. He always said his great curse was not being an only child. Anyway, Marty was some kind of big-shot construction engineer, and they lived all over the world. Every time Matilda got pregnant, they'd come back to my hometown so she could have the baby. My father said he came back "to dump her off to domino." But all their kids—my cousins—were born in the same hospital I was, had the same doctor. Once in a while, they'd visit when she wasn't pregnant, and they liked to drink. They had a ritual they called "our cocktail hour," which always happened right at five o'clock. About four-forty-five, my mother and father would take a walk. They never took walks any other time, but if Matilda and Marty were there, rain or shine, snow or sleet, they'd bundle me, my brother, and sister up and haul us out of the house during the "our cocktail hour." My mother would yell instructions at Aunt Matilda about what to do about dinner, and we'd walk, and walk, and walk. After about an hour, we'd come back, and then we'd sit down and have dinner just like it was the most normal thing in the world. But I *could smell the booze, you know, in the glasses, on their breath, and it made me want some, even when I was little.*

I remember the first time I tasted real alcohol, though. I guess every kid from Baptist parents and a dry county remembers that. I and Billy Hatcher and Carl Abbott went to this basketball game. We must have been sixteen or seventeen, since we all had summer jobs, and we had saved enough money to pay Daryl Hendershot and some of his cronies who were home from Cisco Junior College to make a run up to Oklahoma and buy us some stuff. I think we paid about fifty dollars for a six-pack of beer, some peppermint schnapps, slo-gin, and Carl insisted on a half-gallon of port.

Port! Can you believe the guy? Carl read a lot more books than any of us, and in one of the books, he read about all these guys sitting around in Oxford or someplace sipping port. I guess he didn't have an idea of sipping, since a half-gallon of Gallo port would last even the heartiest Oxford dons about a decade. And Gallo port had the consistency of motor oil, anyhow.

Anyway, we were at this basketball game when Daryl showed up with our haul, and we left. We had already planned to take our sleeping bags and stuff out to Carl's father's farm and spend the night, so we drove around a while mixing the schnapps and slo-gin with Cokes until we got a little sick, then we hauled out to the country. When we got there, Carl rigged up a hammock between these two hackberry trees and spread his sleeping bag in it. He always had to be different. We ate some hamburgers we brought out with us, and he drank—excuse me, sipped*—his goddamn port for about an hour while Billy and I finished off the liquor and started in on the beer. Carl offered to let us sample the port for a dollar a shot, but we didn't take him up on it.*

We all got sick. I threw up for about ten minutes, and Billy followed me. We were feeling pretty rocky and kept dry-heaving for a long time. But Carl didn't throw up, at least not right away. He pulled his sleeping bag over his ears and snuggled down with that half-gallon jug and kept saying "Never mix, never worry," a line I thought for years he made up until I found out he stole it from Edward Albee. But he offered to share the port for free. We didn't.

After we felt better, we climbed into our bags and lay there and talked, the way guys do, you know, about girls, about getting laid, though all of us were still virgins. But that's what guys did then. That's what they talked about. You know what? They still do, and age hasn't got one goddamned thing to do with it.

Anyway, about two o'clock in the morning, the wind came up,

82

and Carl's hammock started swinging. He kept yelling at us to help him get out of it, but we wouldn't. In fact, Billy was so pissed off about the way Carl had been acting, he reached out his foot and kept the hammock going back and forth, back and forth. Pretty soon, Carl was offering to trade all the port he had left if Billy would quit, but Billy just kept rocking the hammock, and Carl kept yelling.

Then he leaned out and lost it: all of it. Two, three hours of port sipping right into these nifty new hiking boots he had ordered out of an Abercrombie and Fitch catalogue. Filled both of them right up.

He had to bury the boots, and he never spoke to Billy after that. I saw him several years later, after we both had finished college— he went to Harvard, natch, and then on to Oxford for graduate work—and he told me with a little grin that he still couldn't stand even the smell *of wine. That made it hard to get on at Christ College, I'll bet.*

I threw up a lot after drinking in those days. My first college drinking experience put me off rum forever and ruined this guy's MG. A few weeks later, we were in this big hotel. We rented it to celebrate this guy's birthday. About four in the morning, I was hanging out the window blowing beets from ten floors up. Vodka and Hawaiian Punch: deadly goddamn combination. It would have been funny if I hadn't felt so bad the next morning. And then, during my first year of graduate school, I got drunk at a party at this professor's house and wound up in bed with his wife after he passed out in the living room and everyone else left. Her name was Doris, and she had these long arms—you know, "downed with light brown hair"—and a huge set of knockers, and I'll bet she was good. To tell you the truth, I don't remember. I blacked out the whole thing.

We did a lot of dope in college, grad school, too. No acid. I saw too many guys having bad trips. Just grass and a few ludes, maybe, bennies for finals' week. When I got out of school, I stayed with beer or, if I drank hard stuff, whiskey. Whiskey gets to you before you get to it, mostly. I stayed away from tequila after a couple of bad experiences in Mexico but came back to it later on. In a way, I guess that caused me a lot of problems I wouldn't have had if I had stuck to whiskey.

Some lessons are harder to learn than others.

I also have quite a tolerance for alcohol. I'm not bragging here, and I didn't come by that naturally. I just learned to pace myself, and after a few years, I just got to the point where I could hold it.

A lot of poets tell you that they write their best work when they're drunk or high. I think Dylan Thomas said that. Or it was said about him. And there's Poe and that whole gang of three-named Romantics who weren't shy about firing up their opium pipes or chugging laudanum and absinthe. They say Proust was stoned the whole time he was scribbling Swan's Way, *and even Kipling liked his pipeful of funny drugs. But I never could do it. I mean, I'd sometimes get fantastic ideas when I was really zonked, and I'd get all excited and write them out. But they didn't work when I sobered up. Not once.*

Every poem I ever wrote, I wrote when I was stone cold sober. I needed a clear head—and no hangover, either—to write well. That's a lesson I learned easily.

I guess the poems were like my folks. They just didn't want to be around during anybody's "our cocktail hour." I told my wife that they came from a dry county.

She didn't laugh. I don't think she ever really thought they were there at all.

New York

"I can't believe I'm really here," he said to Felix for the tenth time. His feet hurt in new shoes. No one told him that New York was such a walking town. He must have hiked five miles that afternoon, following Felix from bookstore to office to bookstore. Then back to his hotel, and then across town again for the awards banquet. He should have taken the subway or maybe a cab. But he couldn't figure out the subway—and he was a little afraid of it, as well. Cab money was something he just didn't have. Merely coming up to New York had almost bankrupted him. Thank God, Melton House was picking up the tab for his room. His credit cards were maxed.

But it was his first time there: the Big Apple! He'd been on the circuit, toured for years, visited almost every major American city at least once, some several times. But New York was restricted. A writer had to be *invited* to come to New York, asked in by people who mattered. It was an unwritten law of contemporary poetics, and he had observed it, bided his time until he got the invitation. It was a long time coming: long overdue in his opinion.

He could barely believe he had finally made it, even so. The North American Poetry Awards was the Big Time. It mattered. He had dreamed of being there, but he secretly doubted it would ever happen. Almost every poet in the room was a household name.

Those who weren't were officers in the Association or major contenders. And he was there as a nominee, an invited guest. There was no getting around it: This was New York. This marked him forever: a success and one of the unquestionably elite.

He was seated between his publisher, Claude Melton, and Felix DeMarco. Felix was gay, Italian, and full of himself, but he was a damned good poetry editor. He once said he had descended from Petrarch's family, that poetry was in his blood, but since he couldn't write it, he took up editing it. It was Felix who had taken his first book to Claude Melton and put it in front of the old man, himself a failed poet. When it was approved, Felix called him and told him that so long as he could write with that control, that power, Melton House would publish him. And they would pay him for it.

"Now we go for the big time awards," Felix said. That had been years ago. Eons, it seemed. They had made sure both *Free Falling, Free Flying* and *Towers of Glass* were put before every awards committee in the country, but neither had made the cut. Not once. Not even honorable mention. *Touring Taos and Tahoe*, his next volume, was completely ignored as well, although it garnered more and better reviews than the first two books put together. Then they touted *Opaque Images*, a cycle of heroic couplets intended to be a play on Alexander Pope. It was centered on confusion in a media-broadcast world, a modern mock epic using well-known actors, news anchor people, TV personalities and cartoon characters as principal figures. Unbelievably, it had been the one to take fire. He had put little real effort into it, and for the first time, he wrote the poems in it even when they didn't seem to be there. He thought every section was mechanical, strained, lacking in inspiration. But the critics loved it. Felix loved it. Because of it, this was to be his *annus mirabilis*, and he wasn't in any mood to argue.

His sex life had gone to hell, partly a result of his trying to show some restraint, to concentrate on one woman at a time—or nearly. And with the decline of activity in that area, the decline in inspiration had come also. But he was determined to be serious about what he was doing, to cease playing games with his art. If he was a poet, he was a poet. It had nothing to do with his prick, he kept telling himself. But, as he put together *Opaque Images*, he realized that he was lying. The connection was there, no matter how much he denied it, and he sought new women, new inspiration continually.

It had been a grand evening so far. James Dickey was speaking and would then read, then another nominee, then another poet, and then him. Those poets who followed on the program—interspersed as they were with other nominees—represented the major poetic forces in the country: W. S. Merwin, James Wright, Adrienne Rich, Gwendolyn Brooks, Imamu Amiri Baraka, Richard Wilbur, and others. He would also read. It was incredible, thrilling.

"I really can't believe it," he said and shook his head.

"I don't know why you keep saying that," Felix whispered. "You deserve to be here. You have four books out, and *Opaque Images* made the front page of the *New York Times Book Review*. You're a *major* poet. Why shouldn't you be here?"

"Well, I'm not black, Jewish, female, or gay," he said. "Aside from Dickey and D. Snodgrass, half the program falls into one of those categories. All the nominees do."

"Well, I'm Jewish *and* gay," Felix hissed, "and Italian. I can tell you that you're a better poet than any of them." He gave him a kidding smile. "You're better looking, smarter, too. For macho, goy white bread."

"If I'm so smart, why ain't I rich?"

"You ever heard of a rich poet?" Felix grinned. Claude Melton frowned and put a finger to his lips, and they turned their attention back to Dickey's reading.

The Great Southern Poet was droning rhymed quatrains from a children's book he had published a few years back: ballad-stanza, predictable and bad. He wrote it for his daughter, and to a child, it might be wonderful. For this audience of quasi-sophisticated New York *literati*, it was a burden. There was a lot of sucking at empty glasses and crossings of legs. Impolite whispering was going on. People in the darkened recesses at the rear of the room rose and escaped to the restrooms.

"Ever since he got to read for the President on national TV he's been insufferable," Felix whispered.

He nodded back, careful not to speak and offend Claude. But when he looked, Claude was asleep. His bearded chin rested on his ruffled shirt, and a light snore was audible.

He elbowed Felix and nodded toward the old man, but the young editor only shrugged and folded his arms across his chest. Claude must be nearly eighty, and he held onto Melton House only because no major corporation had offered to buy it. Poetry and expensive art books just weren't selling, and that was his specialty. A series of cookbooks for newlywed vegetarians was keeping him afloat.

He settled back and tried to remain calm. He had trouble keeping his mind on the ceremony. It was too unreal. New York itself was unreal. All his life, growing up in a small West Texas prairie town in the middle of nowhere, attending a cowboy-ag school in a bigger middle of a bigger nowhere, then climbing the rungs of graduate school and faculty advancement in the great anonymity of the midwest, still nowhere, he had always dreamed of being honored here. But now that it was happening, it seemed anticlimactic: like waking up from a pleasant dream about forthcoming events that would never be as good as they were in his imagination.

He doubted he had a shot at the award, any of the three for which he was nominated. When Felix called and insisted he come up, he had balked.

"I'll never win," he said. "They've never given one to anyone who published with a commercial press."

"The way our profits are going, it's debatable whether we're commercial or not." Felix laughed. "C'mon, what have you got to lose?"

He thought about it and decided he had a great deal to lose, not the least of which was the seven hundred dollars it cost him for the last minute round-trip ticket to New York. If they had announced the nominees early enough, he could have gotten a Supersaver, but with only three days to make reservations, he paid full fare. And there were other things as well.

The banquet was scheduled in the middle of final exam week. He had a stack of student poetry to get through before grades went in, two exams to give and mark in his other classes, and a half-dozen books awaited review. The deadline was the same week. He would miss all of it if he flew to New York for three days.

"We need you up here," Felix insisted. "We're reissuing all three of your earlier books in paperback this year, and I can get you some signings, a TV appearance, likely, maybe a shot at an NPR interview."

"But can you get me any money?" he finally asked. He hated that, but he had no choice. His daughter started college the previous year—Bryn Mawr, no less—and his commitment to pay for the education of the child he had seen but a dozen times in as many years was killing him. No one asked him to do it, of course, but he made her that promise when she was too young to understand anything more than the words of it. Now, she held him to it. Gently, perhaps, but a hold nonetheless. He didn't mind. It bound him to her in a way that his ex-wife couldn't sever. Not that she wanted to sever it. Her constant complaint over the years was that he was never close to the girl, didn't care enough about her to make even one birthday, one ceremony in her teenaged life. That he had been denied shared custody, visitation rights, or even a voice when she skipped from

state to state and job to job—and man to man, he figured—
sometimes not even notifying him of their whereabouts until he got
a Christmas card—or a notice from her attorney that he was late with
a child support payment did not mitigate.

He suspected the girl had had an abortion—maybe two—but he
didn't know for sure. Couldn't find out, and honestly, didn't care. He
just paid the mysterious doctor's bills for "gynecological
procedures" and kept his mouth shut. There was no way to ask a
question like that of a girl—woman—who was now past twenty and
living on her own, with his financial support, naturally. But he
couldn't begrudge her. She was too important to him, an abstract bulwark against what he deeply suspected he was becoming: a failure.

He was also still paying for a child he had never seen, would
never see: Rae Ann's child. He didn't even know its name, its sex,
or where its mother lived. He sent his checks to a lawyer in Cleveland,
but she had left there long ago.

To make matters worse, Betsy, his current girlfriend, the
graduate student would-be poet who had originally found his
frequent sleeping with other students stimulating—then revolting—
insisted that he fly with her to New Mexico for a Christmas break ski
trip. She put her pretty little foot down about it and made it clear that
he could come along with her—handle their expenses—or he could
find another apartment. On his own. He wasn't sure which would
cost him more. The only thing he was sure of was that since finishing
the book a year before, he hadn't written a word of decent poetry and
he hadn't had a decent lay. For a while, he determined to be serious
about what he was doing, to cease playing games with his art. If he
was a poet, he was a poet. But he hadn't had a single poetic idea.
Behind his closed eyes, his mind was an empty room, a wasteland.

"Have you already spent the advance?" Felix asked, somewhat
incredulously.

"Had it spent before I got it," he replied.

"All of it? That's not possible."

It was, he thought. But he couldn't make Felix or anyone else
understand that.

Opaque Images had brought him his largest advance ever. But
it didn't go far in a budget already ravaged. *Dissonant Voices* had
folded, finally giving in to a changing critical atmosphere which was
no longer tolerant of the sulfuric winds of honest criticism. What
free-lance reviewing he could get was spotty and uncertain and
didn't pay nearly so well. His well-established reputation for
savagery made his opinions hard to sell to editors—most of them

under thirty and without a clue as to what constituted a poem—who now saw the promotion—not the destruction—of poets as their primary mission. Most of his queries came back with what he was sure they imagined were amusing comments scrawled across the pages. "When we're ready to go out of business, we'll call you." Or "We're not quite willing to set ourselves up as Grand Wizards of 'what works' and 'what doesn't.'" His name was poison to more than half the magazines in the country, and that astonished him. One editor called after he reviewed two books—favorably—and told him that they had forty cancellations after his name appeared on the masthead. No, he responded, they wouldn't run him under a pseudonym, either. His critical style was too well known. His reviews had been consistently bitter and mean for the past decade, and he was a pariah to struggling young poets. He would never shed the reputation as a wicked hatchet-man, mean-spirited and vicious, dedicated to eradicating anything that wasn't up to what another editor called his "impossible and arbitrary, if not somewhat archaic, if not arcane, standards."

What little money he had saved would have to provide seed for the two tours he had lined up in the spring. The honoraria would restore the funds, maybe, but for the time being, he didn't have the cash flow to go to New York. He ignored Felix's further questions about what he had done with the advance.

"It'll cost hundreds to fly up there. This is goddamn short notice."

"It's important," Felix insisted. "Melton hasn't had a nominee in the past ten years. You're the first in what we hope will be a long line." Felix paused, let his voice take on a slight guilt-casting whine. "The old man wants to publish more poetry, revitalize his image." He took an audibly deep breath. "Confidentially, he's in trouble, and he needs something like this to keep him from declaring chapter eleven, or selling out." Felix let that sink in and then added, "Claude thinks you need to be here. He's put a lot of faith—*and* money—into your work over the years. This is the first time we have a shot at some return. I don't see how you can let him down. He wants you here."

"Then, let Claude come up with some cash. He can write it off."

"We'll cover the room. Or you can stay with me."

He had met Felix face to face only once, at the ABA when *Taos and Tahoe* came out. He pictured the editor's narrow body and dark, pretty, girlish face. "No," he said. "I'll take the room. If I can raise the airfare, somehow."

"Use a credit card. The cash awards are five thousand."

"That's all three combined," he pointed out. "My chances of winning any one of them aren't that good."

"You're a shoo-in for the Gideon Memorial," Felix said. "His book is out, and you're the star."

Felix was half-right, he thought. Gideon had made him famous, or infamous. The dedication to his book of criticism read: "To a Heckler's Heckler—a Man With No Friends," and then his name followed. It caused a wave of controversy that hadn't yet settled in the world of poetry. But the first essay, the title essay for the book, "Through a Glass, Once More and With Rhythm," had named him the "most important poetic voice" in America. He was compared to Walt Whitman, Thomas Hardy, W. H. Auden, Ezra Pound, T. S. Eliot, Stephen Spender—all to their disfavor. In short, Gideon had gushed, overgushed, embarrassed him.

"Reading these poems," Gideon wrote, "is like observing a marriage of form and content that could never be dissolved. It is fission, an explosion of metric heat that drives the image into the reader's mind with a nuclear force that seems never to climax but only to grow ever larger, mushrooming, until the clear significance of its meaning spreads across the imagination and permeates every thought. It has a half-life of a million years," he concluded, "and will be read long after the detritus that is other contemporary verse has returned to the molecular vapidity from whence it came."

It was the only positive essay in the book. The next five chapters vigorously attacked contemporary poetry and took no prisoners. Gideon dismissed the major poetic voices in the country with a wave of his critical hand and a litany of insults: "trite, stale, unimaginative, unformed, uncultivated, derivative, dead." In an essay called "*No habla* Sweet Poesy *aquí*," he laid waste to the little magazines, to their contributors, to what he called the "lying in state of American poetry." He wrote, "Contemporary American poets have exterminated the poetic voice from verse as certainly as Terminix kills cockroaches, and by their hands the loss to American art is comparatively the same."

But in each of the chapters, Gideon evoked his name as a positive comparison to the negative products of every living American poet's pen. "He maintains the sublime in a new sense," Gideon insisted. "His poems *speak*," Gideon italicized. "They *evoke*, *exhort*, *extol*, but they also *exhume* the American poetic from the premature burial into which the present-day versifiers and poemcrafters of the American contemporary literary scene have consigned it," Gideon concluded.

The dedication became prophecy. If he had friends before it was published, he certainly had none afterwards. Not even Gideon, for Gideon was dead.

The Heckler struck once too often and in the wrong place. He was in his usual back row seat at a reading near UCLA. It was off-campus, a collection of dilettantes from the college and others as well. They took over a café and read in support of each other. As usual, Frank was surrounded by buxom "cousins," a couple of girls from the university, who, it turned out, had tipped off several of their friends that the Heckler was planning to be present.

He never heard for sure what remark came from Gideon the Heckler, only that the reader, an anemic Arabic-American, stopped dead when the voice interrupted one of his poetic introductions which, he heard, was little more than an anti-Jewish diatribe on behalf of the PLO with an emphasis on the impulsive violence of the Israelis and their knee-jerk reaction to critical rhetoric. Gideon's only comment, reportedly, was *"Oi, vey!"* But it was enough. The poet expected the disruption, apparently, and he was prepared. He pulled a .22 automatic pistol from his pocket and shot Frank Gideon, The Heckler, right between the eyes.

The irony was that the poet fled the country and never was arrested.

Gideon's book was published a month later with his long-secret sobriquet right on the cover, and it became an instant best seller. Everyone had heard of The Heckler, everyone had heard of Frank Gideon, and everyone now heard of the poet, the infamous critic so extolled. Amid rumors that he and Gideon were lovers—*that* was a laugh, he thought when he pictured the booze-washed, drug-laden orgies Frank and his many female "cousins" arranged whenever they were in the same city—demand for his books soared. Melton reissued them in hardcover, and now they were coming out in paper. He was nominated for the North American Poetry Awards, and his life as a poet—if not a well-paid critic—was in danger of improving. If he won, it could turn his career—which he often envisioned as sliding into a fur-lined toilet—around and put him on the high road forever. Next year, it would be he who was one of the invited "distinguished" readers, not some second-tier nominee in an eighty-dollar rented tux who was scared half out of his mind. A win here would mean that he had made it at last.

Except for one thing: He couldn't write any more. He hadn't been able to for a year, and he wasn't sure what was wrong—unless it was the sex, or the lack of it. Living with a woman was no better than being married to her, he discovered. Commitment of any kind kept the poems at bay. He also learned that fantasy was a poor substitute for the real thing when it came to conjuring the poems. Betsy was good in bed—great really—but her toleration of his other women ended the moment they took up housekeeping together, and much as he enjoyed living there, fond as he was of her, it seemed that she was ruining his poetry. It was the nightmare of his wife all over again.

"Faithful love will never turn to hate," he reminded himself every day, but he also knew that when Cupid's arrow struck, it was usually a near thing to tell whether the sharpened point was lead or gold.

And there was another thing: He was broke. Too broke to move out, too broke to make it on his own. Certainly, he was too broke to even think about going to New York. But he came anyway. He had to.

He sold his car, an eight-year-old Audi he bought used, and funded the ticket for New York. Betsy was pissed off about it, but he promised her that if he won, he would fly out to Santa Fe and meet her there. He had no intention of doing so, but it prevented a scene. He would deal with her later. He abandoned his classes to a teaching assistant, bundled up the student poetry to critique on the plane, and flew to New York. This was his big shot: He couldn't let it pass.

Dickey wound up, and another nominee, a Japanese-American woman from California, named Kenji, read a dozen haikus, all pretty good, then W. D. Snodgrass took the stage. This is a great poet, he thought. Snodgrass's verse worshipped form, idealized it, played with it. He was one of the few working poets in America Gideon hadn't castigated in his book. It was all to do with tradition, he suddenly realized as he listened to the jolly poet reading and laughing with his voice as his tongue melded form into function. Gideon was a traditionalist, and so was he. So were all the really great poets. Eliot's system of epistemological, political, "art-emotions," it seemed, was right. At least insofar as Frank Gideon was concerned. It was, to contradict Pound, "right from the start."

The ballroom was full and dark apart from the bright spotlight on the lectern. Smoke hung off the floors and he opened his second pack of cigarettes for the evening. Claude Melton continued to sleep through Snodgrass's reading, as well as through a Native American poet, Lance Yellowfeather's, sing-song imitations of the hymns of his ancestors.

He nearly drifted off. Only the cigarettes kept him awake, but they made his throat dry, and he sucked down more wine as he smoked. He had hoped to have time to visit some of the sights, take a "literary tour" of Manhattan. He didn't want to admit to Felix that he had never seen the Statue of Liberty, Empire State Building, Washington Square, Central Park, the Brooklyn Bridge, that "harp and altar" shrine, it seemed, to some of the greatest American poetry. All the sights of Manhattan, some of which he had even used in his poems, had existed in his imagination for so long that it frustrated him to be so close to them without visiting them. He wanted the chance to play tourist, but his Sunday morning flight back would be early, and he didn't have cab fare, and he was almost certain his feet wouldn't stand much more walking.

Yellowfeather accepted a tepid round of applause, arrogantly flipped his braid behind him, and stalked off the white man's stage. Then it was his turn. Felix squeezed his arm while a strangely familiar man in a burgundy dinner jacket rose to make the introduction. He glanced quickly down at his program. The introducers were listed on the back.

"I am flying a bit under false colors," the man began, "having to give an introduction to a poet—and a critic—who has never had a kind word to say about me. Or anyone else."

"David Brittlestein," he found the name and hissed at Felix loud enough to awaken Claude Melton. "That son of a bitch! He hates my guts!" He slumped down in his chair. This *wasn't* happening.

"I've known this man—this poet—this critic—for more than a decade," Brittlestein said brightly. "We first met in St. Louis, at a panel discussion held in conjunction with the Popular Culture Association. He had a pretty fair book of poetry out, then. Pretty fair," he repeated.

He groaned. Brittlestein had sworn to have revenge, and this was it. How could Felix let this happen to him? He looked at his editor, but the young man's eyes were focused on Brittlestein. They were curious but wary. Felix *knew* Brittlestein, he realized, and well. There was something stronger than admiration in his eyes.

When they met in St. Louis, Brittlestein had just completed his MFA at Iowa and had a new wife, Sherlyn. She was lovely. Sweet, and shyly blonde, she hung back while her husband cut what he hoped would be a wide swath through the convention. He also had a new book, his first—*Brittleverse*, clever title, his master's thesis, University of Chicago Press—and he was rolling in newfound recognition. He was also obnoxious, egocentric, and much too sure of himself.

Brittlestein ignored Sherlyn completely as he shook hands, signed books, and engaged in heavy discussions in corners with anyone who wanted his attention. She wore patience like a hair shirt.

He was not there as a reader, himself. He was there to lecture on the emptiness of contemporary free verse. In fact, that was his paper's topic. He was to be at the reading as a panelist following the three poets who had been invited to showcase their work, all of which was in open form. Brittlestein was the moderator and had set him up—which was usual—to see if he would go ahead with his familiar challenge or back off in the face of those who he often attacked. He knew none of the poets personally, and Brittlestein was young, anxious to make his reputation by shooting down the big gun in public. It didn't work. The young poet had underestimated just how fast on the draw his adversary could be.

After the session, during which he grossly embarrassed all three of them as well as Brittlestein by suggesting that they gave new meaning to the idea that poetry was only "prose badly written" and befuddled them with obvious quotations they couldn't identify from almost every major twentieth century American poet, he wandered off, alone as usual, to the coffee pot where he found Sherlyn, also isolated and waiting.

"Robert Frost," she said when he walked up.

"Huh?"

"'The Road Not Taken.'" She smiled. "When you finished, you told them 'And that has made all the difference.' That's 'The Road Not Taken.' It was obvious, but a little pat, don't you think?"

"Right," he said. He thought he had used Frost well. It was a spur of the moment idea, but it seemed to have worked. She obviously didn't entirely agree.

"I love Frost," she said, "but I never thought of him, of that poem, that way. I guess it can be applied any way you want it to." She gave him a knowing grin, then blushed. "It was a little mean."

"Do *you* think I was mean?" He was prepared for her to defend her husband.

"Actually, I think you were probably right. But I don't know. I'm not a poet."

"Guess I won't be asked to the Poet's Hour." It was a cocktail reception for the creative writers in the association. Drinks were free, and admission was strictly by invitation. His name wasn't on the list.

"I really don't know much about all this," she said to him. He drew two cups of lukewarm coffee and handed one to her. "I'm pre-law. Ohio State. David's going to start teaching there next fall."

He nodded. Brittlestein was watching them furtively, but he was also talking earnestly with a collection of young men who had gathered around him with copies of his book. The crowd was, if anything, thicker than ever in the small conference room, and it was Brittlestein's chance to repair the damage the discussion had done to his barely emerged reputation.

He felt ignored and trapped, wanted a drink. "I'm going up to the bar," he said and set down the coffee. "This stuff is left over from this morning." She looked at him, an unmistakable appeal in her eye. "You want to come along?"

"Let me ask David," she said and gave him a long, narrow look. She had on a nice suit that complimented her figure. She was pretty but no knockout, only gentle, midwestern, innocent. Her hair was flaxen and looked freshly washed. Beneath the hem of her skirt, her calves curved deliciously before tapering into strong, narrow ankles. The arch of her foot rose slightly from her low-heeled pumps. She was tan in spite of the early season and wore no stockings. If there was a word to describe her, he thought, it was *ripe*. Something in him made him want to touch her.

After a moment of mutual silent examination, he shrugged, and she moved over to the corner where her husband continued to be the center of attention. If there was one straight guy in the whole bunch, he thought, he'd buy them all a round of drinks. Brittlestein glared at him a moment, then broke away and came over.

"Sherlyn says you asked her up for a drink."

"Not exactly." He shrugged again, mentally noting that Brittlestein had as much trouble with concrete communication as he did with concrete imagery. "I said I was going up to the bar, and I asked her to come along. You're busy." He shrugged again. "I'm not real popular around here."

"That's your own fault," Brittlestein accused. "You could join in the post-modern movement instead of fighting so hard to hurt it. You think you have to go your own way or not at all, don't you?"

"Out walking in the frozen swamp one gray day," he said with a smile at Sherlyn, "I paused and said, 'I will turn back from here./ No, I will go on farther—and we shall see.'" He looked at her, but her face was a blank. So was Brittlestein's. "Robert Frost," he said, and she brightened, but not much.

"Some people want to talk to me," Brittlestein said to her. The boys in the crowd looked anxious at his back, as if fearful he would vanish before their eyes. Sherlyn stood beside them, uncertain.

He dropped his eyes and studied the slight rise of her foot. "Well, no one wants to talk to me," he repeated.

"After what you said, I'm not surprised. You're stuck back with the pre-Raphaelites. You're a dinosaur."

He warmed immediately and lifted his chin to face the challenge. "Yeah, well, you're an imitative asshole. I've read your book: Derivative."

Sherlyn smiled pleasantly, apparently ignorant that her husband's face was red, his fists clenched. Either she was unaware of how serious they were, or she didn't care. Either quality endeared her to him.

Brittlestein pulled his shoulders back. He was a good-looking kid, he thought: Blue eyes, dark hair, only one long eyebrow, but that was the single serious flaw, at least physically speaking. "Well?" Tough as he wanted to appear, he knew how much he could use a positive notice from a major critic.

"There can be but one Robert Browning," he deliberately misquoted, but Brittlestein's face continued to question his. He shook his head. "Read my review. It'll be in *American Poetics*," he said, turning to Sherlyn. "I'm going to the bar. When he makes up his mind whether you can come along or not, that's where I'll be. The offer of a drink stands."

"I don't want to hang around here any longer, David," she said quickly. "Why don't you come, too."

"I can't," he said with a glance at the crowd of young men awaiting him with impatience.

"Well, I'm going up to have a drink," she said.

He raised his eyebrows toward Brittlestein. It was the younger man's move. He was still red-faced with anger, but he swallowed hard. "If she wants to go with you, that's her business. I don't tell her what to do," he said, reaching out and taking his arm. "But you listen: I know your reputation. I know all about you. You lay one hand on her, and so help me—"

"David!" she exclaimed, her eyes wide with shock. "What are you thinking?"

"Let me go." He looked hard into Brittlestein's eyes, and his arm was free. "If she wants to come, I'll escort her, entertain her while you're busy with your admirers. I think she's old enough to know what she's doing."

"I certainly think I am, too," she said pertly. "David, you apologize, right now. To both of us."

Brittlestein was even redder now, but he composed himself. "I'm sorry," he said, but to her. Then he turned to him. "We just got married. And I'm a little touchy." There was a beat of embarrassed silence. "You two go on, and I'll be along in a few minutes to join you." He turned away and walked to his gaggle of fans.

So they left. And they talked. And Brittlestein didn't show up. Three martinis later—which she gulped down like an amateur trying to act like a pro—she passed tipsy and started the road toward sloppy. She confessed that even though this trip was the end of a two-week honeymoon financed by her father, she and Brittlestein had not yet made love. The revelation came drunkenly, startlingly, but he couldn't say he was entirely surprised.

"Why'd you marry him? Hadn't you slept together?"

She looked startled behind the alcoholic daze. "Of course not! We just dated. I'm not like *that*. I would like to be, though," she giggled. Then she composed herself falsely. "I just couldn't. Couldn't," she affirmed with a nod. Then she looked at him and made a fan of her hands in front of her eyes. "I can now, though. I mean, I *think* I can." Her smile became sly. "I mean, I'm a married woman, now. What the hell, right?"

"Why did you marry him?"

"Oh," she said brightly. "He's talented."

"Now, there's a unique reason."

"Oh," she sighed, "I *like* him. He's handsome, and very romantic, don't you think?"

"I never noticed." He was thinking of his poetry. "Maybe a bit Gothic."

"He's going to be the poet-in-residence next year," she confirmed with another nod of her head toward the bartender to bring another round. "At OSU."

"Really?" He was surprised by that news.

"Sure. Daddy fixed it. I started at Iowa. Then we moved to Ohio, but I had already met David, and we fell in love." She nodded yet again, as if making sure she was reciting her facts correctly. "Yes, we are. Daddy said we could bring him over as soon as he finished. Publishing the book just made it work. It's a *good* book. David said it will mean a lot to us. To our kids. If we ever have kids," she said doubtfully. Then she returned to the script. "He's going to be a great poet. Daddy thinks so, too."

"And Daddy would be?"

"The assistant provost. At Ohio State. Since last year, anyway. He was a dean at Iowa. It's a big move up."

"And he thinks David is a great poet."

"Yep." The waiter brought the fresh martinis. "I do, too. Don't you?"

He shouldn't have—he knew that then and he knew it later—but he told her he didn't, and he told her why, and she listened, intently and with the fervent attention of a sophomore. Then she asked him to quote his own poetry to her, and she admitted that his images, his insights were superior to her new husband's, to any she had ever heard evoked by a living poet. All the while, she was drinking and she almost fell out of her chair before he pulled her up and practically carried her to the elevator. They didn't stop at her floor. They went to his room.

He had promised himself he would *not* seduce her, that they would just talk. But she was drunk and vulnerable, and he was weaker than he thought. The longer they talked, the lower their voices dropped. Soon they were sitting next to each other on the bed, and it seemed natural for them to kiss. They did away with a bottle of champagne on top of all the gin, and everything descended into a seamless fog of touching and petting. There was some crying, some guilt, then a lot of rationalization and more necking and groping. The rest just fell out as it always did. Her carefully protected virginity melted away in a tearful recrimination against marriage—as an institution and a disappointing reality—and she fell completely into his power. But the sex was tentative, uncertain, dissatisfying, bouts of drunken guilt and streaming tears. He delighted in her innocence, her shyness, her naiveté, her self-conscious protection of her body from his eyes, her surrender. The phone rang off and on all night, but they ignored it, covered it with a pillow, and at some point there was knocking on his door, which they also ignored. After a while, they passed out and forgot where they were, what they had done.

He thought of her tenderly the next morning. He was horribly hung over, but before coming down for breakfast, he roughed out three new poems because of the experience. None of them turned out to be any good.

He saw Brittlestein the next evening. He was waiting in the lobby for the airport shuttle when the rumpled and furious young poet charged him, knocked him down with an off-balance, half- formed fist thrown toward his upper lip. He still felt none too well, and now, with the space of several hours between him and the night before, he barely remembered most of what happened.

"I'll get you, you son of a bitch," Brittlestein yelled at him after two bellboys and the concierge pulled the young man up and held him back. "I looked *everywhere* for her. Called the cops! And she says she was with you! *With* you! You shit! You won't get away with this."

A crowd had gathered, and his head was spinning from Brittlestein's blow. He felt of his lip, which was swelling, and looked at the irate young poet's eyes and felt anger welling inside him. "Boomlay, boomlay, boomlay, BOOM!" he said.

Brittlestein's fists were clenched, but he stood his ground. "You think you're hot shit, but I'm telling you, I'll bring you down."

"'The maiden fears, and fearing runs/Into the charmed snare she shuns,'" he growled, picking up his bag and looking about for his briefcase. "If I were you, I'd shut the fuck up before I say something I might mean."

"I'll get you back, you son of a bitch. You'll pay for this."

"I already have," he said. "I had to read your poetry. Now, you read my review," he said. He straightened his clothes and took his bags outside to wait for the airport bus, nursing his swollen lip and feeling a vague struggle between guilt and satisfaction going on inside him.

He hadn't thought seriously of Brittlestein again. But now the angry young man was on the podium, and he had the microphone and the audience's undivided attention.

"So, even though it pains me to bring up a man who has dedicated his life, as well as his work, to the destruction and impediment of contemporary poetry, such is my duty," Brittlestein concluded his remarks. They were outrageous. Brittlestein was almost shaking with emotion, but he held his voice steady. "I therefore give you a man who has written much good poetry but no great poem and who has done less for the advancement of the genre than any living writer."

Even Felix was now staring down at a napkin he clutched in his fist. "I had no idea he was going to do this," he said quietly.

"What the hell did you do to him?" Claude leaned over and whispered. "He's a voting member on the committee."

"He's only *one* vote," Felix said through gritted teeth. "And only on one award." He turned to face him. "Why didn't you tell me about this? I knew he didn't like you, but I never thought . . . ." He drank off his wine. "I could have stopped this. Why didn't you tell me?"

"I had no idea he would be here," he said. "I didn't know he was alive." He didn't. After the first book, which his review had a hand in killing off, there was no more poetry. Sherlyn annulled the marriage, he heard, and Brittlestein didn't get the job at Ohio. He came out of the closet a year later, just after he was named president of The Poet's Alliance, a gay organization of versifiers centered in Boston. But after that, he dropped out of sight, out of memory. Until tonight.

He finally heard his name, stood and dropped his napkin on his plate, and went to the stage. Brittlestein's smile was a razor slash across his beardless face, a red parallel to his single eyebrow. The failed poet had enjoyed his slanderous introduction far more than the real poet had enjoyed having sex with poor, innocent Sherlyn. For a moment, he wondered whatever became of her.

As he climbed up to the lectern, he recalled he had been drinking steadily all evening. He had reason to recall it: His head swam, and he had to concentrate to keep from swaying. Up to that moment, adrenaline had kept the alcohol at bay, but now, standing here with the familiar old nervousness returning, he was too numb from wine even to feel the embarrassment he should be experiencing. He looked down when he reached into his jacket pocket for the four poems he planned to read. A bright red stain—wine or meat sauce, he couldn't tell—covered his rented shirt's white front. When had that happened? He looked like a drunk, a sloppy drunk, a bloody drunk. And he felt like one, too.

He unfolded the poems carefully on the lectern. Thank God that he never gave long introductions to his verse. He would have enough trouble straightening out his tongue to read the poems.

"Side Glances," he said hoarsely into the microphone. His voice boomed back to him from the cavernous ballroom. He looked out. The spotlight blinded him. The room was a black hole. He thought he could see Dickey and Snodgrass at the same table, but he wasn't sure. He did see Richard Wilbur rising, but whether he was going to the men's room or leaving, he couldn't tell. It didn't matter. What the famous translator was about to hear wasn't important enough to stay for. He could see Brittlestein, also. He was at the head table, next to Betty Adcock, and he was grinning at him: triumph, revenge. He started the poem.

When he finished the four selections, he stumbled through the tables back toward his chair. His eyes wouldn't adjust to the relative darkness after the brilliance of the spot, and he felt his fingers drifting over people's shoulders. Most shrugged him off. Some made angry remarks. Applause followed him, but he couldn't say if it was enthusiastic or polite. It didn't matter. He had fumbled words, lost his place twice, leaned on the lectern for support, and dribbled water down his front when he paused to gather his senses. In short, he generally made an ass of himself. Wilbur hadn't come back, and when he glanced over toward their table, Snodgrass and Dickey were also absent. So was Brooks. If they had been there at all. Maybe it was all a nightmare. His stomach raged at him, but he poured a glass of wine into it anyway. It seemed to settle, but he felt feverish.

"How bad was it?" he asked Felix. Melton was asleep again.

"God help us," Felix said. His forehead was in his hands.

The name poets all returned to their tables while another poet completed the program, and then the room settled when the president of the Association stood to make the awards. He won none of them, didn't even make honorable mention. The Gideon Memorial Award was split between Yellowfeather and a transsexual Canadian poet named St. Paul.

"You fucked yourself," Felix whispered. "Why didn't you tell me you were going to fuck yourself?"

"I didn't know about Brittlestein," he said in his defense. "How *could* I know about him?" His speech was slurred. Focusing was hard. "You should have told me. I could have called him. Apologized." He wondered what kind of apology one made to an avowed homosexual for seducing his wife.

Felix said nothing, left the table before the ceremony was over. Melton continued to sleep, and he walked the ten painful blocks back to the hotel alone. There was a phone message from Betsy saying that if he didn't show up at the ski lodge the next morning, he might as well move out before she returned, but if he was coming, could he wire her two hundred to cover "early expenses."

The next morning there was a note in his box from Felix.

"All signings and appearances are cancelled. Have a good trip home. I'll call later. PS: Fuck you."

When he checked out, he found that the entire bill was charged to him.

VI

"He went whoring to find satisfaction
But with whores, though accomplished in action,
He never could capture
That wonderful rapture,
For the thought of his wife was distraction."
— Unclaimed

Women. Boy, that's tough. Sometimes, I think about nothing else, not even poetry. But not for long. Of course, there's that connection, and that's why, but in the beginning, I didn't know that. And the distaff examples of human life were still always in my thoughts. You know how some kids have imaginary friends, well, I had imaginary lovers. I still do. I think I've probably had more imaginary lovers than real lovers, and I've had a lot of real lovers. And most—not all, but most—of them were knockouts. The kind of women guys lie around and imagine having. I suppose that makes me lucky, but actually, you know, it's not luck. It's really more of a curse than anything else, not because of the risk of pregnancy, AIDS or anything like that. It's a curse because it was something I needed. I could have lived without it, but I couldn't write poetry without it, and I guess that's why I never could resist women. I never had the courage to live without poetry.

Pretty conceited, right? Sure it is. But it's true. Anybody who knows me knows it's true. Hell, people who never met me know it's true. I didn't ask for it to be that way. I wanted what most guys want: a wife in the Junior League, two-point-five kids, two late-model imported cars, a preferred-rate mortgage, Gold Card. All that. And, ironically, I had it. Okay, I know, only one of the kids was legit, and I lost the wife, who was never Junior League material, and there was most definitely a mortgage. Also child support, alimony. But we had two cars, and they were both imports. We had that much, at least. As for the Gold Card, I never could rationalize the annual fee.

Then it was gone. Poof. Just like that. Just like it never was. I drank it away, fucked it away. But that's not really true, either. It would be a lie to say that: a self-pitying lie. The whole and bitter truth is that poetry took it away from me. And poetry was connected to the women. And the women connected to the drinking. Poetry to women to drinking. Double-play. Classic, right? And I didn't strike out much, either. Every night I wanted it, there was joy in Mudville. Most afternoons, too. No measured life in coffee-spoons for this boy.

"Pleasure's a sin, and sometimes sin's a pleasure," Byron says, but sometimes it doesn't have a thing to do with pleasure or sin: Sometimes you just can't help yourself.

I know what people think. Hell, I heard it often enough whispered just loud enough for me to hear. How does a guy like me, who looks like me, get so many women into bed? And good-looking women. Young, too. Up until I was nearly fifty, I never went to bed with any woman who wasn't at least average-looking, and on average, so to speak, most of them were half my age. And I was never more than ordinary looking, like I am now: short, slightly built, balding before I was twenty-five, paunchy at thirty, near-sighted, but not bad enough to need glasses, and bad teeth. I guess I was what the witnesses on the cop shows call "medium" in height, weight, looks. Always was, even when I was a kid. "The Most Likely to Be Ordinary" would have been my yearbook category, if they had such a category. The goddamn truth was that I was too boring to be anything but average.

Later, though, all that changed: I got grotesque. And old: "a tattered coat upon a stick." And fat: "a true hog of Epicurus' herd." I was more afraid of exercise than of cancer. The "four ounce arm bend" was the only thing I did reps and sets in, if you know what I mean, six ounces if I had a double on the rocks. "Going the distance," to me, meant having to climb two flights because an elevator was out. I was never handsome, but I truly got ugly. The girls weren't, though. For the most part, they were still pretty good even after I lost whatever I might have had in the way of appeal. But over time, even an old player has to move to the bullpen, play for the save, not for the win. I lost my consistency, lowered the old standards a bit. Frequency was good, though. That never faltered any more than my luck did. You know: "To strive, to seek, to find, and not to yield," and all that.

There was a while there, though, I prayed for impotence. I thought that it might change things. Can you imagine praying for something like that? Tell you the truth, though, I think a lot of guys *do. I mean, just not be able to do it. But you should be careful what you pray for. You might get it too late. That's what happened. It was humiliating, I can tell you. And the poetry stopped, so I didn't have that, either. I kept telling myself that I didn't care, but I did. When I got it back, I prayed that I wouldn't ever lose it again. And I didn't.*

I'm talking in the past tense, but I can still get it up. Don't ever doubt it, and if you have me over to dinner and have a really pretty wife or daughter or fucking maiden aunt, you'd better lock them up. Or lock me up. Don't leave us alone. Oh, I won't jump her between the main course and dessert, but if she's inclined that way at all, it'll happen. I swear. That's just the way it is. I can't help it. You pour an alchy a drink, you get the same reaction. A wink's as good as a nudge, as the saying goes.

I really don't know how I got so many great-looking women to sleep with me. It sure wasn't that way when I was a kid. It got easier as I got older, and it was a snap when I got old. I guess age truly doesn't matter. At least not for men. The older the violin, the better the music, or so they say. The older the wine, the better the vintage. Experience counts, right? Bullshit. The old clichés are still the best ones. They don't lie.

> *My poems guarding the house, well-made watchdogs*
> *Ready to bite.*
> *But time sucks out the juice,*
> *A man grows old and indolent.*

Indolent? Me? No way. I was always too horny to be indolent. In fact, the older and fatter I got, the less fucking indolent I felt. The truth is I don't know how I did it. Half the time, I was too drunk to remember the preliminaries. The other half, I woke up with some-body and didn't even know who she was, how she got there. But I was never too drunk to get a poem or two out of it. I might have been down, you know, but I was never out. Not while I could get it up.

What would I be "without the sexual myth," as Stevens puts it? "The human reverie or poem of death." Not me. Hell, no.

I guess every guy remembers his first piece of ass. That's a crude way of putting it, but that's the way guys put it. Women hate that expression, and, anatomically, it doesn't even make sense, you know. I apologize for it, not just to women, but to men, too. Using expressions like that got me a reputation as a male chauvinist, which I probably am, although I never saw myself that way. But "more of that anon," as they say. I love women. I mean, I respect them. As individuals. But I love them the other way, too. I can't help that. I'm just being honest.

Like thousands and millions of other guys, my first time was when I was in high school, when I was fifteen. It wasn't like later, when I was in control, when I could make the distinction between fucking and making love. I was only fifteen, and she was a year older and practically raped me. It wasn't me she wanted, not for sex, anyway. It was put best by everybody's favorite funny uncle, Oscar Wilde, you know: "Love passed into the house of lust." Or maybe it was desperation. She was already pregnant, and she was trying to lay it off on me. Hey, listen, that happens more than you'd think it does. When I found out what was going on—the guy who really knocked her up said he would marry her and boom, I was out of the picture—I was afraid to tell anybody, even my closest friends. And all the Baptist crap my parents laid on me had me screwed for guilt. I was sure I was going to hell, probably got some kind of disease, all that. Hell, I was so screwed up, I didn't masturbate until after I was in college. But that's the way with a lot of guys. Half the time, we don't find out how bad our parents fucked us up until we've already fucked up our own kids with the same shit.

Wordsworth was right: "The child is father to the man" [my italics!]. Kids could do so much better if adults would just leave them alone, let them figure out things for themselves.

Anyway, my first time didn't really count. The second time, though, that was different. Her name was Suzie Lynn, and she was kind of plain, but she had great legs. We went out a couple of times, and one thing led to another, as it almost had to. In high school, if you didn't "do it" after the third or fourth date, you just weren't interested in each other. We "did it"—but "it" was just barely sex— on a blanket in a state park near our hometown. It was messy and uncomfortable: hardly "splendor in the grass," hardly Keats' "elfin grot." More of an elephantine grope, truly. Honestly, I got a bigger charge out of seeing her naked than I did out of any of the rest of it. After it was over, she cried a little, and I might have, too. I don't remember. I do remember feeling sort of lost and disappointed. I was so stupid, and the first time had happened so fast and was so confusing I didn't notice that girls had pubic hair. That confused me. I remember us sitting there with her crying and me trying to figure out what else there was I didn't know.

There was plenty, of course. But that wouldn't come until later.

So after a while, I took her home. Then, the next night, I was out cruising around with some friends, and her big sister Donna—

she was a senior—flagged me down. She was Head Cheerleader—which in high school was like being Head Goddess—and she had two other cheerleaders with her. They had this '58 Impala, fancy, nice: rolled leather seats and red cherry pin-striping. I was thrilled to death, and the guys I was with when they stopped and picked me up were absolutely green. I'd been telling them what a boss stud I was—since the night before anyway—and now senior girls—cheerleaders—were inviting me to make the drag with them. It must have looked like I was about to go to Pussy Heaven when I climbed in the back of that Chevy. Tell you the truth, I thought I was, too.

Well, it was far from heaven and a long way from pussy: It was the goddamn third-degree. They had Suzie Lynn with them, hidden, crouched down in the back, crying and whining and stuff. All I heard for the next two hours was that now that we had "broached the sea of love" and other rock and roll bullshit, that we were going steady, engaged to be engaged, and all that. She had told them about "it," "about us," as she put it, and now they had their hearts set on us being a couple. All of them. They'd already picked out the colors for their bridesmaids' dresses. Here I was, not even fifteen hardly, and the bitches had my whole life figured out.

> *Ah! Well-day! What evil looks*
> *Had I from old and young!*
> *Instead of the cross, the albatross*
> *Around my neck was hung.*

You ever notice how Coleridge is always around when you need him? Particularly when the bullshit starts flying.

Anyway, a lot of guys would have given in, I guess, or pretended to. Anything to get out of that Chevy. But something in me wouldn't let it happen. I just sat there and didn't say anything and let them call me all kinds of foul names, make me feel dirty and guiltier than I already felt, in spite of all the bragging I was doing.

Sandy, one of the cheerleaders, was really down on me. She said I was a "foul sinner" and a "fornicator" and my "thing" would rot off if I didn't do right by Suzie Lynn. Sandy's daddy was a Methodist minister, and she knew all about it. She quoted more scripture at me that night than I heard in a year of Sundays in our own church. And we were Baptists, *like I said. I have to admit, it almost got to me.*

But when I looked over at little Suzie Lynn, I just couldn't see myself hooked up with her. She was sort of mousey and not really pretty in spite of her long legs and cute little boobs. And even though I had thought enough of her to take her out, to "do it" with her, I wasn't about to hand over my letter jacket or anything. At that point, I couldn't really see what all the fuss was about, anyway. If that was sex, I figured I could live without it. It wasn't nearly as good as peppermint schnapps and Coke, and the only thing I really had wanted to do afterwards was go take a shower. A hot one. After an hour or two, they could see that I wasn't going to give in no matter what they called me. I must have said that Suzie Lynn was a "real nice girl" about a million times, but that was as far as I would go. She got sick of hearing it, I guess, and made them take her home. Then they started all over on me. Mean stuff. Wicked stuff. After a while, they ran out of names to call me and put me out of the car five miles from town. I had to walk home.

But the next weekend, I was out cruising again, and Sandy flagged me down—by herself this time—and we buzzed out to the same state park and I found out that there was more to sex than pubic hair and more to a preacher's kid than scripture. We had a pretty good year together before she left for college, even though we never told anybody about it. She was going steady with a guy named Biff: big time jock who, she told me, couldn't get it up, or wouldn't, at least not until they got married in the Church of Christ, which they never did. Suzie Lynn wound up going steady with Chip Guyman. They married, and she dropped out of high school to have the first baby. They bought a mobile home and he went to work at the railroad and they had four more kids. Last I heard, he'd busted her nose three times, and she'd given him a concussion with a tire iron: marriage made in heaven. So far as I know, they're still living there, still together, growing older by the day and wondering what the hell happened.

I was with other girls in high school: four, five. Not all at one time or anything. It was a small town, and a guy with a perpetually wet wick could get in trouble just the same as a girl who "went down like the Titanic*" could. A bad reputation is a bad reputation, and it doesn't matter if you're a man or a woman.*

It took me a long time to learn that. It was an expensive lesson, I can tell you.

I don't want to give you the idea I was some kind of stud or anything. Or thought I was. I wasn't and I didn't. I don't. There were guys who were getting it with greater regularity and variety than I was, and there were a lot of weekends and dances and parties when I couldn't have gotten a date if I'd put an ad in the paper and offered a new car to anybody who'd go out with me. But I was no virgin when I hit college, not by a long shot.

I just hadn't made love, yet.

I hadn't written a poem, yet, either. And in a way, they sort of went together. I learned that thanks to Joy, as I said before.

I sometimes wonder if that's what screwed me up, ultimately. I mean, if healthy young bodies could copulate at will without all the bullshit, all the guilt, all the sneaking around and worrying about what people will think—people who are doing it or want to do it just as much as the kids do but who won't or won't do it openly anyway—I think there would be a lot less pain in the world. I know for a fact there would have been a lot less pain in mine.

There's something else, too. All the way through college, even into graduate school before I met my wife, I never fucked a friend's girl. Not a close friend, anyway. I just didn't have any respect for guys who did that. For the girls, either. Now, the operative word there is friend. *I slept with a lot of women who were going with— even sometimes married to—guys I knew. But I didn't like them, didn't respect them. To tell you the truth, I didn't respect the women much, either. I never went looking for it, but I never turned one of them down. I guess that says something about me.*

"Don't shit where you eat." That was my philosophy long before I heard it, even though I didn't always follow it. I tried though. I respected the spirit of that law if not the letter.

There was a lot of opportunity for that kind of thing in college. A lot of couples were on-again-off-again so much you needed a score card just to keep them straight. But that was when I began to get the *reputation, which most of my friends and roommates never could understand, since, like I said, I'm really below average-looking, sort of small, and I had already started to go bald and get a paunch before I was twenty-one. They'd talk about it around me, like I wasn't there. "How's he do it?" they'd ask and look at me funny. "He must have a twelve-inch whang."*

Well I didn't, don't. And it wouldn't have made any difference anyway. Women don't think like that except in the porno films. I just understood technique. Most guys' idea of romance was to lower the lights, put on some soft rock and roll, maybe some Elvis or Buddy Holly or, if they were really hot, a whole stack of Johnny Mathis records. Then, they'd give their dates a drink that was about half Coke or 7-Up and half 100-proof vodka, on the theory that they couldn't taste it and would get drunk, give in. I must have seen that a thousand times. Even tried it myself once in a while. It never worked. Sometimes booze greases the skids, but it won't change anybody's mind.

They almost never did. There's a truth here: Nobody gives in who doesn't want to in the first place. I'm not talking about rape or "date rape" or anything like that. Rape has nothing to do with having sex, with making love. Rape is a whole different thing, and it's not good. I'm just saying that all the vodka in the world won't make anybody reverse course, have a change of mind and have sex when it wasn't in the game plan to begin with. All that happens, if anything does, is that two drunks wind up rolling around in the sack until one passes out or throws up. I've seen a lot of great relationship potential go down the toilet—literally—because some guy thought that he could get a girl drunk and then make her forget that she wouldn't sleep with him if her life depended on it. Sex and booze don't mix.

They ought to put that on the buildings at the colleges, instead of all that Greek and Latin bullshit they carve out for inspiration. "BOOZE DON'T WORK." *How'd that look over the university library?*

What my roommates would do is get them down under them on a sofa or floor out in the living room or in the back seat of somebody's car, lay on top of them so they couldn't move, and in between feeding them big sips of the Mickey Finn, they'd get in some kissing and petting, figuring to make up what the booze wasn't accomplishing by hitting the right erogenous zone. Usually, though, they'd wind up getting their teeth rearranged, or a knee in the nuts, or they'd spend a lot of time in the bathroom holding wet cloths to their date's forehead while she tried to retch up a kidney. "What dire offense from amorous causes spring," *you know?*

I never did that. Any of that. I just talked. Quoted a little poetry, maybe. We'd have a little music, maybe a little wine or beer, usually, and then after a while, I'd get around to my own poetry. Then we'd go into the bedroom where the light was better or where my poems were, and we'd sit on the bed, and I'd read a few. Then I'd say something like "You want to make love," and she'd say "Yeah," or we didn't say anything at all. Sometimes it worked. Sometimes it didn't. Even when it didn't, though, I got to try out some good poems on a new audience. I was writing a lot of good shit in those days. Eventually, I published almost all of it.

When it was over, after she would leave or I took her home or even if she just turned over and went to sleep, I could close my eyes, and the poems would come: All new stuff, and I'd feel great about it. Which was another argument for not drinking too much. I usually lost that argument when I got older, though. It took me a while to learn that drunk poetry is bad poetry, after sex or any other time.

There was a connection there, you see? Sex and poetry. Maybe a little booze, but not too much, just enough to work up my nerve. But the idea of poetry being tied to love-making. A connection. There had to be. At least for a while, because they always came right afterwards, even when I let myself go and had too much to drink.

> *And though it in the center sit,*
> *Yet when the other far doth roam,*
> *It leans and hearkens after it,*
> *And grows erect, as that comes home.*

Sex. Good sex, bad sex, any sex at all brought my poems out: sent them to me in armies, especially when I was with a woman.

Every woman but my wife, that is.

You won't believe this—sometimes I don't believe it myself— but my wife was a virgin when we married. I mean, she lost it right there on the honeymoon in Waco—Jerusalem-on-the-Brazos— Fucking Texas, right across from that bastion of Baptist guilt, Baylor University. And our daughter came along nine months later. I wasn't like a lot of guys—had to marry a virgin and all that—it's just that she was a super Catholic, which just italicizes the irony of the whole thing. She really bought into the whole religion game, and there was no way some guy was getting into her pants without putting a ring on her finger first.

Funny thing, though, being Catholic didn't stop her from getting a divorce. Education can go a long way toward breaking down religious superstition, I guess, which is why I suppose fundamentalists hate secular humanism so much: makes them think.

I couldn't believe I asked her to marry me. I don't think I loved her when I married her. I don't think I ever did, and we were togeth- er twelve years, nearly fourteen if you count the separations. But that was all right. I don't think she ever loved me, either. She was sort of a challenge. I don't mean the sexual part—if I'd kept after her, she might have given in long before we stood up together. She challenged me to grow up, to be normal, whatever the hell that means.

We dated a long time: two years. I was still sleeping with other women right up to the wedding. I balled Laura, her maid of honor, the night after the rehearsal dinner. It was a kind of farewell performance. In fact, that was the title of the poem I wrote the next morning, right before we left for the church. A Petrarchian sonnet. I didn't think of us as being married in the sense that we were a couple of lovers. It was like a contract, a rite of passage. I made up my mind that I would be loyal, faithful, loving, and I was. For a long time, I was. But it didn't have anything to do with women. It didn't connect. And the poetry stopped, too.

I blamed that on being busy with scholarship, with criticism, with all that stuff. I said that I was through with other women, turned down lots of chances, even blatant offers. I was married, and that was it. It was for life. And no parole.

I didn't count on divorce, though. Divorce is like a pardon, an excuse. It's like a marriage never happened. If it weren't for my daughter, I'd have trouble believing that it did.

And I didn't miss the poems, even when they came to me. I didn't see myself as a poet, then. I didn't see much of anything other than ambition. She didn't miss it either. She just didn't give a shit. I don't think she ever read—I mean really read even one of my poems. She pretended to, and I guess that's the only thing I have trouble forgiving in her: the goddamn pretense. But I wasn't writing many when we were still young enough in our marriage for it to register. I hadn't put those connections together, yet, and I still carried around a lot of guilt.

You know, they say Catholics invented guilt, but the Baptists have the patent on it. You bet.

We were married over ten years before I was unfaithful, if that's the right word. Actually, I think making love to someone you don't care about is the worst form of infidelity, it's being unfaithful to both of you. Sleeping with someone you're not married to when you're married to someone else is only half an infidelity. If you're careful and can handle the guilt, it's not even an indiscretion.

Ten years, though: That's a long time. It's a seventh of the average person's life. Her name was Laura, too, although my wife didn't know her. She was married, too, but hers was on the rocks. She had married a guy two years younger than she was, and like me, she had hit her late-twenties and was feeling it. Okay, it was a precocious-menopausal thing. So what? Her husband was some kind of computer whiz, and they had a lot of money. She was in one of my classes, and one morning we wound up going to lunch at her place. It was really nice, nicer than any place I'd ever been in when I knew the people who owned it. We ate out by the pool, and then we went swimming. She had a great body, and I was turned on. We started fooling around, splashing each other, playing tag, in the *water, and then we made love under water. It was a new experience for me. Both things: the submerged sex, and the adultery.*

I wanted more of at least one of them, and I knew that my wife would never make love under water. It was all I could do to get her to do it in bed. I don't think she came once the whole time we were married.

And she never gave me a poem. I got a half a dozen good ones out of Laura before she re-read their pre-nuptial agreement and decided it was better to hang on and make a go of it. Better "a queen for life" than a hopeless "rake," as Pope, that frustrated dwarf, points out.

Anyway, we were married a long time for two people who really couldn't stand each other. She put me through graduate school, then I put her through graduate school: tit for tat. When our daughter was a baby, she stayed home and played housewife, and when she went to school, I was the Troop Mom, or whatever the hell they call it, for Brownies. I was the one who hauled her around to sell the fucking cookies and went to her school as the Homeroom Mom, and did all that stuff. I made every goddamn birthday party and school play, too. My wife didn't, not if she had a class to go to, a paper to write. But she didn't remember that, later on.

But we were good parents. I was a good father as long as I was allowed to be.

The first years after I started teaching—right when she started her first post-graduate degree—were the hardest. I was writing my first book—an extension of my dissertation on the importance of closed form in modern poetry. It was called A Validation of Modern Verse, *and it was outrageous. It was meant to be. It got a* New York Times *review because I took on the major names: Ginsburg, Snyder, all of them. I defended Richard Wilbur and W. D. Snodgrass, and I revived T. S. Eliot as* the *oracle of modern poetic theory. I had gotten over my aversion to his middle name by then.*

In a way, it was the same old thing: Crush the competition. Only, I didn't see the publishing poets as competition, then. I only saw them as idols that needed to be either worshipped or brought down. I didn't bring any of them down, but I sure drew attention to myself. It wasn't the same as other critics would do later. Hey, I was just a kid. But I had potential. Every review—even the negative ones—said that.

Her parents were supportive as hell. They loaned us a lot of money to buy a house, a couple of cars, paid our bills when my salary wouldn't stretch to that, her tuition, too, when there was a shortfall. *Promotions came hard in those days, and pay increases for academics—hah! My dad was dead—stroke—and my mother was a drooling victim of Alzheimer's living with my sister who never married—or even dated. My brother got zapped in Vietnam. He did get married. His wife lives in Michigan with their kid. She remarried, I think. But my wife's parents never got over my turning to "nonsense," which is how her old man always referred to my poetry. He could barely understand why I wanted to teach in the first place when he had a place all cut out for me in his business— highway construction—I guess trying to understand poetry was asking too much of him. He'd rather me be out on some fucking interstate shoveling hot top and smoking cigars.*

No, not that. He hated my smoking worse than anything about me. He said I was a compulsive addict, a pathological addict. It was the only thing about me he ever got right.

I moved up in academics fast. Same way I moved into it. If some hotshot was threatening me, I found him another job, sent him to MLA with a basket full of references, or smeared him with rumors of scholarly ineptitude, and he was gone. Poof! *I outpublished my seniors, forced them to promote me. I was the most popular teacher in the fucking department. I was on my way to being one of the best-known scholar-critics in the country, too: at twenty-five. I was faithful to my wife, a doting if imperfect son-in-law, a good father to my daughter, and a supportive member of a university faculty. Then I hit the slide, and it was all past tense.*

So what happened? Poetry happened. That's the point, remember?

The Rubber Chicken Circuit

The ballroom was ultra modern, cavernous, and crowded with tables. Along one wall were photographs of donors and benefactors. All the men seemed to look like George F. Babbitt, all the women like the Queen Mother. Every face was identical, only the clothing changed. The men uniformly wore white shirts and club ties beneath black, gray, and blue suits. The women—blithe spirits all—seemed to all wear various shades of pink, purple, and yellow. The men were balding and wore outmoded spectacles. The women's hair was dyed and swept up toward heaven. Taken together, they looked like a hellish dinner party ensemble designed for any wayward soul with a scrap of imagination or conversational ability condemned to sit and make small talk with the brainless for eternity. If any one of the heavily retouched faces—blank and happily ignorant as they were—fronted a mind capable of forming an abstract thought, the discovery of it would have rocked the foundations of the universe.

The opposite wall held a huge gilded cross with a fish, the ancient symbol for Christ, painted in red at the cross bar. There were curtains across the near end of the rectangular room, a bank of swinging doors leading to the kitchen lined the distant opposite. Overhead, huge chandeliers hung at regular intervals, and smoke detector-sprinklers dropped ominously between them. Although there was an echo of hubbub from one end of the hall to the other, the acoustics were excellent. No speaker, he had been told, ever needed a microphone to have THE WORD OF GOD—which was always spoken in all caps—heard anywhere in the room. It was designed that way and had, he was assured, cost over two million dollars to build. At that, it was in the third least expensive building on campus. He also noted that a microphone protruded from the lectern in anticipation of his secular reading.

There were two, three hundred people there: faculty, guests, trustees, a handful of selected graduate students. No undergraduates unless they were members of one of the prestigious honor clubs on campus, and then they were seated in the anteroom, which doubled as a foyer. He had been assured of that, as well: It was for their own protection.

He left the buffet line and stood uncertainly for a moment before accepting a reluctant but inviting wave from a party of four women and three men seated close to the near end of the room. They were near the lone lectern well in advance of the curtains, well off the platform that held the pulpit. He settled himself into the chair around the overlarge round table and offered a weak smile in return for the rapid introductions that he instantly forgot. Three of the women were either old or ugly or both, and the men were all portly, well-barbered, clean-shaven, prosperous-looking, and as interesting as a box of hair. They weren't as ordinary—or as beatifically countenanced—as those in the photographic portraits, but they were no more originally attired, as if all of them were extras in a Frank Capra movie. And they were so painfully polite, their smiles made him frown in spite of himself. If there were a word to describe them it would be "self-satisfied." Thinking of it made him frown even more deeply.

What he really felt like doing was laughing in their faces. But he didn't dare.

He realized he had interrupted something one of the women was saying. She wore a purple chiffon dress—a "garden-party dress," he mentally classified—had on an absurd straw hat with bright plastic cherries ringing the brim, and her over-rouged cheeks bobbed up and down for a moment while he placed his plate in front of him and scooted his chair under the table. She didn't go on, but put her hand to her throat and looked away. He could tell that beneath her heavy pancake makeup, there was a blush.

She overcame it and offered him a too large smile that proved the value of extensive and expensive dental attention, thrust an arm manacled by a heavy gold bracelet across the table. He shook hands with her lightly and met her dark eyes. She was the best looking *mature* woman he had seen on the campus, and there was intelligence behind her eyes in spite of her get-up and pasty cosmetics. He tried to read her age: Could be fifty, could be thirty-five, even younger. With these people, it was always hard to tell.

She had been talking about him, he guessed, as the others coughed nervously or exchanged embarrassed looks while he arranged his plate. As his eyes ran around the table, no other pair would meet his glance. Good goddamned deal, he thought. There was *plenty* to talk about, and they at least had the decency to be ashamed of themselves.

I'm not a freak, he wanted to say. I'm not all that unusual a commodity in the "real world."

No one said anything for a moment, until the youngest of the men commented on how nice the weather had been. He agreed enthusiastically, although he had barely noticed. They all smiled again at him, grateful for his innocuous remark. The Devil in their midst, he thought. It must be hard on them. No one had touched a morsel of food, and they all sat with their hands folded over their laps, staring at their plates.

He finally understood what they were waiting for: Dr. Gloria Chambers, Ed.D., matronly head of the English Department. She ceremoniously rose from her seat, stalked certainly to the lectern, and announced that "Grace" would be said by the Reverend Dr. Timothy Abernathy, an acerbic little man who had been introduced to him yesterday as both "sometimes poet" and missionary to Kenya. He couldn't figure out which role took the good Reverend to Africa, but he reasoned that of the two, probably Dr. Abernathy's verse was the most pestiferous. He had been presented the afternoon before with Abernathy's single chapbook bound in what appeared to be animal skin—lion or possibly water buffalo—and he had glanced through it briefly. Abernathy might be a candidate for the worst poet in

Christendom—or Islam—and was certainly no paraclete for American cultural development.

Everyone in the ballroom allowed the food to get cold while Dr. Abernathy evoked the Deity's blessing upon it. He went on in strained metaphor to thank God for the afternoon's schedule, for the "fine Christian university" with which they were blessed, for the "morally upstanding nature of the youth of America, the hope of the nation's future," and for a dozen or so other abstract and sometimes mixed blessings, all involving the spreading of THE WORD OF GOD in one manner or another. He then wound into a series of requests for guidance for the President of the United States, several other heads of state who were currently in the news, the President and Founder of this university, Dr. Vernon T. Bigelow, its several dozen vice-presidents and deans, its faculty, and those others who "labor in the vineyards of knowledge to produce the fermentations of truth and the distillations of faith."

He felt he could have used a sip or two of "distilled faith" right then, preferably Jack Daniels. He glanced down at the watery iced-tea in a glass in front of his plate. Why was it, he wondered, that these fundamentalists insisted on calling up images of wine when a glass of Perrier with a twist would frighten them?

"Malt does more than Milton can / to justify God's ways to man," he muttered, and the red cherries bobbed up and revealed a disapproving frown revealing deep and hitherto disguised wrinkles.

Fifty-five, he mentally tabulated, not a day under fifty-five. He also guessed that major foundation garments were diligently at work beneath the purple fabric. "We are betrayed by what is false within," he silently mouthed Meredith's warning.

This gig was Felix's doing. A sort of peace-treaty between him and his now estranged New York editor. After the fiasco in the Big Apple, they hadn't spoken but three times. Felix believed his career was probably over. His financial career was in ruin, that was sure, and he hadn't written a poem—not a good poem—in over eighteen months. Now, Felix finally came around and responded to the several dozen letters, phone calls, and pleas for understanding. And he put him onto a circuit, one that could make him some money.

It wasn't much of a circuit. It was, indeed, the weirdest he had ever heard of. Twelve schools in fourteen days and every one of them associated with some of the more extreme fundamentalist Christian sects in the country. In the past he had visited every sort of college, he thought. He had been at large state universities and tiny, backwater technical schools, ag schools and junior colleges, even one or two so-called "institutes." He had read or spoken at all kinds of private and parochial institutions ranging from the very exclusive to the religious old timers of Brigham Young, Baylor, and ORU in Tulsa. But this was different: The colleges on this circuit belonged to the lunatic fringe of their self-proclaimed Christian institutions of higher learning. Not one of them was associated with an established church, faith, or denomination, although several subscribed to the more severe interpretations of neo-Calvinist dogma flying around the country. It amazed him that they had faculties, let alone students. It also amazed him that they were accredited. It amazed him even more that they wanted a poet to visit, at least a poet who was not one of their own.

He wasn't stupid enough to believe that Felix had arranged his place on the circuit out of any sort of loyalty or even charity. There was a healthy margin of self-interest involved.

"Everyone's saying you've peaked," Felix warned him. "It's time to prove them wrong or throw in the towel."

"Everyone's saying I'm burned out," he corrected. "Why can't you be straight with me, for chrissake? I've heard that I'm in an alcohol rehabilitation center, a drug center, and that I'm dying of AIDS. The goddamned *LA Times* published my obituary three months ago."

"That was an honest error. They confused you with that playwright, what's his name?"

"He's not dead either."

"Anyway, they published a retraction and an apology."

"Some apology. They ran a half page on me in the Arts Section and claimed that I had burned out."

"Peaked."

"*Burned out.* That's what they said. Half the fucking poets in California took the trouble to cut it out and send it to me. I'm rolling them up and smoking them." He paused and tried to cool off. It was their first conversation in too long to allow it to end in a blow up. "Anyway, 'burned out' was the very phrase."

"Peaked, burned out, it's the same thing," Felix said. "The point is that you haven't produced any new poetry for a long time, too long to sit on your butt—"

"The phrase is 'laurels': 'to rest on one's laurels,'" he again corrected his editor, thankful that they were separated by a thousand miles, courtesy of AT&T, and he couldn't see the pained look on Felix's face.

"Sit on your butt," Felix insisted in a tone growing more impatient. "The point is that you need to get back on the road if you're not going to continue to publish. Hell, even your criticism is drying up."

"It's not my fault. I can't force people to publish my stuff."

"You seem to have had pretty good luck with me."

"You always were a sucker for a pretty face."

"That's not funny," Felix said. "You're headed for serious trouble. You may already be there."

Felix was right. And he knew it. The editor had been too deeply committed to bringing out the paperback reprints to write them off after the New York fiasco. As expected, they had foundered. Rather than send them to the pulpsmith or hand them over to remainder buyers for two cents on the dollar, Felix wanted to put him on the road again, to give him a chance to hawk some of them and reduce old man Melton's loss as much as he could. This was the only deal he could get on short notice, and this was the deal that was.

Felix ought to be here, he thought. A homosexual Italian Jew should feel right at home among these social and philosophical misfits.

"So get me a real tour," he begged. "Send me to some real colleges."

"It's too late in the year to get you on most places. You'd wind up spending everything you made on airfare. This is a sweetheart deal. They pick up your travel, lodging, even meals, and since you're the first one of the bunch, they'll be enthusiastic. They'll buy books."

"Do those people *read* books?"

"I don't give a shit if they wipe their asses with them. They'll buy them. That's what counts. Listen, you're up against the wall. Whether you take a dive for the rest of your career or bounce back to outsell Richard Bach is up to you, not me. What is up to me is that you have a chance for a turnaround here, and you're goddamn crazy if you don't take it."

"But for chrissake, Felix," he pleaded, "these are Jesus-freak schools. Jerry Falwell, Jimmy Swaggart, all that shit. Can't you get me at least one good gig?"

"You take this, and I'll see what I can do for the spring. But you take it. Damn it, take it."

So he had. But weak as the deal was, reluctant as Felix was to do anything personal for him after the embarrassment in New York, he was more thankful for it than the Reverend Dr. Timothy Abernathy was for "this bountiful land of plenty where freedom abounds and religious choice is the law of the land," a phrase that led him then into interrupting his "Grace" for numerous miscellaneous appreciations.

His stomach rumbled, and he coughed slightly to cover the noise. Around him every head was bowed in fervent prayer. He was the only one whose eyes were open, whose hands were not folded over his plate. Another gastronomic noise grumbled from his stomach, and he coughed again, louder this time, harder. A stabbing pain from his forehead raced back toward his neck. He almost gagged.

He was starved, hungover from last night, and, he thought with a renewed twisting of his stomach, worried about how he would come off in front of these pleasant puppets of semi-organized religion. He also was not particularly interested in the food in front of him. On the way over that morning, he had spotted a diner inconspicuously squatting on a corner across from the campus. It was one of those old dining cars from the days of passenger rail service, removed from the tracks and converted into a bona fide short-order house. It looked filthy, fly-blown and rusty amidst pollution-choked loblolly pines on the corner. But the very sight of it caused his body to long for a greasy cheeseburger-all-the-way, fries, maybe a side of red beans or potato salad. Maybe wash the whole thing down with crankcase coffee and chase it with an Alka-Seltzer.

He would love to be flatulent, bad-breathed, and top-button-open-stuffed before he shuffled off for a much-needed afternoon nap. This was, after all, the South, he thought. He wanted to eat, belch, and fart like a Southerner. He looked at the lady in purple and wondered what she did when she needed to fart in public.

But he would not have a chance for the nap, or for the cheeseburger, or even for a decent gas explosion. He was being paid to eat what was offered him, and to perform, to read. Or sort of. He studied the food and winced.

The imitation bone china plate before him held a congealed batch of noodles sprinkled with parsley, a cluster of undercooked broccoli slathered in melted nondairy cheese-food, and what apparently had once been a breast of a living chicken, lying sideways on the rim of the plate, congealing in a moat of canned mushroom soup in the full—and confident—expectation of being left completely alone. At least by him. Rolls hard enough to pave streets protruded from a basket next to a stack of melting margarine squares.

He surreptitiously touched the meat with his finger: ice cold. Rubber chicken for a rubber reading.

With a sonorous "Amen," repeated in a mumbling echo throughout the room, the prayer gracefully ended, and Dr. Abernathy toddled back to his table and chicken dinner. The minister was furiously mopping his brow with a cloth napkin, and he remembered someone saying that the missionary was suffering from one of two or three tropical fevers. He glanced again at the ruined food and silently wished the Reverend a quick deliverance from life's perils for the sake of his black African flock if not for the poetry of the world.

He was to read at the luncheon, but they were to eat first. It didn't matter. He couldn't foresee being able to do more than force a bite or two of the garbage in front of him down into his acid-washed stomach. He pulled a Rolaids pack from his coat pocket and pushed two tablets into his mouth. The roll was half gone, and the day was far from half over.

Dr. Chambers arose to take command of the lectern again. She wasn't much over forty, he guessed, and wore a severely cut mauve business suit and open-toed shoes that revealed the darker shades of her stockings' toes. He wondered if they were pantyhose or real stockings. Imagining her in a black garter belt brought a smile to his lips that one of the men innocently shared.

"She's a gem," the man said. "An absolute gem. She's just thrilled to have you here to kick off the circuit. It's something she's been working for since she came. Cultural exposure."

He wondered about his mental exposure of her body, and looked at her again. She had a nice figure, pleasant auburn hair that showed life and softness in spite of a couple of cans of hairspray applied to hold it in place. Her face, though, was severe: drawn-on eyebrows, too much mascara, lipstick smeared from drinking something. No, he grinned again, she wasn't the type to wear a garter belt, black or otherwise. Girdle, maybe, foundation bra, and sanitary napkins. No nasty French stoppers for her. She caught his eye and smiled quickly at him and then overcame a sudden squawk of feedback to invite them all to eat.

His seven companions immediately dug into their plates with the frantic zeal of people who hadn't had food in a month. He chewed his Rolaids and rinsed his mouth with the tea. Across the room, a young black student-aged waiter moved about with a coffee pot. He turned his cup upright and hoped that he could catch his eye between the youngster's obsequious bows and well-practiced step-and-fetch-it act around the rich Christian white folks. Everyone else at his table was concentrating on trying to slice something off of their piece of chicken. Each breast utterly defied its attacker with passive indifference. Gummy noodles drifted off the rims and stained the linen table-cloths.

This was the first school on the circuit. Like the others, it was religiously funded with the nickels and dimes, CDs and IRAs of the faithful. They had responded to the evangelist Founder and President Vernon T. Bigelow's televised pleas for their support to create a bulwark of higher learning against the forces of Satanic Darkness and Sin, to say nothing of Communism, Crime, and Capital Gains Taxes. The rumor, he recalled, was that the minister raised close to fourteen million dollars in his first year of appeals, much of which went to pay back the money he borrowed to support three unsuccessful tries for a seat in the United States Senate and a presidential bid that never made it past the Illinois primary.

He had not met the esteemed evangelist. He had been given to understand that he would not.

The take, it was also rumored, ran close to a hundred million dollars in the first five years. It was probably an exaggeration, he figured, but even if the figures were inflated by three or four times, this school started with a better budget than many state university systems had after a century of operation.

But that was a decade ago. The place now must be worth five times that, and new buildings were going up every day. The maintenance budget, he had heard, was greater than combined faculty salaries at universities four times its size. But he'd heard as well that no individual faculty member's salary here would equal the cost for chalk at any other school.

He glanced around the room and received dutiful nods from the faculty. Teachers here were obliged to work for the love of God, or the love of Vernon T. Bigelow and his personal monument to Christian education, or for both. After meeting and talking with a number of them, he couldn't see that they made much distinction.

He was disgusted, and after last night and this morning, he was a little unnerved. Still, he needed the tour. He might break out of his financial woes by the end of the year, pay off a huge IRS tab, maybe cover his travel, and his MasterCard and his American Express with it. With luck, he might even come out ahead, especially if Felix came through with a real tour in the spring.

But much as he needed the cash, much as he needed the exposure, he felt guilty taking their money. He thought every one of these fortresses of faith was nothing more than a nest of narrow-minded hypocrisy. Just being among them made his skin tingle, and then it made him angry. He told Felix that, urged him to try to find at least one or two better places to even out the tour, but Felix had not been sympathetic to his ethical qualms.

"They pay damned well—best honoraria in the country—and they pay in advance, through the circuit. They'll also buy a hundred copies of each title per school on a non-return basis. This may get you back in the game. I'm telling you, you're against a wall." There was a pause while he chewed on that. "And listen, they *know* about you. I had to talk like crazy to get you in on this. But they're all on their guard. Be careful. Don't fuck it up."

"What do they know?" he demanded. "Just what do they *think* they know?"

"Just don't fuck it up," Felix repeated. "Think with your head, not your prick, for once. I'm warning you."

He had already come close. In fact, he probably had already gone too far. His obvious discomfort at being surrounded by so many monuments to faith, the most obnoxious of which were represented by the students themselves in their well-scrubbed nicey-nice attitudes and almost military courtesy shown to anyone from the outside, soon manifest itself as cynicism, and he was having an increasingly hard time hiding it. He felt like a heathen among the faithful, a secret infidel who had somehow invaded Mecca as Sir Richard Burton had done a hundred-fifty years before. And he had felt like that since he arrived. There was little chance, he thought with a wry smile as he toured the campus, met the plastic smiles and vapid expressions worn by the emissaries of the student government, English Honor Society, and Poets and Writers Lunch Bunch, that he would discover anything so interesting as the *Karma Sutra* to translate or experiment with.

But he found he had been wrong about that, too. Every garden has its serpent, every serpent has its Eve. Only in this case, her name was Rachael, and he was trying to figure out just how badly he had fucked up because of her. The only thing he was sure of, he thought with a satisfied smile, was that it had been worth the risk.

Prayer before anything—dining, lunching, sporting, moving one's bowels—was both anticipated and expected here, he learned. He estimated that he had been involved in more and longer oral community prayer in the past twenty-four hours than he had experienced in his entire life. Cecil, the squeaky-clean young man who had picked him up at the airport had even stopped on the exit ramp from the parking lot to intone a heaven-bound hope for their safety in their journey across town to the campus. That Cecil had also thanked God profusely for the "safe arrival of this eminent poet and critic" did not impress him so much as the several cars lined up and honking behind them. Cecil's devotion was unshaken and impervious to commuter urgings, though, and his "Amen" was in no way rushed.

He looked down at the jellied food on his plate and sent up a silent and unhopeful prayer of his own. If Jesus changed water into wine and fed the five thousand with loaves and fishes, he asked the Deity, would it be too much trouble to request that this reprocessed mess be transformed into a hot plate of steak and eggs? He'd even forgo biscuits and gravy, he ironically added. But, he thought with another searching look toward the waiter, who spun around as if deliberately ignoring him, he *would* like a cup of coffee. And a cigarette, he mentally amended the supplication.

Right then, he thought he might sell his soul to Satan himself for a smoke, half a smoke, two good puffs: enough for some "solace in time of woe," he silently bargained.

"So, anyway." One of the men at the table noticed his looking around and attempted to attract his attention with an expansive gesture. He gave up on the coffee, arranged his napkin on his lap, and continued to ignore his food and wish for caffeine. The man was continuing to gesture and talk. One cheek was full of food, but the words escaped from the white and green mass he tried to chew. He remembered that the speaker was dean of something: nothing academic, parking lots or Bible distribution, something like that.

"What do you think of our little school? Ten years ago, there was nothing but forest and empty fields here. We have poured over a thousand square acres of concrete. It's quite remarkable, isn't it? Quite a blessing, wouldn't you say?"

It's full to brimming with narrow-mindedness, an educational philosophy so backward that it recalls the Inquisition, and a faculty workload that would make slavery on a Roman galley look like a vacation cruise, he thought, and mentally concluded: "Seek true religion, oh where?"

"It's fine," he said. "Very nice. You have some beautiful buildings. Obviously a generous endowment."

"Some of our biggest donors are *Jewish*," an older lady confided in a whisper and quick glance at the portrait gallery. She was Mrs. Pickery, Somebody Important's sister and a trustee, he remembered. The purple lady in the cherry hat nodded to confirm. "Isn't that curious for a Christian school?" Mrs. Pickery asked more of the purple lady than to him. He filled his mouth with icy, tasteless food and nodded. Eating semi-frozen broccoli was better than trying to talk to these people.

"Dr. Ferguson—he's our Assistant Vice-Provost for Religious Education," Mrs. Pickery announced, "said that's because those people have a profound respect for quality education. They always have. That's why so many of them become lawyers and doctors."

"There *were* the Pharisees," he noted, but they ignored him.

"Did you know that 'rabbi' means 'teacher'?" Mrs. Pickery asked the table at large. Everyone nodded wisely, and she seemed disappointed.

"Have you seen our law and medical schools?" the dean asked and went on without waiting the negative shake of the head. He was having trouble swallowing, he discovered, and a large piece of food was lodged in the back of his throat. He slurped tea, but the dean continued. "We keep all our facilities right here on one campus. Have our own hospital—well, it's a clinic really—but it *will* be a hospital. Dr. Bigelow conducted the ground-breaking last Christmas. It had been snowing—here, if you can believe it—but no sooner did his silver shovel touch the ground than the skies cleared and the weather warmed. It was a definite sign, don't you think?" He only stared at him and wondered if there were specialty shops that sold ugly ties that lay completely flaccid against the chest.

"We're looking for a grand opening in two years," the dean went blithely on. "It will join our graduate school. It will be a blessing to have all our needs right here."

"Do you have your own court system?" he asked quietly. His eyes were watering from the effort to fight off choking. The last thing he wanted was for someone to have to perform the Heimlich Maneuver on him.

"Beg pardon?" the dean asked. His eyes blinked behind rimless glasses.

"For the law school?" he asked. He wished he hadn't, but the dean didn't rise to the bait. Or he didn't get it.

"Uh, oh, I see!" he laughed. "That's a good one. A corker! I'll have to remember that for the next faculty meeting."

"Save it for the student paper, Harold," the purple lady ordered. "They always need something for their 'Humor on Campus' column." She turned to him. "There's not a lot of humor among students these days. Did you ever notice that?"

He grunted and attacked the chicken breast without success. He wondered if someone had slipped a plastic piece on his plate as some sort of practical joke. His knife was useless against it.

"The hospital *is* going to be lovely," Mrs. Pickery offered from behind a bewildered mask, as she had completely lost the thread of the conversation. "A thousand beds and a trauma unit. Prenatal care, a cancer research center and a chapel that will seat a hundred people."

"It's going to be taller than the dorms," the purple lady affirmed.

He remembered that Dr. Bigelow had made his start in a second-hand circus tent as a faith healer. Apparently prayer was taking a back seat to high-priced medicine these days.

"How large is the library?" he asked. They all looked at each other in confusion.

"Did you want to *see* the library?" Mrs. Pickery asked. She turned to Dean Harold and fluttered her hands in confusion. "He was *supposed* to receive a full tour of the campus."

Dean Harold leaned forward. "Confidentially, your being here, this whole program, is sort of a recruiting move." The purple lady nodded in agreement. "Do you think the library is important? For recruitment, I mean?"

"I'd say the library is very important," he said, putting down his fork and conceding the chicken its victory. Dean Harold removed a notebook from his pocket and made a note as he added, "I can't think of anything on a university campus more important than a library."

"Except the principles underlying the philosophy of the education," the purple lady inserted. "I should say that those are more important."

Mrs. Pickery agreed. "We've had to be *very* selective about the books in the library."

This time, *he* let the bait drown and finished off the tea. He had serious doubts that the library contained much "philosophy" at all.

"All our buildings are designed by the same architect," another man offered in an attempt to steer the conversation toward a more comfortable subject.

He struggled to remember his name: Dr. Something. They were all called "Doctor Something" or "Dean Something": never "professor." Cecil had warned him about that by explaining that "professor" was "a secular term often associated with humanism. Did you know it's an Arabic word?"

He pleaded ignorance.

"He's very famous, the architect," the purple lady assured him. "Dr. Titus Andrews. He's designed office buildings and churches all over the country."

And theme parks, he silently added: Disney World, Epcot Center, Six Flags Over Texas, Georgia, Alabama, and Missouri, WonderWorld, and a hundred other outlandish fantasy places. Any time a piece of natural wilderness was in danger of impeding human pleasure or progress, Dr. Titus Andrews was undoubtedly the man to call. The school looked like a futuristic amusement park rather than a college. No two buildings were alike, but each bore the markings of the "latest design" in Titus Andrews' arsenal of imaginative academic architectural fashion. The six high-rise dormitories looked more like vertical ice-trays that had been somehow transformed into rocket ships, ready for take-off, complete with spiked bell spires that offered electronic chimes in synchronization on the hour. The administration building was a long, low triangle in the center of which was a replica of the Tower of Pisa—not leaning—which served as yet another bell tower that tolled the quarter hour.

"Do not ask for whom the bell tolls," he had quipped when Cecil explained the intricate system of time telling on the campus. Cecil was not sure if he should be offended or not and only stared at him.

The most obnoxious structure on campus, he thought, was an enormous statue of Jesus that bore an uncanny facial likeness to Vernon T. Bigelow. It stood on a slight rise of ground Cecil identified as "The Mount." The Savior's arms were outspread, his eyes lifted toward Heaven—which likely wasn't more than a few yards above him, given the colossal height of the thing—his marble robes an alabaster white. Ingeniously, his shadow cast the time on an enormous—adjustable for daylight savings time—sundial that surrounded his golden sandaled and properly scarred feet. He dwarfed even the dormitories, dominated the whole campus.

Hell, he thought when he first realized what he was looking at, the statue dominated the entire south end of the city. All that was missing were more bells.

However ugly the campus was during the day, night transformed it into an otherworldly dimension of the grotesque. Cecil called it "Heavenly." Strategically placed lighting gave the buildings the illusion of movement, the youngster explained, the sidewalks a golden aspect, and if one were standing just so on a hill just above the campus, he would have the impression that they were gyrating and rotating under the benevolent hands of Christ.

A most recent scandal, Cecil informed him, was that someone— presumably students from the cross-town state university, a major basketball rival—had painted Jesus' toenails a bright red the week before. Nothing anyone could concoct would remove the crimson stain from the Savior's feet, so now his toes were covered with canvas tarps soaked in mineral spirits.

"It's a sinful disgrace," Cecil assured him when he was given the obligatory tour of the campus the previous afternoon. "And I'm praying for the juvenile delinquents who did it."

Praying that they burn in everlasting fire, he presumed. But then he retracted the thought. Young Cecil loved benevolent prayer above all things. They had stopped for two, three minutes at the campus entrance while the youngster prayed for the safe delivery of "this esteemed artist and poet" from the danger and death of the airport freeway. He listened patiently, studied the "Thank You for Not Smoking" sign on the van's dashboard, and finally considered Cecil himself. It was hard to compare him with the scruffy bunch of kids who usually filed into his own English classes. Cecil wore a neat sleeveless sweater emblazoned with the school's logo—praying hands over an open Bible—their mascot was The Apostles—over a short-sleeved shirt and clip-on bowtie. He also wore starched and creased khaki slacks, penny loafers, and argyle socks. Such sartorial standards made even the best dressed fraternity men appear slovenly.

To his shock, it appeared to be some sort of uniform. There wasn't a pair of jeans or shorts visible—or permitted, he learned—anywhere on campus. No mustache or beard, either. He wondered if they wore long trousers in P.E. Every young man he met was similarly attired, although colors and fabrics varied, and the sweaters were often replaced with cardigans or sleeveless sweatshirts, and one or two wore expensive imported running shoes instead of loafers. They all cut their hair painfully short, though still combed, and he did not spy one crooked tooth, pimple, or other physical aberration or deformity among any of the students. The phrase "Hitler Youth" came to mind along with a possible poem, but he reminded himself of his promise to Felix that he would behave, and he squelched the idea.

He had trouble stifling a laugh about Jesus' colorful pedicure, even so, in fact, kept trying to smother snorting chuckles about it, about the whole absurdity that lay around him, and Cecil became increasingly sullen as the trip concluded with a round-robin tour of the English department and loud, smiling introductions of every faculty member, secretary, and any ultra-polite student who happened by.

Although it was after four in the afternoon, every office was occupied with some diligent "doctor" flailing away with red pens at neatly typed manuscript pages and recording grades in open books on immaculate desks.

The only major problem, his young male charge reluctantly admitted as they drove to the administration building where he was to meet with Dr. Guidry, the Dean of Arts and Sciences, was that for some reason, grass wouldn't grow anywhere on campus. As a result, those portions of the grounds that weren't paved or bricked or landscaped with trees and shrubs, ran to mud at the slightest hint of moisture. It was a mystery that had confounded every biologist who was consulted.

"Maybe God isn't pleased with all this idolatry," he suggested with a kidding grin and gesture toward the huge statue when they left the university van and strolled up the steps toward the building. He knew immediately that the remark was a mistake.

Cecil froze. "This *isn't* idolatry. This is the glory of God!"

He nodded and smiled to show he understood, that he was sorry, but the damage was done. Cecil paused, gave him a withering look, lowered his head, and breathed a barely audible prayer, he supposed, for the soul of this ignorant sinner before him.

He would, he thought, have rather had a cigarette, or a drink, or both. Now, stuck at this table in the middle of this huge ballroom—which, he had been informed, doubled as a sanctuary during televised revivals—he felt a panicky desperation setting in. Sweat steamed up from beneath his coat, and his stomach felt as if a rock had been dropped into it.

"The Jews like basketball." Dean Harold tried to pick up the conversation after an awkward period of silent chewing of the inedible food passed. The others seemed to be relieved that someone said something. They had apparently noticed his growing discomfort, and wanted him to talk. "Nearly as much as the coloreds. Uh, Negroes."

"I think they bet on it," Mrs. Pickery said. "The Jews, that is." Her voice fell to a whisper. "They're notorious gangsters, you know."

"How many blacks are enrolled here?" he asked with a fervent glance at the waiter who continued to ignore his signals for coffee. Another mistake, he tabulated as he saw the party around the table exchange quick, confidential looks. He shouldn't have said "blacks." It tipped them off: He was not only a sinner, he was also a *liberal*. He was also a libertine, he thought, and they knew that for sure.

"Oh, we have a number," Mrs. Pickery piped up. "Quite a number. I don't know the percentages. Do you, Bart?" She looked with panic at Dr. Something: Bart. He shrugged and sipped his tea.

Another woman at the table was more helpful. "There are forty-five Negro students here," she assured everyone with pride. "That's almost two percent of the total enrollment." She dabbed at her mouth with a napkin and spoke with brusque authority. "Undergraduate enrollment, that is. We don't have a lot of them in the graduate school. As a matter-of-fact, I don't think we have any. Not yet. So far, our minority recruitment has targeted freshman admissions and transfers."

And all of them are six-ten and play basketball, he thought. The school was notorious for accusations of recruiting violations, of grade inflation, for admitting no black student who couldn't hit a three-point fade-away from center-court. In the ten or so years of operation, no black student had ever been graduated from here, although quite a number of the former "student athletes" were making a healthy six figures in the NBA. Somehow, they had escaped penalties, so far, but now the NAACP was in the act, and the press had hold of it. He figured that their days as a Final Four Powerhouse were numbered.

The interview with Dr. Guidry to whom Cecil had finally escorted him had not gone well at all and, if anything, had almost driven him away, screaming for a taxi to take him back to the airport, out of this city of madness back into burnout for good.

Dean Guidry was a painfully thin man with razored white hair who received him from behind a desk that was just a few inches smaller than his own faculty office back home. No paper or pencil blotted the desk's smooth mahogany surface. Only a small, leather-bound *New Testament* interrupted the grain. The office was void of books, typewriter or computer terminal. The only artwork was a badly framed Joshua Reynolds print, an architect's rendering of a huge building—presumably the new hospital—and a portrait of Jesus praying in the Garden of Gethsemane. Loutish disciples sprawled on a grassy knoll just behind the Savior's heavenly-lit face, and the painting was underscored with calligraphy that read, "Abide With Me."

"I want you to know," Dr. Guidry said after he shook hands and invited him to follow him to an expensive leather sofa and chair in the corner, "that I was originally opposed—fundamentally and firmly opposed—to this whole visiting writer business."

He sat down heavily and searched for a response.

"I find that the students are exposed to far too much secular influence as it is, and I was severely disappointed to learn that none of the writers Dr. Chambers engaged on the circuit were avowedly Christian writers." Guidry folded his hands across his narrow lap. "You are *not* a Christian writer," he asked without looking directly at him. "I am correct in that supposition."

He nodded weakly. "I am a Christian. If that makes any difference."

Guidry nodded slowly. "Well," he said in a dark voice, "there are Christians and then there are *Christians*. Do you mind my asking what sort of Christian you profess to be?"

He looked at him carefully. Guidry's eyes were on the Jesus portrait and had a beatific cast behind his glasses. He had the uncanny feeling of being in a confessional.

"I was raised a Baptist," he said.

"Baptist," Guidry repeated with a sagacious nod.

"Southern Baptist." The nod deepened. "But I've been attending different churches off and on," he lied. He hadn't been inside a church in years. The last time was a memorial service for one of his elderly retired colleagues whose widow asked him to be a pallbearer.

"Roman Catholic?" Guidry asked quietly.

He was too quick for that. "No," he said. He didn't elaborate. He wondered what Guidry would say if he knew that his latest girlfriend was a shapely young girl fifteen years his junior whose last name was Rosenstein and whose father was an Hasidic rabbi.

But Guidry didn't push. "Well, be that as it may," he said, "your personal beliefs—or lifestyle—are not my concern—not my *professional* concern—nor are they the reason for this meeting. I wanted you to know that I've decided to allow you to go ahead with the reading, but I've also decided to cancel the poetry workshop that was scheduled for tomorrow morning."

He was more relieved than anything else, but he was also curious. The workshops were optional, and only a handful of the circuit schools had requested them. He dreaded holding a session in this center of Christian piety, imagined with horror the numbers of poems about personal conversions, confessions of imagined sins, supplications for guidance: devotional verse at its worst. Impossible to critique, impossible to improve. He felt he should question the decision, however tepidly.

"I'm sorry to hear that," he said, offering a conciliatory lie designed to make Guidry regret his decision. "I had planned, really, not to conduct a formal workshop, but rather to talk to them about serious poetry. Traditional verse. I thought I might read some elegiac poetry, Coleridge, Gray, perhaps, maybe some confessional poetry. Then, of course, I wanted to emphasize the verse of Donne and Swift. Some really fine poets have been clerics, you know."

Guidry's reaction was not what he expected: The dean blanched, his teeth locked and head rocked back as if he had been slapped. For the first time since greeting him, he turned his eyes on him.

"Weren't they Catholics? *Roman* Catholics?"

"Well, no," he said. "They were Anglicans. Church of England. Actually, Swift was Irish. He was dean of St. Patrick's —"

"*Saint* Patrick's!" Guidry's index finger shot into the air. "That's what I mean right there! Anglican is just another way of saying 'Roman Catholic.' Isn't that right?"

"Well, not really. I mean the Creed is the same, or similar. But the Reformation—"

"The whore of Babylon," Guidry intoned. "Papal slaves. Idol-worshippers and lost sinners. I was afraid you might be planning to do something like that."

"What about Milton?" he asked. He didn't know whether to be amused or outraged by the man's deliberate ignorance.

"Milton is dirty," Guidry explained patiently, as if he were talking to a novice. "He writes of nothing but sex and makes Satan a hero."

"Milton was a Puritan," he offered. "*Paradise Lost* is—"

"Milton was truly an Anglican," Guidry insisted. He clenched his fist and gently placed it in the palm of his other hand. "I don't see that there's any difference. A Puritan, perhaps, but a tool of the 'Established Church' nonetheless. Sin by any other name is still sin! The Puritans were a calming force, reduced the Roman influence in the church, understood the proper role of women, the importance of family, to be sure. But they were not—and are not—entirely correct as subsequent interpretations have shown. In any event, we do not teach such writers or allow them to be taught. The students," he added quickly, "are free to read anything they wish. But I do believe in exercising some control over the curriculum."

"I see," he said. He decided to leave. Right then, right now. But he realized that his airline ticket wasn't refundable, couldn't be exchanged. "Don't fuck it up," Felix had warned him. He had to stay. There was no easy way out, but his anger simmered inside him. "I guess you don't teach Eliot, either."

"T. S. Eliot? The turncoat, the Catholic? Of course, not. Nor the homosexual, Walt Whitman, nor the madman and traitor, Ezra Pound, nor the Jew and panderer of obscenity, Alan Ginsburg, nor any poet who writes of filth and vile suggestion. There are ample poets of high moral values who have rejected the misleading teachings of secular humanism." He caught his breath, removed his glasses and wiped them carefully. "Some Shakespeare is all right—the histories, perhaps, most of the sonnets—and there's Bryant, of course, and Whittier, Robert Frost, certainly, and Ransom and Tate—the Southern poets. Emily Dickinson is mostly good, although I have heard that she's agnostic, and I rather like Ogden Nash and e.e.

cummings's lighter verse. I'm also fond of James Thurber. Robert W. Service, of course."

"What about Emerson?"

"Emerson?"

"'I like a church; I like a cowl;/I love a prophet of the soul; And on my heart monastic aisles/Fall like sweet strains, or pensive smiles,'" he quoted. "Ralph Waldo Emerson."

"'Yet not for all his faith can see/Would I that cowled churchman be,'" Guidry completed the quotation with a wry smile. "No. Although I admire some of his essays—certainly 'Self Reliance' and 'The American Scholar,' I must forbid the teaching of that poor confused man. Unitarian, you understand, is *not* Christian."

"I thought he was a Congregationalist."

"It amounts to the same thing."

"May I ask what your degree is in?" he inquired. Although the administrator repulsed him, he had a grudging admiration for the scope of his knowledge. He knew the enemy: that was sure.

"Why," Dr. Guidry turned toward him again and grinned broadly, almost warmly. "I have a Doctorate of Divinity, but I know what you're suggesting. I also have a Master of Arts in English literature. From Brown University. I specialized in American poetry."

"From Brown. I see." He was surprised, and dismayed. He thought Brown too good a school to produce such a bigot.

"Let me make myself clear," Guidry said. "There have been, uh . . . shall we say 'reports' on your behavior elsewhere. We know that you have a weakness for hard drink and . . . uh, for other sinful pursuits, involving young women, or so we're informed. I wanted to meet with you, speak with you, let you know that none of that sort of thing will be tolerated here. We may have to have this program, but we do *not* have to brook a corruption of our young people. Do I make myself absolutely clear?"

He set his teeth and looked away. "Yes," he said. "I will try not to introduce 'the wrong' literature into your students' minds." Or sex, he thought, right, wrong, or otherwise. He couldn't believe he was saying this. He couldn't believe he was taking it. Oh Felix, he thought, why have you forsaken me?

"And there's one more thing," Guidry stood and suddenly shoved out his hand. He realized that the interview was coming to an end and rose to his feet. "I have looked over your . . . uh, poems. I have read your books. I will not forbid their being sold through the bookstore, although I am sorely tempted to do so. However, I urge you to make your reading selections for tomorrow's luncheon with the utmost care." He stepped to his desk, opened a drawer, and pulled out a sheaf of typed papers.

"Utmost care," he repeated. "I have taken the liberty of asking Mrs. Waters, my secretary, to type out those I think would be most appropriate." Guidry put out his hand to meet the protest he was preparing as the administrator spoke. "You are *not*, repeat *not*, restricted to this list. And I hasten to assure you that these poems have in no way been altered or changed." He smiled. "These are merely suggestions, typed anew for your more easy perusal and," he added with a thin smile, "to aid you in avoiding any mischievous temptations."

"I see," he took the papers and folded them into his pocket.

Guidry nodded and opened the door to the outer office. "I have restricted the invited guests to adults, which would include most of our graduate students, of course. But the undergraduates will not be seated inside. I urge you to bear this in mind." A bright smile lit his face as they passed through his office door. Every tooth was perfectly aligned. "I want to welcome you to our campus," he said with plastic amiability. "I apologize for canceling the workshop, but I think it's for the best. I am sure most of the faculty and guests are looking forward to your reading tomorrow, and that will be sufficient." He offered his hand for a shake.

"It's the same honorarium," he said defensively, as an after-thought. He felt burned, somehow, as if Guidry's hand was full of fire.

"The fee is arranged by the circuit. We may use your services as we see fit. I believe that was the agreement." He steered him toward the outer office door, past Mrs. Waters, whose huge yellow spiral of hair was mounted on her head. "I just don't believe that much would be gained by the introduction of seditious and potentially damaging literature into the curriculum, even briefly." He stopped and physically turned him so they were face to face. "I caution you not to try to do it otherwise. I urge you to be on your best behavior."

He only nodded. "I assure you—"

"Assure me of nothing," Dr. Guidry said as he opened the door to the hall. "But *you* may rest assured that I—and Dr. Bigelow—will pray for you."

With that, he was in the hallway, casting his eyes about for Cecil. But instead of the young SS-man driver, and he supposed, spy and bodyguard, he was met by a gentle strawberry blonde woman who had a sly smile and narrow blue eyes that flashed when she approached.

"Hi, I'm Rachael," she said. She stopped and gave him an even, appraising look. "Cecil said he didn't feel well, so I said I'd take over. I'm sort of a poet-groupie, and it'll give us a chance to talk. Where do you want to go?"

He didn't answer. He could only stare at her smile, her piercing eyes, and try to keep his heart still and out of his throat. She was pure, innocent, lovely.

Everyone had finished eating when he saw Dr. Chambers rise once more and move to the lectern. He didn't much feel like reading, hadn't since his interview with Guidry. But he felt like writing, more than he had in a long time. Rachael had proven to be more of an inspiration than he ever could have hoped for. Her effect on him was profound, frightening, and at the same time electrifying. He was completely in her power, but he didn't care. A sense of renewal overwhelmed him. Maybe Felix was right. Maybe this sort of thing would move him off the wall and back into the action. "If winter comes, can spring be far behind?" he asked himself. But spring and the promised circuit, a *real* circuit at *real* schools, would demand new poems. He had no doubt that Rachael could summon them.

But it couldn't begin until this ordeal was behind him. He longed to leave the room, to find Rachael, to try to capture the poems she so easily summoned to his mind. A sense of euphoria gripped him when he thought of her. God, he thought, was it possible any woman could affect him so?

She was, she said as they walked back to the van, which Cecil had obligingly parked in front of the building, an English major, but they weren't teaching her much about what she called "real literature."

"I take courses back home in Atlanta during the summer," she said while they walked. "At Georgia State. They have some really neat poets and writers there, but the best ones don't teach summers."

"Why not go there permanently?" he asked.

"My folks. They say if I will finish here, get my degree from here, with honors, of course, they'll pay for me to study for two years in England. Or Paris. My choice. I'm good in French, but I can't make up my mind. Which would you choose?"

He got into the van and didn't answer. He was having trouble reading her, and just being near her distressed him in a way he couldn't entirely define. She wore the standard "female uniform" of the campus: calf-length skirt under a sleeveless sweater over an oxford-cloth shirt, sneakers and bobby socks. But when she climbed behind the wheel, she hiked her skirt up, and he saw a tiny rose petal tattooed on her left knee. Something in him stirred.

"Do you write poetry yourself?" he asked.

"Yeah," she said casually. "Who doesn't? Not very good stuff, though. I'd like you to look at it. But you don't have to. So where to?"

He swallowed hard, decided to test her. "I need to get to the hotel," he said. "Lie down, I guess, before dinner. I don't know if they," he jerked a thumb toward the building behind them, "have anything planned for dinner."

"Nope," she said. "I checked the itinerary. I'm to drop you off, and there's nothing until I pick you up for the luncheon tomorrow. I even get to keep the van. Or Cecil did." She backed the van out of the parking space. "I'm free for dinner, though," she said. "In fact, they let me sign out overnight." She winked. "I'm staying with my aunt."

"Your aunt?" The stirring heated up and tightened.

"Yeah. Aunt Margaret. She's in town for the night. Asked me to stay overnight with her." She winked again. "She comes in a lot, lately."

He studied her thoroughly. She had small but well-formed breasts under the sweater and a narrow waist where the skirt's belt gathered it. Her fingers were long, graceful, the nails clipped short and unpolished. She wasn't really pretty, but she had a wholesome, attractive look complemented by the color of her hair that picked up and accented the amber freckles that sprouted across her perky, upturned nose. She looked every inch the student at this school: except for the tattoo, of course, and for the cunning expression on her face when she smiled at him, as if she were planning something that she might or might not let him in on. He felt his chest tighten another turn.

"Don't fuck it up," Felix's voice warned him from somewhere inside. Guidry's stern face swam before his eyes. Fuck you, Felix, he thought, fuck all of you, and he lit a cigarette.

"Do you mind?" he asked as he blew smoke out his nostrils. It felt like his first smoke in days. His lungs burned.

She shook her head and held out two fingers. He passed it over and she took a puff. "I've read your work, you know," she said as she turned out of the circle and headed back toward the campus entrance. "All of it. They—that is Dr. Guidry—told us we shouldn't, that it wouldn't be required, but I did it anyway. Several of us did."

"Even Cecil?"

"Oh no." She laughed. "Not Cecil. He won't read anything not on the 'approved list.' He thinks we're all cretins."

"We?"

"We have a little group that meets in the dorm. It's not really secret or anything. Just some of us who see what a load of bullshit all this is. Of course, if Cecil and *his* bunch knew about it, he'd tell Dr. Guidry or Dr. Ferguson, and that'd be that. We had a meeting last night, and I read some of your poetry. We were all disappointed they cancelled the workshop tomorrow, but we'll come hear you read anyway. We have to sit in the hall, but I can't wait. I *love* your poetry."

"It's pretty sinful stuff," he said. The sheaf of papers seemed to burn through his coat pocket. He was curious what Guidry had found "appropriate."

"Oh, I don't know. It seemed honest to me. Really good. I liked it. It turned me on."

He looked at her hard, trying to see if the figure of speech was just that, or if, as he thought, hoped, it was a leading remark. "Really?"

"Really," she said. Her eyes flashed again. There was warmth in them, and it made his heart boil.

He looked at the statue of Bigelow-Jesus picking up the late afternoon sun. Then he glanced at her again. "You have your poetry with you?"

"Yep," she said with a nod. Her eyes were on the road, both hands on the wheel. "But don't sweat it. You can just read your stuff to me. My stuff's no good."

"You'll hear me tomorrow, you said."

"Oh, sure," she laughed. "You won't read the *good* stuff. They wouldn't let you get away with that."

He smiled. All or nothing, he thought. "Say, is there possibly a liquor store somewhere on the way to the hotel?"

"Yep." She nodded.

"I'd like to stop. Get a six-pack."

"I prefer scotch," she said. "On the rocks."

Dr. Chambers began her introduction, and he moved his chair back and patted the sheaf of papers that Dr. Guidry chose. He hadn't looked at them, but he figured he could guess which ones they were. He smiled to himself with the thought of the watchful administrator going through his books, searching for any poem with anti-religious or immoral references, hunting for subjects from nature and straining to avoid any that raised serious metaphysical questions. It wasn't an easy task, he realized, but likely Guidry found a half-dozen he felt were either harmless or too sophisticated for these Philistines to comprehend. It didn't matter. All he wanted was for this reading to be over.

He heard his stomach growl once more. His head ached, and he realized that he was closer to being physically ill than he had been in his adult life. And for the first time in his professional life, he realized that he didn't want to read. What he really wanted to do was to find Rachael and go back to the hotel. Maybe take a swim.

Then he remembered the signs. "Men's Pool" and "Women's Pool." There was to be no mixed-gender swimming at the University Lodge, which doubled as a practical laboratory for their school of hotel and restaurant management. Nor, he had learned to his chagrin, was there to be any smoking. He and Rachael got a frightening lesson about that the evening before.

No sooner had he returned from fetching ice and begun reading his first poem, a roundel with a different double entendre in each refrain, that suggested something more than love could be achieved through the joining of two bodies in passion, than he stopped in mid-line. They looked silently at each other, measured the tension in the room, and then scrambled across the bed that divided their distance. Their hands, legs, mouths and tongues became a living whirlwind of groping, grasping probes and clutches. They fell onto the bed, both finding delight in a cascade of giggles and kisses as they stripped off their clothes and plunged into one another, licking and tasting each other's bodies before they found a strong single rhythm that ended, finally, in a sweaty, noisy mutual climax that left them both spent, panting.

Rachael pulled free from the wet, tangled sheets and garments and mixed their first drinks. He lit a cigarette and watched her move through the wisps of silvery smoke. Her body was long, lithe, and seemed almost comical in its naked innocence, particularly with the not one but four rose tattoos she had placed strategically all over her lower body. He studied her every move with something he defined to himself as awe. It was all he could do to keep from leaping up, grabbing her, pulling her back to him, and the restraint he forced onto himself was deliciously painful.

"They're my single form of rebellion." She smiled when she came back to him. He ran his fingers from one to the other in a sensual game of connect the dots. "I call them 'My Sensuous Roses.' My parents would die, and old Dr. Ferguson would have a cat if he knew anyone on campus had a tattoo anywhere. He says they're 'brands of the Devil.' This one," she pointed to the rose petal on her knee, "is the most daring. But since no women are allowed to wear skirts that show their knees, only my roommate knows for sure." She winked. "She has one here," she pointed to a spot high on her inner thigh next to her light brown pubic pelt. "It's a penis, erect and squirting. If old Ferguson knew about that one, he would have every woman on campus stripped and inspected."

"I doubt Dr. Guidry would like it, either," he said. His breath was short, and he knew he wanted her again, right then. No woman had ever moved him in this way. He felt hungry for her, anxious to touch her, to never stop touching her. But there was something else, also. There was something about her that warmed him, made him feel secure. His self-esteem soared, and he felt as if his mind were bursting.

"The *Reverend* Dr. Dean Guidry?" she asked with a playful lilt in her voice. "He would fucking *love* it! I could tell you tales about some of the girls who've been called to his office for 'prayer conferences.' Believe me, there's a lot more than hand-holding going on. Hand *jobs* is more like it."

"Why do they put up with it? Why don't they tell?"

"How do they prove it? Besides, it would mean flunking out. Oh, it doesn't happen a lot, I don't guess. But it does happen. It happened to my roommate, Claire."

He took thought:

There once was a co-ed named Claire,
Who had her first "conference affair."
As the dean her legs spread,
She gasped and she said,
"I prefer to be opened with prayer."

"That is *sinful!*" Rachael cried as she collapsed with laughter. "I'll have to remember it. Wait! I've got one, too:

The dean undressed with heaving breast
The errant girl to lie on.
He thought it lewd
To do it nude,
So he kept his old school tie on."

They went through five or six more before they ran out of clever rhymes. She was still laughing while she refilled their drinks.

He lay back and closed his eyes: Poems danced across his mind. This girl was good. Very good. Good for him. Good forever. She made him feel ten years younger, athletic, proud of himself. She could well be his ticket back. Maybe Felix was more right about his taking this tour than even he knew. He blew smoke rings toward the sprinkler system that crisscrossed the ceiling and smiled. He was buoyed up by confidence. For the first time in over a decade, he thought about marriage, about living with her, loving her. It was ridiculous, but it seemed inevitable, destined. It would happen.

He shook his head to clear away his thoughts. She misread the gesture and flopped down in a chair, crossing her naked knees and holding her chin in one hand.

"The administrators don't like anything," she said sadly. "But we're not all what we seem. To them, at least. If they only knew. . . ." Then her face took on a defensive look. "This is a good school for some things. Our SAT scores are in the top ten percent. Almost everyone goes on to medical or law school—and not just here, either. And our parents are *thrilled* we're here. We have to give up a lot. Our freedom, for one thing. They want to know where we are every minute. Force us to lie about everything. But there are enough of us who don't agree with all the bullshit that life stays bearable. Besides, maybe it's worth the sacrifice. I'm on the Dean's List, have been every term."

He reached for her, but she rose, smiled brightly, and danced away from him. "What I miss most is music," she said. "Dancing. If it wasn't for the summers at Georgia State, I'd have died long ago."

He watched her move through the whirls of cigarette smoke and admired her vitality, her immodest sexuality. She looked like a young doe when she skipped over to the glasses, and he knew he could never let her get away, not just because of the poems she summoned, but because of something else. It was absurd, he insisted while he watched her, but he was falling in love with her, with the idea of her. He wanted to eat her alive, consume her, own her.

She continued to dance, slashing seductively at the tobacco clouds and demurely covering her breasts and pubic mound when she turned to face him. She was having the time of her life, and so was he.

"More smoke," she ordered. "I'll dance the dance of the Seven Veils, and the only head served up'll be a pleasure to both of us." He obliged her by lighting another cigarette and puffing out clouds for her to interrupt with her narrow arms and jutting breasts. He was hard again, and he flung back the sheet and exposed himself to her. She grinned and moved toward him with a seductive sway.

Suddenly, he heard his name being called from directly overhead. They both froze, her skin broke out in gooseflesh, and her nipples went taut. His erection shrank, and he rolled over, pulled the sheet up to his chest, and looked around, panic in his eyes. His name was repeated, and they both stared at the ceiling.

"Are you by any chance smoking in the room?" the disembodied voice asked. The tone was young, sexless. A student, doubtlessly, paid to monitor smoke detectors and harass violators. He spotted the recessed speaker next to the air-conditioning vent.

"Yes," he said, "I am, as a matter of fact. It's *my* room." He was still frightened, but now he was growing angry. What the hell was this, anyway?

"Smoking is not permitted in the University Lodge," the voice announced as if he were reading from a brochure. "There is no smoking permitted anywhere on university grounds, indoors or out."

"I'm sorry," he said and tried to control his voice. He realized his heart was thudding, thundering in his ears. Rachael was still frozen, but now a smile crossed her freckled face, and a set of long fingers came up to cover her grin. "If there's no smoking, why in God's name do you put ashtrays in the rooms?" Anger now overcame his voice. "It's *my* room, for God's sake."

"Please observe this rule," the voice concluded with monotonous cold authority. "There is no smoking or consumption of alcoholic beverages in any room of the University Lodge. Have a pleasant evening, and God bless you." He heard a definite click as the intercom shut off.

"That does it," he sighed in an exaggerated whisper, heaving his legs over the side of the bed. "I've got to find another hotel."

"Nope," Rachael said in a clear voice when she moved over to him and handed him a fresh drink. She put a finger to her lips, then went to her purse. She took out several rubber bands and a handful of small boxes: Condoms.

"Uh . . . no," he said, confused. "We don't really need them. I've had a—"

"It's not for you, silly," she said. She stood up on the bed and stretched high to strap the rubber over the combination sprinkler-smoke detector overhead. It was too ironic, and she was too tempting, and he encircled her thin waist with his hands, but she pushed him away and completed her deceptive task with the other three spigots in the room.

"How did you learn that?" he whispered.

"In the dorm," she smiled. Her eyebrows narrowed in mock conspiracy, "I knew they had these there, but I didn't think they'd bug the goddamn hotel rooms too. The walls have noses."

"Quiet. They have *ears*, too. They could be listening."

"Without you knowing?" she laughed. "They'd never do that. That would be a 'sinful deception.' The intercoms are strictly one-way. You should hear what we say back to them in the dorms. We'd all be expelled if *they* heard. Besides, this place has a hundred rooms. They can't listen to all of them. But the smoke alarm goes off if you work up a sweat. We're okay now, if we flush our butts and ashes. So," she reached down and grabbed his penis and allowed it to grow once more and fill her narrow hand, "give me a cigarette and finish your drink. I want to hear some more poetry. And then," she smiled her sly grin as if to say that she knew all his secrets, "we'll see what we can do about making some."

"You didn't eat much," Mrs. Pickery offered helpfully while Dr. Chambers rattled off his credits and publications. "Aren't you feeling well? You look a little pale."

He *felt* a little pale. Last night's room service dinner—ordered for one and ignored by two—had been no better than this fare. Stuffed flounder was the supposed entree, but his was colder and deader than the luncheon chicken, and apparently they brought over the left-over noodles from the lodge. Even the lemon pie looked wilted and badly used. The filling had run out and was brimming on the plate.

"I'm fine," he said. "I'm just not hungry." She looked so sorry for him, he felt he should say something more. "I'm working on some new poems, and I usually don't eat much when I'm writing."

It was a lie, but she seemed satisfied. The mysteries of creative effort always befuddled the dull-minded. He waited until Dr. Chambers finished her narration of his credentials, and then rose and made his way to the lectern.

As he mounted the small podium, he looked out over a bobbing sea of bright and expectant faces. Even so, he knew those false smiles and blinking eyes hid deep suspicions. He felt as if he was facing a hostile tribe, a group of people who were ready to crucify him if he made a false move or dared utter a secular humanist truth.

A sudden movement from the doorway distracted him. Then he saw Rachael. She was standing there, one hand over her mouth to suppress her cunning smile. She was surrounded by students, undergraduates, all dressed alike, who had left their assigned tables and ganged up in the anteroom doorway and were looking into the ballroom like well-washed waifs, allowed to watch the wealthy eat but forbidden admission to this inner sanctum where secrets might be revealed.

She had changed, but her uniform was still intact. The sneakers were replaced by low-heeled pumps, which emphasized the muscles of her ankle and lower calf and made his chest go hollow with want. She stood with one leg crossed over the other beneath her long skirt. Her hand dropped from her mouth to a cocked hip, and she winked at him. He saw himself leaving the podium, moving over to her, taking her arm in his and walking away. For a moment, he thought he actually might do just that.

Dr. Chambers caught the direction of his attention and half-rose to see what was going on. Her frown clouded the room.

He had to read and quickly, he thought. Otherwise, that battleaxe was going to run them off, run Rachael off. He didn't want that.

He fumbled in his pocket for the papers Guidry gave him, but when he pulled them out and spread them open on the lectern, his mouth fell open in astonishment. These were not the poems Guidry had selected. He knew that he couldn't read the verse in front of him at all, not to these people.

Sweat broke out on his forehead. "Just a moment," he muttered. "I'm looking for a particular piece."

From the corner of his eye, he watched Rachael. Her smile was now wide, and her eyes were bright with her private, practical joke.

He had awakened at six-thirty, earlier than usual for him in any case, but particularly early considering that he and Rachael had done away with almost an entire bottle of whiskey, finally drinking it without ice to keep from having to get dressed and go down the outside hallway for more. He had lost count of the number of times they had come together, but he knew that his penis was raw and sore when he got up to urinate. In the bright light of the bathroom, his entire groin was angry, red and tender.

It was without a doubt the best sex he had enjoyed since he could remember, and he was euphoric in spite of the discomfort. She had seduced him, had insured herself the role of his companion by usurping the stale and stodgy Cecil's job. But best yet, in between their wild cries and passionate rollings around on the rumpled bed, his sleep was interdicted by a virtual army of poems. He had never seen so many "ghosts of beauty glide" across his mind, never felt such urging to write. No, he thought, spring is not far behind at all.

Finally, he could lie there no longer. He left her sleeping and went to the desk and began writing. To his surprise, the poems he tried to capture began to coalesce into one, a mock-epic: heroic lines that stunned him with their ingenious wit, their careful expressions of true love. The measured couplets flowed from his mind through his hand, and their rhythms and rhymes filled the page almost automatically.

It was, he realized after looking over four pages of completed draft, the most complete poem he had ever conceived at one sitting: ironic and erotic, yes, but somehow poignant, seeking in the same way the narrator described the quest of the poet-hero as he moved from woman to woman, searching for the perfect love in the furious depths of depravity.

After he finished six pages, he returned to bed, rolled her gently over, and before she was completely awake entered her once more. She responded slowly but with growing enthusiasm, her freckled, tattooed legs lacing themselves behind his calves and pulling him into her ever more deeply. "Closer," she whispered between long, dark kisses, "come closer." She didn't make the same small cries she had every time she came the night before, but instead gasped out a surprising quote, something he dimly remembered from Lawrence.

"A flood/Of sweet fire sweeps across me, so I drown/Against him, die, and find death good!" she breathed into his ear. She grasped him to her, clung to him with a kind of girlish desperation and hunger that electrified him when she reached a shuddering climax that brought tears to his eyes.

He had never made love to any woman like this. He realized, stunned, that he wasn't making love to her at all. He was simply, completely, and totally possessing her and at the same time being possessed by her. The thought disturbed him. He felt out of control, maneuvered by this blonde girl and her cunning ways. But he felt helpless to prevent it.

When they finished, his penis burned horribly from the exertion, but he pushed himself out of bed, allowed her to return to sleep, and returned to the desk, where he finished the first draft of the ballad he had already named "Song for My Sensuous Roses."

He worked on it the rest of the morning, cursing his lack of a computer or typewriter, but finally satisfied himself with a bold hand-printed version that took up the remaining hotel stationery, front and back.

"I want you to read it," she said after he awakened her and plied her with coffee and forced her to sit up and listen to it. Her eyes were wide now, steamy with the sexual adventure of the night before, but at the same time eager. A tear ran down her cheek. "It's beautiful. Read it to them. It's mine! I want them all to hear it. It's so fucking beautiful. It's so fucking wonderful! It's me. It's mine. You *have* to read it. For me. For us!"

"I can't," he explained. "I would be boiled alive." He didn't tell her it could cost him much more than the displeasure of the luncheon guests, that it could cost him this whole gig, his place on the circuit. It could push him off the wall in a disastrous direction, new inspiration or not.

"They'd understand. When they heard it, they'd understand. Oh, I love it!"

Although she was moving him nearly to tears, he shook his head. He had never before read a completed poem to one of the women he picked up during a reading. Sometimes, he had done so to those he lived with, those he had a sustained relationship with, but even then, he was reluctant to tell them that they inspired it. In this case, though, after so long a time without a meaningful inspiration in his life, he had gone ahead, and besides, he argued with himself, she had picked *him* up.

Still, she deserved to hear it read aloud, in public, he argued with himself. But now, seeing resignation on her face, he knew he had made a mistake to let her know it existed. She wouldn't understand why he couldn't do it, and he was in danger of hurting her.

"I just can't," he said. "You don't understand."

"But I love it! I fucking love it! I love you."

His head snapped up to look into her eyes, and the explanation for all he felt with her rushed over him. "Love?" he asked. She said she *loved* him. God, how long had it been since any woman had said that to him? Had any *ever* said it? Had his wife *ever* said it? It touched him, pushed him deeply into himself, and he felt an unfamiliar heat now swimming to the surface.

"Yes! Oh, yes." She flopped back onto the pillows and kicked her naked legs high overhead. "It's orgasmic. It'll *kill* them. You *have* to read it."

"I can't," he said quietly. His voice seemed far away to him. An angry swarm of emotions circled his head furiously, compounded his hangover, made him nearly ill. "Maybe some other place, some other time. But not here. There's too much at stake."

She pouted a while, but seemed finally to accept the disappointment, though, as she rose and dressed. While he showered, she emptied the ashtrays in the toilet and washed them in the sink, removed the rubbers from the spigots, and stood waiting, holding his coat for him, when they left to go to the luncheon.

That, he realized, was when she shifted the poem out of his briefcase and switched it with the Xeroxed pages Guidry chose for him to read.

The little bitch, he thought, but his heart swelled.

The audience shuffled. Some of them took a tentative taste of the watery pie or sipped coffee the waiter had provided, finally, to the tables nearest his own. Dr. Chambers raised an eyebrow as if to ask him if there was some problem. A thunderstorm raged in her eyes.

He looked up and shuffled the papers helplessly in front of him. Rachael stood back with her companions, and everyone was waiting. Then he decided.

Fuck them. Fuck them all.

He was one of the most important goddamn poets in the country, and here he was, planning to pander his weakest work in front of them just to hold onto some silly contract, just to please a bunch of assholes whose necks were the only thing that ever got stiff or red. They could never know what he knew, never experience what he had experienced. But he could tell them, and he would.

Besides, he thought, he had Rachael. She *loved* him, and, he realized to his astonishment, he loved her: That was enough.

He looked down at the poem and sought courage to match his anger. They would find the poem indecorous, he thought, almost nasty in places, but it was so beautiful at the same time that maybe they wouldn't care. Images such as he had never sensed before spun their way through the measured lines. The careful irony, the subtle humor in the account of a slim, blonde seductress dancing through wispy clouds at last to mount her lover's staff, to swallow his tongue— ultimately to blend his juices with her own in a scalding cascade, like a waterfall sluicing through a humid, pubic forest sur-rounding the spire of his passion. And all to lead them to bliss, to mutual dependence, a melding of their hearts in a thicket of thorny roses.

God, he thought, it was funny: It was good.

"Just a moment," he repeated and glanced at Rachael once more. She had a finger in her mouth, as if biting the nail. She was as nervous as he. But was she so frightened? He didn't know, couldn't imagine that she was. This was all her doing, but she had nothing to lose: They had each other, no matter what.

He swallowed hard, sought to bolster himself. God, he wanted a cigarette, a drink. This was the only way to keep her, the only way to keep the poems she demanded. If he went on and read it, she might be discovered, might be thrown out, abandoned by her parents, forced to go with him. The idea took full shape in his mind. This was his future, he insisted, the only shot he had left. When it was over, nothing else would matter. They could leave together, and that would be that.

Sweat broke out on his forehead, and his fingers fumbled with the pages. Her eyes were accusing him, gently submitting irony toward him, daring him, praying in a way no one in five miles had ever prayed for something no one in five miles could even dare to hope for.

"I . . . uh, have a new poem. Just one, but it's rather long. I hadn't planned to read it, but well . . . what the hell? You only live once, no matter how many times you're born again."

"I believe you had a prepared agenda," Dr. Chambers came instantly to her feet and offered hopefully. There was an edge on her voice, a warning, but he ignored her. Rachael's face was alive with color, beaming with pride, warm with love.

He looked up, let his eyes dance over the filled room. He couldn't imagine what their reaction would be to the explicit imagery, the exquisite detail, the sensual descriptions, the marvelous images.

"Don't fuck it up," Felix's voice warned, but he knew it was too late. Felix was out of this: way out. He could never understand, would never understand. It was over: He was done on the rubber chicken circuit, done with these bigots. And he would go out with a bang, not a whimper. He smiled at the puns.

But, he realized, there was never any chance that he *wouldn't* read the poem. Never any chance that he could refuse her. She really didn't have to trick him. All she had to do was ask, really ask. He loved her utterly: He could never deny her a thing.

He smoothed down the stationery once more. "There's an epigraph for this," he said, and Rachael looked momentarily confused. He looked up and began:

If we shadows have offended,
Think but this, and all is mended,
That you have but slumber'd here
And this weak and idle theme,
No more yielding but a dream.

Everyone smiled, and he saw several confirm the source and nod with affirmation. Dr. Chambers resumed her seat.

He looked down once more, nodded his head to confirm a last minute change in the finished product. "It's dedicated to one of your students who both inspired and illuminated it. I speak truly when I say that I couldn't have written it without her." He paused, took a breath and deliberately avoided Rachel's eyes. It was a bold decision, he thought, but a right one. That he was certain of.

"The title of the poem," he said, "is 'Rachael's Song.'"

The silence that followed the reading was like a shroud dropped over the expansive hall. He looked up, swallowed hard, listened for the bright echoes of hedonism and free passion the poem proclaimed. Every eye stared at him and shot bolts of hatred toward the lectern. He felt like a lump of toxic waste, irredeemable, disgusting beyond description.

But he felt proud of himself, even so. Fuck them, he repeated. Fuck the circuit, fuck Felix. He would make it as he always had. On his own, with Rachael, with the best poetry he could write.

He wanted to look at Rachael now, but he didn't. He wanted to save that moment, the contact that he knew would be there. It was a triumph. And only she knew it, only she could validate it.

He remained still and met the hateful gazes from the audience until Dr. Chambers stood at last and announced in a choked, strained voice that the "program for today is over."

Indeed, he thought, the entire circuit program was over. He had screwed it good, and all for one poem, one goddamn poem. But that was all right: He had Rachael.

He folded "Rachael's Song" and thrust it back into his pocket. If they could find a Xerox machine, he intended to give the original to her, and then he began thinking of ways to bring her home with him. Could he afford it? Would she come? He had discussed none of this with her, he suddenly realized. What would she say? Would she defy her parents? The questions tortured him, and before stepping away to face the combined wrath of Chambers and the rest of the hostile group already rising to assault him, he gave in and looked over toward her.

Rachael stood alone, abandoned by her friends. Her smile was also gone, and in its place was the tortured expression of bewilderment and pain. She moved quickly to him. She suddenly appeared to him like a frightened child, a mischievous little girl who had been betrayed, slapped down by someone she trusted. "You *told* on me," she said. "How could you?" He saw rather than heard the words leave her lips.

"You *told* me to read it," he stammered. "You wanted me to read it. You insisted." He opened his hands between them in a gesture of supplication. "You *wanted* me to read it."

A general hubbub filled the room as those in front tried to decide how best to deal with him.

She was crying. "But you gave them my name. How could you do that to me? You *named* me." Her hand covered her mouth. Shock filled her eyes. "My God! You made a *whore* out of me. What do you think they'll do to me now?"

"It won't matter," he said hurriedly. "You'll come with me. We'll work it out. You can finish school, and—" He stopped. Her eyes, no longer wide with incredulity, now slitted, narrow and sardonic. Her mouth, no longer open in shock and fear, drew now to a thin, cruel line.

"What the hell are you talking about?"

"With me," he dumbly repeated, "You'll come with me. You don't need them. Any of them. I've got . . . well, I thought we might . . . ." He trailed off as she stepped away from him. He felt dirty, evil. "I thought we might get married," he muttered, helpless. "I'm in love with you," he whispered.

At that moment he realized that it had all been false, all some sort of sophomoric prank that he had not understood. Instead, he ruined her life by turning what she saw as a flirtation with sin into something far more than she was capable of understanding.

"Are you nuts? Are you out of your mind? You're old enough to be my father. *Married*? Are you nuts?"

"But last night—" he started. He saw Dr. Guidry make his way from the anteroom into the hall. He was pushing his way through the crowd toward them. "This morning . . ."

"Was *that* it?" she asked. "Was that your idea of proposing? To totally fuck up my life? Man, you're weird. Sick-o."

Dr. Guidry reached her and put one dark arm around her shoulders. She offered no resistance but instead turned and put both arms around him, clinging to his chest.

"I'm taking this child to my office for a prayer conference," he called over his shoulder to Dr. Chambers, who continued to stand where she was as if transfixed. "There will be a vigil to pray for her soul—indeed for all our souls—this evening in the Bigelow Chapel." Guidry shot him a withering glance. "Dr. Chambers, get that foul sewage off this campus."

Then they were gone, and so, he thought suddenly, was he. So was the circuit. So was Felix. So, he feared, was his poetry.

VII

"What's the Latin name for 'parsley'?
What's the Greek name for 'Swine's Snout'?"
—Browning

I read somewhere that when George Bush (the Elder) was President of the United States, he declared that he didn't like broccoli, had never liked broccoli, and would, now that he was the Chief Executive, Commander-in-Chief, head honcho, main wimp, and all, refuse to eat it wherever it was served.

I didn't much like George Bush as President: Didn't vote for him, and was glad, for a while, when Wild Bill Clinton took him down. But on that vital domestic issue, the honorable Mr. Bush and I were in one hundred percent epicurean accord.

Broccoli is nothing more than a tasteless, semi-edible weed.

If you went out onto your front lawn and saw something like broccoli shooting up, you'd probably go call the Lawn Doctor and have the entire property sprayed with herbicides and defoliants. It was never meant to be digested or enjoyed. I never understood its appeal. Unless you douse it in cheese sauce, smother it in salt, or smear butter all over it, it has no taste whatsoever. It's chewy, hard to cut with a fork and it looks like little green bronchioles.

That's what broccoli looks like, even sounds like: something that came out of some diminutive alien's lungs.

But people—especially the food police auxiliary of the politically correct—love it. They'll serve it whenever three or more are gathered together in the name of any damned thing at all. It's like a kind of vegetable communion, a stringy green Eucharist. "This is my inedible, unpalatable vegetable. Choke this down in remembrance of something tasty."

Now, asparagus is a truly noble vegetable. And it grows wild and tastes great. Or the onion. There's no more delightful a food in the world than the humble onion in any of its multiple varieties. It *grows wild, too. Both onions and asparagus are easy to prepare, easy to eat, and they require no harmful, fattening additives, except maybe a little salt. But the onion is cheap and gives you bad breath, and asparagus is expensive and people are afraid of it. Broccoli gives you gas. Onions and asparagus give you flavor!*

I made up my mind long ago that anybody who says "hold the onions" or prefers broccoli to asparagus is doomed to a life of mediocrity, afraid to take chances. You don't have to eat jalapeños, *garlic dill pickles, and leeks to prove your originality. But broccoli can't be anybody's idea of food. It's obscene.*

So—now, stay with me, here—it figures that Wallace Stevens is wrong when he says that poetry is the "supreme fiction." Most contemporary poetry is a lot like broccoli. Everybody talks about it, everybody serves it, everybody pretends to like it. But the truth is that thinking people prefer prose, fiction, and the uglier and seamier the better. Fiction is the asparagus of literature. Sometimes the onion. It grows wild and with very little cultivation. It gives you halitosis of the mind and is easy to digest and only rarely causes gas. People go to readings to hear poetry, fawn over the poets, tell everybody how fucking great they are, and they memorize the shit out of it. But they truly only pretend to like it because it's somehow intellectually *correct to do so. When they drop by their favorite bookstore, what do they buy? Prose. Novels.*

Where people spend their money reveals a reality you can believe in.

Prose writers and poets don't generally get along. Poets think the prose writers get all the press, all the money. Prose writers think poets get all the respect, all the meaningful attention, as well as all the grants and better readings, too. And it's true, mostly. Still, there's a balance to it: You see, poets get laid a whole lot more than novelists do. I mean, how long does it take to read a student's novel? Even a short story can take a half-hour, forty-five minutes. But I could skate through a whole ream of bad verse, comment on it, make some groupie feel good, even look over her revisions and be smoking in bed afterwards in that time. Poets work faster. Novelists plod. In prose, the foreplay takes too long. I know some novelists who've never been laid at all. But otherwise, they've got the advantages.

You get two novelists together in a room, and wham*: they're comparing contracts, agents, movie deals, and talking about six-figure, multi-book offers. "Well," they'll say, "I don't know if I can get Ron Howard's company to take the option or not unless Tony*

Hopkins is interested, but that Fonda gal is hot right now, and there's a chance that Helen Hunt might come on the project as well." Know what I mean? You've heard those guys talking like that.

You get two poets together they talk about other poets and compare their vegetarian diets, which consist mostly of what else? Broccoli. That's the way of the world of modern letters. The prose writers may get the gravy, but the poets get the vegetable plate. Go light on the starches, too.

You ever see a fat poet? I mean a really fat poet, one of those guys with a beer gut hanging down over his buckle so that he has to buy his pants four sizes too big just to button them around his crotch? Hell no. At least, not normally. Or one of those women who has to wear maternity smocks to hide her paunch? Well, you might. You might see both from time to time, but they're the exception that tests the rule, and I'll tell you something: I've never seen a really fat poet worth his or her weight in pork chops.

But fat novelists, well, hell: that's a norm. I mean poets may spend a lot of time hunched over the old writing desk, but they also are famous for taking those long Wordsworthian walks through the rill-laden meadows, those Whitmanesque tramps across the country-side and woods, those Frostian detours among birches and snowy trails.

Novelists drive. Fly first class. Drink a lot, eat well: lots of steak and potatoes. No sushi. No goddamn tofu. Ribs and a big old slab of pork. That's what novelists are made of. When novelists're working, writing, they're not propped up in bed or squatting under some box elder someplace scrawling down lines on a piece of foolscap. They're sitting over a typewriter—or, today, a key-board—all business, hours at a time, letting their guts take on meaningful literary dimension.

But poets, good poets, are always well-built, athletic, in tune with goddamn nature, just like Emerson. Was Emerson fat? No way, José. He was in tune with nature.

Then there are the playwrights. Playwriting gets left out entirely. Playwriting is a lot like carrots: You know they're good for you, and they're easy to digest, and can be tasty—trendy, too— but somehow, you never quite get around to serving them very often. I mean, you have to peel them and all that.

Screenwriting. Ah, well, that's like truffles, a delicacy devoutly to be wished. But most poets and prose writers, too, know that they're rooted out by trained pigs, so lovely as screenwriting may be in terms of money, fame, and getting laid, screenwriters don't get one hell of a lot of respect, you know? If you doubt that, next time you go to a movie—any movie—wait until they flash the name of the screenwriter on the credits, and see how brief it is. It's like four seconds, on average. The goddamn best boy gets more. The point, though, is that playwrights and screenwriters don't fit either mold. I mean Orson Welles was fat, real fat, but Neil Simon is thin, and Edward Albee is just all right.

Generalizing about screenwriting and playwriting is no fun at all.

But nobody reads plays, or screenplays. People just watch them, and then they get fat. It's all those raisinettes and buttered popcorn at the movies, sweet snacks at the theater, you know. Champagne on opening nights, too. Nobody ever got fat reading poetry. Or prose. If prose got people fat, you can bet everybody would be a real tubbo.

That's a good thing because I read a lot more prose than I do poetry. I think most poets do. Somehow, reading other poets' work is painful. It always made me want to go forth and do better, but I rarely did. If you're not careful when you try it, you wind up being imitative, or, worse, you wind up being awful. But you won't admit it. I never did. Again, the food thing: You want to invent your own recipe, but you can't. So you wind up stealing someone else's, and then trying to improve on it. Add a little of this, leave out a little of that, fail to mix it properly or overcook it. It doesn't work very often. The truth is that it doesn't work at all.

Literature and food. There's a quid pro quo there someplace. I'll let you figure it out.

But on tours, readings, and so forth, poets always command a larger audience than do the fictionalists. It's hard to read any meaningful selection of prose in twenty minutes, but a poet can cram in one hell of a lot of verse in that time. Poetry sells for less, too. Of course, those who buy the books will just take them home and put them on the shelf. They won't read them. A lot of poetry loses something on the page. In a way, prose probably shouldn't be read aloud at all. Poetry shouldn't be read any other way. It took me a long time to figure that out.

Of course, most writers, prose writers and poets, read their own work so goddamn badly that it doesn't make much difference one way or another.

Broccoli is also an awful lot like love. It's supposed to be good for you, as I said, but in the end, it's just too hard to take. In the end *you wish you'd just settled for sex. Sex is like asparagus. Or onions: spicy, smelly, and just plain good. And it thrives with almost no cultivation. See how these things work out?*

In all those years, the only woman I came close to loving— really loving—was a prose writer. Her name was Rosemary, and she had published four novels with small but decent imprints in New York, although she wasn't much over twenty-five. She never let me know how much more. Maybe my emotional attachment to her was based on the fact that she didn't need me to do anything for her, didn't demand anything from me, wouldn't give me anything I wasn't willing to match in kind. She was already succeeding in her own right, and we enjoyed a wary but mutual respect.

I actually met her in a bookstore, not one of those kitsch places where they serve croissants and overpriced coffee, but a throwback Mom and Pop store that had somehow been overlooked in the massive free-standing chain store juggernaut that crushed anything—and anyone—who really loved books right out of existence and put the marketing of literature on the same basis as the selling of Big Macs and Japanese televisions. We were both browsing, shelf-reading a little, and it turned out that we both had a similar fondness for musty old shelves where titles long out of print were still offered in brand new first editions. It didn't take long to find a real coffee shop where they served real coffee—with a big old slab of apple pie to go with it—and it only took a little longer for us to realize that we got along very well.

Oh, we had a sexual relationship—you bet—and it was good. But, for once, I didn't read any poetry to her. Tell you the truth, I didn't get any poetry from her either. But in those days, I wasn't writing much. I couldn't: It just wouldn't come. They wouldn't come. Instead, I let her read sections of her new novels to me. It wasn't seductive as an experience, but it was good. I enjoyed it. Hey, we were in love: it was comfortable. We felt really Jamesean, sitting around the fire in our jammies and mucklucks, sipping sherry— although I preferred whiskey or beer—me listening to her romances as they unfolded.

That's what she wrote: romances. Each one was like the other. A count or duke or king or prince or millionaire meets up with the heroine who is an American or British heiress who is naïve because she's been in a boarding school, convent, or home where she is the apple of her rich daddy's or uncle's or brother's eye. They have their first encounter in London, Paris, Monte Carlo, Florence, Venice, or Rome, and even though they are quite taken with each other, they are prevented from actually consummating their affair because he is married, gay, in trouble with the KGB or CIA, accused of murder, smuggling, gun-running, or cheating at baccarat, *or maybe, if he's royalty, he's restricted in his associations to blue blood. This angst goes along for a while and she confides to her governess, mother, companion, or best friend what the problem is, and, after a harrowing series of close calls that might either kill, imprison, exile, or ruin him socially or financially, a solution is eventually worked out as he is cleared of whatever difficulty exists, and they marry, even though he must relinquish his throne, fortune, or political power, and they will be forced to live in poverty, or on her money, or, God forbid, go to work.*

They all went along pretty much like that. Sometimes, Rosemary would give one an historical twist and he would be a pirate or general or frontiersman or explorer, and she would be a princess, duchess, Indian maiden, frontier woman, or queen of an Amazon tribe, but they were all really about the same. I didn't see that there was much challenge to it.

Still, sitting there with the firelight flickering off her platinum-blonde hair—no dye job, either, I guarantee—and watching her gray eyes illuminate with excitement and steam with sex whenever she got to those scenes where their "troth was ultimately consummated" amidst an ocean of heaving bosoms and firm touches of passion was truly one of the great experiences of my life. It was love: more rewarding than poetry, really. Really.

I sort of got to the point where I identified Rosemary with her standard heroine, who was always named Jasamine or Truella or Cynthia, or Camella, and who thought in adverbial italics and spoke in exclamatory adjectives. And I guess I identified myself with her usual hero, who always was named Lance or Conrad or Jacques or Eric or Ivan (pronounced ee-vahn), and that's when the trouble started.

You see, I came to understand that prose writers play the roles they create, and their readers do too. But I was just a broken-down college professor and about to be a has-been poet. She was a highly successful nobody romance writer who had never visited half the places she wrote about, never met anybody like her characters. And I realized that it was all something of a lie.

Prose is a lie. You heard it here first.

So is love. You probably heard that before.

But poetry is true. It may not be honest, but it doesn't create any false hopes in the reader. It's always true.

So is sex. I told you this would work out.

You don't find yourself wanting to wear a tux or black chiffon to dinner when you read poetry. But you do when you read prose. You can't help it. You tend to want to live *prose, because feeling it is so goddamn hard. I went through nearly a case of vermouth when I read all of Hemingway's novels. Smoked my tongue sore on a pipe when I read Conan Doyle's tales. I wanted a sports car when I was reading Ian Fleming, and felt a terrible urge to drive across the country when I read Kerouac.*

But when I read Browning, I had no urge to paint, and Gray didn't send me padding out to find churchyards any more than Whitman gave me homo-erotic urges to "celebrate myself." Joyce Kilmer didn't turn me into a naturalist any more than Wilfred Owen made me into a pacifist or Lawrence converted me into a savior of whales. God knows, Robert Graves didn't stymie my wanton sexual urges any more than Sylvia Plath made me want to stick my head in the oven. I had no yen for borscht *when I read Pushkin, and I had no urge to replace my commode with a porcelain bowl when I read Joyce's "Chamber Music." I didn't shut myself up in my "own society" when I read Dickinson, and Frost didn't send me out past snowy fields for lobster and spoon bread.*

The only thing poetry makes me want is a new worn-out corduroy sports jacket. Maybe a joint and some good jazz, if it's Ginsberg. Ferlinghetti, too.

Poetry affects the reader differently, affects the writer differently, the same way love and sex do, the same way broccoli and asparagus do. And you can see it in the reactions people have to both.

So, Rosemary and I didn't last. I think it was as meaningful an ending as I ever went through, and it truly ruined me for love. Here's what happened:

We were at this dinner, a lecture-slash-banquet, believe it or not, at one of those super parochial religious schools, one of those places where they put pictures of Jesus all over the place and everybody says "God Bless You" and they have all those shitty "Thank You For Not Smoking" signs posted on every fucking door and hallway in sight. It was part of a convention of Romance writers and Christian poets—odd combination, don't ask me—and Rosemary and I were there. She was supposed to talk after dinner, which would come right after this guy, Dr. Clarence Shumaker, DD, Th.D., Ed.fuckingD., finished his talk on the values of Elizabethan poetry as a translation of scripture and read representative selections from the King James Bible.

Nobody knew me there. Or at least nobody admitted to recognizing my name. There is some value in being an asshole critic and a secular humanist poet. I was totally incognito for the first time in a long time, and I was loving it.

So we had been smirking through his talk, which preceded the big feed, and finally he sat down, and they prayed for fifteen or twenty minutes over "the food we are about to receive," and then the freshest faced bunch of kids you ever saw came out with the groceries. Now, Rosemary wasn't a big feminist or anything, not militant, but she noticed right away that my serving of ice-cold, stuffed flounder was larger than hers, that, indeed, every man in the room had a bigger piece of fish than was served to the women.

She sent for a waiter, who sent for the food service manager, who explained foolishly to Rosemary that since women are smaller and eat less, it would be a waste of food to give them equal portions to their larger and obviously more virile counterparts.

"But the people who paid for this all paid the same thing, didn't they?" Rosemary practically yelled at the man, who gave her his best I'm-a-Christian-so-fuck-you-smile and assured her that such was the case. "And their money is the same goddamn size, isn't it?" she demanded. He nodded again, rolling his eyes at her language. "Then, they deserve the same amount of food," she argued. She was almost yelling at this point, and I began to feel sorry for that poor sucker. He had really screwed up, and he wasn't used to running into women who didn't just blush and say "Aw, pooh, that's all right. Just don't do it again."

But I also felt sorry for Rosemary. It was hopeless, you see? I grew up with people like that: self-complacent super Christians who know they're on their way to heaven and you don't stand a chance in hell of coming in after them. I knew you couldn't attack them with reason. They operate with a different set of attitudes, alternate value structures. Logic has never stood a chance against religion.

By now, the guy is shaking his head in a pitying gesture—boy, that was a mistake with a woman like Rosemary—and everybody's looking at them, so she stands up and grabs him by his coat lapels.

Did I tell you she was good-looking? Well, she was. I mean a knock-out, a real head-turner. Legs to her neck and a set of honkers that were utterly perfect. But none of that matched her face, which was gorgeous and could, when she got as serious as Ailene or Arcadia or Allyson or any of her other imaginary heroines, become a mask of terrifying condemnation. I mean, all she would have had to do to this guy was act *like she was going to touch him or even just talk to him, and he was past tense. It would be incomprehensible for someone so lovely to be so angry that she might actually* touch *him. But before he could puddle up and flow away from her grasp, she grabbed him, and then she was "in his face," as the kids say, talking to him, and their noses were about two inches apart, and he could probably smell her perfume and see up close that those platinum locks did not have dark roots, and her gray eyes could get colder than chrome steel in the arctic, and all of a sudden there wasn't much left of him.*

"Listen, you bigoted sexist prick," she yells at him, "if a woman pays the same as a man, then she should get the same amount as a man. Whether she eats it or not!" The man looks around for help, but nobody's moving. He's on his own, and his knees are jelly. "Now, you go and bring me a full serving—and a hot one, I might add—and what I don't eat, you can shove up your chauvinistic ass, you sanctimonious son of a bitch!"

That did it. He practically runs away, and he doesn't come back. So after it finally became obvious that no one in the room would ever stop staring at us, we leave. We go back to the motel, pack our bags, and we're out of there tout de suite.

But she doesn't speak to me all the way home, and it's nearly a two hundred mile drive. You see, she could tell I was embarrassed for her. I didn't want to be, but I was. I mean, I knew she was right, and she had every right to do what she did, but I still wished she hadn't made such a big deal out of it. She could have used a little finesse, you know.

When we got home, she said I was mad because she forfeited her speaker's fee—and it was a big one, three grand—but that really wasn't it at all. I just felt bad for her.

I guess I just saw something in her I didn't like, a kind of impetuousness, maybe, if that's the right word, maybe petulance, maybe immaturity. I don't know. Basically she was strutting her stuff, showing off, and she was doing it about something that didn't matter in front of a bunch of people who didn't matter. Still, I wished later that I had supported her. Orally, I mean, even after the fact. But I hadn't. I hadn't said a word. She was a better than fair writer, and she deserved better support, better treatment.

But even though I knew she was right, and even though I knew she deserved me by her side, I just couldn't do it. It was like the time I came out of a bar and saw this guy watching two other guys beat the shit out of each other. I asked ,"Don't you think you ought to do something?" And you know what he said? "Hey, man, it ain't my fight."

And he was right. That was Rosemary's fight, and I just didn't want to get in the middle of it. Somehow, I don't think she really wanted me to. Somehow, I think I just reminded her of the whole thing, and the memory was painful. She just didn't have the experience I had in making a fool of myself.

After that, though, the magic was gone. Every time she would sit down and read, I'd see that snarl on her lips, see her fists full of that poor jerk's coat lapels, see his cheesy, helpless smile, and I'd get sad and a little afraid of her. We just fell out of love, if we'd ever been in it in the first place.

I didn't know how to know whether or not it truly was love. But what I finally came to terms with was that while I still believed I loved her, I didn't like her anymore. You see, you can like someone you don't love, but it's goddamn hard to love someone you don't like. That kind of thing festers and grows and pretty soon you come to resent the person for making you love them when you really can't stand the way they are.

After the incident, we kept on going through the motions, of course. It's hard to admit that a change of that magnitude is real and lasting. Our routine stayed the same, but the changes crept in "on little cat's feet" and stayed. I kept falling asleep when she was reading, allowing my poems to come and visit, but they never stayed long enough to do any good, and I didn't pay close attention. The sex soon slowed down, too, and finally, it ended. We slept side-by-side, like two homeless people sharing a cot in a public shelter.

Then, one night I got a little drunk and I told her my theory of prose. I also told her that the money she was making was just proceeds from prostitution. I said that, but I didn't really mean it personally. All writing is prostitution: It's just that writers sell their imaginations to someone to use as fantasies instead of their bodies. She didn't agree. Violently disagreed, as a matter of fact. That tore it, and she threw me out and said she had never loved me.

Love is sort of prostitution, too. I figured that out a long time ago.

It hurt when she told me to pack up and get gone. I'd never been hurt like that, not even when my wife left—any single one of the times she left. I mean, I'd been thrown out before, and by women even better looking than this platinum beauty. But this time, it hurt. I didn't like that feeling, especially when I didn't actually do anything to cause it. I guess it was more what I didn't do, in a way, *but still, I was hurt. Guilt is a whole hell of a lot easier to deal with than rejection when love is involved.*

I moved in with a poet after that, a doll-like redhead who I met in a goddamn Starbucks next door to a Barnes & Noble. She reminded me of a cross between Holly Hunter and Sandy Duncan. We didn't get along much better, but I think we understood one another. We both wanted raw, self-indulgent sex. And we both hated broccoli. And that helped. You see, among poets, there's no danger, really, of falling in love any more than there's any danger of learning to like something that's good for you. If you fall in love, you're going to get shit on. Love should come with a standard-issue brown helmet. You let yourself go, give in a little, and then that's all she wrote. You're left standing there, your feet on the edge of the purple shaft, looking down and knowing there's no bottom you'd ever want to touch, wondering how you let yourself in for such a fall.

Still, love is like poetry. You have to count on it, and you need the hurt now and then.

And, I guess, love is always there, always available, and there are times you have to settle for it. Or starve. But in the meantime, there's the poetry, and in spite of the quid pro quo, *that's better than broccoli.*

Tenure

He swung his legs over the side of the bed, reached for a cigarette and lit it. His mouth tasted like wet ashes, but it was rasp-dry. By the flare of the lighter, he checked his watch: 6:30. It felt cold, and he reminded himself of the snowfall outside the motel room. He should have brought his heavy coat, he reminded himself for the twentieth time in as many days: Winter comes early to the Northwest.

He had to think for a moment to remember exactly what state he was in. Montana? No. Wyoming? No. Colorado? Yeah. Colorado. Northern Colorado. Six-week tour: readings, workshops, lectures, signings, booze, and girls. Whirlwind swing through the colleges and universities of cowboy-creative-writing-land: Ten thousand dollars and all the pussy you can eat.

He smiled at his own weak wit. Then he frowned. Who was he kidding? He had to hustle his way onto this circuit. Beg. He was on the slide, and the bottom was coming up, hard and fast.

He had hit the wall, and he had bounced. But not back. There was no question which way he would fall. Now it was only a question of slowing the descent. "Lost, lost!" Browning's priest's lament came to him all at once, "One moment knelled the woe of years."

A cough itched in his lungs, and he let it out before he remembered that he wasn't alone and cupped his hand over his mouth to stifle the noise. Smoke came up through his nose, and his eyes watered. It was too dark to see, so he walked over and pulled the heavy curtains aside to let in a beam of arc light from the parking lot. The amber shaft picked up a reflection off the snow and fell across the bed where a young woman turned quickly in her sleep to avoid the brightness. Her head buried itself into the pillow. He shuddered when he saw her. He couldn't quite picture what she looked like.

"So there stood Matthew Arnold and this girl," he quoted softly. But he was a long way from Dover, a long way from the ocean, a long way from Sophocles, a long way from anywhere. And this particular girl, he mused, was even further from being a "mournful cosmic last resort."

He took another deep drag and opened the curtain a bit more. She was two years younger than his daughter, twenty pounds lighter than either of his thighs. Her hair was shorter than his, her talent probably greater. No, not probably: definitely. He'd looked at her stuff. Not one of them wasn't publishable. It frightened him to see how good she was.

But, he reminded himself, she *was* another workshop pickup, a poetry groupie. She had read all his books, most of his reviews, thought he was "the greatest living poet," she said. And, like most, she wanted him to read her work, get her published, fuck her till she cried. He had obliged her on the last item, anyway, and he couldn't decide who was more surprised, her or him. As usual, she was appointed by the resident creative writing program to drive him around, show him the sights, see to his needs. Especially the most primal ones. The only need he had was her naked in his bed. Skinny little thing, he thought, tight belly, slender and lean, chest like a boy.

He tried to remember her name: Linda, Melinda, Glenda? He couldn't recall. He barely remembered their sex, but he was sure it went all right, better than it had been going lately, that was sure, since there had at least *been* sex. He dropped his hand and scratched his crotch. Her fragrance, a perfumed sexual odor, rose from the irritation. Yeah, he thought, it was all right. Not like Sioux City.

That had been humiliating. *Her* name was Glenda. She was short, too, pretty but chubby, with a face full of freckles and strands of brown hair hanging down over her droopy little tits. But kind of sexy all the same. Good mouth, nice eyes. And she was married. He drank

160

almost a whole bottle of whiskey trying to talk himself—*will* himself—into it. When he failed, she got hurt, then angry. Threatened to tell her husband all about it, called him a fag. Then she sat there naked and cried for an hour, letting her mascara run down and black-streak her breasts and fall onto the slight bulge of her abdomen. It was disgusting. She left him feeling more drained than if she had taken everything he had. But lately, he hadn't had much to give anyone. It was a wonder he had anything last night.

The half-empty tequila bottle glistened in the light next to the bed. Good grass and cheap tequila, he thought: deadly goddamned combination. He used to get sick on it, but now, it seemed to work better than anything. Bourbon and scotch fucked him. Tequila made him fuck.

Another cough tried to claw its way out of his lungs. He went into the bathroom and hacked up several globs of phlegm. The effort made him clammy, dizzy. He was still shaking when he pissed. His urine burned coming out, and he worried vaguely about disease. He didn't worry about knocking up anybody any more. He had a vasectomy years ago. Used the last royalty check to pay for it. It was Felix's suggestion after Rae Ann contacted Melton House—or her lawyer did—checking to see if he was worth enough money to sue him for it. Or, at least, that's what Felix told him. It didn't matter. There wasn't enough money: There wasn't *any* money. That's why he stopped the support payments. Let her sue, he thought.

"You don't need any more of this," Felix warned him. "And since you obviously can't control yourself, you need to take some drastic measures to insure that it doesn't happen again. Hell, man, they put you in jail in some states for child abandonment."

He agreed and went under the knife a week later. Still, with all the herpes and shit and something new called AIDS going around, he worried about his safety, and he kept rubbers in his briefcase. For all the good it usually did him.

"I can't feel it if you wear that," the girl said when he unwrapped the condom. "I want to *feel* it. Feel *you* probing me." He discarded the sheepskin and said the hell with it. He was too drunk, too stoned to care much, anyway, happy enough to be erect. What's the worst that could happen, he wondered. Get syphilis and lose his mind and wind up in a padded cell playing with himself and quoting Sir John Suckling? He was damned near there, anyway. She didn't quote Suckling or anything so metaphysically mundane. Instead, she quoted lines of his own poems to him, shouted them out when she came, he suddenly recalled. They were from his first, second book.

He barely remembered it, and when he realized what she was doing, he was embarrassed, felt like a bad actor in a worse movie. A farce. If he hadn't been so near the end of the ordeal, he would have lost it entirely and collapsed in laughter.

Now *that* would be embarrassing, he thought.

He got the bottle and poured two fingers into a plastic glass, drank it off. It burned his throat, but it was too early for coffee. No place to get any, anyway. He had come down in life. The motels he arranged to stay in weren't the sort to have all-night restaurants. At least this place was cheap. They sent out for pizza when she arrived. Pizza, grass, and tequila. The supper of champions.

He remembered lines from her poetry. Good stuff. Same old open form shit at first glance, but as he read it, he found it was astonishingly controlled: vivid images, original phrasing, startling metaphors, lean, sensitive diction. A little Ann Sexton, maybe, but not derivative. Too much humor in it for that, too much integrity in her syntax. It had none of the romantic schmaltz or erotic titillation that usually came from sexually active undergraduates. He thought he might send some in with a recommendation, try out his name again. He hadn't done anything like that in a long time. He wondered if anyone important remembered him. He tried to think of a journal editor's name. Any journal. All that came to mind were retired, dead, or bankrupt. Aside from Felix, no one in publishing would still speak to him, and Felix only did so out of pity, he thought.

Good old Felix. After all the shit he'd put him through, he hung in there, kept his books out of the remainder houses. Some of them anyway. He couldn't remember which ones they were, though.

His memory, he had feared lately, was going the same way the poems did. It was like having a memory of a memory, like writing poems about poems.

He closed the commode lid, sat down, and lit another cigarette, took another hit of the tequila. Overhead, the heat lamp warmed him. He didn't feel like going back into the dark room, sliding in next to her, maybe nudging her awake for another round before breakfast. He doubted he could get it up again, anyway. Recently, he found he needed to be drunk, really drunk, to get hard, stay hard long enough not to make a fool of himself as he had with Glenda in Sioux City. After he calmed her down, got her dressed, got them both dressed, the chubby little bitch turned mean. She just stood there and laughed at him. Called him old. Well, he was. Old and on the slide. Needed to rest. Needed to write.

He wondered all at once but idly how his daughter was doing,

162

his "real" child. Her first baby was born two weeks ago, and he hadn't even sent a card. At least he had managed to keep the checks going to *her*, even though it meant that some months he survived on noodles and canned chili.

He meant to call, he reminded himself. He always meant to call.

A thought of the snow outside reminded him suddenly of Minnesota. A year ago. Four colleges in a week, all in or near the Twin Cities. What was *her* name? Debbie? That didn't sound right. She was his driver, too, he remembered, another groupie. But she didn't gush, didn't cry, didn't quote his poetry to him. She was all business. She stayed right by him all day, never cracked a smile, just made little suggestive remarks about nasty sex. She punctuated her diction with words like "fuck" and "cunt," pointed out every motel where she had had a nooner as they drove around, so when he asked her into his room for a nightcap, it looked like a sure thing. Took her in the back way, up the stairs, got her a drink, then tried to kiss her. And she had laughed, pushed him away. But she hadn't called him old, just "too sure of himself." Well, he was that, too. And she hung around, didn't run, didn't fight back, just sat there smoking his grass, drinking his scotch—he hadn't discovered tequila yet, what it could do for him—giving him a flash every now and then when she crossed her legs, getting him hot, then leaving him hard-up, wanting her.

Prick tease, he thought. At least she hadn't shown him any of her poetry. At least he hadn't had to go through that.

He poured another dollop of the yellow liquid in his glass and tossed it back. Cuervo Gold, he read the label. Good shit. Good friend. "José Cuervo, You Are a Friend of Mine," he said softly and almost giggled. He couldn't remember the lyrics. "Shit," he said. "You can't even remember the bad stuff."

He had to get Brenda or Linda or whatever up and dressed and out of here before . . . before what? What *was* his itinerary this morning? He thought hard, studied the red coal of the smoke. It seemed that he had a breakfast session, a reading for the Student Poetry Club. More bullshit students looking for a break, more sheaves of half-finished poems thrust into his hands as he left the room. More stuff for the next motel's dumpster.

"Goddamn personal computers, anyway," he said softly. "Makes it so any asshole can be a circulating poet."

"Circulating poet," he repeated. Good line. Good image. That's what he was: a fucking circulating poet. That wouldn't work. Too many participles. He rubbed his whiskered chin and wondered if there was a poem there even so. Maybe.

"Where is the bard, whose soul can now / Its high presuming hopes avow?" he whispered. Then he smiled. Hell, that came back easily enough, and he hadn't thought of Collins in years.

He rose, dropped his butt into the commode and turned on the shower. When the water was warm, he doused his head. "Circulating poet," he gurgled into the spray. "Rotating asshole." He hadn't felt this bad since he left teaching. At the time, he had felt free, euphoric, liberated from the tedium at last. But it hadn't sustained him for long. Now, he wondered if the depression that had settled over him like a low-pressure system was merely stalled or had become permanent. "A sea change," he said. "Shift in climate. From trouble to big trouble, and now, you may lose it all."

"You have to realize that you're still on faculty *here*," Ross Turner, his department head, said to him the morning when the balloon went up. He'd been summoned. Command performance in Ross's office. He knew what was going to happen, but he was still in denial.

"In the past four or five years," Ross continued over tented fingers, "I don't think you've been on campus more than three or four weeks running. We've let this go on far too long. You're in trouble."

"It's my work," he said. It was a weak defense. He hadn't published more than a handful of poems in two years. And the review writing had dried up.

"If I need an executioner," the last editor he spoke to told him, "I'll call you. You haven't liked a book of anyone else's poetry in years. You've got a rep, and it hurts us to publish you. Besides, until you do something new, you're yesterday's news." Same old song. He couldn't even get occasional work anymore.

"Nobody likes a professional cynic," Felix told him when he complained about it. "You'd contradict God about how good David might be. You're a fucking heretic."

"The *Psalms* are repetitive and trite, and they don't rhyme," he grumbled, but Felix didn't laugh. He hung up on him. That was Felix's stock response when he figured out that he was trying to reason with a frustrated reprobate and a drunk, not the cool, rational poet he had discovered years before.

Ross Turner, of course, was an asshole, a disappointed seeker. He had written one book—*one* goddamn book—on homophobia in Hemingway's novels. It came out with one of the smallest university presses in the country the previous spring, but that and a handful of articles stimulated him to ride everyone in the department like he was the cock of the fucking walk. No one liked him, but everyone feared him, and everyone sucked up to him. He was the only faculty member to wear a suit and a white shirt and tie every day of the week, even when he had no classes. *Martinet* was the word. Ross used reading glasses, although his eyesight was perfect. He liked the image. He should have, it was image more than anything that put him into the head of department's office when old Marion Dunphy died. Dunphy was a prince. He was also scared shitless of anybody who could publish so much as a letter to the editor. Ross wasn't scared, though. He was too stupid to be scared.

"Your work is here," Ross said. "You draw a pretty handsome check for an associate professor every goddamn month, and your evaluations are shit."

"My courses are shit. All but the workshops. They're good. Why not look at *their* evaluations?"

"All A's," Ross sighed. "You give everybody an A, unless they die, in which case you give them an incomplete. Of course, you score evaluation points with them. It's a crib course. You score something else, too, if what I hear is right."

"You can't grade creativity. It's not a crib. Half the students have gone on to publish. More than half. You can't grade creativity."

"You have to grade *something*! For Christ's sake, you fail two-thirds of your other students, but these dilettantes all get A's. How does that look?"

"You mean, how does that make *you* look?"

"Well, it *doesn't* reflect well on the overall departmental average, but that's not the point. The point is you. You're just not making it in the classroom. In the *real* classes."

"I've got to have my writing time."

Ross looked down at his list of publications. "For what? You're not doing anything anymore. You've a few poems, and that's all right—"

"Since when is 'all right' not good enough. And it's not *all* poetry. Most of what's there is criticism."

"Reviews," Ross corrected. "Most of this is review work. And most of it's two, three years old. You haven't done anything in two years other than an occasional poem. Some of those are reprints."

All of them were, he thought, but you're too stupid to check, asshole.

"You know it doesn't really count as much as scholarship," Ross went on. "We used to count it. Just for you. But then you wrote scholarship as well. After a fashion. At least you were reviewing for major publications. Now, you're not doing anything."

"I'm a poet. Dunphy understood that."

"Dunphy's dead. Anyway, you weren't *hired* to be a poet. You were hired to be a teacher, and a scholar. When you were doing books . . . well, that was different. But a poem here and there doesn't add up. It's just not the same. Anybody can do that. Anybody can write a poem."

"Have you?"

"No, and you know I haven't. But I write other things: scholarship. That's what a university is supposed to be about: scholarship, books and articles, teaching." Ross folded his hands over his desk. His voice was sonorous with a constant whining undertone. "A poem, even a good one, even in a major national magazine just isn't the same. You know that."

"I know I need another book." He pretended to agree with what hadn't been said. "I haven't had a new collection in five years. I'm as aware of that as anybody. But I need my time to think. Scholarship—bullshit footnotes, gets in the way, takes up my creative energy."

"So does booze."

He ignored that. "I need time. I get frustrated. Listen, you know as well as I do that I've been named the most promising poet in this region. I've—"

"That was years ago."

"And *four* books! In *New York*. Not some bullshit little mono-graph press at Fuck-More-Ewe."

"That was years ago," Ross repeated and waved aside the implied insult. "You aren't even under contract for a new book. You aren't doing anything."

"My load's too heavy. I need time to think when I'm writing."

"Nine hours is *not* too heavy, especially when six is in workshop. Half the department's carrying twelve, some fifteen just to make room for you."

"Half the department's just marking time, waiting out retire-ment," he said. "Hell, most of them don't even lecture any more. They just read the fucking stuff to their classes and give them multiple-choice tests. Jesus, Ross, the fucking Scantron room is the busiest place on campus during midterms. Why don't you have some of that deadwood in here chewing them out? We're *supposed* to be teaching literature and writing."

"You're off the point. You aren't here at midterm anyway. You're never here." Ross sat back and laced his fingers over his chest. "Cancel some of your trips. That's really the problem. You're all over the map. Half the time, we don't know what state you're in. Any time any two people are sitting down anywhere in the country, you think you have to go and read to them."

"The trips sell books," he muttered. "Show the school off. Besides, it's not coming out of your budget. I pay my own way."

"Your teaching responsibilities come out of my budget, and the student complaints come out of my hide." He sighed deeply and furrowed his brow in a carefully rehearsed expression of sober concern. "The dean's all over this. He says you have to get these scores up, publish something decent, or—"

"Or what? I've got tenure."

Ross's eyes clouded. "There are ways around tenure. You know that."

"Fuck you, Ross."

"That's good. Real good. Is that what you're going to tell the dean? The provost? Face it: This is a state university, and this is a poor state. We're accountable to all kinds of people. Regents, politicians who haven't read a word of poetry or anything else since they left high school. If they ever went. And I won't even get into the local community's reaction to having a man like you teaching their youngsters." He sighed again, adjusted the clear glasses on his nose, though there was nothing in front of him to read. "The deal was we'd give you two workshops a semester if you'd handle the rest of your load and committee work. You're not. You ignore meetings and cut your own lectures. We can't afford somebody who doesn't carry his weight. And . . . ." He tilted back his head to take aim with the glasses twin lenses. "Who doesn't keep his name out of the papers."

"I carry my weight," he said, but he winced slightly. He had been named as "participating cause" in three divorce actions in the past year and arrested twice for DWI. It wasn't a good image for the school. In that, at least, Ross had a point.

"You don't carry anything. These prove it." He held up the computer print-outs that held his evaluations. "You're five, six points below the worst of the graduate TAs. Your students hate you. You show up . . . ." He trailed off in frustration.

"Go on, say it."

"You show up *drunk* half the time. Your lectures ramble. You fell asleep in your own class a few weeks ago. You get angry for no reason, throw students out of class. You have a clearly discernible bias against blacks, women—"

"Young Republicans," he added.

"You know . . . this is serious." Ross picked up a pen and pointed it at his face. "The Student Women's Caucus has complained to the provost. They say women in your lecture classes have to sleep with you or risk a C."

"That's not true. I've always given A's for sex. Good sex, anyway. Bad sex is a B-, bottom line." He smiled. But Ross wasn't taking anything for a joke.

"This is goddamn serious. I wish you'd try to understand that. I'm trying to save your butt, but you make it hard. I've got Affirmative Action on my ass because of that student you threw out of class last week."

"He threatened me."

"That's not what the other students say. They say you called him 'a stinking nigger.'"

"That's not true, either. I called him a 'flatulent ape.' Why don't you check with Miss Simpson?"

Ross's face reddened. "Who?"

"Your little spy in American Lit. The one with the mini-tape recorder in her bra. C'mon Ross, you think I'm an idiot? One tit is twice the size of the other. She's lopsided, and you can see the microphone. Tell me, does she just give you the tapes to be transcribed? I know she doesn't type them up herself. She can't type or spell well enough. She probably did spell 'ape' n-i-g-g-e-r." He grinned thinly. "Is she any good in the sack. I'll bet she's a moaner."

"You're disgusting."

"I *knew* she was a moaner." He snapped his fingers. "I've never known one with freckles on her knees who wasn't. You ever notice that?" He made a kissing noise with his lips.

Ross looked away. "If you're not going to be serious, I'm going to end this interview."

"Is this an interview?" he shouted, now genuinely angry. "I thought I already *had* the fucking job. Matter of fact, I've had it six years longer than you have. Dunphy hired me on the spot. You were a fucking TA when I came here. The only reason you have the job is that no one else would take it for the paltry salary they offered. The fucking dean won't turn loose of enough money to hire someone decent. Just because you leap-frogged into full rank and put your ass on a padded desk chair doesn't give you the right to look down your nose at me. I had a goddamn book in print before you finished your master's."

"That's off the point, too, and it doesn't matter. What matters is that the black kid's suing." Ross stacked the evaluations. "And I've got to defend you to the dean."

He opened his hands helplessly, lowered his voice, and tried to explain. "He refused to read *Huckleberry Finn* because he said it was racist. The truth is that he was too damn lazy to get through it or anything else I assigned. He kept mouthing off, complaining, distracting everyone. He also kept farting out loud. So I threw him out. He was a disruptive element. I don't need defending."

"You do. According to you, half your students are disruptive. Your male students, anyway. I don't know how you know that, since you're never in class. Do you know you missed nine out of fifteen weeks last semester?"

"I was touring. Doing readings."

"That's my point: You're supposed to be teaching."

"I *am* teaching. I lecture, run workshops."

"Our students!" Ross yelled, then took a breath and controlled himself. "*Our* students. Here! They're the ones paying tuition. They're the ones writing complaints. Their parents pay taxes in *this* state."

He shrugged. Ross played with his pen a moment and chewed his lip, then went on. "That's why I asked you to come in here, to tell you that. You're in deep. The complaints have reached monumental proportion."

"Don't exaggerate."

"I'm not exaggerating."

"Then, don't be trite. Jesus, Ross, you're the department head. You're supposed to set an example."

"To save yourself, you've got to stay here. On *this* campus. Do some real teaching. What happened to you? You used to be our most productive faculty member. The students adored you."

He rubbed his eyes and wished for a cigarette. The NO SMOKING sign glared at him from Ross's desk. "Some still do. The workshops prove—"

"The workshops are two-thirds women, almost none of them are full-time students, and you're screwing half of them. And a lot of them are married. I read the papers. I'm surprised somebody hasn't shot you. You've got the worst reputation on campus. Hell." Ross shot him a narrow look, and then said with a pained expression, as if this was his best shot and he hated to waste it, "I heard you even hit on Becky Templeton."

"Don's wife!" he was genuinely shocked. "That's a lie!" It wasn't. Not exactly. She had hit on *him*. They had a hot flurry of kisses and a grope in the kitchen of the faculty club after the Christmas party last year. She was twenty-five, black-haired, green-eyed, well past tipsy, and hot. Don, her husband—a new junior professor in classics—"just didn't satisfy her," she said to him in a humid whisper, dark with sensuality. But he hadn't followed up. He had to maintain something like a standard of behavior with regard to colleagues' wives.

Ross stood. "Didn't anybody ever tell you not to foul your own nest?"

"I've said that, myself. Often." He smiled at the coincidence, but Ross was too angry to soften his attack.

"Well, you should have listened."

"I did. I have. I might have dated a few students—"

"Or lived with them."

"Or lived with them. There's nothing in my contract that says anything about my personal life. What I do, who I sleep with is my business."

"Not when it affects the school's reputation. And not when it affects grades."

"You have no proof," he yelled. "No proof of that at all. There is nothing except empty accusations of a bunch of petty, jealous little bitches to go on." He paused, swallowed, tried to control his voice. "Yes, I have slept with some women who were students. Yes, I have lived with women who were students. I'm living with one now." He choked a bit. Tonya left him three days ago. Without her trust fund to support him, he'd have to find a cheaper apartment. He gathered wind. "But I have *never* exchanged sex for a grade. Never! Jesus, Ross, give me a fucking break."

"It doesn't matter," he said. "I'm sorry. I hoped you'd look over these." He pointed to the evaluations. "Be contrite, apologize, shape up. Promise to get yourself together. Give me *something*. The dean wants a meeting in the morning, and he's on the warpath. You need to be there to save your scalp. Nine sharp. Wear a tie, if you own one."

"I've got a class. Western American Poetry."

"Walk it. I promise no one will notice." He went to the window and looked out over the quad. He had the only office with a window in the whole department. It was a jealously guarded privilege. "I'm afraid you should prepare for the worst."

"Let him fire me." He stood also. "Let him try. I'll have the goddamn AAUP all over his ass."

"The AAUP doesn't frighten anyone," Ross said quietly. "Not even the AAUP. They're just a bunch of ivory tower blowhards who like to be written up in the *Chronicle of Higher Education*. You know that. This isn't California. We don't have a union."

"I'll sue if he fires me. I can sue."

"He won't fire you," Ross said quietly. "He'll make you leave on your own."

And he did. Four sections of remedial English, to begin with, and no workshops, and no raise, not next year, not ever, was only the beginning.

"Sue me," the dean insisted. "Oh, please do! I'd *love* to get your ass in court. Hang out all your dirty laundry. It'd finish you in academics for good. You're a disgrace to the profession."

Then he went on to recite a litany of punitive measures: no more excused travel absences, no more excused duty from standing committees, no more sick leave without written doctor's approval, and they were moving his office to the basement. A single complaint about his being drunk in class would mean immediate suspension. So would one more complaint about his love life. He would no longer receive merit credit for publication of individual poems. It would all be by the numbers, a formula. He had to publish six individual pieces to receive equal credit for one review, a dozen for an article. That meant the pressure was on for another book. And he knew it would be a long time coming. It might not come at all.

That was the verdict, and there was no appeal. "You should know that the provost said to go ahead and fire you," the dean said. "He said we'd take the heat, censure even. You're a filthy son of a bitch, an embarrassment to the department and the college. To the whole university, in fact. I want you gone. But I won't fire you. I won't buck the faculty senate and anyone else you might get to help you out of pure principle. No sir. You'll leave on your own, and I'll dance a jig on the quad while you pack."

He thought it over for an hour, then resigned, but the dean didn't dance. Tenure was gone, the school was gone, but somehow it didn't seem to matter. He realized that he hadn't had his head in the classroom in years, didn't care anymore. He never re-read a single work he assigned and was lecturing from memory. He decided that he gave up teaching the day *Opaque Images* was published. After that, he was only going through the motions. In a way, it took the albatross from around his neck, but he was now only sadder, not really a wiser man. Now, he was only depressed as hell.

The real impact of the decision to leave came when he cleaned out his office and understood that he didn't want to say goodbye to anyone. No one in the department was a friend, no one had shared so much as a cup of coffee with him in years. He was a stranger, and he couldn't name half the junior faculty, wouldn't know them if he sat next to one on a bus. His last act was to pile up on his desk all the student papers and lecture notes he'd collected over the years. He climbed onto a chair, dropped his trousers, and pissed on the stack. He wished someone had been there to take his picture. He wanted to send it to the student newspaper. "There is some shit I will not eat," he quoted the imaginary caption, "I will not kiss your fucking flag."

Good old e.e., he thought. He did his time in hell, too.

He called in every favor he could recall and lined up five separate tours and in a flurry of enthusiasm applied for a dozen grants. He got none of the grants. Two of the tours fell through—largely because of his reputation—and his retirement money was gone in three years. Now, he whined and wheedled his way onto second-rate circuits and managed an occasional visiting writer position at podunk backwater colleges where he made less and lived worse than most of the graduate students. More than once he'd been let go at mid-semester because of complaints filed by some irate co-ed or because he couldn't stay sober long enough to get through a class. The number of schools he could never return to because of some scandalous, drunken, salacious behavior was growing. And there was still no book in sight: not from New York, not from anywhere. He didn't have the poems even if he had had the contract. Felix had been hanging up on him more and more during the past two years: not slamming the phone down, just brushing him off, but hanging up, just the same.

The more he drank, the more miserable he felt. The poetry became harder and harder to write, also. Then, it didn't come any more at all—*they* didn't come at all, no matter what he did, who he slept with or how often. When he tried to write anyway, to force it, his words seemed stilted, wooden, as if someone else was writing them. He thought of it as "false verse," and he wrote it best when he was drunk or stoned or both, then the next morning little of it made sense. He could still stay in the forms, though. He just couldn't make the words sing or express anything like a true emotion.

He tore up more than he kept, and much of what he kept was in fragments, isolated lines and ideas wadded up in his battered briefcase. The poems in his mind stayed just out of sight, around corners of his imagination, crouching in shadows. He could sense that they were there, but he couldn't lay a mental finger on them, sense them in any tangible way at all. It made him want more to drink, more to smoke, more to fuck, more of anything to keep his mind off what he really couldn't do.

Often he wished for a friend, and more than once he cried himself to sleep thinking what a goddamn waste it was that Frank Gideon was dead. Or that Gideon had left him still alive.

He shut off the shower, toweled off, and took another shot of tequila. It made his head spin, and he had to grip the sink to keep from falling. His knees hurt as if he had been running or climbing stairs, and his breath cracked hollow in his ears.

Finally, he gained his balance and snapped off the light. In the darkness he stumbled against a suitcase and whispered an oath. The motel's built-in slab of Formica-coated particle board that served as a desk was in disarray, and he would have to turn on a light to find paper and something to write with. But the inspiration was gone, back into the shadows. Poetry mocked him.

"Circulating poet," he whispered the repetition. "Rotating asshole." He pushed the chair back, sat down, then quickly rose and whispered:

No coward soul is mine,
No trembler in the world's storm-troubled sphere;
I see Heaven's glories shine,
And faith shines equal, arming me from fear.

Brönte, he thought as he rubbed his gray, unshaven face. It would take a woman to write such simpering, romantic pap as that: a frustrated woman.

"Hell with it," he hissed. And he slid back into bed. The girl— Sybil: her name was Sybil—spooned her body against him and her hand fell to his groin, fondled him gently. His body made no response, but it didn't matter. She was still asleep. In the light, her face was pouty, pretty, young, but somehow masculine, sharp in the silver light. He reached over and picked up another cigarette, lit it, and lay there in the amber beam from the curtain, smoking, looking up at the ceiling, waiting for daylight and thinking about nothing at all.

VIII

"The artist is the creator of beautiful things.
To reveal art and conceal the artist is art's aim."
—Oscar Wilde

I saw an article about me in Poets Magazine—*you know it? It's one of those publications devoted to literacy that refuses to use an apostrophe correctly. The writer, a woman, a kid from New Jersey, an assistant professor at Princeton, said that I ruined any chance I had for success because of my pronounced hatred of women, blacks, and "any other minority that asserted itself into the literary arena." It doesn't do much good to say so, I guess, but the truth is that I'm really a genuine liberal. I voted Democrat, when I used to vote, and I give, or used to, a lot of money to World Wildlife Fund and Greenpeace—"Save the Whales" and "Save the Snail Darter," and all that. I supported the ERA. I had a bumper sticker in favor of it on my office door. I wouldn't care if my daughter dated or even married a black or an Hispanic or a Jew—although she never did, I don't think—and I've made love to women of all three distinctions.*

But saying you're not a bigot or a sexist or a racist isn't ever enough. In fact, it sort of tips everyone off that that's precisely what you are. It's like when Nixon said "I am not a crook." Everybody who heard that, everybody who heard about it, even those who really liked Nixon—and there were one hell of a lot more of them than you would imagine if you ask around today—everybody knew right then when he said it that he was a crook: no doubt about it. Same thing happened when George the Elder said he wasn't a "wimp," or when Billy Boy from Arkansas said he didn't actually have sex with chubby little Monica. Denial is the sincerest form of admission.

And don't be taken in by that old saw about actions speaking louder than words. I mean, you can vote right, treat people right, never discriminate, be equal in all your dealings, but if you tell an

174

off-color joke, a racial joke, a religious joke, an ethnic joke, or even use the wrong word now and then, you're fucked for life: branded. I mean, it's brought down cabinet secretaries, heads of corporations, governors, generals, presidential candidates and mayors. Never mind that somebody is ripping off the taxpayers, snorting coke, and balling everything with a slit between its legs from Hell to Dallas: Just make goddamn sure he's not retelling some joke he heard on a comedy special on cable TV last night. That'll end his career and quickly.

Don't ever let anybody tell you that words aren't more powerful than anything else on the planet. Faith may move mountains, but a few well-uttered phrases can shove whole continents around.

The truth, though, and for what it's worth, is that I don't have any real prejudices in the conventional sense. I don't hate anybody but fakes and phonies. It's just an unfortunate fact of our culture that most of the people I've met in the "literary arena" are fakes and phonies. My only real prejudice is against bad poetry.

Sometimes, I think you ought to have to have a license to write any poetry at all.

This business of politics and poetry, though, is a bad one. That's one place where I disagree with the postmodern critics, the multiculturalists, and all those who think poetry ought to be political. I know that to a great extent, it always has been—even Homer salted his peanuts a lot, and Shakespeare did, and so did Milton and Pope and Wordsworth and big Jimmy Dickey. We sort of forgive Poet Laureates, though. Political poetry goes with the job. But Browning was certainly political, and there's Sassoon, and Auden, Ginsberg. And poor old Ezra. Politics and economic theory fucked up his poetry worse than they did his life. I doubt that anything I say can change the idea that politics always will be part of the poetic. But, God knows, there ought to be some art to it, as well.

Stephane Mallarmé said it best: "You don't make a poem with ideas, but with words." But half the dumb shitheads writing poetry today never heard of Mallarmé. Half haven't read any real poetry, either. And I doubt if any of them have ever had an original idea.

You know, in the Poetics, *Aristotle says that poets are truer to their culture than historians or critics because they have no hidden agenda in their writing. By that, I think, he meant politics. But he saw* The Lysistrada *and* The Birds, *the* Orestia, *and the* Oedipus *plays, and if we can see they were political, I'm sure he could. So what did he mean? And I don't know if the old boy was right or not,*

175

but I wish to believe that he was being prescriptive for once, saying that poetry shouldn't *have that hidden agenda. It was okay for Moliére, maybe, even for Milton or Tennyson or Matthew Arnold, but when poetry gets mixed up with politics, then the politics takes over, at least in modern times. And that creates problems for the poet and the critic as well.*

The biggest dilemma is that some poets can mix politics and poetry successfully. Ginsburg did, and Howl *is one of the great poems of the modern era. And, lyric poets like Bob Dylan had tremendous success with it. Even Merle Haggard: "The Fightin' Side of Me." or "Okie From Muskogee." But* real *poetry, serious poetry should focus on the poem, not on the message. Fuck that form into content shit.*

You know what I mean. Everyone knows what I mean, even if no one will admit it. See, I think that when you get a room full of people sitting around discussing somebody's poetry, or listening to it, they spend more time looking for the goddamn thesis than trying to appreciate the beauty of it. That's all I've tried to say when I've attacked bad poetry: The poem has to come first, the truth of the verse has to be more important than anything else. Even if it doesn't have a thesis, an idea at all, that's okay—to hell with Aristotle on that point, anyway—beauty is everything: a joy forfuckingever. Keats had the right ticket on that much, at least.

But those same people are scared to death to say they don't like the poetry, because that means they don't agree with the politics. And if they agree with the politics, then they have to like the poetry. See? It's lunacy. God, it messes up the art:

> *St. Joseph feared the world would melt,*
> *But he loved the way his finger smelt.*

Great poem, right? No, of course it's not. But it's not political, either. Old Dondi was right about Yeats, for the most part, anyway.

I heard once that Cleanthe Brooks said that "Wordsworth's contribution to poetry" was that he "liberated the imagination." I like that. It says in a nutshell what poetry should do, and Brooks wasn't talking about the goddamn "Prelude" or anything, I'll bet. He also wasn't talking about the kind of necessary junk that Tennyson put out: "Charge of the Light Brigade," and "Maude," even though that stuff made his career a lot faster than Idylls of the King *or* In Memoriam *did. And there's goddamn Henry Wadsworth—the only real American who has a spot in Poet's Corner. But*

176

that was a different era. "Occasional poetry" was big then. A "Paul Revere's Ride" or "Arsenal at Springfield" was money in the bank. The Victorians ate that shit up.

But when I see one of these self-righteous activist types stand up and try to bend poetry around some social issue, particularly when it's the poet's social issue, it just frosts my balls. I mean, if they want to write a fucking essay, they ought to go off and write a fucking essay. Leave poetry alone. That's what I say. Said. And I said it a lot.

And every time I said it, I got in deeper and deeper shit. If the poet in question was a feminist, especially, watch out. She'd have my balls for bells in a heartbeat if I so much as suggested that her verse stunk worse than a sanitary landfill at high noon in July. Which most of it does, not because she's a woman, not because she's a feminist: because she's a lousy poet. And if I fight back, I get this rep as a woman hater. Like I said, that's ridiculous, but it went hand-in-hand with my rep as a bigot and racist, so it seemed to fit. But there you are. You can't win, not if you're honest.

Love me, love my poetry. My art: love it or be a bigot.

In a way, it's a kind of silly, reverse logic. Here I am reading work by a woman whose whole wardrobe consists of opaque hose, black dresses, and sensible shoes, and whose poetry all turns on the subjugation of women. If she says a poem by Whitman or Milton or Sandburg or somebody is lousy because it's sexist, everybody around nods wisely and feels bad that these really fine poets were so blind to the liberation of the female of the species. But if I—or anyone—suggests that her poetry sucks the clouds out of the fucking sky—then suddenly it's I who's violating her civil rights. I'm the chief pig in the room because I dared to be honest about my opinion of her verse.

You ever notice how most feminist poets feel that they have to work in words like "cock" and "penis" and "vagina" and all the rest of the anatomical catalogue into their poetry? Why is that? Are they that hung up on genitalia? You can feel the tension in the room every time one of them says the word "fuck" out loud. If I say "fuck" it's expected—naughty, maybe, but expected. If they say "fuck" it's a mark of their liberation. One feminist poet I know—and rather like—hasn't ever written a poem without a couple of those words in it. I asked her about it, once, and she said that she felt obligated to use what she called "frank language" to prove that she, a woman, wasn't afraid of it. It's sort of a like black poets using the word "nigger" or Hispanics calling each other "greasers" or

177

"spicks." It's like if they use the words, they won't have to be afraid of them anymore.

What she—and her sisters in ball busting—really wants, is for everyone to accept lousy verse by women because women were treated like shit for centuries. And, if you point out that there were a couple of pretty fair female poets in all those years of subjugation, she'll shoot right back that you're right, there were a few, but only a few, and that's the fault of men. Men, after all, are the critics. Still are, for the most part.

You get the same shit from the blacks. And gays. The Hispanics don't use it quite as much, and Indians—Native Americans, to use the politically correct term, which most Indians I know hate—hardly argue from that point at all. They don't have to: Their poetry is either good or bad because it's mostly all drawn from their own tradition. They don't expect anyone else to like it. Or even understand it. And they don't condemn anyone who admits that. Asian American poets feel the same way, I think. But for women and blacks, it all too often comes down to the same thing: Like me, and love my work for what I believe, not for whether my stuff's any good or not. But dislike my stuff, and you disagree with me, and my politics, and that makes you a sexist bigot: bullshit.

But that's the problem, isn't it? Another woman I know—but not a friend—who's a really militant feminist always tells me that I hate women's poetry because it's women's poetry, and when I say I don't, she asks me to name one great living woman poet. I do. In fact, I'll name a couple, and then she asks me to name some really great living male poets, and I do that, too. "Who's better?" she asks. If I name one of the women, then she says I'm patronizing her: lying. If I name a man, she says I'm a sexist. You can't win. Not with feminists.

This same old gal got the damned McCarther, too, you know, the certified genius award mysteriously handed over to two classes of people: those who don't deserve it and those who don't need it. In my experience they're often one and the same. Anyway, this broad got two hundred fifty-thousand samoleons for cranking out a whole cycle of poems about menstruation. She was invited to read at the gubernatorial inauguration in her home state, and she not only read these verses filled with graphic allusions to female plumbing, she concluded her performance by announcing that to "inculcate the image in her mind," she wrote them out originally in long hand, using her own menstrual fluid for ink. I wasn't there, but I heard about it. Apparently the governor was less than impressed with this *display of feminism. His wife got ill and left the room. Personally, I felt sorry for the poor son of a bitch who got the manuscripts to edit.*

Oh, and you know what the exclaimed poetess did with all that money? She blew it all on shoes. Every dime. Custom made footwear by world-class designers at an average of $15,000 a pop. And women wonder why men stereotype them.

I campaigned for a female senatorial candidate once, and this same woman called me a "mole," accused me of infiltrating the candidate's organization so I could "prowl" for women to take to bed. She was partly right, of course. I mean, there's a lot of horny women in politics. It's a rarefied atmosphere, full of power, and any Freudian knows that power is sexy. So in politics the mood is right, and most of them are too business-minded not to be vulnerable to poetry, when it's presented right. But she was wrong, too. I mean, hey, I got laid a lot, but I really believed in that candidate. I voted for her, and I was sorry she lost.

I tried to practice what I preached, what was preached at me. I mean, over the years, I worked closely with a lot of women: colleagues, student assistants, associates, friends. And I didn't try to take them to bed all the time, regardless of what you probably think about me by now. I mean I thought about it. It's normal to think about it, but I didn't do anything about it, not every time, not even the majority of times, not even some times when I knew, sensed that if I had made a move, it would have been positively received.

Listen: There was this woman named Faye. We were shoved together to write a new curriculum for English majors. It was scut work, but back when I was teaching, I had to do it sometimes, you know? I was in one of my self-reclamation phases and tried to take it seriously. So we worked hard on it. We burned the midnight oil right there in the Gregorian Memorial English Building, and we kept it all business. Never got close to a bed. Not even a sofa. But we worked on this thing every day and most evenings for about two months. This was "P.C.," pre-computers, and everything had to be typed up whenever we had changes to make. It was long, tedious work.

Faye was nice-looking: long legs, nice little bottom, pretty face, prematurely gray hair—white really—and she was a self-proclaimed feminist. She was about my age, also a professor, and married to a pilot for American Airlines. He was away a lot. Anyway, he came to pick her up one night, and she introduced me to him. He was cordial, invited me to join them for a drink. But I

179

knew, you see, that he'd been gone for like ten days or something, flying overseas routes, so I didn't accept. I tried to be courteous, considerate. Reclamation progress, right? Didn't work.

When we finished the project a couple of weeks later, we felt pretty good. It was about five in the afternoon, and she suggested we step across the street to a pizza joint for a beer to celebrate. I said, "Sure," and off we went. We got as far as the front door, and she said, "You know, this isn't such a good idea." She went on to tell me that her husband was jealous of me. And I hadn't laid a hand on her, not even a suggestive wink. I hadn't done a goddamn thing. We were colleagues, co-workers, equal partners in an important project. That was all. That was it.

I was cool about it, but it bothered me, you know. Here I was giving the Devil his due, so to speak, behaving as if she was just like anybody else, any other colleague, no thought or reference to gender at all, what do I get? Hanged for a goat. Or is it sheep? Well, it doesn't matter, and that's the point of the cliché.

I mean, I guess I had that reputation, but I was trying, and she didn't have any grounds to make me feel like that. My biggest regret was that I didn't hit on her. Maybe that was what was at the bottom of the whole thing after all. Maybe she did that to let me know that I should have hit on her. But you know what? I'll bet if I had made a move, she'd have taken my fucking head off. Now that I think about it, maybe that's why I didn't make a move. Rejection, as I've said, is the toughest thing in the world.

Militant feminists became the nuns of the nineties. They spend most of their time contemplating their departure from the real world, pissed off as hell that they have to isolate themselves from playing women to men, and taking it out on the rest of us. They want to be desirable, but woe to any man who suggests that he desires them. They want to play with the boys, but they want to be treated special because they're not boys. It's not that they're better, it's just that they're different. Sometimes, I think they get up every morning just fundamentally pissed off that they were born female.

Some of them want to be forgiven somehow for being women, paid back somehow for being female, like it's a liability. The truth, I think, is that they really want to wear drop-dead clothes, make-up, and get their hair done so some poor slob will pant himself to death chasing them to bed. But they're more afraid of that than anything else. They spend so much time denying that there is such a thing as physical attraction between the sexes that they forget that it's that attraction that makes things work. It sure as hell *makes poetry work, and I suspect that it makes everything else work as well.*

Hey, "Black is Beautiful" is a great slogan. Female is what? Pissed off, as I said.

It doesn't bother me much, except when it comes to poetry. I mean, I've slept with a lot of self-proclaimed feminists over the years, and most of them are pretty good in bed. They usually want to do it to prove they can, for the same reasons they pepper their poetry with four-letter words: prove they're not afraid of sex, prove that they're not lesbian, too. The question in my mind, though, is whom *are they proving it to? They seem to think that having multiple orgasms is some sort of requirement for womanhood. If they don't come, then they fake it, though. Really. There are hookers that could take lessons from some of the liberated women I've known, because they're not faking it for me: They're faking it for themselves. They couldn't look at themselves in the old mirror if they admitted that a man somehow could do something they couldn't.*

They deny it, you know. They'll claim that's wrong. But the truth is, I think, that they really don't want a world where men and women are equal. They want a world where there are no men. Period.

Jill was one of those, but I sort of forgave her from the first time, because she was—maybe still is—one of the best friends I ever had. She may be my only friend, in fact. And she's Jewish, or her mother was. Her father was Scotch-Irish, and I think he was a Presbyterian or something. And she's married to a black guy, or was when I last saw her. But none of that is more important than her art. She's not a poet, you see. She's a painter. Nudes are her specialty, and she's won some awards, gotten top money for some of her paintings. But none of them are political. When you take a person's clothes off, it's hard to tell what he or she stands for, you know.

She's political, but she kept it out of her art, and out of her bed. Politics—"sexual politics," as the phrase goes—were important to her, made her mad, but she left it in that part of her life that was political, and that's where it stayed. She didn't believe in pushing it into anything else. She always said, "It doesn't matter what a person thinks or does. What matters is what's in the soul." I liked that. I wrote a poem about it. She's the only woman I never slept with who inspired my poems to appear. I had a feeling that if I had gotten her into bed, they would have abandoned me, ashamed to be seen.

Maybe that's because she was happy with who she was. She

didn't need me or any bullshit political movement to define herself. She was too self-confident for that.

When politics carries over into poetry, it screws it up. It really does. And I attacked a lot of it over the years. How to lose friends and make certain everyone thinks you're a narrow-minded asshole? Tell the truth. Works every time. The irony, of course, is that the whole reason these poets are writing in the first place is what chiefly makes their poetry bad, and when I point that out, they think I'm attacking them as women, blacks, or whatever. I'm not. Never have. I just attack them as bad poets, and because they have their politics so fucked up with their art, they can't tell the difference.

Jewish poets seem to have a better a handle on it. Jewish poets I've known don't go around demanding anything. They just write what they feel, and if what they feel has to do with being Jewish, that's fine, too. It's usually better poetry. But blacks feel that they have to work in something about being black, and women feel they have to work in something about being women, and that usually kills off the verse. The difference, maybe, is that Jews like being Jews, are comfortable with it. Women and blacks, well . . . sometimes it's hard to tell where they stand on what they are, at least that's true in their poetry. If their "militant verse" is any indication, I'd say the poets aren't comfortable with it. But what can you do? You can't change what you are—at least not ordinarily. So they try to put it into their verse. And, not to be too repetitive, that screws up the poetry.

As I said, let them go write a fucking essay.

The whole problem with most of them is that they've spent so much time reading sociology, political science, history, and all that other crap, they haven't had time to read any poetry. If they read some poetry, they'd see how bad they really are, and they'd be embarrassed.

But what that article missed was that I've written a lot of praise for poets who were women, black, or otherwise identified as minority writers. The difference, though, was that they're good poets. They have a sense of what Mallarmé was talking about: they're poets first, and whatever the hell else they are second. Can you imagine me trying to sell a poem about how great it is to be a white male? It ain't all it's cracked up to be, I can tell you. And so far as I know, very few poets have even tried to write about it.

There was this one two-day workshop I did up in New Hampshire years ago. It was one of my first tours, long before I had made much of a name as a critic. But I already was developing the rep as a womanizer and a woman-hater, or maybe all men were. I can't remember. The school was one of those small universities that used to be a "women's college" until the late sixties when a lot of men started going there. Anyway, the workshop was filled up with women. I don't know if there were no male poets at the school or what, but there they were, and some of them were pretty fair writers. More of them looked likely for a warm night, but that just didn't happen. Not with them.

Well, the first day we all exchanged poems, talked about a few that we read, and on the second day, I was supposed to tear into a couple they gave me to read overnight. When we met for the next day's session, I was in the process of writing one of the particularly bad ones on the board. It really wasn't a poem, I didn't think. It only had four words: "Fine Feathers," which was written high in the right hand corner of the page, and "Female Fingers" which was down in the lower left margin. I wrote it on the board and was about to start trying to analyze it, when the door bursts open and in comes this woman.

She was older than the others, and she wasn't on my roll sheet, but I didn't say anything. Feminist? You bet. She not only had the uniform on, she also had a bun pulled back so tight I wondered how she could close her eyes. No makeup, no bra, either. As usual, she had done everything she could to be both provocative and sexless at the same time. But she couldn't completely hide the fact that she was attractive. She was too pretty for that.

Anyway, I leaned against the board while she took her seat, and then I started working on the poem. I pointed out the fact that there was no poetic relationship apparent in the ideas, and she stood up and immediately contradicted me. She was ready, locked and loaded.

"Of course there is," she said and looked around for confirmation, which came in the form of a small lake of bobbing heads. "The very fact that you can deduce 'Female Fingers' from the expression 'Fine Feathers' points out the fact that the poetic image is clearly established. How could you come to the idea of 'Female Fingers' otherwise?" She actually pointed a paintless nail at me. "You are just blinded by your sexist tendencies and can't even admit your own deductions from the obvious."

I didn't know what to say, and then I realized that I was still standing in front of the two words on the lower left. She hadn't seen them, although everyone else had.

I didn't say a word, merely stepped aside and revealed the whole "poem" to her. There was a silence, then a lot of nervous laughter.

It was like Gilda Radner on TV, you know? She turned red as a ripe boil, said "Never mind," and left the room.

She came to dinner at the dean's house later that night and to my shock, she apologized. She confessed that in a review I had attacked a collection written by a friend of hers, and she had come to the workshop to get revenge. She planned to embarrass me in front of the students, show me up for the sham she believed I was. She said she still thought I was a phony, even though she finally admitted that she liked my poetry. She was an instructor there, she said, and she said what she did was "inhospitable." She then asked me to forgive her rudeness.

I accepted her apology, let her drive me back to the hotel, and we wound up having a nightcap or two, and she took down her hair, and we enjoyed a decent roll in the hay, so to speak. We did okay together, and I saw her a couple of times over the years. If she ever faked it, I couldn't tell.

I got a fairly decent couple of poems out of it, too. The connection isn't political. That's important.

But the general point is the same: Bad poetry is bad poetry, and good poetry is good poetry. It doesn't have much to do with anything other than vision. And in my case, it has a lot to do with women. There have been entirely too many women in my life, but without them, there wouldn't have been any poetry at all. They didn't ruin me. I ruined myself for their sake, and for the sake of my poems.

How in God's name could I hate them?

The Arts Council

The first meeting of the lecture and readings series was in her home: a two-story, red brick, antebellum affair surrounded by magnolias, pines, and breezy patios overlooking lawns that appeared to have been manicured with nail scissors. She was tall, willowy, and rich, and when she moved across the room in her loose-fitting black hostess' dress, refilling glasses and picking up the occasional empty bottle, he could think of no one but Byron.

It was an apt allusion. She wasn't truly beautiful, but she walked "in beauty." She had the kind of sophistication that came with money, position, power: ice-cold on the outside, a blast furnace beneath the surface. Moreover, she looked available, eager even, particularly when she noticed him staring at her and gave him back one of her furtive, dark and sensuous looks. Better yet, he was physically aroused for the first time in two years and thankful for the library table that shielded him from the crowd. Her name was Gladys, and she captivated him utterly.

The drone from the other end of the table came from Teddy Wilbarger, a ripe candidate for the oldest living poet in America. As an undergraduate, Teddy had worked with Ransom, Tate, "Red" Warren, the other fugitives at Vanderbilt, and while his own work had found its way only with the greatest difficulty and string-pulling into the occasional anthology, he was now regarded and usually billed as the "last of the Agrarians."

Last of the Mohicans, was more like it. It was a wonder old Teddy lived long enough to make the flight in from Atlanta. Everyone had heard of him, but he was well past his time, and he had nothing new to say. Nobody did. Everything these days was "pre-text," "sub-text," "polymorphs," and other "reader response" horseshit which had nothing to do with anything to do with the poetic. The philosophical revolution begun by Northrup Frye and Bob Scholes, Wayne Booth and Stanley Fish has spawned a host of disciples any messiah would envy, and like most of the religiously fervent, they had no idea what they were talking about. But they had the indecipherable and vapid rhetoric down pat.

Teddy was from the Old School: the Moderns, the New Critics, art for the sake of art, historical imperative, objective correlative, tradition and individual talent as precedent, requirement for poetic expression. Ezra Pound was their savior, T. S. Eliot their pope. For angelic saints, they looked to Whitman and Dickinson. But that was old hat. Here, no one was listening, no one cared. He didn't care, either. The worst thing that could happen to poetry was for someone to try to explain it. He stopped listening to Teddy after his third word.

The formally printed program—embossed gold leaf on creamy parchment—was open on the table, next to a legal pad that supposedly contained his notes. There were no notes. There were only snatches of phrases, a handful of idle thoughts he hoped would forge themselves into something solid, something metrical. There were poems there, too. They were back for the first time in years: real poems, his poems: two sonnets, an ode, a fucking envoy, couple of others in rough draft. He hadn't decided yet. He was too excited. He had needed them and they came. It was a good feeling, like the stirring in his long-dormant groin when he looked again at Gladys, something else that felt as familiar as a long-lost friend. He hadn't had either sensation for a long time, and he sat back and enjoyed them, entreated them to stay a while.

Teddy would be followed by Vida Carruthers, one of the original far-left former hippie-radical poets. She had credentials with the SDS and the Weathermen, had been in Chicago in sixty-eight, Woodstock in sixty-nine. In the forefront of the early feminist movement, she'd supposedly slept with Timothy Leary and H. Rap Brown and rode around for a while in Ken Kesey's bus, then took up with Richard Brautigan. She was implicated in some ROTC building burnings in 1970, then she dropped out of sight. She'd been in hiding in Peru up until last year, when she came back, called a press conference right in La Guardia airport, and publicly offered to turn herself in to the FBI. But the FBI wasn't interested in her, never had been. They didn't even show up for the big surrender. She was only wanted for questioning, it turned out, and no one seemed to remember what the questions were about. For anyone else, it would have been god-damned embarrassing, but Vida turned it to advantage. Her new book, *Twenty Years in Hiding: A Poet's Crusade*, was selling well among the cokeheads who still remembered what it was like when getting high and getting laid were both unique thrills and political statements.

He had read the book, even got a shot at reviewing it for the *New York Times Book Review*. He wrote them, sent photocopies of his old clippings, and they shocked him by calling him up and saying okay. But they only wanted three hundred words. By the time he got through trouncing Vida's militant musings, he had over eight typed pages, and they wouldn't take it. Instead, they sent it back to him and commissioned Norton Hargood, a twenty-two-year-old Pulitzer winner to do it in his place, and the little snot-nose, who hadn't been born when Vida was balling Stokely Carmichael, had raved about it. So Vida was raking in the royalties, and he didn't even get a kill fee.

Following Vida on the program was Vanilla White: black poet. What more was there to say, except that she wasn't a poet and she wasn't very black? Her book, *We BE the Beauty* consisted of long, periodic sentence-poems, sixty-five of them, with line breaks every five or six words. No rhythm, no meter, just a lot of poverty and ghetto misery. She managed to work in the word "motherfucker" every other page, truncating it to "mu'fu'k'r" to keep it on school library order lists. It was little more than semi-obscene rambling about the long-haul of the black experience, and the continuing need to keep white guilt alive, something that was hard to swallow from a woman so light-complected and obviously affluent. If her skin was any darker, he thought, she could pass for Hispanic.

She also had a book of rap verse coming out, he was told. Rap verse. What the hell was that?

Then there was he. He wasn't entirely sure why he was here with this group: a traditionalist, a radical, a black. They were billing him to talk about the "Old New Formalism," which he took to mean that he was as usual and once again supposed to defend poetry written in recognizable forms, but it was still confusing to him. But then, he knew why: Gladys.

He saw the ad for the job in an AWP job list in a faculty lounge of one of the small colleges where he still could get an occasional reading. "Director of New Arts Council. Published artist preferred, degree required. Manage large city's arts budget, arrange meetings, conferences, showings, and readings. Fund raising, grant writing experience a must. Salary commensurate with experience." He had experience, and he had written enough grants to fill a warehouse. That he never received one was beside the point.

He borrowed a computer terminal from the departmental secretary, whacked out a vita and sent it in, using Felix's number in New York as a contact. He had no permanent address at the time.

They still weren't as friendly as they had been, but Felix had softened over the years, especially when he realized that there was no chance he was going to be pressured into publishing another book of his poetry. Melton was dead. Felix was now president of the company, which now specialized in publishing manuals for technical writing courses: Felix was cleaning up.

Gladys called Felix, and Felix passed the word that he was expected there for an interview. He pushed his old Toyota to the limit to make it by the appointed date.

"I heard you read when I was in college," she said to him when they met at the Civic Auditorium in the Arts Council's office. "At LSU. You were wonderful. Your poetry was the most sensational— and *real*—stuff I heard the whole time I was in school." She lowered her eyes, breathed out the next words. "You turned me on. I wanted to talk to you, but you went off with a friend of mine. Shirley Tilden. Do you remember her?"

He didn't and shook his head. "It was a long time ago."

"Shirley remembers," Gladys said with a bright wink. "I *know* I would have remembered, too. From what Shirley told me." She licked her lips. "She said that when you were bad, you were much, much better."

Most women would have blushed when they admitted that, even after so many years. Not Gladys. She held his face in her dark eyes and gave him a level stare: a proposition, he thought. He knew one when he saw one. He ought to. He felt shabby in a garage-sale sport coat and shiny khakis, but she didn't seem to notice. Her eyes held his, and they sent messages that he hadn't seen in a long time. Or if he had received them, he hadn't been able to respond. To Gladys, he responded.

Then he went to work. This gathering was the first in a series of programs featuring name writers. They had the money. He was to spend it. It was a good job, and he had a decent apartment for the first time in years. He was sober, clean, and had no local reputation, was truly not known in the state. He thought that he might actually get some writing done. Again. The poems were back, but they were hazy, ghostly things, emaciated from neglect, skittish as young colts from their lack of exposure to a human mind. He didn't push it. He had learned long ago that he *couldn't* push it. If they didn't come to him on their own, he couldn't write them. So he just waited and poured his energies into organizing the new Arts Council, into keeping Gladys at arm's length: close enough to bring the poems, far enough to keep from fucking up.

He wanted to do this without taking her to bed. He felt that if he could capture the poems without having sex with her, he would transcend the old curse, defy the old humor. And he was close. He was writing now, and he believed it would work. He also needed the job. Screwing Gladys would mean screwing himself, and he had done that once too often already. The trick was to avoid it this time and come out ahead. It appeared it would work. But Gladys might have other ideas. The way she looked at him certainly suggested that she did.

He looked again at the program. All his books were listed, all his credits, even his current stint as "Advisor of Arts" to the city: bullshit job. They needed someone to front an office to disperse NEA and state council money to young artists, galleries, theaters, and other wastes of the taxpayers' cash. Fifteen-grand for the year was his salary, but they paid for his digs, gave him an office, a pretty young secretary, Elise, who he was sure he would have in bed in another week or so as a bulwark against Gladys if nothing else, and they got him gigs like this. He was sure that with all this positive stimulation, he could write.

He used his first check for a new wardrobe. It was pure K-Mart, but better than anything he'd owned in years. In the mirror, a handsome if somewhat pudgy, short, and rapidly balding middle-aged man stared back at him. He looked goddamn confident, and he felt the same way, not just of himself, of his potential. He hadn't felt this good since grad school.

But it was all a sham. He soon learned that he was being set up for a better deal, a real job. Back in a college, back in the classroom, and that was Gladys's doing, also. The Arts Council was running on soft money, and it couldn't support him more than six months. By getting him a salary through the local school, part time, he could do both. He thought about it and decided that it might be all right. He figured he had five or six more years left in him. He could learn how to teach again. If he couldn't forget how to eat, then he'd damned well better learn how to teach once more.

Actually, the prospect excited him. He had missed teaching far more than he ever thought he would when he left it. He missed the excitement of watching students discover things for themselves, their anxious abilities forming slowly. He couldn't remember what had put him off it so, what had made him give it up so easily. It didn't matter. He needed to get back into the classroom, and Gladys was his ticket.

He just couldn't figure out her angle, what she wanted from him, besides a tumble. She had it made. What interest could she possibly have in a bald, fat, aging poet who had trouble remembering which fork to use at the dinner table? A twenty-year-old streak of envy for a sorority sister's fling? He doubted it. Whatever Shirley had been like, she couldn't have been moved to that dimension of bragging.

On the other hand, he reminded himself, "Time doth transfix the flourish set on youth/ and delve the parallels in beauty's brow." Maybe when he was younger he was that good: Maybe he could be that good again.

He tugged at his tie and watched Gladys make another pass through the room. She shot another deep, suggestive look toward him: a slight smile, hiding something that was too obvious to keep hidden. This was her house, or hers and her husband's. Robert. That was his name. Not Bob, Bobby, or Rob, or anything that sounded warm or human. Robert. Robert D. Ludlow, attorney-at-law. He told everyone who came in that night that he "didn't know from poetry," but if this "art stuff" made Gladys happy, then that was fine. He then disappeared, probably to the upstairs to watch porn on the VCR. Or to boff the maid.

The maid was worth boffing. She was really French. Long legs, Wonder-bra tits, black mesh stockings rising incredibly out of black spiked heels. She had a voice like crystal. She was such a cliché, he couldn't believe she wasn't an actress hired to play the role. It was like something out of Feydeaux. Or Plautus—no, Sondheim. "Everybody Ought To Have a Maid."

It didn't matter to him whether old Robert was boffing the maid or whether he "knew from poetry" or not. Robert was chairman of the board of regents. It would be up to him whether the local cracker school could afford the luxury of a poet-in-residence. And since Gladys apparently got anything she asked for, he felt confident that Robert would decide that it could. Robert struck him as a man who never took no for an answer to anything.

"It can't be tenure-track," Robert said casually at dinner, "or full time, of course." Gladys smiled sympathetically. She called and asked him to come by early. They were dining *al fresco* on the patio before the meeting began: *paté* sandwiches, light wine, Russian caviar, and imported potato chips Robert fingered with his highly buffed nails. "I mean, you know it can't. But I think we could work out something year-to-year. The VPAA owes me a favor or two. The school needs some culture, something to balance that goddamned losing football team they finally dropped last year. It's a tech school, basically: forest management and marine science used to be their forte. Now they're sort of lost. But you might bring a dimension of class to their act. Class." He shook his neatly barbered head and smiled. "That's something they could use."

"What's the academic standing?" he asked. He knew the answer, but he wanted to hear them admit that anyone with a warm body and cold cash could go there.

"Poor. But that's likely to change, now that we've eliminated football. Basketball's next. That's the plan. Anyway, the Arts Council needs a director, or so Gladys tells me. I don't see why she doesn't to it herself."

Gladys said, "Oh, Robert," and struck her husband lightly on the arm, then cast a dark wink in his direction.

"So, that'll be the deal. Your contract with the city is good for a while, but I don't see why we can't start you off with a couple of courses in the spring term. Get your feet wet. Then, if the AC money runs out, you'll have a place to fall." Robert concluded his remarks like any attorney finishing his litigation: smooth as shit under water. "I foresee no problems."

He smiled and nodded. Money was welcome. "A place to fall" was unimaginable. The school, a four-year-junior college disguised as a university, was a commuter college: Classes were jammed with out-of-work pipe fitters, former oil-field roughnecks, unemployed general refinery laborers, all now mowing lawns and chopping firewood for money, now trying desperately to retool themselves into high tech or real estate before those markets dried up as well. The school gave more degrees in industrial arts and cosmetology than in anything resembling academics. "Air conditioning engineering" and something called "industrial management," which he suspected meant janitorial training, were also popular. They hadn't had a forest management graduate in five years, and no one could remember the last time anyone majored in marine science. Teaching creative writing out there was laughable. Two thirds of the students couldn't write above the eighth-grade level.

But he wasn't laughing: He hadn't had a regular paycheck in a long time. And he was getting too old to move around like he used to. And he needed—desperately wanted—an address. The prospect of even temporary job security and a double-dipping deal was grand. He sensed his poetry would come back as well, like an errant dog that finally made his way home. This had all the earmarks of a "last ditch effort," but he was determined to make the most of it. Every time he looked down, the bottom looked harder and more solid. And closer.

The best part of the whole deal was that his daughter and her family lived within a hundred miles of here: two-hour drive. He could be there and back easily on weekends. He hadn't seen her but four or five times in the past seven years. Missed her high school graduation, missed her college commencement. Missed the birth of his first and second grandchild. He planned to be there for the arrival of the third. She and her stock-broker husband had already invited him to come up for Thanksgiving, and there was a chance for at least a day-visit at Christmas. Her mother would be there from Denver with her CPA spouse and their two kids, but what the hell. It had been years: It was time for bygones.

He never thought he would be glad that he had kept up the child-support all those years. Never missed a payment. Sometimes sent extra, even though it meant eating soup over a sink for a month and putting off new underwear and socks. He paid for most of the girl's college as well. Now, it would pay him back. *Pater familias*, he thought. He had rights he'd earned.

It occurred to him, especially lately, that he had actually supported two children to adulthood—well, one of them all the way to adulthood, anyway—yet he couldn't come up with a mental picture of what either looked like. Rae Ann's child, he had never seen, though. His daughter was another matter. That was a guilty spot that ached when he touched it.

Gladys cast a smile at the four panelists and glided out of the room. She was younger than he, but no kid: maybe forty-five. Wrinkles around her mouth and eyes said she'd been around the block: knew the way things worked. She kept her figure, although photographs sprinkled around the house suggested she had three, four children, all teenagers or older. He wasn't comfortable being on the program he had himself arranged, but it was Gladys's idea. She insisted. He was given to understand that it was really a showcase for him. There were four members of the board of regents present, and the college president and his wife were out there somewhere. Two members of the so-called English department as well. He had to be careful, Gladys warned him: They had sensitive "bullshit detectors."

How they found and convinced these other poetic losers to come and present their wares was a mystery. "A Discussion of Poetic Directions," was the billing, "With Four Distinguished Poets," was the subtitle. *Distinguished*, shit, he thought. This was the biggest collection of forgotten souls he'd imagined possible this side of hell, himself included. Not one of them had any serious reputation as a poet or anything else. Not one had the respect of even the worst of the poetry journals or reviews in spite of a temporary success in publishing. He didn't, either. He hadn't in years. He didn't have a book left in print.

That could change, though. He glanced down at the legal pad. One of the unfinished poems began to take shape as he stared at it. Four quatrains, he thought, *a-b-c-b*. Some slant rhyme for flavor, play with the metrics. That was the scheme. Tetrameter. No: iambic pentameter. Shakespeare's line. He thought briefly of Frank Gideon. It would work.

"Beware! Beware!" he thought with slight smile. "For he on honeydew hath fed, / and drunk the milk of Paradise." The old poet was right, but this was fine. He felt reckless for the first time in years. The poetry was good. He felt his heart swelling. He felt younger than he had for a long time. He did a quick mental check and saw the bottom receding, momentarily, at least.

Teddy concluded his remarks and peered hopefully out into the audience to take questions. He wore Yeats and Joyce-style glasses and squinted hard through them. Wonder if he'll keel over, he thought. That'd be a laugh. He envisioned the headline, "Poet Dies in the Saddle." Or "At the Table." Although he had a Pulitzer and six other antique awards gathering mold on his southern mantel, old Teddy hadn't published a new poem in a decade. But then, he reminded himself: he was nearly a decade without anything at all himself. Not even a greeting card. But that was about to change. He was sure of it.

A job, a position. He would have the confidence he needed. He could do it. Keep his nose clean, his wick dipped in nothing but ink. Stay away from women, he lectured himself. Even Elise, he promised in a sudden upsurge of moral certitude. Certainly the students. Masturbate every damned hour on the hour if he had to, but just stay the hell away. "Poetry is the underwear of the soul," he quoted to himself. It's best to keep it on.

If he couldn't write without fucking some woman, then he just wouldn't write. He'd teach, eat, have a roof over his head, and retire. That was that.

And he'd quit drinking. That was the hard promise.

There were three tentative questions from the small group. Maybe thirty, forty people: high-society types in a hick town. Dressed to the nines for the evening at the attorney-at-law's estate. It occurred to him that Robert might be considering political office. Except for the department members, whoever they might be, the main idea of poetry here was something out of their sophomore English classes. Classic literary chic. Classic literary shit. Any one of them was wearing more cash in clothing and jewelry than his net worth, crummy salary included, even if he got the job with the college.

The questions were abstract, polite, and Teddy handled them with obtuse ease. No one understood his answers, but everyone nodded in sympathetic agreement and, he thought, wondered who would win the Superbowl that year.

"Courtesy is a debt we owe the old," or something, he tried to remember the whole quote without success.

"There's only one important thing to remember about modern poetry," Teddy wheezed in conclusion. Emphysemic, he thought, or maybe consumptive. The Poet's Disease. "It must be an expression of the depth of the soul's beauty. Without that, it is meaningless." Teddy sat back, relieved when there were no more comments or questions, and Vida began.

"I don't entirely agree with my distinguished colleague, or with Keats, who he's ripping off," she snarled. "There's a shit-load more to poetry than beauty. There's the need to raise the social and political consciousness of a whole civilization. *That* is poetry's principal responsibility." She pressed the table with her fingers and her raggedly chewed nails turned white. "Always has been. Always will be. Look at Sappho. Look at H.D. Look at Plath and Sexton. They weren't afraid to fuck or to talk about it!"

He could tell that she wanted to stand up, pace, lecture, but there wasn't room. In a way he was reminded of himself, and for a moment he remembered how good it felt to be teaching, really teaching.

Teddy sighed and sat back. Vida went on. He had not noticed how truly ugly she was when he first met her. She had on a sleeveless purple sweater that was stretched tightly over her braless, flaccid nipples. Her breasts seemed to stick out in opposite directions, like some weird kind of wall-eyed monster. She wore an ankh between them on a leather thong, providing a weight that increased their separate absurdity. Wiry hair poked from the sweater's seams, and when she reached up to push back a strand from her eye, the shock of the dark swatch under her arms forced all eyes to look away and mouths to cough in embarrassed disgust.

She finished her none-too-subtle destruction of everything Teddy said, called him an old idiot in five or six ways, then started reading from her own work. Readings were supposed to come later, after a "light buffet supper," as the program billed it, but she wasn't going to abide by any rules. She called herself an "Anarchist in Verse," according to the program notes, and nothing so mundane as a planned agenda was going to deter her any more than rhyme, meter, metaphors, images, indeed poetry itself would interfere with her work.

Her poetry was hard stuff: driving, angry, old-hat—or old hair—militant, anti-establishment and pro-populism, guaranteed to induce catatonia among serious poets. The audience stiffened. Half of them had been hippies—at least they pretended to be—twenty-five years ago. But beads and tie-dye were replaced by diamonds and mink, VW vans and spare change by BMWs and Platinum Cards. They weren't outraged by this old activist's anger. They weren't even offended: They were nostalgic. She was an entertaining recollection of the way they once were, of the way they might have been if they hadn't come to their senses, converted to Republicanism, and started making money. Vida, on the other hand, was patent-ed. She was still fighting the same old battles and hadn't yet figured out that the "enemy" was made up of former comrades: deserters.

"We have met the enemy and he bought us out," he scrawled on his pad.

His eyes roamed the room again, searching for Gladys. He spotted her in the hallway, emptying an ashtray. He was reminded that he could smoke here—that Gladys herself smoked—so he pulled out a cigarette and lit it, fighting back a gag and desire to cough up his heart when he drew in the first cloud. He needed to quit, but self-imposed sobriety and celibacy seemed like enough of a challenge for the time being. She seemed to sense he was looking at her and looked up, smiled, and made a motion to ask if he needed anything to drink. A half-full glass of pretty decent sherry sat in front of him. He shook his head. Not unless it's got some kick, sweetie, he thought and smiled back.

Vida finished her reading and began her analysis of the role of poetry as a political force. He sighed and tried not to roll his eyes or to smile ironically. Teddy's liver-spotted hands moved slightly on the table in front of him, tapping out the rhythm to a tune only he heard. Vanilla stretched long, slender, caramel and thoroughly unshaven legs out under the table and shuffled her notes. Several members of the audience shifted uncomfortably as Vida began attacking the President of the United States personally, as if it was she, not some liberal minded Polish-American intern who had put a fatal liplock on the presidential love muscle, but their smiles were grafted on. There wasn't a democratic impulse in ten blocks, and Gladys's Robert was the head of the county's Republican Committee. No one would think to contradict her, or to argue with her. There were no questions when she finished.

They took a break after Vida growled an ironic "thanks for your indivisible, comatose attention," then added, "the steel-trap convention will meet in the next room." The crowd broke up quickly, women escaping to the powder room to titter over her crudity, the men shuffling past him toward the porch to grumble over her naïve politics and giggle about her underarms. "Be like fucking a woman with three pussies," he heard one of them saw over a new cigar.

Vida herself must have heard the remark, but she ignored it and made a bee-line for the snack table. Vanilla wandered off to a corner by herself. No other blacks were present except for a cook who had made a brief appearance to replace the *hors d'oeuvres* tray, and Vanilla was being self-consciously self-conscious. Teddy remained at the table, signing thumb-worn copies of his books and nodding to platitudes mouthed by the handful who came up to say they had "read you for years," and were so glad they could "lure you out of Atlanta to this corner of the world," and so forth.

He set his course for Gladys. "How long's the break?" he asked, catching her at the foot of the stairs. She was on her way up, probably to check on Robert.

"Oh, twenty minutes, I guess. Maybe thirty." She looked concerned. "This is going much faster than we had thought. The food for the buffet isn't here yet. I told the caterers not to come until nine-thirty. I thought there would be more questions." She smiled, shrugged. Her lipstick was slightly smeared and her complexion was blotchy.

His watch told him it wasn't even eight yet. "Well, take your time," he said with a smile. "I didn't plan to speak that long myself. Saving it for the readings." She smiled back, warmly. "Say, do you think I could have something to drink? I mean, a *real* drink?"

She looked down at the tiny sherry glass and frowned. "Is something wrong with the—Oh! I see. You want something stronger." She grinned.

"Well," he tried to look sheepish. "A Diet Coke would do. This is sort of sweet. I'm getting older. I've got to watch it. Still, if there's any whiskey, bourbon or maybe even some V.O. or Canadian Club." He hesitated, considered his promise. "A Coke. Really. A Diet Coke will do fine."

A sly expression came on her face, and he thought he saw something behind her eyes harden, struggle with itself, then yield into a melting softness. She looked lovelier, sexier than he had seen her before. When he occasionally met with her in her capacity as the chair of the advisory committee, she seemed severe, cold and a little distant: a little afraid of him, too flirtatious, but arm's length. Now she was warm, inviting. She wasn't pretty, never had been, but her eyes were pure jet, and her hair, pulled behind her head, was dark, thick, and sensuous. She had the kind of attractiveness that money buys. Social standing makes up for a lot of flaws, he thought. So does a fat checkbook.

"A Coke? Are you sure?" she asked. Her smile cut through him like a blade of fire.

"'I shut my eyes and turned them on my heart.

   'As a man calls for wine before he fights,

    'I ask one draught of earlier, happier sights,

     'Ere fitly I could hope to play my part.'

"How's that?" He stood back, pleased with his ability to remember.

"Tennyson?" she asked.

"Browning," he corrected. "A Coke will be fine."

"You don't fool me," she said softly and leaned toward him. He smelled liquor on her breath: strong stuff, not the sweet sherry she was serving. "I know what you like. Robert's got some single malt. C'mon."

She took his hand in her slender fingers and led him through a doorway into what he realized was the library. Floor-to-ceiling glass-fronted bookshelves flanked a large fireplace. There was a mahogany partner's desk, greenplush chairs, a leather chaise, deep pile carpet. She went to a cabinet and fanned open the top. A rack of bottles and glasses rose magically from the inside. She selected a decanter of light-brown liquid and poured a Waterford tumbler half full.

"Join me?" he asked as he accepted it. She smiled again, coy this time, turned and fixed herself a highball.

"To poetry," he said grandly, and he downed it. It felt good: smooth and warm going down. One was enough, he lectured himself. Well, two. "Think first, fight afterwards—the soldier's art: / One taste of the old time sets all to right." he mentally completed the recitation and tipped his glass in her direction.

"To poetry." She sipped, then drank deeply. Her hands gripped the fancy glass. Her nails were long, clear, beautifully tapered. She had a large emerald ring on one hand, a cluster of two-carat diamonds on the other. A light silver bracelet encircled a perfect wrist.

They had two more without conversation. She kept giving him the same, penetrating, admiring looks she had shot at him in the office and from across the room before, and the familiar tightening in his chest and pressure in his crotch reminded him of the danger of what he was feeling. He was suddenly alarmed. There's a lot at stake here, he told himself. Don't fuck it up. Don't shit where you eat, especially before you have a chance to get to the table.

She poured a third shot for him, glanced at her diamond wristwatch. Cartier, he noted.

"I can't wait until you're at the college," she said softly.

"Yeah, me, too. I miss teaching. Miss the students." He downed the drink.

"I mean, *I* can't wait," she repeated. Her tone was dark, her eyes steady. "Can *you*?"

He coughed slightly. "Uh, no. Do we have time?" He tilted his empty tumbler, wanting more. It was good scotch, and he was feeling a strong buzz, wished for the first time in two years that he had a joint. He had sworn off dope somewhere in Idaho when he awoke in an alley behind his motel, beaten, robbed, soaked by a September rain. He'd given up reading his own work long before and had started lecturing more and more. He'd given a talk on Jewish confessional poetry, then read several fairly good representations: wrong decision. When he came to a swastika was spray-painted on his shirt, and someone had pissed all over him.

Good smoke covered more than pain, he thought. He stayed the hell out of Idaho after that—and Utah and Washington and Oregon. And he stayed the hell away from dope. It was one resolution he had managed to keep.

"I think so," she breathed softly instead of answering aloud, set her glass down on the table and came to him, enfolding his neck in her long arms and pulled his mouth to hers. It all seemed so natural, so automatic, he took her into his arms without thinking. She thrust her tongue against his teeth, pushed through, probed his mouth, and pressed her thighs against him. He dropped his empty tumbler on the rug and grasped her hips. He was surprised and pleased to find himself fully erect as she folded herself into him. She thrust her pelvis firmly against his abdomen, her legs spread beneath her skirt and grasped his calves. Her lips were all over his face.

"I didn't mean . . . ," he gasped when she broke for air.

"Shhh," she cautioned and kissed him again. He backed up against the leather chaise, trying to find his way down onto it, but the position was wrong. He felt her weight on his shoulders, her legs climbing his, wrapping themselves around him. Her hands groped for his fly.

"Your hus—" he warned, but she shook her hair out behind her, let it fall, and closed his mouth with hers once more.

"I'm leaving him," she gasped. "Touch me. See how wet I am, how wet you make me."

Her legs climbed around his waist, her long skirt bunched between them. She grabbed his hand and thrust it up under the fabric. He felt her, moist and naked, and he gave in. It wasn't difficult. It was familiar. He completed her work on his trousers, let them drop, then pushed toward her and pulled her to him at the same time. She gasped deeply, gasped again, and he pushed himself into her. She whimpered, then cried out and chewed his lip.

He was too old for this shit, he thought when his back twinged with her weight. But he didn't stop, didn't shove her away. They developed an awkward rapid rhythm, and her whimpering became regular between gasps. God, he wanted her. He hungered for her.

"Just what the fuck is going on here?" Robert's voice came across the room and froze them *en tableau*. He felt her teeth bite into his lip, hard this time, and he tasted blood. Her eyes were wide. The hard black coldness came back into them, surrounded now by fear, guilt. There was a madness there, too, he saw before she turned her face away.

"Goddamn it, Gladys! Goddamn it!" Robert slammed the door behind him.

She pulled herself off of him, stepped off and straightened her skirt. He pulled his trousers up, felt ashamed as he zipped them closed. Robert strode across the room, deliberately spun her around and slapped her. "I thought we had this shit behind us," he barked.

"I thought . . . oh shit." Robert put his hands on her shoulders. Her head dropped down to her chest. His handprint was vibrant on her cheek. "I'm sorry," the attorney said.

He looked at Robert for a moment, then retrieved his glass and went to the bar, poured another drink, tossed it back, poured another. He felt the need to be cool, sophisticated. He lit a cigarette.

"Is this your idea of gratitude?" Robert demanded quietly. He realized he wasn't speaking to Gladys, but to him. She was slumped into the chaise and stared at the floor, legs akimbo. Confusion etched her face, and her eyes were unfocused "You come in here. Ask for a job, eat my food, drink my scotch, fuck my wife," Robert continued.

"Your order of priorities is intriguing." He didn't smile, though he felt like it. Old times, he thought. Shades of the past. Fucked up, he thought, and now he was in the middle of a Noel Coward farce.

"Poet. Shit." He turned back to Gladys. She had risen and crossed the room. Now she studied herself in a mirror, pulling her hair back into place, straightening her dress. She looked calm, collected. "Get back to your fucking guests," he said. "Intermission's over."

"I want a divorce," she said to his reflection in the mirror.

"Yeah," he said. "I've heard *that* before. You'll want it tonight, maybe tomorrow. But you really *don't* want it at all. You can't survive without me, and you know it."

"I want to write. You won't let me write."

"I won't let you fuck writers either," he said. "Or anybody else. We've been through all this before. Now get out there. Get it started. Get those people out of here."

"What about him?" She was smiling. It was as if he was a stick of furniture or, he thought, a trick dog, or the man who wasn't there.

"He got ill. Had to go." Inside him, he heard a distinctive noise, like the cable on an elevator snapping. Then the plunge downward started. "Make the announcement. Go on," Robert ordered.

She looked at Robert passively, smiled briefly around the room as if an audience were present, then turned her deep gaze on him.

"I can't *wait* until you're at the university full time," she said. She licked her lips and gave him one more penetrating look. Then she left.

"I guess that's it," he said. The sensation of downward motion picked up momentum.

"That's it." Robert sat down on the chaise, put his head in his hands.

"I'll get my stuff and cut out. Sorry. Really. I needed this gig."

"Forget your stuff. I'll mail it to you."

"I'll pick it up. Tomorrow."

"Tomorrow," Robert said and rose. "Tomorrow your ass won't be in this town. In this state. If I ever hear of you anywhere in five hundred miles of here, I'll have you arrested, thrown in jail. I can do it." Then softly: "I'm connected."

"C'mon." He opened his hands. "I'm sorry about this. It wasn't all my idea. In fact, it wasn't really my idea at all. I've got better sense—"

"I'd like to say 'I'll bet,' or something," Robert sighed, "but the truth is, it's not the first time. You're not the first one. She's been away for it. A lot. I keep thinking it's over, that she's cured. But then some asshole like you comes along, and it starts all over again." He slitted his eyes, looked away. "Two years ago it was musicians. Year before, she was into artists. When we had the baseball team, it was athletes. She'll fuck anything that moves. Even an old fart like you. I guess it's a good thing the naval base didn't come here. She's a sick woman."

"She's a sexy woman." He groped for words. "She's attractive."

"She's sick," Robert insisted. "I know that. Three psychiatrists know that. Two hospitals in Europe know it. Now, you know it, and that makes you dangerous. So you're going to have to leave." He sighed again. "She's been out of therapy for over a year. I thought she was over it. Thought this Arts Council thing would take up all her energy. They said it would. Charged me thousands and said it would. Shit. Said I should be supportive of some of her projects, she'd turn it completely around, put it all behind her once and for all."

He gave him a hard, appraising glare. "When you came along, I thought you were too old for her. She's always . . . well, younger men. You know. Shit." Robert looked at him like he was a project that failed. "Get the fuck out of here."

"Look, I need this job." He thought suddenly of his daughter, of her children. His stomach tightened. "I really do. I'll stay away from her. I swear. But I *need* the job."

"Tough. I'll see to it you get a month's severance from the bullshit council. But your being around is just plain bad news. I'm serious. Once she starts something, it just won't end. If you're here, she'll be like a bitch in heat every time she gets a drink inside her. I won't lock her up, so you've got to go. Out of town. Out of the fucking state. Don't try to find work here. I mean it. I'll bust you. I've got friends. I can do that."

Robert looked hard across the room. "I know about you, about your reputation. I checked and I let you come here anyway. You're supposed to be over the hill." He slapped himself on the forehead. "I don't know what's wrong with me. I must have been out of my mind. Invite the fucking fox into the henhouse and expect him to be on a goddamn diet." Robert looked at him once more. His tone turned dangerous. "You're gone. If I can't do it legally, then . . . well, I've got *those* kinds of friends, too, you know what I'm talking about? I've got the money. You'll wind up . . . ." Robert put his head down again. "I can hurt you," he said. "Bad."

He felt a thrill of fear run up his spine.

"Just . . . just go," Robert said. "Make it easy. You'll get a check. Just go."

He swallowed. His fear kept rising like bile. "I need the poems. On the legal pad. I need them."

Robert kept his head down, said nothing.

"Would you send them, too?"

The attorney merely waved his hand weakly. "Get the fuck out of my sight."

He turned and left. Gladys was in the hallway. Vanilla White was reading some of her long sentences, and the audience was back in place, nodding toward her in sympathy to the black struggle in America, probably wondering what kind of excuse would get them out before she started reading the Rap verse.

"You know," he whispered when he passed behind her, "it's all bullshit anyway."

She turned and smiled. "You're so sweet," she said. "And I'm sorry about Robert. He gets so jealous. But I'm leaving him. I mean it this time. I'll meet you at midnight if you like. Your place. I know where it is. We can drive to Florida in the morning. That's where Shirley lives now. She'll understand." She put her long fingers to her lips, kissed them, and then placed them on his mouth. "Midnight," she whispered.

At midnight he was driving north in his packed Toyota. He desperately hoped Robert would mail him the poems. He didn't think he had any more in him or that they would ever come again. "It's all bullshit anyway," he said to the moonlit highway. But he wasn't convinced, not yet.

IX

I look into my glass,
And view my wasting skin,
And say, "Would God it came to pass
My heart had shrunk as thin!"
                                   —Hardy

I missed teaching. I really did. And not for the reasons you probably think, either. It wasn't the women, the girls, although I have to admit that, more often than not, they were a "principal motivating factor," as my wife's psychology professors were fond of saying. At the time, all those years, I genuinely looked forward to going into the classroom, in seeing the mixture of fear and admiration that always filled students' eyes—men and women—since they knew there was something I knew that they didn't.

In the early years, even when I was just a teaching fellow in graduate school, I got off on it. It was a kind of high, a performance, you know? But that wore off after a bit, and when I had a real job, started teaching for a living, then I realized that how much I enjoyed it was directly proportional to how good I thought—or believed— I was at it. I still think I was pretty good. Up until the very end, I didn't get that many complaints. And it wasn't because I gave a lot of A's, either. It had to do with my attitude. You see, I respected the students, even the bad ones.

In a state university, even a good one, there's lots of bad ones.

I mostly taught poetry, of course. Not the writing of poetry: just poetry. Literature. And after a while, that got old. I got pat with it, lost what some teachers call their "evangelical edge." Teaching literature, maybe history, too, is a lot like preaching. You have to sell the idea of committing your soul to something that won't make you a living, only a better person.

"Better person." That's a goddamned laugh. Look what it did for me.

I also got old, and I realized that the doe-eyed female young-sters who could give me that "high" and just as often make me hard as a post were getting fewer. I also probably was getting pretty gross. That was one thing my former colleagues were right about. I got sloppy about everything sooner or later, and my hair all fell out, and the teaching just went right along with everything else. Including the poetry.

After I couldn't teach any more—that is, after I knew I couldn't teach any more—I should have quit. Going through the kind of humiliation I had to endure was too much. It would have killed a sane man. But I wasn't sane: I was desperate. I kept thinking the poetry would come back, would save me. I had no idea in the world that the all important connection had less to do with the women I was taking to bed than with the whole teaching thing, with just being in a classroom. Even those air-head, would-be poets who fawned all over me after a workshop or reading someplace weren't interested in me. Or in my poetry. They were interested in what I could give them, teach them. I didn't understand that until it was way too late to do much about it.

You know, the most ironic thing of all is that I've always been a slow learner.

Even years later, after I was out of the academy for good, on my own and trying to scare up any kind of reading or job I could, trying just as hard to scare up a bed partner—which, to be honest, was easier—and trying even harder to stay sober most of a whole week, or day, was when it finally dawned on me, at last, that teaching was important to me. I missed it, that I had to have it.

It's a hell of a thing to miss, you know. Teaching, even in college, is the hardest job in the world. And it pays less than you could earn picking up roadkill for the highway department.

I just never could master what I finally came to think of as "dilettantism," the idea of being an artist, confident enough of my own abilities, confident enough of my own poetry to sit back and not worry. I needed an audience for what I did—not just readers, but a living audience. That was the real connection all along. The sex, the women, the drinking: None of it had anything at all to do with making the poems come. It was the teaching all the time. When I let my teaching go, then I was on the slide for good. The one thing that ruined me could have saved me. Ain't that a kick in the ass?

I lived with a total of thirty-one different women before I got kicked out of my teaching career and told not to come back. Ever. That number includes a half-dozen or so who only let me stay a month or less, but it also includes one or two who let me hang around and eat their cooking and piss on their toilet seats for as long as a year.

More than once I was living with two at a time: Agility is important for the modern poet.

They were all younger than I—some by decades—and they were all good looking. I always had standards like that, like I said: uncanny luck. But standards or luck or no, none of them ever did much for me. I got a couple of good poems out of the best of them, no poems at all out of the worst. And all the time, I kept thinking it was the sex. It wasn't, it was the teaching they wanted me for. For most of them, I was nothing more than a pedagogical prostitute, a live-in tutor, and when they decided they had learned as much as they could from me, they kicked me out. Whammo! Just like that. Not once in all thirty-one times did I ever break off a relationship myself. Every goddamned time, I got kicked out. It's kind of humiliating when you think of it. It's more than that: It's pitiful.

The best of them, though, were good to me. And I don't mean just sexually, either. They were kind. They made me feel good, and even though I was never faithful to any of them, I think I respected all of them, even those who were cruel at the end. A lot of them were cruel, too. It's easy to be cruel to an old drunk poet. It's like running over a squirrel in the street. You may feel bad when you do it, but by the time you get home, drink a beer, eat a meal, you've forgotten it ever happened. Squirrels don't belong to anyone. Nobody misses them when they're dead. So, in terms of sex, that's what I was to most of them: a squirrel in the fucking street.

The absolute best, I guess, was Jeanette. She was Italian by birth and temperament. Her early education came out of a convent. Sisters of Mary. They know how to fuck somebody up almost as well as the Jesuits do. She had a hot temper and a high intellect. She also had nice legs and breasts that looked like they were sculptured: could have been a "Playmate of the Month." She was the quintessential European, too: passionate and uninhibited. She came over to this country when she was eighteen to study at the University of Massachusetts. Some hotshot from MIT met her at a mixer of some kind, saw this dark-eyed, black-haired beauty standing around speaking with a Mediterranean accent, and latched onto her. He seduced her the same night, married her two months later, and brought her down to the Southwest where he went to work for this big electronics outfit. He made beaucoups of money and was a big-deal executive when I found her looking up at me in my Modern

American Poetry seminar. After class, over a cup of espresso, she told me that her husband was an asshole: He expected her to entertain the corporate wives, be his grease on the ride to executive heaven. He also expected her to sleep with key vice-presidents, which she was more or less willing to do, if she liked them, but not willing to do merely to help out her chickenshit husband.

We were in bed regularly before Thanksgiving, and she moved out on Got-Rocks Hotshot before Christmas. We set up an apartment, and I guess, for a while, we were happy as hell, although I have to admit our fights resembled high opera.

Making up was great though. She did things in bed I swear only a Roman could think of.

And she goddamn loved my poetry. And she was good to me. The problem is that she wanted kids: a family, something to meld her Italian background and her new American identity. When she asked me to leave, it was like something from La Dolce Vita. No shit. No condemnation: We both cried. It wasn't until I heard that she went back with the Platinum Card Asshole that I realized that she had used me, gotten me to teach her how to be a liberated American wife, responsible for herself and proud of what she knew, what she could do: Gave her the courage to tell her husband to go to hell and to be a person in her own right. And what did I use her for—other than the sex? Poetry, of course. I got more poems out of that relationship than any other I ever had, and I spent more time teaching her things than sleeping with her, too. I think I even loved her a little.

Then, I fell in lust, sort of, with Andrea. She was Costa Rican, or so she said. Actually, I think she was a Mexican, but in that part of the country, being a Mexican was just one cut above being white trash, so she claimed to be a Costa Rican, and that sort of worked. She had green eyes and reddish-brown hair, and she hated my guts. I never understood why she let me come on to her, and I sure as hell never understood why she allowed me to move in with her.

She was Catholic, too. I wonder why it is that a Baptist boy like me is so attracted to Catholic women? Of all the women I've had more than a one-night stand with, I think more than three-quarters of them were Catholic. My wife was Catholic, and maybe that has something to do with it. And, like Jeanette, she had been seduced by this huge jock when she was just out of the convent. Same story with Andrea. This time, his name was Billy, and he knocked her up before she knew much about sex, let alone birth control. He paid for the abortion, but that didn't help her guilt much. They broke up, and that's when I came into the picture.

Andrea was in my poetry workshop, and she was wonderful in her sensitivity to verse. She couldn't write worth a shit, but then, almost none of them could. We knew each other less than a week before we set up housekeeping, and things went along all right until I showed up one afternoon and found everything I owned piled out in the parking lot in front of the apartment. She wouldn't let me in or even speak to me. I couldn't even find out what was wrong. She dropped the workshop and married Billy over Christmas. I never knew if the baby she had in the summer was mine or his. I suspect it was mine, but he had been there first, so to speak, so I guess that's the way it went.

Besides, I already had one kid that wasn't mine—not in anything but the most real sense of the word, the guilty *sense—and that's enough for anybody.*

Nobody wants a retired professor for a father for her kid, not when she's barely twenty and has a healthy jock on the string.

I got no poems at all from that relationship, even though it lasted two months. But I didn't teach her a thing. Not really. I think she was a slow learner, too.

All that time, though, all the time I was with my students, boffing them, living with them, traveling around and sleeping with one woman after another, I was kidding myself. Andrea was just like all the rest. My attraction to her was what I thought I could tell her, teach her. Not my great prowess as a lover. Hell, by then, I was impotent half the time anyway, or too drunk to care one way or another. That's just the way it went. I just didn't recognize the truth of it. Maybe if I had tried harder to teach her something, she would have let me stay. Kid or no kid. Maybe I would have gotten a poem or two out of it, at least.

By then, you see, I needed a poem. I was on the slide, and I thought I could see the bottom.

I told myself it was the sex causing it all. The sex and the drinking and the drugs. I was drinking a lot, an awful lot. I was losing whole days, but that didn't stop me. It just made me drink more: "Down in lovely muck I've lain," and all that. My capacity was as big as ever, and it was harder and harder to get drunk. One night I drank a whole fifth of bourbon and didn't even get buzzed. That scared me.

But the booze, scary as it was, wasn't as important as the sex. I told myself that so often that I believed it. I mean, it was self-evident. When I was having a great relationship with some woman, the poems came. When I wasn't, they didn't. What I never understood was that when I was having this great time with a woman, I was teaching her something. And it was the teaching that made the poems come, not the sex. The sex was just a catalyst, a sideshow. If I had known that earlier, I would have understood it. I might have saved myself.

It took a long time to realize what was happening. The last chances to teach, though, those were tempting. I would have played Van Gogh and cut my whang off to have it, I decided. But that wouldn't help, either. And it wouldn't restore me to what I wanted. It was too late. I had fucked up, and I had fucked my way back by fucking too much. Women and booze: shit.

Eventually, I'd let my famous standards drop so low, I didn't care. I felt like a junkie, and I guess I was. For sure an alchy. My habits fed on me and I fed on them. I just didn't know that it wasn't the habits that were the cause of the slide. I was the cause of the slide. I was fucking myself.

When the bottom came up at last and for real, it came hard. Every day I'd get up, shave, look into the mirror and think I'd hit it at last, that there was no place lower to fall to. But then I'd know that it was still coming, that the worst was still yet to happen. Because, see, even after losing everything—wife, family, job, even the fucking poetry—I still had my pride. I hadn't learned that until you lose your pride, you haven't hit bottom.

That's a lesson you have to experience to learn. No one can teach you that, no matter how fast you catch on.

It was in the middle of South Dakota, at this little Lutheran school, when the bottom finally jumped up and hit me in the eyes. I didn't hit it then, not yet, but I got a notion of what it was going to be like when it came. And it was going to hurt. I was pretty close to the end of my string by then. I was doing two workshops and a reading for $335.17, exactly the cost of replacing the alternator and plugging the radiator on my car, which I planned to drive to I didn't know where. Everything I owned was in it. I didn't even have a post-office box that year. I just broke down in South Dakota, hiked over to the college and struck a deal with the department head in the English office. He was glad to have me, said he remembered me—and let me tell you, there's nothing to strip you of pride like being told that somebody fucking remembers you, like you're dead or something—and agreed to the price.

And I was pretty good. Because I was teaching again, see? It was one of those little clientele schools where the students are jerky and cock-sure that if they fail—or even make a C—that their daddies will cut their contributions to the endowment, and that's that. But they were smart little fuckers: high SAT's, National Merit quality. I read some of their poetry, which, bad as it was, was better than the average shit I'd seen over the years—and I was polite about stomping on it. They were respectful, although I suspect my rumpled, agéd self did little to make them take anything I said seriously. Afterwards I got one of the women on faculty to give me a ride to my car.

Her name was Barbara, and she was so skinny I wondered how she could stand up in the South Dakota wind. On the other hand, she provided so little resistance to force that I guess the gusts out of the north just went around her. We had to stop by her place for her to "change," which meant, of course, that we went to bed: for an hour or two. I was feeling pretty good, then. I'd been sober for a while, and even though she had no tits at all and a butt like cottage cheese, I enjoyed it. She wasn't that pretty, you know. In fact, she was goddamn homely, the ugliest woman I'd ever taken to bed. But I'd given up on standards at that point. There had been a couple of likely prospects in the workshop, but I didn't have the old confidence anymore: I was willing to settle. But she was good to me, liked me, and we lay around for a while and I held forth on the "state of modern poetry" for the first time in a long time.

It was all *bullshit. I hadn't* read *a new poem by anybody important in years, and I was out of touch, out of the loop as the* patois *went then. My brain had stopped working. I just didn't give a shit any more. I had trouble remembering her name.*

Afterwards, she offered me a drink, some wine, but I wanted something stronger—whiskey, tequila, something to make me feel like I thought I ought to feel. I had talked so much, I guess, taught *so much, that when I lay back and closed my eyes, a poem came. Just like that. It was the first one in what seemed like forever. I drafted out a line or two, told her again how much I wanted something to drink, and she was so taken in by it all, she jumped up and went out to buy some real hootch, something with some goddamn kick.*

When she returned, I finished the poem, an epyllion, really more of an exercise in esemplastic verse, and I had the idea it might be the first stanza of something important, a real narrative account of my life, seen through the eyes of a self-pitying failure. It had potential. She invited me to stay for a couple of days, said her roommate—another professor named Kathleen—wouldn't mind, since she was out of town attending a family funeral.

I hung around for most of a week, got my car out of hock, and had the first real food I'd eaten in months. And I worked on "Dakota Blue," which was really taking on a nice shape. Barbara cleaned and mended my clothes, helped me organize what passed for my earthly possessions, typed up my revisions as I made them, and took me to bed every night, where I would grapple with her skinny body and try to make the rest of the poem come. It was fine, you know, even if she wasn't that good looking, even if the poem wouldn't come along like it should. She was kind to me, and she loved to hear me talk, listen to me teach.

*Kathleen returned on Sunday. Barbara had gone to the library, and we had the place to ourselves while we got acquainted. Unlike Barbara, Kathleen was gorgeous—Queen of the Prom fresh and well stacked—*voluptuous *is the word—and her field was modern poetry: ten years younger than Barbara and centuries apart in attitude. She broke out some decent grass—and I had tequila—and the weather was turning nasty, so we built a fire, and I read part of "Dakota Blue" to her, instructed her on the finer points of the application of the heroic past to the satiric present. And while* Sixty Minutes *was coming on the tube, she and I started necking on the sofa. It was like old times. It felt so fucking* good, *you know? I was just enjoying the whole thing too much, and then she asked me to read more of the poem, talk about it while she worked on me, and she was in the process of demonstrating the finer points of* fellatio gratias *when Barbara came in just ahead of the first blasts of what would become a record-setting blizzard.*

When I saw the look on Barbara's face when she walked in and caught us in our "pubic beards," I realized I had hurt her. Really hurt her. I think that was the first time in my life I realized I had hurt another human being—other than my daughter, of course—that someone cared enough about me to be *hurt. Something inside me broke apart. I mean it. That's how it felt. Like a wall shattered or something. I don't think anything I had ever done made me feel that low.*

I thought that was the bottom, for real. It wasn't anything like what I had expected. It was worse. But it wasn't the bottom. It wasn't even close.

She threw me out, of course. I had to walk around in the apartment parking lot in nothing but a shirt for about two hours until Kathleen talked Barbara out of burning my clothes and brought everything out and gave it to me. She also gave me fifty dollars and a kiss on a cheek.

I felt like a whore, because I was one. I felt like shit, because

I was. But I had only passed the hashmark. You see, I still had some pride left, enough to feel bad about it all: "We poets in our youth begin in gladness;/ But there comes in the end despondency and madness."

I was on my way down for the last time, and when I hit, I was going to splatter. The bottom always comes up hard, as I said.

After that, I decided to change for real. But it was too late. I was too far down, too far gone. I had the velocity, you know, like a melon falling from an airplane. So I mostly went through the motions. I was only beginning to realize that the poetry wasn't that connected to sex at all. It was connected to something else. I just hadn't figured out what, but I made up my mind to try. I could see what was coming, and I wanted to avoid it. The only way out I knew was poetry, even though it was poetry that brought me that low in the first place, and even though it was poetry that made my ultimate arrival at the bottom inevitable.

The Grant

He sat on a bar stool in the club of the cut-rate motel in the small eastern Tennessee city and listened to the music while he contemplated his surroundings. Cheapo-depot, he thought to himself, small town chic, but better than he had any right to expect. They let him park the camper in the lot for ten bucks, but not without an argument.

"Rooms are only thirty-two-fifty," the pimply little girl at the desk had argued in a wide-mouthed drawl. She must have been working on twelve sticks of gum at once, he thought. "We ain't supposed to allow nobody to park and sleep in the lot," she chewed on. "People sell them drugs out of outfits like yours." Her chipped metal nametag identified her as Denise, Assistant Night Manager. At maybe nineteen years old, she was, perhaps, the most unattractive woman he had ever directly spoken to.

He told her he was there at the invitation of the college. He didn't want to be robbed, and he didn't believe in drugs. "Just say no." He smiled, turned on the charm. He assured her he would love to pay for a room, but he truly lacked the funds. "I'm a writer," he explained, "a poet. Poetry just doesn't provide a great income."

"Poet?" She cocked a crusty eyebrow. Dandruff or psoriasis, he couldn't tell.

"I am."

"Never had no poet staying here, before. All of a sudden, we're overrun with 'em. What kind of stuff you write?"

"Oh, traditional verse. You'd like it. Maybe you could come to the reading."

"Couldn't afford that," she said and offered him a well-rehearsed speech: "Can't even afford to go the show. They want six dollars just to see a show. Can you beat that?" She looked out the window. The streets were dusty and dry. It was hard to believe there was anything like a college within a hundred miles. "They charge us townies like shit to come to stuff over to the college, too. Think we're bunch of white-trash hicks. Don't know nothing. It's our *tax* dollars pays for that college outfit."

He knew better than to think there would be any charge for his reading. "I'll get you a free ticket," he promised. "C'mon, let me park out there. Around back."

She studied him and chewed a fingernail. Her teeth were stained, and she had a slight mustache. "Well, okay. But it's ten bucks. Cash. No credit cards."

He peeled a ten-spot off his small roll. She stuffed it into her blouse. Just like in the movies, he thought.

"Way 'round back, hear? You can forget that ticket, I guess. I really don't know nothing about poetry if it don't rhyme or nothing. Like in a song. I never was no good in English."

"Can I get a receipt?"

She smiled craftily. "Don't push it, cowboy."

He had finally received an NEA Grant. It took over two decades and a small fortune in photocopying and postage, and he had to practically get down on his knees and beg Felix to let him use his Manhattan address, but it worked. He kicked himself for not using the New York zip code before. He should have figured that out. He had figured out almost everything else.

But the money was there. It came in right on time, and by the time he paid the taxes on it, paid off some bills and put a down payment on a used pickup with a camper, he barely had enough left to send out the mailers to try and get another tour. This time on his own. It wasn't much, he told himself when he started out, but it was a start. A way back. It was the only chance he had left to keep from cracking up.

"Crashed and burned," he sometimes repeated to himself. It was an expression he recalled from high school. It had to do with failing to find a date, being turned down after weeks of anxious build-up. The irony of using it in a different context appealed to him. He had had no trouble finding "a date" for a long time, but he was no stranger to prolonged anxiety. The prospect of crashing, burning, finally losing what little pride he had left was tangible.

He had no new poems. Nothing worked anymore. The ideas and visions he had sometimes seen flickering on the horizons of his imagination vanished completely when he sat down and tried to form them into verse. Like mirages on the highway, they evaporated when he approached them, reached to touch them. As he drove from school to school, he scoured garage sales, used bookstores, junk shops, hunting for ten-and-twenty-five-cent paperback anthologies to re-read, searching for the inspiration he once had relied on utterly. But it wouldn't come. It wasn't there. The verse in the books lay on the page, flaccid, dead. It wouldn't sing.

He hadn't been to bed with a woman in two years. That, he told himself over and over, was the cause of the whole thing, the complete blank-page impotence that came over him. He needed to get laid, and well laid. There never had been inspiration in the printed page. He had always found it in moist, tangled sheets in cheap motels. Sitting down and quietly reading poetry was never a substitute for that.

For a while, he tried hookers, but that didn't work. He tried older women, the worn-out hags who hung around the fleabag rooming house-hotel in Austin where he set up headquarters. Those who would have him made him gag. Half of them were addicted, if not to drugs or some medication, then to booze. Those who were the least bit attractive looked at him as if he were a leper. He couldn't score with anyone who might inspire him. No way. He had lost it. He was old, gross, worn out. Beautiful women were apparently a figment of his memory, and so, apparently, were the poems. They wouldn't come to him, and that fact was more real than apparent.

But he still had his old stuff. All of it was out of print, forgotten, and a new generation of young poets and would-be poets were teaching the creative writing classes. They had only heard of him, most of them, remembered reading his work a decade ago when he was hot, and they were thrilled when they read in the self-printed flyers he sent out that he was available.

Available, he thought. *Shit*. He was desperate.

"I remember you!" they invariably said when they called him on the pay phone at the rooming house. He usually had to kick aside two or three winos and crack heads to get to it when it was ringing, fight them off while he was talking. "I heard you read when I was in college—or maybe high school. That was a long time ago. You were hot stuff a few years back."

He had been. He still was, he assured them. He had been out of circulation for a while, but he was now an NEA Fellow, working on a new book, a major departure from his old stuff, and something different from the current directions in poetry: a comeback. It was still closed form, but different forms, new ideas in new poems. He wooed them with his old argument: Strong stuff. Good stuff. True verse.

"The mighty line," he quoted Gideon's old compliment. "It's back, and it's better than ever." There was hope that X. J. Kennedy or maybe D. Snodgrass would do the introduction, he blatantly lied. The professors croaked back in their adolescent-sounding voices that they would *definitely* get him a reading. It would be an honor, they said. He lined up twenty-four schools for a twelve-week, four-state tour across the South, gassed up the pickup, and set out.

And he worked cheap: a hundred for a reading, fifty for a workshop, fifty more to judge a student contest. Lectures he threw in for free. He covered his own expenses: slept in the camper, ate canned soup heated on a hot plate plugged into the cigarette lighter, drank cheap beer, and smoked generic cigarettes, kept the battered old Dodge rolling on retreads. Retreads, he thought when he sat on the spares in the bed of the truck and ate his soup: That's exactly how he felt. But he was confident. It would take time, but it would work. It had to. He was building something new. He could make it back. One school at a time. One reading at a time. If he could only find the poems. If they would only return to him.

He lit a cigarette and ordered another shot and draught. It was ladies' night at the bar. A country band grunted and groaned in the corner, and a few rednecks polished their belt-buckles on their sweethearts' tight, flat bellies while they shuffled around on the floor. Two or three single women eyed him, decided he was too old, too fat, too bald, too whatever, then returned their bored stares out to the multi-colored lights that flickered on the dance floor. It didn't matter to him. He had other plans, reluctant as he was to implement them. But every sip of beer moved him closer to a decision.

This small city was just like Frank Gideon's old hometown, he reminded himself while he watched the imitation Southern cowboys push their partners around on the floor. How in God's name did a critic of that caliber ever emerge from such a backwater as San Angelo, Texas? It was laughable, ludicrous. This was Tennessee, but it didn't matter. Small town America was small town America, he reminded himself: Skoal, Budweiser, Tony Llama, and Willie Nelson. It was a national cult that defied geography.

There were three other poets at the same motel: Jack Something, Ray Something, and a Pakistani-American named Afgar. He'd seen none of them, knew none of them, not even by reputation. All were more than twenty years younger than he, but tomorrow he would headline the session, and they would follow. He'd pull out his best stuff, poetry he knew had worked before. Start with comedy, then hit them with that long sad one about the kid who kills himself right in front of his father. It always left an audience worn out, wrung completely of emotion. If he followed with the narrative he finished two years before, the long one set on the Kansas plains that turned its phrasings with such compressed wit, such controlled chagrin, he would exhaust them, leave nothing for any reader who followed him, no matter how young, energetic, and potentially successful any of them were. He called it "Sea Bed: Meditations on Undulations." It was the only new poem he had, and it was unfinished. But it built his confidence to know it was in his arsenal.

He was back, he told himself: Fucking-A.

The kid at the college—Associate Professor Steven P. Randolph, if you please—who ran the creative writing program had set this up on his own, with little help from a hostile administration, showed up and invited him into the motel restaurant to eat. It was probably the best spot in the whole county—redplush leather booths with actual tablecloths, dark paneling and candlelight. A three-star menu in a one-horse town. The other poets weren't there yet, and he was relieved. They had drinks, then more drinks, and then dinner with wine, and he'd told the kid about his experience with cretinous colleagues of his past.

"You were right to get out," Randolph agreed. "Even if it meant resigning tenure. I get *no* credit for publishing creative work. I mean, I've got a collection of stories and twenty poems published, but they don't care. They gave *full* merit credit to Rita Johnson—the new *assistant* prof—for a *quarter* page in *Notes and Queries*. A *quarter* page! Can you beat *that*?"

He liked Randolph: he talked in italics. He nodded in sympathy. "Is she black or just a she?" he asked.

"Gay," Randolph whispered. "But only our chair*person* knows for sure, if you get my drift."

He nodded. "It's a cold, cruel world, kid," he said.

"If you're white *and* male, it is." Randolph shook his head. "If I were a woman or a minority, I'd have a *decent* job. I've got *my* Ph.D., published my dissertation. Or I will next year. But *here* I am, at the corner of Copenhagen and Kudzu, my thumb in the air."

"Better than where I was with mine: Up my ass," he said and emptied the wine bottle into their glasses.

"Anyway," Randolph said and signaled casually for a new bottle, "I'm getting the money for this whole gig out of Student Services. The director's a friend of mine. *She* doesn't know it. And when she finds out, she'll have a fit. But *I* don't give a damn. I've got tenure. What can they do? *Fire* me?"

"Believe me, kid," he said with a sad shake of his head. "They can do a hell of a lot more than that." He started to tell him more, but instead just recharged their wine glasses. He gave up years ago offering advise based on his experience. No one listened to the horror stories. They all believed too much in happy endings. He wondered if he did, too.

Randolph's college was mostly a tech-ag college in the southwest end of the state where the Cumberland Gap gave up trying to be pretty and descended into Arkansas ugly. Too far from Memphis to be trendy, it was actually closer to the crackers of Mississippi and inbred jugheads of northern Louisiana. The surrounding terrain flat, red, and dusty, more like West Texas than anywhere in the South, he thought. The college itself was small, totally overshadowed by U-Tennessee and Memphis State, Ol' Miss, Alabama, and Auburn. But they had a good enrollment, and they were making money, more than any other college their size in the region. Still, it was an underdog with a struggling football team and a new president who wanted to tear down the art building and put up a new gym. Randolph moaned when he turned the conversation to a complaint about his pay, his course load, the general lack of support anyone who did anything important received.

"Anyway," Randolph concluded with slurring speech. The second bottle of wine was gone. He ordered two brandies and wound up drinking both of them. Randolph was getting sloppy, holding onto the side of the table for support. "That's why the *goddamn* honorarium is so low. We just didn't have enough to go around. And my buddy wouldn't kick in the money for just *one* reader. But these guys who're on the program with you are unknown: nobodies, kids, really, hotshot shitheads, for the most part. Part of that Southern Poetry Circuit that thinks so goddamn much of itself. You're a *big* name. They'll have to take notice when they see how much the students like you."

"You think they will?"

"Hell, yes. They're *hungry* for good stuff. They'll eat it up." He lowered his voice. "Listen," he whispered, "I've got *friends*. I'm connected with a whole fucking *network* across the South. Alabama, Georgia, Florida. The Confederacy of Creative Writing Teachers'

Association. I can get you a reading a week, if you like. You're *good*, and your stuff should get a lot of play. I can do you a lot of good."

"And what do I have to do for you?" He was interested, excited in spite of himself. Randolph might be a kid, but he was serious. This could be the key to the whole thing. If he didn't blow it. He made up his mind not to blow it.

"Nothing," Randolph slurred. "Not one goddamn thing. Just be yourself." He gave him a cockeyed grin. "We'll show them. *Damned if we won't!*"

They staggered out into the lobby, him supporting Randolph as if he were walking wounded. He wouldn't let Randolph drive, and he wasn't about to give up his own parking lot spot. He finally got a number for a girlfriend, Millie, from the young professor and made the call for her to come get him from the motel's lobby while Randolph slumped on a sofa and fought unconsciousness. When she arrived, she was a surprise: Short, pretty, and unbelievably cute with perky little tits under a snap-button yolk shirt, high heeled boots, and jeans so tight they looked painted on her firm, tubular thighs and firm buttocks. When she bounced into the lobby and flashed a smile bright enough to blind the sun, years fell away from him like so many unnecessary clothes. Nostalgia swept through him for a self he believed had abandoned him long before. Her bright brown eyes stirred the old fires in him, made him feel the familiar tightening across the chest when she took his hand in introduction: She held it too long, he thought, flashed her big eyes too much when she said his name, grinned too slyly.

It was like they had known each other forever. In a way, he thought, they had. She made him deliciously uncomfortable.

But he turned away and concentrated on an ugly painting of a pioneer woodsman on the wall. He fought to put his mind on other things. There was a glimmer of a poem approaching from the alcohol laden shadows of his mind, and he shook his head quickly, tried to clear the dust away from it. It disappeared.

"Do you need a ride, too?" she asked. "I can only carry one at a time. I got a new car. One of those little bitty ones. A Miata. Just two seats."

"No," he said firmly. "I'm here. Staying here." He pulled Randolph to his feet and steered him uncertainly toward her.

Randolph swayed and leaned over on her. "He's *staying* here," he repeated. "Right *here*. He's a real poet! *All* the poets stay here!"

"He's a little drunk," she said and smiled again, this time with apology.

"Yeah," he said. "The wine seemed to hit him all at once." Her smile warmed him, gave him an uncomfortable feeling once more.

"Wine! You drank wine," she scolded Randolph. "You know you can't drink wine." She looked up to explain. "He has no tolerance for wine. Two glasses is his limit. And that's with food."

"I fear we split two bottles." *I fear*, he thought. He sounded like an English fop. Why he hadn't added a "my dear" or two he couldn't imagine. He was old enough to be her grandfather. "We seem to have had a few cocktails as well."

"No wonder in the world!" she cried. "He'll be in fine shape tomorrow. I'd better get him home." She looked up, blushed. "To *his* home."

"I'm sorry. I didn't know about the wine," he said. "I would have stopped him." *His* home, he repeated to himself, searching her chocolate eyes once more. Did he mistake the inflection, or did she speak in italics, too?

"Oh, that's all right. He knows. He ought to." She shouldered his weight. "I like wine, too. But I can handle it."

Would you like to have a glass? he mentally asked her, a bottle? Then bit it off with a helpless grin. "Do you need some help?" Randolph was dangerously tottering, now singing slightly to himself and swinging his arms akimbo.

"No, that's okay." She sighed deeply. "I've done this before. I guess I'll do it again. He's just a big baby. Bet y'all were talking politics."

"School."

"Yep. I knew it. Departmental politics: His favorite subject, especially when he gets like this. C'mon, Stevie, let's get you home." They staggered off, him towering a good foot over her, leaning heavily on her. "Say," she turned. "You sure you don't need anything? A ride anywhere? I can come back. He only lives a few blocks from here."

He looked at her, at her eyes, her legs encased in the tight jeans, the empty circle between the tops of her thighs. Her voice was moonlight. He shook his head.

"Might have a drink, later," he offered, hating himself for it. Don't blow it, he pleaded with himself. *Don't blow it.* He bit the inside of his cheek and relished the pain.

"Maybe. I'd really like to talk to you about your poetry. It's interesting to me, especially the way you make abstract things seem so real. I have a degree in English, you know. Teach high school. Don't let this cowgirl outfit fool you. We had 'Western Day' at school today." She giggled, then blushed. "It's early yet. Why don't you call me after while? You've got my number, right?"

"Right," he said. "Goodnight, Professor Randolph. See you tomorrow."

"I just hope he can see *you* is all," she said, and she and Associate Professor Stephen P. Randolph limped out into the parking lot. While he watched her hips move beneath the tight denim, he tried to decide if she gave him one more knowing—or was it telling?—look before they left.

He was burning inside. He hadn't felt that way for a long time. It almost hurt, made his breath short.

He went into the bar, nursed four shots and beers at a buck apiece, smoked a half a pack of cigarettes, and watched the dancers, sought for a dizzying buzz, wished time would pass more quickly. He felt a terrible sense of loss, of missed opportunity. But he vowed he wouldn't call her. Randolph was a good boy—a good man—and he was a real fan of his work and, not incidentally, he could do him a lot of good. Of all the regions besides California, the South was the hardest to penetrate. Even when he was at his best, when his books were selling well and he was a name, he couldn't get more than a half-dozen readings at a time anywhere below the Mason-Dixon. They took care of their own, first, and they were notoriously hostile to outsiders. This tour was only possible because he would work cheap, as cheap as the relatively unknown youngsters who were billed with him. But Randolph promised that his connections could put him into the circuit. He liked him well enough to do that. He deserved better than to have his girlfriend boffed in the back of a broken-down old poet's pickup.

He would *not* call her, he told himself.

But the old yearning was there, like a hunger that worsened with every sip of beer or whiskey, and none of the girls in the bar—pros or not—seemed at all interested in him. The poems would come back if he called her. He knew it. He also knew that unless something or someone else turned up—and fast—he *would* call her in spite of all. He couldn't help himself. The feeling of loss was almost overpowering, and the more he drank, the less important his resolve seemed.

He felt the need of a woman more now than he had in years, not since the grant came through. It wasn't just for the poem—or poems—he thought she might summon, either. He just wanted to be with someone. Not with some impersonal whore or barroom pickup, but with her. He shook his head and knocked back another shot. No, he said. With another woman: *any* woman.

He scanned the room, but the girls alone at the bar were young, younger even than Millie. They returned his gaze with flat, disinterested eyes, sized him up for the fat old coot he was and ignored him. He imagined giving them a line, inviting them to his camper to hear some poetry. It used to work, he thought, there was a time when it couldn't miss. Here, he observed with a look at the rednecks who had begun to take narrow, sideways notice of him now that the crowd was thinning, he could get his butt whipped. That, too, had happened before.

But it would work with Millie. He knew that as certainly as he knew anything. And he also knew that sometime before it became ridiculously late, he was going to call her.

"I find that I can't sleep," he would say.

"Let me come over and keep you company," she would say.

"It's too much trouble, sorry I bothered you," he would say.

"It's okay. I wanted you to talk to me about your poetry, anyway. I'll be right over. Shall I bring some more wine?"

That's the way it would go, he knew. That's the way it always went.

He groped for the poem he had sensed when he was speaking with her. He could almost feel it, see it. But it eluded him as the band swung into their fourth bad rendition of "Cotton-Eyed Joe" that night. He was still searching as they finished and tried out a rock and roll medley which was utterly ruined by an out of tune twin fiddle.

"Something about a steel guitar just fucks up rock and roll," he said to the bartender. The squat man frowned and pointed a stubby finger at a sign over the bar. **NO PROFANITY**, it said.

He finished the beer, left a dollar tip on the bar, and got up to leave, knowing exactly where he was going. The vision of the pay phone in the lobby beckoned to him. Then a grossly fat woman barreled into him and almost knocked him over.

"My name is Tina Louise, and you're going to dance with me, cowboy!" she announced, and she swung him out onto the floor.

She was grotesque, huge, outweighed him by more than twice, and she whirled him about like he was a sack of grain. He felt as if he were being pushed around by a truck. The musicians watched the show, laughed, and segued into a high-gear bluegrass breakdown that added momentum to their mad cavort.

He was no dancer, had never been a dancer, particularly a country dancer. He hated country music worse than anything. His feet flew from under him as she whipped him around on the floor and banged him against the other dancers. His breath came in gasps. The lights swam around him, and the alcohol in his system began to make him sick.

"I gotta get out of here," he yelled over the electric fiddle that squawked a Cajun polka in his ear. "I'm gonna throw up."

Tina Louise laughed and swung him around one more time. Her palms were wet, and he slipped loose, thudding into a knot of high-hatted, heavy-booted men who had spent the evening blocking the bar's entrance. They stepped back slightly and let him fall onto the floor.

"Say, you better watch where you're going," one said in a low voice.

"Sorry," he said. "I was—"

"You're a clumsy son of a bitch. Ruined my shine," another said, holding up a bright boot toe for his inspection. "I ought to whip your ass."

"I apologize." He got himself together and stood. "I really didn't have control."

"Control this, asshole," the first cowboy said, raising a middle finger in front of his face.

"Hey, where you going?" Tina Louise barked at him when she rushed up, breathless. She took his arm and led him away from the belligerent would-be cowboys.

"I don't feel well," he said. "I need some air." He peeled her fat fingers with their gnawed nails from his wrist. His eyes sought the exit.

"Well, you come right on back," she warned. "Else, I'll come looking for you. There ain't a *real* man in the joint." She gave the rednecks a mean look while she reached out and squeezed his groin painfully. The men gave him dark looks but shuffled out of his way as he plunged toward the men's room.

He couldn't vomit. He tried. He stuck a finger down his throat, tried to force it. But nothing worked. He washed his face, used a dirty Rollo-wipe to dry it, then lit a cigarette and studied himself in the mirror. His reflection looked alarmed. What was left of his hair was white. When had that happened? He couldn't remember it turning gray all around the ring that raced backwards from his forehead. But there it was. And he needed a shave. Salt and pepper bristles stuck out all over. His teeth were gray from neglect, and wrinkles covered his forehead. He felt greasy, dirty, tired.

"When did you get so fucking old?" he wondered aloud. "'The longest journey/ Is the journey inwards of him who has chosen his destiny,'" his reflection commented dryly back.

Then he thought of Millie. Had he imagined the look in her eyes, that familiar, "I'm willing if you are" look? How could anyone in her right mind be interested in a worn out old man like him or in ten-to-twenty-year-old poetry? Hell, she couldn't have been out of junior high when his last reprint was remaindered. The poem he sensed when he looked at her flitted again across his mind, but when he reached for it, it moved away, out of sight. He wanted to cry.

"You're done," he said. "Washed up. Kidding yourself." He envisioned himself taking a swan dive into an empty swimming pool. Crash and burn, he thought, lean in to the pitch: Do the world a favor. Do women a favor. He looked at his watch: 1:30. He had a workshop at ten. Then the full-scale reading with the other three at noon. Then a long drive down into northern Mississippi for the next gig. Then Biloxi, Mobile, Marion, then back up to Birmingham—or was it Chattanooga? He couldn't remember, didn't know or care. There wasn't a real college in the bunch, not one first or even second-tier university. But it was his last chance, and success in most if not all of them could herald a real comeback.

The poem he sensed before was gone. Back into the whiskey-laced shadows. He wondered if it had ever been there, if it was the last one he would ever have so much as a glimpse of. He knew that if he called Millie, if he took her back to his truck, talked a little poetry, undressed those thin thighs and crawled between them, filled that wonderful space between her legs with pure lust that it might come back, that it *would* come back. But at what price? he asked himself.

The poems were whores, he told himself, prowling the darkened street corners of his mind. They had something to give, sure, but they charged for it. They charged too much. They had always wanted his pride, his self-respect, his health, his life. Now, they wanted his soul.

"Road back," he said aloud. "Road to hell."

A pair of rednecks came into the room just as he spoke, stopped and stared at him peering into the mirror, talking to himself. He immediately turned on the tap, washed his face once more. They went into a stall, and in a moment he heard a lighter strike, smelled pungent odor of the drug, and broke out of the door in a panic. *This is all I fucking need*, he silently screamed at himself. The booze was bad enough. Did he really want to dive into a needle or a pipe, as well? It was worse than a nightmare, and then he spotted the pay phone at the far end of the lobby. No, he warned himself and rubbed the heels of his hands into his eyes. *No*. But the phone loomed large in his eyes. It *was* a nightmare. It wouldn't let him go.

Music still thudded out from the bar, but he took a breath,

composed himself, turned left, and went into the lobby. Then he stopped, turned and looked once more at the phone. One good poem, he thought in a half-promise. Just one really good one to prove that he still could. He stopped and pondered the promise. Did he really mean it? he asked himself. Could he stop with just one? Would Millie be the end of something or only a new beginning—a U-turn? Was there anything wrong with it, with fucking Randolph's girl in exchange for what might or might not be a different road back? Or would she just accelerate his fall? The debate froze him, and he realized he had become the object of observation from the lobby.

Three young men sat around in the threadbare, overstuffed chairs. A bottle of bourbon was on the table, and they poured from it into plastic cups and exchanged knowing glances when he looked over toward them, noticed them staring at his rumpled, tortured form.

"Say," he stepped toward them, stopped, hesitated. They were all well-dressed, casual, but carefully studied style: not business-men, not redneck salesmen. L.L. Bean chinos, a little Land's End tweed to soften the effect: the other poets. He was sure of it. A small clutter of chapbooks on the table next to the bottle confirmed it. "Could you spare a shot of that?"

They looked at each other, a little embarrassed, and one, a tall youngster with glasses, nodded. "What the hell," he said. "It's late. Have a seat."

He fell into a chair, took a cup half full of whiskey from the one who had spoken, and held it in both hands as he sipped it. The tall one was Jack Something. He tried to remember the flyer and pictures Associate Professor Stephen P. Randolph had sent him.

"Well, I thought he was dead." Jack ignored the newcomer and sat back with a refreshed drink and picked up the interrupted conversation.

"Everyone thought Penn Warren was dead, too," another, who he identified as Ray, said. "Spender, as well, and Auden."

"Spender's not dead, Ray," the first one said.

"How can you tell?" the darkest member of the trio—the Pakistani-American, Afgar—asked. There was laughter.

"Old poets never die," Jack said. "They just drink themselves away."

"I hear they get AIDS," Ray replied and laughed.

"Not this old boy. He's a lech, not queer."

"I don't believe half of it," Jack said. "Nobody gets that lucky all the time. Besides, he's an *old* fart. He's always *been* an old fart." He poured their glasses full. They were drunk, or nearly, paying no attention to him at all. He heard his name again.

"Well, I think it's true," Afgar insisted. He had no trace of an accent. He was considerably more American than Pakistani. "I've got a friend who was at U-Iowa when he came through. He hit on half the women in the workshop, scored with three, I hear, and hell, he was only there two days."

"I heard he did the same thing at Cincinnati," Ray offered. "Only it was four days, five women, including the department head's daughter." He shook his hand as if something was stuck to his fingers. "She was something, too: stone fox, professional model. Did a spread in *Playboy* two years later: Miss May. But that son of a bitch got there first. Took all the fun out of it."

"You're just jealous," Jack accused. "Both of you."

"Maybe." Afgar leaned forward and refilled his glass. "But I'm telling you: Greg, my friend, he says he was unbelievable. Like a one-man fucking machine. He was over forty then. I hate to think what he was like when he was young."

He thought back for a moment, remembered, reflected. Iowa: He barely could recall it. Diana, that was one of them. And she was. Diaphanous: clear and light. That's what he had told her anyway. She was the only one who took him up on it, though. The others chickened out. But she was worth it: sophomore sensuous. He had no recollection of Cincinnati, except that he had been there, but it was too foggy to recall. *Playboy*? he asked himself. Had he ever done that well? He shook his head and accepted another drink from Jack, who was waving the bottle around.

"Well, I've got a buddy from South Carolina," Jack said. "I tell you, he says he's nothing but a drunk and a blowhard. Alcohol and ego all mixed up together. Hell, when he was there, he passed out during the reading." He pointed a finger at his friends. "Fact: You cannot *fuck* when you're too drunk to *read*. He was, according to my buddy, too drunk to see, let alone read. Or fuck."

That's not true, he thought. He had been drunk. Awfully drunk. He had leaned on the podium and remembered having to struggle to stay awake between poems, but he got through it, and he didn't pass out. Shit, that wasn't that long ago. What? Five years. Seven? Eight? It was hard to remember. In a sudden flash he recalled buying dinner for—how many was it?—seventeen, eighteen people. Insisted on paying. Got *damned* insistent about it, made a big show. He told the waitress to put it all on one ticket, sent everyone away, then used an expired credit card, the only thing he had on him. Then he had to call the school and get someone to come bail him out of the restaurant's office where the manager was threatening to call the cops. Eight-hundred-dollar tab.

Damned embarrassing, he guessed, but he remembered laughing about it later, with a sweet little strawberry blonde named Mary St. Something. He had teased her about that, called her "St. Mary." She wore a bra that hooked in front, and had tiny but perfectly formed breasts, firm, red little nipples, and almost no pubic hair, just a gossamer covering, soft as down. He remembered her well, had two poems come to him because of her. The rest of the experience was a haze. But it was clear that he was *not* too drunk to fuck.

But she hadn't been at the reading, he suddenly recalled. He had met her later, at the reception. Maybe he had sobered up by then.

Who was he trying to impress back at the restaurant? he wondered. What could her name have been? What had she looked like? The only thing he was sure of was that it was a *she*. When he thought back on his life, it was nothing but a steady parade of shes: young girls—like Mary, like Randolph's Millie—like all of them. And the more of them there were, the more he wrote. That was true, too. That was where his energy went. That was where his poetry came from. But that was where he had gone, as well. Into the shadows, into the topaz haze of beer and booze and wafting smoke from delicious dope. Hey, that wasn't bad, he thought, for doggerel.

"Well, I've got the story to end all stories," Ray spoke up. "I had a reading at Chicago Circle oh, about two, three years ago. Right after I got runner-up for Yale Younger Poet," he added with a penetrating look to make sure they heard it. "They put me up in the dean's guest house. Nice place, sort of a converted garage apartment, but real nice. No Hyatt I've ever stayed in could touch it. There was a liquor cabinet, a big glass thing, but it was locked up. And there was this odd, rectangular hole in the wall by the bed. It had all these loose wires hanging out of it, looked like something had been ripped out. I wondered about that, because, you know, the place was so well kept, so nice, otherwise.

"Well, turns out he was there the month before. He got drunk— hell, from what I hear, he *came* drunk, or stoned. He went through that liquor cabinet like a fox through an arbor, drank it dry the first night. Then, he showed up at breakfast totally sloshed and wondered if there wasn't more around. And the dean's wife went out, bought more, and restocked it."

"So, he drinks," Jack said, refilling his glass again. "So what? I drink, you drink. We all drink. Everybody but Davis Collins drinks, and he's a Baptist."

"He just drinks alone," Afgar said with a laugh.

"Wait," Ray continued. "So, he comes in that night, after his reading, and drinks that restocked cabinet dry. Then he uses the intercom to call up the dean's daughter. She's, oh, maybe seventeen, eighteen. Real airhead. Foo-foo, you know. Showed him some poems of hers over dinner, I hear, and he had offered to counsel her, said he could get her published. Papa and Mama Dean were thrilled to death. He said he'd talk to her that very night."

"Over an intercom?" Jack guessed. "That was the hole in the wall, right?"

Ray nodded. "Whole house was wired. Room to room, the whole thing. Anyway, when he doesn't show up at breakfast the next morning, Mrs. Dean calls him up on the horn, but the "transmit" button's on, so the whole family is treated to the passionate cries of their sweet young daughter going at it hot and heavy in the guest house with you know who."

"Man, that's radio," Afgar said.

"Yeah, well, it sure as hell screwed me. They sure enough hid the liquor and women when I showed up. I was lucky to get a beer. Never did see the daughter."

"Well," Jack said, "it don't matter, boys. He's here tomorrow, and he's got top billing. He's also got an NEA. But keep one hand on your wallet and the other on your poetry."

"He doesn't steal poems, does he?"

"Well, it's been said . . ."

"*And* it's a goddamn lie!" He bellowed and stood. He felt his sparse hair sticking up. He was guilty of a lot of things, of everything they had said—and worse—but not that. Never that. "I've never stolen a poem in my goddamned life! Not a single line, not a single word! Whoever said that is a liar and a son of a bitch."

The three young men sat backwards in their chairs and gaped at him. He could see it in their eyes: madman.

"How *dare* you?" he yelled. "You think you know who I am, think you know all about me!" He snorted derisively. "You don't know a goddamn thing! Not a thing. I could write circles around you. I had books *in print* before you were born. I've got fucking *shirts* older than you. *This* shirt, he tugged at the faded blue denim he wore, is older than any two of you put together!"

He was ranting, and he knew it, but he couldn't help it. The pimply desk clerk yelled something over at him, but he waved her off, gathered more steam. "*Steal* poems? Damn it! I've never read a fucking poem by anybody I thought enough of to *steal* from. Who can write poetry anyway? You?" He pointed at Jack, then at the others. "You? You? Hah! You're not worthy to scrawl graffiti on my bathroom wall!" The echo of his voice came back to him from the lobby walls.

He felt himself deflate like an old basketball. Shame and embarrassment descended on him like a falling dew point, weighed him down.

"It's two o'clock in the morning," he croaked, moving his face to look at each of the young men who squirmed as he scanned them. "I'm tired, sick, lonely. But I've been there, you bastards. I've fucking *been* there. Where you *want* to go, where you *think* you want to go. Oh, 'Success is counted sweetest/ By those who ne'er succeed,' all right. But I can tell you, boys, it's not what you think. It's not that sweet at all. You don't know the first fucking thing about it. And you don't know the first fucking thing about poetry, either."

Spent, he flopped back down into the chair. The three men sat motionless, stunned silent. "Give me another drink, Jack," he said, "and I'll tell you all about it. I won't name names, because I can't remember them. But I'll tell you what was good, what was bad, and what gets worse and worse until you can't stand it any more. I'll tell you what it's like to look up and see nothing but your own asshole."

They exchanged careful, uncomfortable glances, then Jack poured a dollop of whiskey into his cup. He sipped it, held it up to the light.

"You know how much I've had to drink tonight?" They stared and slowly shook their heads, like freshmen presented with a thorny philosophical question. "I had the best part of a bottle of tequila as soon as I got here. Then I went to dinner. Two, three strong scotches—doubles. Split two bottles of wine with Associate Professor Stephen P. Randolph. You know Randolph?"

"The guy at the college," Jack guessed obligingly. "I know him."

"Right! Associate Goddamn Fucking Professor Stephen P.-for-piss-cutter-Randolph. The guy who put this little shoot-out together. Put my name right at the top of the fucking program, *way* up at the top. Way ahead of yours, drunk or sober. Top billing and bigger print. That's no accident, boys. Hell, he knows who can get his dick hard around here, he knows who's a poet and who's not. Well, he and me split a bottle of pretty damned good burgundy. Then we split another one. And right in the middle of my second brandy after our overcooked steaks, right there in the old motel eatery, he went to shit. But did I go to shit? I ask you: Did I?"

"No?" Jack ventured.

"Goddamn right I didn't. I can hold my fucking liquor. I can drink wine, whiskey, tequila, and I can still get it up. I stayed right where

I was and finished my brandy, called up his current piece of ass—little Dale-Evans-cowgirl twist named Millie—to take him home, sober him up for tomorrow's festivities. And then I went into the bar where I drank a shot and a beer, and another, and another. Four, all told. Buck for the shot. Buck for the beer: Eight bucks. Buck for a tip: Nine. That's damn near ten percent of what I'm getting for tomorrow's little run at poetry. What'd'ya think of that?"

"We're all getting the same thing," Afgar said.

"Oh no," he said. "Oh no. We're *all* getting the hundred. You bet. And we'll all get free lunch. But you'll sell a few books, and that'll put you up a bit. And you'll make buddies with old Associate Professor Stephen P. Randolph, and you'll be asked back. But I won't. You know why?"

They said nothing. He was rising to a new peak, a higher and more dangerous one, and they each put hands on the arms of their chairs as if expecting a lift-off.

"I'll tell you why. Because, in about two minutes, I'm going to go over to that phone over there and call old Millie-Dale up. And she's going to come out to my camper, and we're going to climb onto that narrow little single-mattress cot I've got in there, lay right down on the peter tracks and fart stains, and we're going to test out that old truck's dual suspension system. And there's not one goddamn thing that Associate Fucking Professor Randolph—or you—or *anybody* can do about it. Not even God 'will say a word.' Because that's what I do. I write poetry, read poetry, and when I get drunk enough, I fuck women. Beautiful women. Anybody's women. And then, I write more poetry. It's all connected. What do you think of that?"

"I think it's late," Jack said, rising.

"And you think I'm drunk."

"Yes," he replied quietly. "I think you're drunk, and disgusting, and not a little pathetic."

"Well, I wish you were right," he said. "And you are, mostly. I'm gross, and old, and fat, and I'm as pathetic as any roadkill you've ever seen. But I'm not drunk. I wish to God in heaven I was, but it doesn't work any more. I drink and drink, but it just doesn't work any more. Nothing works any more, nothing but that dark hollow feeling inside, that goddamned tight, dark, hollow feeling inside whenever I see somebody as warm and wet and willing as young Millie. But you wouldn't know about that, would you, Jack? None of you would know about that. You're so fucking afraid of failure, so fucking afraid of *life* that you're too scared to beat off. Isn't that right, Jack? Isn't that just the blue-balled shits?"

"Well, where in the name of the cream-colored Jesus have you been?" A shrill soprano voice cut through the tension of the room, forcing them all to relax. They settled down like so many dust bugs. Tina Louise flounced in and filled the room. She moved quickly up behind Jack, slapped him on the back, and pushed him back down into this chair. "I been waiting on you!"

The three poets shifted uncomfortably. She tried to sit on the arm of Jack's chair, but her heft was too great, and she could only lean on him, one massive hip pushing him over to one side. She draped a huge paw across his shoulders and squeezed him with her left arm, then pointed across the room toward where he sat.

"He's my dancing partner!" she announced loudly. "I been in there waiting on him, and he's out here bullshitting with y'all. What is this, anyway? A queer's convention? Don't y'all like girls? I come out here to get him. It's time to dance!"

"Well, you can have him," Ray said. "We're about to retire."

"Whoo," she said and winked at him. "You're too young 'to retire.' Too cute, too. It's the shank of the evening!"

Here under the lobby's blistering lights, he could see that she was even more grotesque than she had appeared in the muted colored bulbs inside the bar. Her cheeks were small red islands swimming in acne-scarred fat and rising to encircle her watery blue eyes. Stringy, badly dyed blonde hair frayed up in a dozen directions. She was squeezed into a pair of corduroy jeans no less than two sizes too small, and her enormous belly bulged out and expanded the flap of the fly to expose the extent of the zipper's strain. Everything about her was obese. Even her fingers seemed two or three times too big for her hands, which were wrapped double around an oversized cocktail glass full of dull orange liquid. But the biggest thing about her was her smile. It dimmed the light in the room, forced each of the men to look away from its brilliance.

Ray failed to read her remark correctly and took offense. "I expect I'm older than you," he said huffily.

"Well, ain't *you* somethin'," she hollered. "Hey, Denise," she yelled at the desk clerk who made a motion to quiet her. "This little peckerwood thinks he's older'n me." She formed a sly grin and winked at Ray, "I tell you what, Sweetmeat, let's head off to your room, an' we can tell each other lies all night." She made a sucking sound with her lips.

The young poet shifted. "God," he muttered.

"Oh, heck, don't pay me no mind," she said, squeezing Jack's shoulder once more and shifting even more of her weight onto him.

"I'm drunk! I've had me two CMCMFM's tonight."

"What?" Ray asked.

He wondered why Ray didn't just shut up. This was her turf, and she was going to win.

"Chase Me, Catch Me, Fuck Me." She beamed at Ray and giggled. "CMCMFM. Get it? Course, they ain't as good as a *cocksucker*," she said with a dour frown. "But they're better'n a *motherfucker*. Not as sweet." She shifted more weight even more onto Jack who squirmed away.

He was suddenly reminded of a short story he read once about a man shoeing a horse. When he lifted the huge animal's foot, the horse leaned its weight onto him. The description in the story was graphic. It had made him tired just to read it. That's the way he felt now as he watched Jack writhe under her mass.

"I don't expect you'd like them," Tina Louise said to break a silence that had fallen over the group. "You look more like you'd like Sex on the Beach. I had me that twice tonight."

"What?" Ray, who was the youngest poet of the group, was genuinely shocked. He hadn't learned a thing from the previous exchange.

"Sex on the Beach," she squealed. "Don't you know nothing? Don't tell me you've never had Sex on the Beach."

"There's no beach in five hundred miles of here," Ray insisted.

"It's a drink, you moron," Jack said. He rose and pushed Tina Louise off of him. "They're *all* drinks. 'Cocksucker' is a drink. 'Sex on the Beach' is a drink. Jesus!" He worked his way out from under her bulk and stood.

"Well, sure." Tina Louise settled into his chair and crooked a fat leg over it. Her pants wouldn't quite bend. A booted foot floated out almost straight. "What'd'y'all think?" Her eyes were wide platters of innocence. "Boy, this is a warm seat," she giggled. "You got a tiny little old butt, but you're a pistol where it counts, I'll bet."

"Going to bed," Jack said. The others rose as well. He stayed put.

"Leave the bottle," he said to Jack when the poet leaned over to pick it up. It was but a quarter full, yet it looked good. "For old times."

Jack stiffened, then stood up. "Look, I'm sorry. We were just talking. The booze was talking. We didn't know you were . . . it shouldn't matter. Whether you were here or not. We shouldn't have said all that stuff. I'm sorry."

"Apology accepted. And you were right. Mostly. But I never stole a poem. Leave the fucking bottle."

"You were kind of a legend, once. I read your stuff. Still do. You were good. Really good. I never heard you read, but I've heard about you. You set standards, took no shit from anybody." He lowered his eyes, swallowed to gather courage for the question.

Then: "What happened?"

"Hell, I don't know," he said, with an exasperated sigh. "I guess I just kind of forgot why I wrote. Or maybe I lost the guts to go looking for it." He sighed. "I just lost it somewhere."

Jack glanced at the bottle. "It was in one of those?"

"Nope," he said with a quick glance at Tina Louise who was about to cop a feel on Afgar's behind. "In one of those."

"Look what I can do," she shouted suddenly and sat up straight. All eyes turned. She flicked out her tongue and ran it over her left cheek and then her right. Then she snaked it out and ran it across the bottom of her triple chin.

"It's kind of a family thing," she said, laughing at their looks of shock and disgust. "I got a brother who can lick his eyebrows. Just like a cat. I think it's cause our folks is second cousins."

"God, I'm going to bed," Ray said and stalked off. Afgar followed.

Jack looked down at him once more. "See you tomorrow," he said. "I'm looking forward to it. And I *am* sorry."

He lifted his plastic cup and pretended to examine the liquid inside.

"It should do good to heart and head
When your soul's in my soul's stead;
And I will friend you if I may,
 In the dark and cloudy day.

"No harm done," he added.

"Yeah, well, goodnight."

"Goodnight, Sugar," Tina Louise called as Jack followed his companions out of the lobby and across the parking lot. "Don't get any on you," she advised in a loud afterthought.

He sipped directly from the bottle, thought again of Millie. He looked at his watch: 2:15.

"Well, what 'bout it? We going to dance, or what?" Tina Louise demanded after a moment's silence. As if in answer to her question, the lead guitar and bass man passed through the lobby with their instruments. The bar was closed.

"Looks like we're out of music," he said. He took another hit off the bottle. He really wanted to be drunk. But he didn't think he could stand to be alone. He looked at her smiling, fat face for a moment, let his eyes scan her from her frowsy greenish-blonde wisps of hair all the way down to her fat thighs and thick corduroy-covered calves as they descended to cover the stressed vamps of low-top purple boots. He shook his head, but not in denial, finished off the bottle at a gulp, and smiled back at her.

"They got radios on the TV sets in the rooms," she said with a wink.

He tried to imagine it. He couldn't. Just looking at her made his stomach churn, his throat close. He couldn't go that low. He wouldn't. Then his eyes drifted over to the pay phone, and Millie's brown eyes and suggestive smile crossed his mind. He felt as if he were standing on the brink of two gaping holes. He had to choose one to dive into, and neither would save him.

"I don't have a room. All I have is a camper shell with a cot."

"Camper shell!"

He nodded. "On the back of a broken-down pickup." And a half-full bottle of tequila, he added silently, clenching his teeth.

"Why, hell, son, I can do better than that," she cried, winked broadly, and came to her feet. "C'mon, I got me a fucking Winnebago!"

X

That low man seeks a little thing to do,
Sees it and does it;
This high man, with a great thing to pursue,
Dies ere he knows it.
                                        —Robert Browning

*S*uicide: *"the sincerest form of criticism life gets,"* Wilfrid
Sheed or somebody *defined it. Yeah, well, I've been there. More
than once, I can tell you. Right there. Even before I bottomed out,
long before. Standing in the bathroom with a razor blade, ready to
make the "beautiful incision," die the "glorious death."* Criticism?
Shit. *It's a subject full of romantic claptrap.*

Yet a time may come when a poet or any person
Having a long life behind him, pleasure and sorrow . . .
May fancy life comes to him with love and says:
We are friends enough now for me to give you death;
Then he may commit suicide, then
He may go

Good advice coming from a woman who wrote under a man's name.
*But I can tell you that taking yourself off is not all it's cracked
up to be. And thinking about it doesn't get you "successfully
through a bad night," the way old Nietzsche said, either. And it's
not "the coward's way out," or anything so grand as that. Mostly,
it's just one more version of the same old song. Some other way of
doing the same old shit: start to finish.*
How's that for profoundly poetic, Stevie? A "gift of life" my ass.
*You know, you can't hardly buy razor blades anymore? I mean
it. I went to four or five different places before I tried a hardware
store. That's where I found them. They still carry them as refills for
paint scrapers and utility knives. Nobody shaves with them*

232

anymore. I mean, you can buy razors, all kinds. You can buy the heavy metal, space-age looking jobbies with the dual or even triple-track, Teflon-coated blades, "guaranteed not to cut or bite," they lift and trim, press and slice, chop and dice. Sounds like a Korean-made food processor, doesn't it? Or you can buy those little plastic throw-away numbers, that kind that lets you whistle while you work and comes in packages of twenty. Fat lot of good any of those will do when you're serious about crossing the old river Styx with a quarter in your mouth and pennies on your eyes. Who the hell would want a razor blade "guaranteed not to cut," anyway? And there's electric razors, of course: cordless and rechargeable so you can't even fake an accidental electrocution. You can use half of them in the damned shower.

But the old fashioned Gillette Blues, sharper than a sophomore on both sides, guaranfuckingteed to cut and bite, to slice open an artery if you look at it wrong. Forget it. No grocery stores or drug stores carry them anymore. Asking one of those anemic young clerks in a dirty apron about them is no good either. You might as well ask where a bucket of lard is, or a fly swatter.

Lard and razor blades and fly swatters. Shades of the past that really mean something.

And church keys: You know, can openers. Not for cans of tomatoes or green beans, but cans of beer and Coke and stuff like that. I remember in high school there was this guy named Marvin Harris who used to wear a church key around his neck. "Never know when you'll run across a cold one," he'd say, if anybody asked him about it. Guys used to hang them from their rear-view mirrors: preparedness. It was required teenage equipment, like Trojans and 45-rpm records. There was nothing like the sound of a beer can being punctured with those two wonderful little triangular holes. Squoosh! they'd go, and there was this metallic click that went along with it. Made you thirsty just hearing it. Then they came out with ring pulls, pop tops, twist-offs and something resembling a punch card: totally fucked up serious beer drinking.

The church key went the way of lard and fly swatters and razor blades and 45s. And I could add fedoras and V-8 engines. At least rubbers have come back into fashion. Civilization has to hold on to something, otherwise it becomes just like old Ezra described it: "An old bitch, gone in the teeth." But rubbers made their comeback out of necessity, not convenience. Nowadays, the failure to use one may be a quicker ticket to the great beyond than a razor—or a church key.

But suicide. Yeah. I tried it: I got the razor blades after driving all over town, stood in the most filthy bathroom you can imagine and tried to ignore the junkie from down the hall who came and pounded on the door anytime anybody was in there for more than three minutes. "I might have to go!" he'd scream. "I might have to go any second now!"

I lived there six months, and I don't think he moved his bowels one time. He just kept getting more and more bloated up. He died, finally. Fell down the stairs and broke his neck. I think he just got bottom heavy and lost his balance. Or maybe he was just too stoned to care: Lucky bastard.

Anyway, there I was, standing in front of this cracked, fly-specked mirror, looking at my fringe of gray hair surrounding Mount Baldy. I had on a torn undershirt, needed a bath. I looked like an escapee from an Erskine Caldwell novel. I held up the razor blade and examined it in the light. It wasn't blue, as I remembered them being. And it wasn't really that deadly looking. I remember when I started shaving and was scared to death I'd slice off a finger with one when I changed them in my old safety razor. It didn't look so dangerous, suddenly.

I put it on my left wrist and made a little line. Didn't break the skin, just sort of scratched the surface: X marks the spot, you know. And then I remembered I'd planned to get into the tub, run it full of hot water, and then just die. "Naked came I," and all that shit. The landlady got bugged to shit if anybody took a bath in more than a half-tub of water—there wasn't any shower in that place—so I planned to get in, open up both wrists, and then just bleed to death. Leave a clean corpse. By the time the water seeped through the floor and flooded the dining room below me, I'd be dead, I told myself. The old bitch—and she was "gone in the teeth," gone in every other way—would be so pissed off about the water bill, she'd probably forget I owed her two months' back rent.

I even wrote my own epitaph: "I did not know that verse had undone so many." Not bad, huh? Sort of syrupy romantic and unoriginal, self-pitying, and utterly befitting a suicide, right?

A suicide ought to be self-pitying. Otherwise, people get the wrong idea.

But when I opened the taps, there wasn't any hot water. Not even lukewarm. Just cold and rusty. And I just couldn't see dying in cold water, or shaving in it. So I made the constipated little bastard happy and postponed my rendezvous with death until the hot water heater refilled, and then I chickened out. I still wanted to die, but I just didn't want to do it to myself. I was afraid it might hurt after all. I didn't want any more pain. I'd had enough of that for a lifetime, or so I told myself. And that's truly self-pitying.

I tried to think of other ways of taking a quick exit. Once I sat down and made a list of ways to go out. I had two categories: out with a ballad, out with a haiku. Wrist-slashing was definitely in the haiku category. So was poison, drowning, taking too many drugs, and other things like that. A gun was just out, period. I didn't own one, didn't know where to steal one, and if I could have afforded one, I wouldn't have been thinking of killing myself. But there were still the ballads: jumping off a building, throwing myself under a train or truck, maybe plowing my old pickup head-on into an embankment or a bus load of nuns or something. But the ballad category was mostly messy, and there were never any guarantees. The haiku category held the most promise for success, I suppose: short, sweet, and it gets the point across.

I spent a lot of time figuring this out.

I also worried about writing a note to go with the epitaph. Maybe a final poem. I hadn't seen a poem in my mind for a long time, but I thought maybe if I really got serious about snuffing myself out, one might come to me. It was chancy, and I wasn't sure just how serious I had to be, how far I would have to go before one might take the trouble to show up. Then, on the other hand, I worried that if one showed up, it might be some kind of magnum opus, *some great poem that would revitalize the whole modern poetic.*

Don't laugh. It's possible. And the way my luck had been going, it would be a fitting irony. When you really hit the bottom, you tend to go for anything that's ironic.

I thought it would be a whole hell of a lot better if somebody would take the job off my hands, even so. I took to walking around in dangerous neighborhoods, trying to act like I was drunk—and sometimes, not acting, when I had the price of a bottle—like I had money on me. It never worked. Everybody left me alone. I hitch-hiked all over town, but that didn't work either. Lots of assholes picked me up, but nobody thought enough of me to kill me, even to pick on me or try to rob me. Ain't that hell? After a while, you sort of feel unwanted.

Maybe that's what took it off my mind for good. I mean, if you're not going to leave anybody mourning, anybody angry about your taking off, then what's the point? I see stories and actually run into all these "homeless" people, and I wonder why in God's name they don't just take the easy way out. What keeps them going from shelter to shelter, from dumpster to dumpster, eating garbage, sleeping on hot-air grates, covering themselves with cardboard, watching their kids starve, finally going completely loony? Why not just take a powder? I can only figure it's because nobody gives a flying fuck about them. No one would care if they were gone. In fact, most people would be happier if they did kill themselves. It would remove the guilt, you see, at least bury it and keep it out of sight.

And I guess they still have their pride. I remember once when I was in Phoenix—Tempe, really. I was still riding high then, still somebody to be reckoned with, and I'd just finished a reading over at the university. I had gone for a beer with this woman named Alice I'd picked out of the workshop. She was a sweet little redhead with gorgeous blue eyes and millions of freckles that—I soon discovered—covered every inch of her creamy skin. After my gig, we'd done serious damage to a couple of pitchers by the time she got around to suggesting that we go back to her place. So we're in the parking lot behind this bar, and we see this old, homeless guy burrowing around in the dumpsters out back. He's wearing about four layers of clothing, although it's high summer in Arizona, like about a hundred forty degrees or something. But he's even got a wool cap on his head, a beard to his waist, and is dragging around a kid's little red wagon packed with all his worldly possessions, I suspect.

We stop and watch him for a second. He's pulling out Styrofoam cartons and bags, pulling half-eaten food out of them and stuffing it into this green sack he has. In the hatchback of her Datsun was a big plate of cookies and sweetbreads left over from the reception. She had grabbed them on the way out so the food-service geeks wouldn't try to serve them again—something she said they were fond of doing—and she got the bright idea to offer them to this guy. She grabbed the plate up and we took it over to him, and she said, "Hey, you want these? They're fresh and they're free."

He lifted up the cover and looked at them with his rheumy eyes. I could see he was really scrawny. His skin was eaten up with something, and he didn't look like he'd had a square meal in a month. But he handed her back the plate and shook his head. "Thankee," he said. "But I can't eat this. Got to watch my cholesterol." And he grabbed his wagon and took off.

Cholesterol. Can you believe that? I mean how far down does a guy have to go before he loses his sense of identity, of pride, or just goddamn caring about whether he lives or dies? I think that may have taught me more about suicide than anything Stevie or *anybody else could teach me. I mean, when we drove off from that parking lot, I felt guilty. Some guy I didn't even know, who would probably be dead in a week from abject starvation and malnutrition, had made me feel guilty. That was a level of suicide satisfaction I could never achieve.*

In my case, though, I didn't want to make anybody feel guilty. I was just an old, worn-out asshole. If I did do it and it did make the goddamn papers, most people would be relieved, since they thought I had died years ago—probably they'd said it out loud to hundreds of people: "Oh, him. He's been dead for years!" Killing myself would just validate their opinions. They'd be glad I was gone for real. So I didn't do it. It wasn't because I lacked the courage. After I thought about it, I just couldn't see the point.

Plenty of poets have offed themselves, though. Some on purpose, some by accident. There was Harry Crosby, you know, and Hart Crane. I always wondered if Shelley drowned himself so Mary Godwin could have that wonderful story to tell about his heart, or if Byron went off to fight in Greece just to get killed and make all those women weep for him. What an irony: to die of a bad cold. Or was it typhus? But that's not really "Crossing the Bar," is it? And it's not crashing on the rocks while sirens sing, or being an athlete dying young, or having a bunch of drunken Vikings put you into a ship and burn it as they push you off for Valhallah and the fat lady sings, or any of that really poetic stuff. I mean, nobody who lived like they lived wants to wind up like Browning's Bishop or like old Walt Whitman, too goddamn decrepit to walk by himself, publishing his final revisions and additions as a "deathbed" edition. God, how self-serving, how morbid, how fucking suicidal can you get?

It would be far better to be like Lorca or somebody. Firing squad and the whole chorus of Tosca singing in the background. Or like Socrates: hemlock cocktail, surrounded by your lovers, or like Cicero, holding out your head and saying "cut the fuck away." Or even like "Aunt Emily," waiting on a fly to buzz and then dying in obscurity, only to be "discovered" later, when she didn't have to stand around and explain why she did anything the way she did.

But I couldn't decide what was worse: Going around and having people say—or look like they wanted to say—"Hey, I thought you were dead," or dying and nobody noticing, nobody remembering, nobody caring. I finally decided that either was bad news. So I abandoned the attempt. Stopped thinking about it for a long time.

But—and I don't mean this as a joke—life goes on whether you want it to or not, even if you're dead. When you think about it, that's about all life's good for anyway: going on. I sort of picked myself up out of that slump and went on. The bottom isn't so bad after you hit it, however hard. I mean, where else was there to fall to? The worst of the pain is in the falling, I found out, not the landing. Once you'd slammed into the pavement, you couldn't do much else that would hurt you or anyone. And bad as I got, as far as my old standards had slipped, I somehow kept my health. I didn't lose anything, not even a tooth.

You'd think any guy who lived as I lived would at least get cancer or something. I mean, where's consumption and the bloody flux when you need them? I couldn't even get a venereal disease. I couldn't catch a cold. And I never once worried about my cholesterol.

The poetry, though, was gone. So, at last, was my pride. So were the women. I had trouble imagining that I ever really had any of it. It was like a series of dreams, something that happened to somebody else. I'd drag out a book of my stuff now and then, look through it, read it as if I was looking over someone else's work. That's the way it seemed, you know? I couldn't see it as mine. There just wasn't any tie with what I was, with what I remembered. It was too good, too genuine, too real. The critics were right: It sang. I mean that honestly, not as a brag of any sort.

I made a list of the poems I thought were really fine. I even called up my old editor and tried to get him to put them together in a final collection. It wasn't going to be like Whitman's final pitiful bow. Rather, it was a kind of testimonial to what I had done, a kind of pre-memorial to one who should have been dead but who hadn't had the courtesy to check out, yet. He didn't like the idea. I was disappointed. But I kept making and revising the list, anyway. I wanted a corrective, you see. I wanted to remember when I was, since I couldn't be anymore. And I wanted to do it without women. But you've probably already guessed that that wouldn't work at all.

There was the connection, you see. Always the connection. That was the point, remember?

I got really into lists then. I sat down and tried to name all the women I'd slept with. I didn't count high school. I started, really, with Joy. Remember Joy? She was sort of important to me. But I'm not sure now whether what she did for me really made all that much difference. Who knows, I might have become a whiz on Wall Street, an attorney, a Mercedes mechanic. I might have followed my brother to a greasy death in Vietnam, or preceded him. I might have been noble—not like Byron—but noble, nevertheless, or I might have wound up like Browning or Eliot: distinguished, a kind of arbiter of taste and quality. I think that's what I really wanted all along.

It was possible. Don't laugh. Whatever you do, don't laugh.

Anyway, I put her name down and found that old copy of "Ode to Joy" and read it. It was still good, you know? And I was glad I never published it. I listed a bunch of other names, but after a while, they all ran together, and I couldn't remember so well anymore. I'd go look at the poems that various women inspired, and I couldn't remember their faces, sometimes, not even their names. I wound up tearing up the lists. I decided I didn't want to remember. It hurt too much. Even when your pride is gone, there's still pain hanging around to remind you of what it was like when you had it.

I made other lists though. I ran down all the colleges I had been to for readings, workshops, visiting professor stints. I listed all the classes I had taught—not the individual classes, just the different courses—and I then listed all the really good poets I personally knew. Then I listed all the really bad ones. There were more bad ones, but you probably already guessed that, too. I listed the cars I'd owned, the places I'd lived, the different hotels and motels I'd stayed in, the states I'd traveled in, the cities where I'd been too drunk to remember, and those I was sober enough to regret. I got really into that kind of thing. I was listing everything I could. Not counting them up, you see, just writing them down, trying to make a sort of chronicle of everything.

And then, right in the middle of the list of every poem I'd written, published or not, collected or not, a series that came right after all the awards I'd won and stuff like that, I stopped. I stared at all these goddamned lists and realized that I'd done exactly what I set out to do: I'd "made it." It hadn't felt like I thought it would feel, and it hadn't lasted as long as I thought it would, but there it was: The history of a poet who "made it." I set out to do something, and I did it. It was all behind me now. There wasn't anything left to do but admit it. I hadn't even bothered to notice: I had been too fucking stupid to notice.

You see, when I looked back on it and tried to identify a time when I knew I had "made it" for sure, when I was absolutely certain that I was on top of the world, I couldn't do it. You see, "making it" in poetry isn't like climbing a mountain or running a marathon. There's no peak, no finish line. There's just a kind of high that comes when you know you're there. I was sure I had felt it, but I just didn't slow down long enough to pay attention to it. I kept wanting more, kept wanting to make sure it would last. And then it was gone. Just like that.

What had happened to me after that, what had been happening to me after that was all a futile attempt to do something I had already done. And I had done it better than anyone ever thought I would, better than most had ever come close to doing.

What a let-down, right? I mean, it's like knowing you had something of value in your hand and realizing that you were too ignorant to appreciate it. Like that "base Judean" Othello talks about. That's the way it was. It was goddamn depressing is what it was. It's just that nobody would take "by the neck" this "circumcised dog" and smite him "thus!" And I didn't have the courage to do it myself. If courage was what it took.

But at the same time, and ironically, it was comforting. I sort of relaxed. I realized I didn't have to try anymore. Women ignored me now, or they just stared at me and pitied me. Not as a man, but as a poor excuse for a human being. I didn't have to have them anymore. But the saddest thing, I guess, was that I didn't care. You see, when I was making all those lists, naming all those names, writing it all down, I came to understand that none of them meant anything to me, not really. I hadn't genuinely loved any of them—well, hardly any—and they hadn't loved me. And that was what was missing. I guess it sounds schmaltzy to say it, but you know it's true, that's what I was looking for all along, with every one of them, even the one-night stands. And even when I could have had it, I was too fucking stupid to reach out and grab it. I'm not speaking romantically here. I think this is the truth.

But it was because of the poetry. Always the poetry. The god-damned fucking poetry. I kept thinking that if I just wrote one more poem, screwed one more woman, then I would make it really big, would be named by people I had no respect for as somebody they respected. I never knew that I was "really big" all along, really something, and I had the respect of everyone, even people who hated my guts. I talked about success, about that kind of respect often enough to impress people, impress myself. I just never believed it, never stopped long enough to appreciate it or to respect myself. It was like when my fifteen minutes of fame finally arrived, I was in the john, whacking off.

But then, right at that moment, I did believe it, and I appreciated it. I understood that killing myself wasn't any kind of answer to anything. Because I wasn't ready to go. I was ready to stay, on my own, without anyone else there to lean on, to hold me up, or, where women were concerned, to go after. I was just I, and I always had been. I didn't need some anonymous validation. I had validated myself. That should have been enough all along.

I remember that night like it was last night. It was a revelation. The "old me" would have gone out, raised the price of a bottle, and climbed into it and tried to forget. That's what I did every time I lost out on a Gugge or some other bullshit contest to some collection of assholes I could write circles around. I mean, it took me nearly twenty years to get a goddamn NEA, and I blew it in two months, produced nothing, abandoned the last tour in mid-gig, ran off with a woman I wouldn't have so much as glanced at a few years before. I gave in to something that had always been there, but this time, it was more deliberate, and you can believe this or not: I did it to save myself from something worse. Even though I walked away when I was faced with one final chance to make something decent of myself, I think the walking away was a more respectable act. It kept me from making the same mistakes over again, from crashing and burning for real.

When it would have meant something, when it might have made me feel respectable, I couldn't do it. So I usually got drunk: stinking, more disgusting than I'd ever been before. I hated the others for keeping me out and locked myself out even more.

But that was the "old me." I was different all of a sudden. I went out to the stockyards and shoveled out some cattle trucks for two weeks, and when I came back, I paid the back rent, packed up what I had, tossed it into a duffle bag, sold the truck, and took off on foot.

This was no "tramp," like Irving or Whitman were fond of, no ramble such as Wordsworth might have approved. It was just a way to get away. I was feeling good, you know. Free of everything. Free of poetry.

But then, that first night out, when I lay down to sleep on the road, all by myself with nothing but my memories for company, they came back. They came back again. Just like they'd never been gone. They trooped through my mind like a fucking army, demanding my attention, my concentration, my pride.

They groaned, they stirred, they all uprose,
Nor spake, nor moved their eyes;
It had been strange even in a dream
To have seen those dead men rise.

Strange indeed, brother Samuel Taylor, strange infuckingdeed. My fingers itched to write them down, and I couldn't sleep. And there was the whole rotten thing starting over. But this time, I was smarter, stronger. This time, I was ready for them, or thought I was. And that, I can assure you, is the real point of the whole damned story.

Malebolge

The dust storm tore out of the northwestern sky and raced unimpeded by hill or tree across the southwestern plains. There was a biting chill in the wind, something that tore a man's voice away from his throat and reminded him that there was ice up there, off the distant horizon, toward the mountains, toward Canada. It wouldn't come, the ice, not this far south, not into the desert, but the cold would. Only a fool wouldn't be ready when it arrived.

He stood fighting back a cough by the squat old fashioned gasoline pump and squinted over a cigarette into the dirty gray clouds scudding out of the northern sky. The brim of a greasy, battered fedora whipped in the wind. A faded silk scarf wound over his head, under his whiskered chin and kept the hat in place. He had no hair to give the sweatband some traction. His khaki trouser legs snapped against his shins like battered flags, and a thick plaid shirt billowed out where the wind sneaked inside and fought against its temporary capture. He calculated the gusts were in excess of thirty miles an hour. It was going to be a hard night for anyone caught outdoors.

It would rain before dark, he thought. And with all this dust in the air, it would probably seem that mud was falling from heaven. It didn't matter to him, though. One thing about being the only service station in ninety-seven-point-five miles: Customers came when they came. They didn't depend on the weather.

He visually checked the stack of mesquite firewood near the back door to the fieldstone building that served as both his residence and office-store for the gas station and what was left of the Llano Motor Courts. Originally constructed in the post-World War II boom that had put Americans on the road and going places, the majority of the white stucco cottages had been razed when the state came along and widened the highway to four lanes. The six cabins that lined out behind the yellow rock façade of the residence-office were all that remained: numbers seven through twelve. They were empty for the moment at least, and that didn't matter to him, either. Guests simply meant more toilets to clean, sheets to wash: work that kept him from thinking about his poetry.

He coughed again when he let the wind propel him back toward the screen that ineffectually blocked the door to the office. A faint yellow light from a desk lamp was visible through the sandy gloom, although it was far from nightfall. The dust and clouds diminished the sunlight to give the afternoon an early evening hue. There might be a poem in that, he thought: "Early Evening Hue." No Sandburgian "little cat feet" fog bullshit either. Out here, on this most darkling of "darkling plains," weather came in wearing high-heeled boots, winter and summer. Had anyone ever written a poem to a blue norther? It was there, he assured himself. It might come out directly. He didn't want to force it, invite it into the open until he could take a good look at it.

The poems were skittish now, like the antelope that had so recently returned to the geography. They came when they wanted to, and they disappeared just as capriciously, easily frightened, disappearing sometimes before he had them fully committed to view. Just thinking about one could cause it to evaporate like a puddle after a spring rain. On the desert *llano*, nothing fresh ever lasted very long.

The driveway was covered with caliche. He had wet it down that morning before the wind came up. Although cold and smelling of rain, the air had dried it, and dust devils rose and danced around his feet. He went over to an electric power box and pulled down a handle, lighting the neon sign that announced what remained of the motor court's existence and alerted wayward tourists that a gallon of unleaded regular cost twenty-five cents more than in the city.

City, he thought. The nearest *town* had but a single Conoco station. The prices there were no lower. Cokes were two bucks apiece, lukewarm. Tee-shirts went for a cool double-sawbuck, and a three-day old tuna sandwich was a five-spot, not including tax. "Do not go naked into the good night," he mentally quipped, for it will cost your soul to slake your thirst, fill up your tank, cover your back, sate your hunger.

It had been a slow day, slow week, slow month, slow year. The interstate ran parallel and forty miles south of the state highway and was the major route for most of the cross-country traffic. Often he didn't see more than a dozen vehicles a day, half of which belonged to ranchers, roughnecks, oil company engineers and the odd Border Patrolman. Most of them drove pickups with twin tanks and had no patience with price-gouging. Most of them lived in Midland-Odessa,

El Paso or Alpine, Ozona or Fort Stockton. Those who lived nearby kept their own gas pumps right on their ranches. Sometimes, even so, they would stop to chat, take a sip of whiskey, smoke a cigarette with him. Tell a few lies about women they had known. One or two had even bought and read his books when they were wasting time in college English courses.

It was still gratifying, he admitted, when someone wanted to talk to him about his work, however old and forgotten it was: however old and forgotten he was. He was delighted to find that many of them had actually remembered poetry they read in school. None of them had ever met a real poet. They were as curious about him, though, as he was pleased with their company. It delighted them that he wasn't a snob. They shared their thoughts with him, even confessed poetic imaginings when they realized that he wasn't opposed to good drink, to "man talk." It made life good. Or at least endurable. There was permanence about this, something he had missed for too long.

The windows of the office were dirty, and he made a mental note to clean them after the storm passed. In spite of the late norther, spring was pressing hard on the south plains, and there would be plenty of tourists—self-sufficient types—whose taste in travel took them off the interstates in search of off-beat sights, strange adventures. They were the sort who would buy books. His books. College professors and graduate students were the best. They disliked the stark sameness of auto-club-recommended routes, sought color and surprise in their lives. Poetry could be surprising, and they usually were interested in the notion of finding it way out here among the cactus and huisache, even though more of them than not were disappointed to learn that he was open and honest and apparently heterosexual. He made sure they could see the volumes clearly from their cars or when they traveled to the restrooms around back, kept the prices posted and an old picture of himself—taken when he had hair and youth—hung over the display in the office. It was a final concession to his long-lost pride.

Early as it was, he took some burlap and covered the series of cages placed off to one side of the caliche drive. His right hip bothered him a little from when he fell a month before, and he had a slight limp. Changes in the weather alarmed his joints, kept him awake nights with deep, mysterious aches. He didn't mind, although he realized that he wasn't nearly old enough for that kind of thing. That was when the poems seemed to come most often.

He had collected a random menagerie of snakes, rats, jack-rabbits, armadillos, lizards, a bobcat, and some desert birds that had fallen prey to other animals or hunters. He had a pair of injured hawks, a buzzard with a wounded wing, and an eagle that had also been shot-gunned. He was nursing them back to health if he could. He had to report all of the injured wildfowl to the game warden when he found them, but he also was the only one in the whole damned county interested in working with them. The warden brought him some pamphlets and even some medicine—vitamins, mostly—as well as a crate of live mice for the birds of prey and the snakes. He also trapped pack rats behind the station, realizing that the buzzard's wing would never heal, and accepting the responsibility of taking care of the bird for life. It was the only tie with nature he had ever had. It alarmed him in its intense demand on his emotions.

Once in a while he drove up and down the highway looking for run-over rabbits or other roadkill for them. But they didn't take to dead flesh as much as their reputation claimed. He discovered, however, that a fresh deer in a ditch dressed out the same as one rifled by some kid with a .30-30. He had developed a surprising tooth for venison, and his freezer was well stocked.

The caged animals made interesting attractions for his occasional customers. He charged nothing for the tourists to look at them, but he discovered that while the kids fed carrots to the jack rabbits or tried to entice the prairie dogs to take a pecan from a dish next to the cages, their parents would sometimes drift into the office and buy beer, cigarettes, sunglasses, tee-shirts, and other assorted junk from his store. Those were high profit items, much higher even than the gasoline. When they occasionally bought one of his books as well, that was the most satisfying, although there was no real money to be made there. He sold them for half their jacket prices and charged no tax.

"Who's the poet?" they might ask, or, in a warmer tone while they studied the blown-up black and white photo, "You know, I've *heard* of him. I read some of his stuff when I was a kid. Did you know him?"

Did he know him? he would ironically ask himself, making note of the past tense. "Yeah, I knew him."

"I heard he was a drunk," they would often say. "Drank himself to death somewhere down in Florida." Or they would recall a more popular rumor. "Somebody killed him, right? In Boston, or was it LA? Caught him with their wife and beat him to death or something like that? He had a reputation, didn't he?"

"Yeah," he would mutter. "He *had* a reputation." But as what? He would ask himself. What, exactly, was he remembered for?

He had long ago stopped being bitter when someone made the automatic assumption that he was dead. If he yelled, "Jesus Christ, you asshole, look at the fucking picture. I *am* him! And I'm as alive as you are," as he did at first, they would gather their kids, herd them into their mini-vans, motor homes, and SUVs, and drive off, looking at him as if he were foaming at the mouth. Or worse, they just stared at him as if he were a ghost and shook their heads with pity.

So, now he just laughed. And once in a while, if they really seemed approachable while they stood their with *Towers of Glass* or *Opaque Images*, or *Touring Taos and Tahoe* in their hands, shifting their gaze from the poster-size likeness to his own weathered face, he would look as shy as he could and admit that he, indeed, was the man in question: the poet. But that could cause trouble of a different kind. Or it did once.

"No!" one woman of about forty exclaimed when he made the confession the previous summer. "You don't *mean* it!" She studied him from over the tops of her sunglasses. "You can't be! Melvin, Melvin, come in here. I want you to meet somebody!" She put on the sun hat she was buying when she was distracted by the books.

For a wild, uncertain moment, he feared that this woman was one of that anonymous parade of female bodies that had inspired so much of his verse, brought about so much of his downfall, led him to a ramshackle gas station-motel in the southwestern desert. In all these years, he had never had such an encounter, but he always worried that one of the days it would happen. There had been so many women, so many different places, the odds were definitely against his avoiding it forever.

"Melvin," she grabbed her short, chubby husband by his Hawaiian shirt and dragged him across the dusty wooden floor of the office. "This is a man I heard read in college! I mean it. He was an inspiration to all of us! I mean it. He read his works *so* beautifully. He is one of the great American poets. And *I* heard him!" She stood back and crossed her arms, staring at him around the price-tag from the hat that dangled down in front of her nose, waiting for Melvin to do something to acknowledge her declarations.

Melvin stuck out a fat hand and gave him a painful grip. "Pleasedtamecha," he said with an embarrassed glance through his expensive sunglasses. "Don't know much about that poetry stuff. Never was any good in English. C'mon Edna, we got to make Deming by dark. How much's that hat?"

"I mean it!" Edna repeated in admonition to her husband. Then she turned to him, warmed him with a soft smile. "I heard you read

246

at the University of Nebraska, oh, twenty, twenty-five years ago. I was just a kid."

"We were all a lot younger," he said. His eyes drifted down to her shorts. Firm, tanned legs dropped into rope-soled, open-toed sandals. The tips of her toes strayed off the ends. The nails were too long and blood red. Why, he wondered, did women's feet get so ugly when they got older? Why did they never buy shoes that fit? A few webby varicose veins raced around her ankles.

"Oh, I say you're right about that. You had more hair, then." She blushed. "I'm sorry. That was rude."

He rubbed his totally bald dome. "It's all right. I've sort of gotten used to it. People tell me I look like a short Yul Brynner. Have for years."

"If you don't quit smoking," she said and wagged her finger in front of his lit cigarette, "it might become a prophecy." She spoke with the familiar ease of an old friend.

It already had, he silently admitted. He had been diagnosed with emphysema the summer before. There was a chance that he had carcinoma as well. His throat hurt all the time, too. Probably a tumor there. After all these years, it seemed fitting that he was dying now, by inches.

"Edna, we got to go," Melvin whined.

"You were *something*," she repeated and removed her shades. Her eyes were almost aquamarine against her dyed auburn hair. She was past forty but still damned attractive, he admitted, and he felt the old warm stirrings. He could imagine the attractive, wonder-eyed co-ed she had been. Her figure was good—lithe and athletic—he silently speculated as to how she had wound up with a lump like Melvin. "I'll *never* forget your reading. Or your workshop!"

"You were in the workshop?" Panic swam over him again. *Was* she one of the women from his past? Was this about to turn ugly? Had they frolicked in some motel in Lincoln twenty years ago? Had he made her promises he never intended to keep? Sometimes they wrote to him for months, even years afterwards. When he returned to wherever he called home, his mailbox would be jammed with cards, letters, bundles of bad poetry he had promised to read, critique, try to get published for them. But he never answered their letters. He never dared. He never looked over his shoulder, never doubled back. One trip to each well was always enough. "Nebraska?" He strained for the memory. "Lincoln?" He shook his head. "When was that? What year?"

"Oh, it was a long time ago." She smiled a mysterious, knowing smile. "I doubt you'd remember me. Or my poetry." She turned to the stack of books near the window. "These *are* for sale, aren't they? I'm going to buy one. I'm going to buy one of each. As a matter of fact, two. One for each of my daughters. They're in college, and I bet they'll love them as much as I did. Well," she winked, "maybe they won't. It won't be as . . . memorable. But it will be just as moving. I'm sure of it."

She clutched her arms beneath her breasts and sighed, still staring at him. "I cannot *believe* it's you. After all these years." She walked deliberately over to the books and began selecting. "And I want you to sign each one. Something personal. Will you do that?" She was speaking over her shoulder and didn't see him nod dumbly, still trying to remember.

"Well, I'm going to wait in the car," Melvin said belligerently.

"You never did have any taste," she shot at her short, fat husband.

"I married *you* didn't I?" Melvin called.

"Momentary lapse," she said absently and removed the hat and tossed her pretty hair. She collected the books and put them on the counter. "He's in insurance," she confided, then winked again. "No sense of rhythm."

Melvin took a can of beer out of the cooler and went outside into the heat, standing so he could watch the screen door. Melvin didn't trust her, he could tell. Seeing her up close, smelling her perfume, and observing Melvin's square little body kicking up dust in the driveway, he decided that she gave him no good reason to. She exuded sex, and he had trouble concentrating on what she was saying.

"Sign them and write something to Marla—that's M-a-r-l-a—in each one, and to Lisa—with an s, though we pronounce it with a z—in the other set."

He began inscribing one of the stock "personal" phrases he had long ago memorized, varying them slightly for each of the girls.

"Where's *Flying Free*?" she asked, glancing at the stack. "That's right, isn't it? Your first book?"

"What . . . uh, oh. *Free Falling, Free Flying*. It's gone. Long gone," he admitted. His first book existed now in only two copies, both damaged by years of being carried around in suitcase, duffle bag, and back pack, finally his trousers' pockets. Outside of libraries, no one he knew of still had one.

"That's a pity," she said. "I loved that one. I remember it so well. That's the one with 'Marla's Eyes' in it. I remember. That's why we named our first child Marla," she said thoughtfully, and her eyes took on a faraway look, as if the idea just occurred to her. She ran her tongue out and licked her lips quickly, and he shuddered.

"Uh, when exactly did you hear me read? I just can't think when I was in Lincoln."

She eyed him closely once more. Mock admonition filled her blue eyes. "I hoped you'd remember. I was Edna Colquit then. I was a junior, majoring in English literature. I *loved* the Romantics: Tennyson and Browning, Auden, Shakespeare, Whittier: all those guys." She sighed and smiled wanly. "I really didn't expect you to remember. It was a long time ago."

"Yeah," he said.

"I hardly ever read any poetry anymore." She looked sad.

"Yeah, it's not a hot item."

"I guess there were a lot of admiring young people in your workshops. You did so many."

"Yeah," he repeated. Hundreds, he admitted. Workshops. It seemed there were thousands of young people. Thousands of admiring girls, women. And she was one. That was clear. But he had no recollection of her at all.

"Anyway," she brightened and went on, "it was right before *Opaque Images* came out. You said there would be a special poem in there for me. Does that help?" Her eyes begged for affirmation.

He looked at her and pretended to think. No, it didn't help a bit. He couldn't find her name or her face in his memory. But he knew better than to disappoint her. "I think I might remember," he smiled as warmly as he could, and she beamed, satisfied, justified. "Look on page sixty-four. The quatorzain."

It was a generic poem. Even the title, "Practical Purposes," was planned to use in precisely this sort of situation. It had never come up before, however. Still, he knew it might someday, and he wanted to be ready.

"I knew it," she almost whispered. She was excited. Her breasts rose and fell quickly, as her breath grew heavy. "I bought a copy a soon as it came out, but I was never sure of which one it was."

She glanced out at Melvin, who had wandered over to look at the animals, then leaned over the counter and quickly bussed his cheek. Her hand squeezed his. Her perfume was jasmine. It filled his nostrils but brought no familiar scenes to mind, only familiar sensations in his chest and stomach. He felt as if he was falling into himself.

"I knew you'd remember," she said. "I thought of you—dreamed of you—for months. Years, really. I kept hoping you'd come back.

I never dreamed I'd see you again. I certainly never thought I'd find you way out here. I just wish there was more time . . . ." She looked deeply into his eyes and he felt her heat. "I mean, then, there was no time. I remember. Everything was so rushed, so messy." She looked out the window once more, quickly, "And there's no time now, either. Damn it."

"Edna, goddamnit," Melvin yelled at the office door. "We've got to go. What the hell are you doing in there?"

"Thank you," she mouthed silently, "for the memories." And she gave his fingers another tight squeeze and moved out through the door, clutching her books to her breasts. "For the poem, especially." She cast one last, long look toward him, turned, and was gone.

"Probably doesn't have a pot to piss in," he heard Melvin yelling as they climbed back into their van. "If he's such a fucking hotshot, what's he doing out here in Bumfuck, Nowhere?"

What indeed? he asked himself. He never heard Edna's answer, and he never remembered her, or what they might have done together or what they might do if, as she said, there had been time. But he recalled Melvin's question every day.

He also knew the answer. What he was actually doing was trying to make a living the only way left open to him. He was also writing poetry again, but that was accidental. He never planned to do that. Still, the poems were coming, he was writing them down, and he wondered what Felix was going to say about it.

Going to New York to beg for something, anything, even a handout wasn't deliberate. He just wound up in a truck stop in New Jersey, and finally admitted that was where he had been unconsciously heading all along. It was as if he was running on some sort of automatic pilot that directed him there. He had nowhere else to go.

He walked up the drive to Felix's house on Long Island. It had been a long road: over two months of odd-jobbing and hitch-hiking from Cleveland, where, the cold, rainy night before, outside a tavern in Lorain, he was beaten badly and his dishwashing pay was stolen from him along with almost everything else he owned. He found his books crumbled and water-logged in a trash bin near the spot where he had been trounced and left for dead. From that point on, he was subconsciously determined to get to New York. It was the only hope he had, and it felt good to admit it, finally, to hit bottom at last and start trying to find a way back up.

Still, he didn't want to arrive on Felix's doorstep looking like a bum. So he took whatever work he could find: raking leaves, mopping out bars, anything that would keep him clean and reasonably well fed. And he stayed sober, mostly. He managed to save enough for a decent set of clothes at a second-hand store in Newark, Delaware, hitched north out of there, and managed a bus ride across the Hudson. He dropped his last change into a pay phone in Williamsburg, New York, to make the Sunday morning call. He didn't know what Felix might say. He might tell him to go to hell, or he might just be his usual, cool, polite self, guarded and fearful of what his old discovery might want. The editor would probably be scared to death that he might have another book ready. Small chance. At that point, he hadn't written a new poem in four years, not even a new line.

He hadn't slept with any woman he hadn't paid for in longer than that. And, for once in his life, they were closer to his own age. Or older. His experience was filled with wrinkled dugs and cracked, black teeth, flabby thighs and age-sparse pubic hair. And his poems had abandoned him, he thought, for good. But when he first spotted the towers of Manhattan across the river, he knew they could come back. He just wasn't sure what forms they would take.

Thankfully, his old editor sounded pleasantly surprised to hear his once-famous poet was in town, and he gave him an address and invited him to come over for lunch. It took him most of the afternoon to hitchhike out to the house.

Felix had prospered, he discovered. After Claude Melton died, the editor bought the whole company and Melton's family estate as well. Publishing wasn't in danger of making him wealthy, but it kept him comfortable, something his branching out into computer software and educational support materials insured. Felix was, if nothing else, in "key with his time." They still published a bit of poetry, but only occasionally, and usually they didn't even consider work by anyone who didn't have an established name. Their forte, in poetry, was anthologies and mixed collections of well-known verse by brand-name writers.

He hadn't been a brand-name in years. But he was still known. Not, however, as a poet or even a critic: He was known as a failure, a has-been, or, in some estimations, a never-was, never-could-have-been.

Over a lunch of cold duck salad, he laid out his plan to do a new collection. They were joined by David Brittlestein, who, it became immediately clear, was living with Felix in the twenty-room mansion. Brittlestein was, if anything, warmer than Felix in his reception of his former rival. He was now editor-in-chief for Melton House, and between the two of them, they really ran the business without much other help. Brittlestein was also, Felix unashamedly revealed, independently wealthy, the result of a fortunate series of family deaths and bequeathals.

He wasted no time with pleasantries or chit-chat. He had an idea that Felix might create a special imprint for a whole new series of verse that might include some young writers, new poets with promise. The idea was born on the way out to Long Island. It died just as quickly.

"It's just not practical," Felix said after listening and nodding politely for a while. "No one really wants poetry any longer. If you're an actor or a rock star, maybe an NFL quarterback or something, yes. But serious poetry just doesn't sell. I thought you knew that. You've said it often enough, yourself."

"You sold my stuff."

"That was a long time ago. Kids bought poetry then. It was a hippie generation, love children, then the children of love children. They believed in art, literature. Now, they buy junk. Romances. Horror. Cyber-sci-fi. Or they don't buy anything. Poetry just isn't viable."

Brittlestein nodded. "It's all post-modernistic clatter," he said. "Bang and boom. Animation and special effects. If you can understand it, it's no good. Hell, we do better with our line of fantasy stories based on video games than with anything else. You've got to 'make it new,'" he added, "but not in the Modernist sense. In the ultra-*post*-modernist sense."

"Which means *non*sense," Felix added, and they both laughed.

"What if it's all *new* stuff," he asked quickly. "*All* new. New forms, no forms. I can write what people want." He felt desperation climbing up his back like a column of ants. Since coming this close to New York, the poems had begun to reappear, but none were clear enough in his mind to be captured. He wasn't sure if he wasn't dreaming, that they weren't mere illusions or hazy memories. As Felix looked at him, he realized that the new imprint idea was only a ploy, just a way of putting himself back into the game so he could have a way of publishing his own verse once more. The salad sat on his empty stomach like so much bulk, and he wanted a drink. Perrier was the only beverage being served, though. He kept eyeing a cabinet in the corner as if it might hide something more substantial.

Felix shook his head and rubbed his clean-shaven chin. "Are you sober?" he asked.

"What? Me? Of course." He felt anger rising. "I've never been anything else when I needed to be."

252

"Well, you might be able to do some editing for us, if you're clean," Felix suggested. "We *are* thinking of publishing a couple of new anthologies."

Yeoman editing: The image struck him hard. Sitting in some cubicle somewhere pouring over others' soon-to-be-published words. It was worse than running a workshop, worse than anything, because he would know that every word, every *bad* word of verse he saw would find its way into print while his own work was forgotten. He would have no status, make no decisions. He would be nothing but a glorified proofreader. All the while, he knew, his own poems would be trooping around, crying for recognition. He shook his head.

"No," he said. "I want to write. I *need* to write. The poems are there." Once made, the admission seemed to relieve the tension that had built up around the table.

"You haven't written anything in a long time," Brittlestein said. Then he put up his hands. "No offense. You just haven't."

"No," he admitted. "I haven't. But I want to. I will. If I can just find a way . . . a handle. I can. I know I can." He looked down at his shabby coat, shiny shirt, ragged tie. He had on almost new sneakers, but they'd become muddy somehow. Brittlestein's sports jacket cost more than he had made in the past three months. He must appear to be exactly what he was, a pitiful has-been. He prepared to beg, if they gave him the chance, but he wouldn't edit. No way. "There's still a market for closed form, for serious poetry. It's just a quiet market. It's always been there. I proved that."

"You were good," Brittlestein admitted. "And you had a certain following. There's no denying it. But things have changed. Poetry has changed. You know that."

They talked a while longer, but he soon knew that they were merely patronizing him. But he didn't have to beg. When it became clear that he had no place to go, no way to get there, they offered to put him up for the night, and he accepted with no idea in the world where he might go the next day. But sometime that night Felix and Brittlestein worked that out as well.

"Listen," Brittlestein said over poolside croissants the next morning, "an uncle of mine died a few years ago. And I have this inheritance."

"I don't want charity," he snapped off the lie and squirmed uncomfortably. It was as if someone else was doing the talking from deep inside him, and his more immediate self was running around trying to shut him up. "I just want to write. To be able to write. I've got poems inside me—"

"Just hear me out," Brittlestein said in a low voice. "Swallow your goddamned pride for once and hear me out."

And he did. And hearing out his old adversary led him to a gas station-motel in what Melvin had correctly identified as Bumfuck, Nowhere. A part of a legacy left to Brittlestein by his mother's brother, a real-estate speculator from Dallas who had a tendency to obtain unsalable properties across the country. He would, Brittlestein explained, buy anything that looked like it was in the right of way of government development, then sell it at a premium. Sometimes, though it didn't work, which is how he came by the Llano Motor Courts that wound up being by-passed by a some engineer's caprice and left off to one side on an usually neglected strip of state highway.

The establishment itself was little more than a series of vermin-infested, tumble-down shacks and a couple of rusty gas pumps when he arrived. The office-residence's roof leaked, and the fireplace was clogged with birds' nests. But Felix and Melton House loaned him— "gave him," was how Felix put it—ten thousand dollars to fix up the abandoned cottages, paint the station, contract for gasoline delivery, buy some sundries and other junk to sell, and to carry him for as long as it would.

"This is all there will be," Felix told him when he handed him the check and a plane ticket to El Paso. "Don't ask for more. I don't mean to sound cheap, but this is really more for old times' sake than anything else."

"I'll consider it an advance," he said and pocketed the small paper. "You'll have the manuscript inside a year." Felix only shook his head and smiled sadly.

The station came with a broken-down seventy-three Ford pickup, a collection of rusty animal cages which had been originally billed as "The Wildlife Museum of the Southwest," and a lot of hard work. But he made the money stretch. After he had been open for two months, twenty-five boxes of his books arrived with a note from Brittlestein.

"We've kept these in storage for years," Brittlestein wrote. "Thought you might be able to sell one or two out of the station." He couldn't tell if it was a mean joke or not. But he put them out, and they did sell, and out of them, he began to rediscover something like self-respect. He came off the bottom, he felt, and he believed he was rising. Or was he kidding himself? He never stopped worrying that there was no returning from that depth, nothing waiting for him but more anguish as he considered the numerous circles he'd descended through. He sometimes felt more deceased than the tourists and would-be poetasters who bought his books made him feel when they discussed him in the past tense. Sometimes, he told himself, he would be better off dead.

But he had had such thoughts before. And he had rejected them when there wasn't so much as this limp-along business to sustain him. He would reject them again and again, he promised the animals he cared for. Suicide just wouldn't answer, he lectured himself: It was too fucking easy.

Then the poems came back in full troupe. They returned as soon as he stopped waiting for them, looking for them, wishing they would come to salvage something of his self-respect. He was writing once more like he had never stopped. Some *vers libre*, as he had expected, but more in closed form, the old way: sonnets and ballads, odes and sestinas. Even the open verse seemed to have structure, to demand balance. And there wasn't a woman in sight. Before Edna showed up, he hadn't even thought of a specific woman since he opened up the business.

The first poem he completed he wrote straight through without stopping and needed little revision. It was a cavalier lyric after the manner of John Suckling's occasional verse. The title was "The Ballad of the High Test Celibate: A No-Lead Lament," and it was, in his modest opinion, hilarious: ribald, imaginative and fresh.

Since that, he had finished thirty new verses, each better than the first. He tried alciac lines, but they remained incomplete and challenged him to come back almost nightly. But other poems flowed, it seemed. They were all hard to write, but not so surrounded with a sense of pending disaster, not so infused with guilt and self-destruction. They didn't all come to stay, and some of them faded before he could capture them, realize them on the page, but they were there.

He finished making sure all of the animals had food and fresh water for the night, then went over to coil up the air and water hoses. The wind was stronger than ever, the sky darker and more ominous. He shielded his eyes against the blowing grit and watched a battered Oldsmobile Cutlass fighting the gusts as it tacked across the highway and into his drive. It chugged and died before it reached the pumps. White steamy smoke seeped from under the hood and evaporated immediately into the wind.

A young woman bounced out, slammed the door shut behind her, and kicked it hard. She had on short shorts and a peasant blouse that showed strong, tanned shoulders supporting a long neck and high, proud head. In spite of the cloudy sky, she wore sunglasses, but her face was pretty, her skin clear. Curly blonde hair was tied with a bright scarf into a tight ponytail that flapped in the wind behind her.

"Shit, shit, shit," she yelled at the car, and kicked it again. Her breasts bounced with the movement. "Fucking piece of fucking junk!"

The Olds had indeed seen better days since it was shiny new in the late 1970s. Each of the front fenders was a different color from the hood and doors, and there were dents everywhere. The windshield was cracked, and one of the door windows was covered with cardboard. The whole car listed dangerously on what was either a bad spring or a broken shock absorber. The tires were bald, and the rear seat was loaded with boxes and piles of clothes and miscellaneous cartons of books and papers.

"Trouble?" he asked when he walked up.

"No thanks, I've already got some," she said, defeated. "It's overheated again. I don't know how I got this far." She kicked it again, but this time, the gesture showed more contempt than anger. "I've been pushing this piece of shit for two weeks up and down every fucking back road in this shit-kicking state. It quits every afternoon, same time. Like some fucking union. 'Five o'clock: Quittin' Time.' Doesn't matter where, doesn't matter how far to any goddamned place at all. Shit."

She reached inside and popped the hood. He walked dutifully over and peered into the motor cavity. He had no idea what he might be looking for. Then he spotted the broken piece of fan belt on top of the air cleaner. He picked it up and handed it to her.

"This could be the problem," he said.

"*Today*, this is the problem," she said. "Yesterday, it was the alternator. The day before, it was something else. Thermostat or something. This heap costs me more to run every fucking mile. God-dammit, anyway." She threw the broken piece of rubber off into the wind. "I'm keeping every redneck mechanic in the southwest in beer and bar nuts. I've spent more on it in the last two weeks than it cost new. Shit!" He looked at it. It was a good deal older than she was.

"I mean, new-used," she said with a half smile, calming down. "I'm sorry. It's not your fault. My old man bought it before he skipped, and he stuck me with the payments *and* the repairs. I had a pretty good motorcycle when we shacked up, but he stole that. I reported it stolen, anyway. For the insurance. I think he's in Montana or some damned place. Hope they throw his ass in jail." Angry all over again, she walked slightly away, toward the office.

She was tall, almost as tall as he. He noticed her narrow waist and her legs, smooth, tan, muscular as she stepped. Her fingers were long and her body was lean, athletic. She had a coltish step, moving each foot high on its ball before shifting to the other. Her breasts were well shaped, her chin rounded but strong. She had high cheek bones and a slight pug nose. She looked proud and sure of herself in spite of her complaints. He admired her the way he had admired so many women in his life. But he felt nothing stirring, nothing uncomfortable, not the way he had reacted to Edna the previous summer, not the way he always reacted to women. Somehow, she struck him as just a beautiful girl, one more in a long parade of his recollected experience, perhaps, but different somehow, distant and unassuming. She was also young. Very young.

"Can you fix it?" she called without looking at him. She was inspecting the cottages, the office, the pumps, frowning a bit.

He shook his head. "Nope," he admitted loudly. "I'm not a mechanic. No parts, no tools, no know-how. You'll have to send for somebody. Tow truck, maybe. You got Triple-A?"

"Are you kidding? I've barely got a car." She looked at the office. "You have a phone, at least?"

He led her toward the door. The wind blew them along faster than they wanted to walk, and he almost bumped into her when she stopped suddenly. Perfume—Tabu, he thought—came to him when his face touched her hair. He realized that she was looking at the books behind the crusty glass. From her position, she had a clear view of the oversized photograph.

"Where is he?"

"Who?"

"Him. The poet. The guy who wrote all those books." She pointed a long nail at the display behind the gritty windows. "That's who I'm looking for." She pushed her sunglasses up and revealed striking green eyes. Her hair, he realized, wasn't curly, but kinked in a series of tiny braids that fell out of a carefully arranged tangle. A line of earrings ran up each lobe, and her smile showed perfect teeth. She was, he realized, uncommonly pretty, lovelier than he first thought. There was a familiarity about her, a déjà vu, as if he'd seen her in a dream.

"That's the guy I'm looking for. Where the hell is he?"

He studied her for a moment. Something in him doubted her, suddenly, feared her. It was different from the experience with Edna, more immediate, darker and more threatening. There were old dangers lurking here: deep dangers. He closed his eyes momentarily to wish her gone, and the poems trooped past like an army of ghosts in the darkness. He opened them again and found her still staring at him.

"What do you want with him? He doesn't like people." He fished a wrinkled cigarette from his pocket. His hands were shaking.

"I want to talk to him," she said, looking around. "I've been all over Texas and New Mexico looking for him. Does he live around here? In one of those?" She pointed at the stucco cottages, then looked hard at him, let her eyes run up and down his greasy shirt and trousers while he finally managed to light his smoke. Then she smiled. "You're him, aren't you?" He nodded, and her smile widened into a huge, satisfied grin and she scampered back to the car.

"Unfuckingbelievable! Get me a Coke. No! A beer or something," she called over her shoulder. "I can't believe it! Lucky!" She danced against the gusting wind, and he waited a beat, then, for want of something to do, went inside and fished a beer out of the cooler. He was confused, unaccountably apprehensive, but he could find no reason to be. He went through physical motions with the care of one who is watching himself, conscious of potential error, bewildered and dreadful.

When she returned, she was almost breathless. She bounced into the office, flopped down into an ancient chair and set a nylon backpack down in front of her. From it she withdrew a small tape recorder and a notebook. He was surprised to see she also had all of his books, even *Free Falling, Free Flying*. She brought them out and stacked them neatly on a table full of fishing magazines.

"I've been driving up and down every goddamn highway in the Southwest looking for you. I called that fag asshole editor of yours in New York, but all he would tell me was that you were running a gas station somewhere out here. 'In the Southwest,' he said. Near El Paso. He wouldn't give me an address, and he said he wasn't forwarding any mail to you. Said you wanted to be left alone. 'Bullshit,' I told him. 'Who does he think he is? Greta Garbo'?" She rose and retrieved a handbag from which she extracted a pack of cigarettes.

"That *was* our agreement," he said. He stood in the middle of the room, speechless, unable to decide what to do next. The girl unnerved him completely. She was all energy. She jumped up and down, flitted from one side of the room to the other, sipped the beer he had opened for her, and smoked as she readied herself for what he took to be an interview, although she had said nothing to him about it. "I don't really want to be found. I don't like company," he added.

She sat again, folded her long legs beneath her and scooched her bottom into the well they made on the peeling plastic of the chair. "I *know* that. Shit, nobody knows where the hell you are. I called every college in the country, and half of them think you're dead. Your ex-wife thinks you're dead, too."

He pondered that. He hadn't contacted her in over five years, had deliberately cut himself off from his daughter long ago as well. "You know her?" he asked.

"No, I just knew her name. It was under your listing in *Who's Who in American Poetry*. Found out she was in Denver and called her up."

"How is she?" He asked automatically, dully.

"Nasty where you're concerned," she said. "Otherwise, just a class-A bitch. Richer than God and twice as important. Her old man's the city auditor. How could you marry somebody like that?"

He ignored the question and wished there were two chairs in the office's anteroom. Thoreau kept three chairs at Walden Pond, he reminded himself, one for solitude, two for company, three for society. He hadn't expected either company or society and wanted neither. He looked at the squeaky desk chair on the other side of the room. Somehow, he felt, if he went over and sat down it would invite her to stay. That, he insisted as he lit another cigarette, was company he especially didn't want.

"Why did you want to find me? I don't like interviews. I didn't want anyone to know where I was. That was part of the deal. I like privacy. Solitude," he corrected. "I need it."

"You're writing again, aren't you?" she asked. Her hands came together in a clap and then rubbed themselves in anticipation. "Fucking-A! I knew it. I just knew it."

"I like to be alone," he repeated, insisted. Go away, he silently said. *Go away now.*

"I know what you like, what you don't like," she said. "I know all about you. I'm did my master's thesis on you. I've read your poetry, your criticism. Goddamn! You're something. Did you know that? You inspired a whole generation of poets who didn't want to write shit. Couldn't write shit. I think half the decent poetry written in the past twenty years was written because of you. Or in spite of you. Did you know that?"

"I imagine that's an exaggeration."

"No fucking way," she said. "Look, I told this asshole Tony Corbett—my thesis director—that I wanted to write on you, and he said—" She dropped her voice and tugged down on her chin. "'He's not significant enough.' He *said* that! Do you know him?"

He knew him. He knew his wife, Carol, better. They were about the same age, same generation, anyway, and had met years ago. Corbett was head of department then, fashioned himself one of the leading critics of poetry in America. He was on the slide then, falling hard and fast, but he was still a formidable name, someone who could come and be a straw man for the "New Wave" critics like Corbett. He took on Corbett and three of his punk-rock and slam-poetry protégées on in a panel discussion and revealed that they didn't know squat—made a fool of Corbett in front of his dean and department—by asking them specific questions about major poets they clearly had never read. He then skipped the reception and screwed Carol Corbett in the seat of her MGB in the deserted parking lot of the university football stadium after two joints and half a bottle of tequila. It was a near record-setting feat of gymnastics, and not particularly satisfying for either of them. Yet she claimed to be enamored of the whole experience and flaunted it right in front of her frantic husband when they returned to the house well after midnight. Corbett never quite got over either humiliation.

He shook his head. "I don't know him. Not really," he said. "Only by reputation."

"Well, that's not what I heard," she said matter-of-factly and sipped her beer. "Most of *his* reputation is exaggerated," she said. "And I know you know that." Then she smiled and his heart jumped a little to realize once more how incredibly pretty she was. In spite of her brassy language, her nonchalant poses, she was soft, almost nymph-like. She had a gentle, anticipatory expression that came naturally to her when she wasn't grinning or frowning.

"He's married and divorced a second time, now, you know. They say he can't get it up unless he's wearing women's underwear. I got that straight from my best friend." She laughed. "But he's the powerhouse in modern poetry there, and to get into a decent doctoral program, you have to work with him. So I did, and I wrote on you anyway. Pissed him off, but he had to go along with it. I knew about his quirks, see? From my friend. Anyway, it was so fucking good, he had to write me great recommendations, too. I had offers for fellowships from the top schools in the country."

She beamed with self-satisfaction. "So, now, I'm going for my doctorate at Northwestern. All I have to do is finish this goddamn dissertation. And I'm going to do it on you, too. There's a book in it. You may not believe it, but I'm about to be the most important fucking critic in the country. And you can take that to the bank."

He smiled. Something about her was fond, endearing. "I expect

Corbett's right," he said. "I don't think I'm very significant, and I doubt writing about my work will make you important."

"Oh, you are," she assured him. "I've read Frank Gideon. Others, too. You're the new Dylan Thomas."

He laughed. "I hope not. I haven't had anything stronger than beer or maybe a sip or two of whiskey in two years, longer. I'm not the drunk I'm reputed to be."

"I don't mean that," she said. "I mean your poetry. Your fucking poetry." She smiled again. "And your criticism. But mostly your life. What you stood for."

"Stood for?" He was shocked. He had never believed that he stood for anything.

"You stood for quality," she insisted. "You wouldn't take any bullshit, wouldn't condone it. You insisted that poetry be poetic. In fact, that's the title of my MA thesis, *The Poetry of the Poetic*. It's coming out of LSU Press as a monograph this year."

"I'd like to see a copy," he muttered. He wouldn't, but he didn't know what else to say, what was appropriate. Why was this girl doing this to him? Why was she making him feel this way? He wanted to laugh and cry at the same time. He finally dragged the desk chair over and sat down.

"This is going to be publishable, too," she said. "Count on it." Again she leaped around the room. "This is *so* fucking awesome! To find you at last. I've been looking for you—oh, I told you that. Did you know that half the critics writing today think you're dead? Just like your old lady—I told you that, too. I'm sorry. I'm just so fucking excited to find you. And you're still writing?" Her voice narrowed. "You *said* you were still writing."

He looked at the tape recorder. "I don't give interviews," he said

"This isn't an interview," she said. "Not unless you want it to be. I just want you to read your poetry, the old stuff first. Then tell me about yourself. Everything about yourself."

"Read?"

"Read. Just like you used to. I hear you're hell on wheels when you read. Then talk."

"What about?"

"About anything you want. Poetry, the poetic. Places you've been, things you've done. Your ideas. Talk about you."

He smiled. Just like he used to, he thought. She had no idea what she was asking, of the danger that used to be associated with his readings, his talks. "I used to be good at that," he admitted. "Talk. And good at reading. But there was a purpose, usually, other than the poetry." He looked again at her legs. She was what, twenty-one, twenty-two? Maybe a little older, not much. A third his age, nearly. He searched himself, sought that old yearning, the familiar tightening across the chest. But it wasn't there. He couldn't quite see her that way, pretty, desirable as she was. And there was something else, something he couldn't quite define about her that put him on his guard, continued to make him nervous.

"You see," she went on, "I haven't just *read* your stuff. I've studied *it. Know it by heart, most of it. Have most of my life. But I* want to hear you interpret it, relate it to your life. And I want to know everything about you. I heard you were awesome when you read your own work. Even Corbett said that no one ever wanted to follow you on a program. It was always an anticlimax, he said." She giggled. "If *half* of your reputation is earned, that's funny."

He blushed in spite of himself. "I don't know what you've heard, but if Corbett—"

She wasn't listening. "You're one of the few successful poets in the past fifty years who writes in all closed form. Some blank verse, but mostly all poetic meters and rhymes. The hard ones, too. You made it against all the odds." She pulled *Free Falling* from her tote, opened it and ran a finger into the middle of poem. "'Blonde on Blonde,'" she read. "Tell me about it, tell me how you came to write it. Who was it for?"

"What makes you think it was 'for' anyone?"

She gave him a sly look. "Because all your poetry was 'for' someone. Usually for some woman. Somebody you balled, right?"

He was silent. How did she know that? No one knew that, no one except the women the poems were for. Hell, most of the time, *they* didn't even know that.

"I want you to tell me all about it. All about how you came to write each of these. I want to know." She sat back and struck a silly pose. "I'm an 'inquiring mind.'"

He was horrified. "For your dissertation?"

"No," she said, "Well, yes. That, too. I'll draw comparisons, conclusions, sure, based on what you tell me. But what I want you to do isn't just for that. It's mostly personal. It's for me."

"It's not the kind of thing I can just talk about," he said and turned away. It was cold in the office, and he shivered. "Not to a total stranger." He suddenly wanted a drink very badly. There was an unreal quality about this whole thing. Who was this girl? Where had she come from? Was she a witch, ghost, a poltergeist of some kind? An ethereal amalgamation of all the women he'd seduced, been seduced by. He felt terrified: all at once frightened of her. What did she want of him? He prayed she would just say all this was a mistake and leave. "Take thy beak from out my heart, and take/ Thy form from off my door," he silently conjured. She clearly had no inclination to leave. She now sat, again crossed her legs beneath her, and readied herself. All she needed was a bust of Pallas, he thought ruefully.

"I'm waiting," she said. "You can start any time. I want to hear it all. All of it. Start when you wrote your first poem. Then read it to me."

"I think you'd better go."

"I'm not leaving," she said, as if startled by the utter absurdity of the idea. "I can't, anyway. It's Friday. I couldn't get that piece of shit repaired way out here till Monday. Go for it. Tell me all. Play Prince Hamlet. Play Browning's Duke. Play Prufrock. 'Tell me all. I have come for you to tell me all!'" She switched the tape recorder on. "I'm serious. I've read your work, thought about you all my life. You owe me a good story." She took a pause. Her smile was fixed but deliberately mysterious, cunning and almost sinister. She was playing with him, and she was enjoying it. "You owe me, period," she said.

Suddenly, another thought hit him. "Beware! Beware!" he thought. Was this the great George Gordon's "Damsel with a Dulcimer"? He rubbed his chin. "Have you come here to hurt me? Kill me, maybe?"

She laughed. "Whatever gave you that idea?"

He shook his head and walked to the other side of the room. The image of her pointing a pistol or holding a knife now seemed ludicrous. "I don't know." He felt like crying. She still seemed ghostly. "I just can't help but think that you're somehow . . . I don't know." He rubbed his eyes shut and checked. Yes, the poems were there: waiting.

His opened eyes fell again on the book open in front of her. "Where did you get that?" he asked and nodded toward the volume. It was in mint condition, more evidence that she was somehow unreal. "Where did you find it? I didn't think there were any more."

"My mother gave it to me."

"Your mother?"

"Yeah." She winked. "You wrote a poem to her, or so she said."

"When?" Fear of satanic visits, ghosts, or even murder vanished. He now faced a different kind of fright, the same feeling he had had the summer before with Edna, the feeling he had dreaded for years.

"Long time ago. She was a student. One of yours."

"And you're . . . "

"Pieria," she said with a coy smile. "I thought you would have guessed that. You suggested the name. I hated it until I got out of high school. My friends call me Pi. So do my profs. Half the time, they think I'm Vietnamese. Can you imagine: Nordic me being mistaken for Vietnamese? Everyone has to make a pun on it. You know, 'Two into pi squared,' or 'How 'bout a piece, Pi?' That sort of thing. I dated a guy whose last name was Horner for a while, and that was hell." She gave him a wry look. "It was all your idea, or so Mother said. But I guess you don't remember. She took off for graduate school right after she found out she was knocked up. I didn't come along for a while after that: Nine months, to be precise. The last time she saw you was in Philadelphia or someplace. She said you were rude. Wouldn't talk to her. And," she lowered her eyes quickly, then looked up, "she said there was someone else. She figured you were ashamed. Were you ashamed? I can't see you in that role."

"Pieria?" he repeated. Nothing stirred in his mind. The birthplace of the Muses, he remembered. Strange name for a child, even a love child of his own. He must have been drunk or mad or both.

"Rae Ann's daughter."

"Rae Ann," he mouthed stupidly. Then the memory flooded over him and carried him back a quarter century: The child he had paid for but never seen, the mother who had dogged him every time he made the national press, every time a new book came out. He looked at Pi and studied her prettiness with this new knowledge. The beautiful young woman sitting across from him, her long, muscular, tanned legs folded beneath her, a beer can in one hand and a cigarette in the other: She was that child. His child.

"I, uh . . . no wonder Felix wouldn't tell you where I was," he said. He remembered the awful letters Rae Ann and her attorneys wrote to Felix, the pleading attempts to enlist his publisher in a lawsuit against him: the accusations, recriminations, threats. They stopped more than ten years ago. He kept up the child support for as long as he could, then he forgot about it. The same way he forgot about everything. He was on the slide then, wanting to forget.

"Don't worry," Pi said. "There's no shyster following me. This isn't a shakedown. I'm not my mother. My interest is *not* financial." She looked at him and around at the dusty office and its antiquated furnishings. "It's a good thing, I guess."

"Then what do you want?"

"It's a quest," she sat back, perfectly still for the first time. "I want to know everything there is to know about you."

264

"Why?" He was alarmed. Confused. "Why would you want that?"

"Because," she said, now serious. "I have the right. I'm your daughter, and I have the fucking right." Her green eyes burned into him, and he looked away. "Besides, you may be the only living poet who has a fucking notion of what a poem is. That's what Mom said, in spite of the way she felt—still feels—about you. You're a first-rate prick, you know."

He nodded. His legs felt heavy, and his hip hurt badly. His mouth was dry, and he wanted a drink. He rose and started putting pieces of mesquite into the fireplace. It was something to do.

"That's what I think when I read your poems," she said. "I want you to tell me why. I want to know so I'll know what you know."

"It's not any of your business."

She slapped her legs with an open palm. Her eyes flared. "Don't tell me that! Don't you *ever* tell me that. I grow up knowing my old man is one of the most famous fucking poets in the country, and he won't even acknowledge me, or my mother. He sends his fucking checks in dutifully enough. That's sure. For a while, anyway. Buys us off, or tries to. Treats me like some turd he shit out and wants somebody else to clean up."

"That's not the way it was at all." He pushed some newspapers under the dry limbs, lit them and stood back. He couldn't look at her.

"That's the way it felt," she insisted. There was no bitterness in her voice. She spoke matter-of-factly. "As soon as I was old enough to know, I found out who my father was, who you were. Mother never married, you know. No, I guess you didn't. You didn't fucking care. Her own poetry never went anywhere, never got published. Because you never helped her, like you said you would." She held up her hands to ward off a protest he had no intention of making. "That's all right. I've read it, or what's left of it. It sucks. But she didn't think so at the time, and she spent a lot of years trying before she found out just how rotten she was. I'll bet it *was* fucking embarrassing when she finally accepted it. Now, she's teaching elementary school in Terre Haute: twenty fucking years of wiping boogers out of kids' noses and telling me that the one goddamn thing in her life that meant anything was you. Because you 'believed' in her, in her poetry. Or that's what you told her."

"Me?" He had to rack his memory to try to conjure Rae Ann's face. The only image he could come up with was a dark scowl cast at him from across a hotel lobby. He wiped his eyes. "Yeah, I probably did."

"I'll bet you said that to all the girls," Pi said with an ironic smile.

"Yeah, I probably did." The fire was catching now. He put a screen in place and wandered about the open space between them. He wanted to sit again, but he feared that if he did he might not get up. He felt dizzy, almost drunk.

"So, I read your stuff. I read it in high school, and I read it in college. I set out to destroy you. I decided I would write the book that would expose you for the fraud I believed you were. I wanted to put you away, drop you off the roster for good. But I didn't have to do that. You did it all by yourself. After a while, there wasn't anything left but your poetry." She stared at him for a beat. "You fucked yourself."

"Yeah," he repeated for the third time. "I probably did."

"And your criticism. The reviews! You attacked *everybody*," she concluded and counted on her fingers. "Women—especially feminists—gays, African Americans, Hispanics, Native Americans, foreigners, old people, young people. Christ, you probably even attacked yourself."

He smiled and opened his hands. "It was never political."

"Bullshit. Your criticism was awful. Mean-spirited, unforgiving. No wonder nobody liked you."

"If all that's true, then why are you—"

"Because you're good," she said. Her smile went cold, a thin slice across her pretty face. "I mean, I hated to admit it, but it's true. You're *really* good. Better than anybody writing then, better than anybody writing now. You're the best, maybe the best there ever was."

"*That*," he said, "is a definite hyperbole."

"Maybe," she admitted. "But that's why I'm here."

He turned went to get her another beer. "Why?"

"Because much as I wanted to hate you, much as I wanted to destroy you, use my thesis, my dissertation for that, I couldn't. You're too good. In spite of everything, your poetry gets inside my head, turns my thoughts inside out. You touch me. You really do. So half way through my thesis, half way through Corbett's direction, I changed my mind. And now, now, I'm ready to write the real study of your work. I want to bring you back, put your work in front of this generation of poets. My generation."

"You're not serious," he said from the cooler. He considered, then raised a can and his eyebrows. She nodded.

"I'm deadly serious. I've got every reason in the world to hate you, and I love you, instead. But I don't understand you. And that's why I'm here. I want you to tell me everything. Don't leave anything out. I want it all, and I want your new stuff. Your new poems. And . . . I want to know your philosophy of life."

"I'm not sure I have one."

"I'm sure you do."

He came over, handed her the beer, then sat down heavily. For a moment his breathing filled his ears. Outside, rain began to pelt the office windows. Did he have one? he wondered. Was there something in his mind, something in his imagination that was worthy of being called a philosophy? He doubted it.

"I just have opinions," he said. "Attitudes. And they're not popular, they're not politically correct, as they say. They're narrow-minded, sexist, bigoted and, for the most part, they're not pretty. You want to know the truth: They're not even right."

"But they *are* poetry, aren't they?" she asked softly.

He nodded.

"Then I want to know them."

"I still don't see why." He gave in, arose and went to a cabinet and extracted a whiskey bottle. He promised he would have but one drink, then he would put it back, find a way to get this girl out of his office, out of his life. "You don't need me in order to write about my work. I don't remember half of it."

"It's not just your old work I'm interested in," she smiled cunningly. "I want your new work."

He paused too long, he knew. He waited for the lie to come to him, for him to say it wasn't any good, that it was only half finished, that it really didn't exist. But by the time he started shaking his head, it was too late.

"You're writing again, so I know you have some," she said. "I *know* you do. And it's good, isn't it? The look on your face confirms it. I want them. All of them. As soon as you've read your old work, you're going to get them, read them to me, then I'll copy them—I've got one of those portable things, a notebook-laptop-whatsit—in the car and a scanner. They're going to *make* my dissertation. It'll be the most publishable fucking dissertation they've ever seen. It'll make my fucking career. Hell, I'll be teaching at Harvard." She clapped her hands in front of her. "God, I can't believe I've really found you."

He sat down and took a swig from the bottle. It made perfect sense, he knew. In the desk drawer, beneath the receipts and a ledger for the gasoline and sundries records, were the thirty-odd new verses. He had been trying to get a total of fifty before sending them to Felix, hoping to change his mind. His plan was to send them in without so much as a letter begging him to consider them. On the way back, there had to be a limit to humiliation. He knew that New York editors, like Greek kings, never changed their minds: It made them appear to be human, mortal, fallible. It was a long shot, but it was the only shot he had. Now there was this.

He looked at her smiling face. He knew what she was planning. It was a brilliant stroke: Find a poet who used to have a reputation, get unpublished verse from him, put it into a dissertation with some well-written explication, and you're made. He never saw himself as the subject of some sort of scholarly study, but there it was. There it was right in front of him. He admired her guts, but he couldn't cooperate. He wouldn't.

"I don't have anything that's finished," he said.

"Liar. I want everything you have, finished or not. This is going to put me into position. I've always known I was going to make it, and you owe it to me to help." She made a thin line of her lips. "You do, you know. We'll talk a while, drink a little, smoke a little—I got some good shit, the only thing my old man left me that was worth a damn. Then, we can eat a little something—I'm a great cook!—and then you're going to read them, explain them, and tell me all. I have looked for you for months. Thought about you for years. I've hated you, and I've loved you. I almost believed you were dead. And now, I'm here, now that I've found you, you are going to go through with it, now."

"It won't work," he said. "What I have," he gestured toward the desk, "it's not ready. It's half finished, half formed."

"I don't care. It's not just for this silly dissertation. Not for anyone else, but for me. I told you: It's personal, and you owe me. I must know them."

"Why?" He lit another cigarette and drank again from the pint bottle. Deeply this time. He was shaking as he removed the cap and took what he dimly realized was his third pull. Shades of the past, he thought, and shifted to the offensive. "Why 'must' you know them? And don't give me any shit. There's more to this than some vendetta, more than some damn degree. Why does this mean so much to you?"

"Because . . . ." She paused, and he turned to look at her. "Because I inherited something from you. Something in here." She put a long finger to her temple. Her green eyes were serious, dark suddenly and they fell to the floor as she spoke. "Sometimes at night, when I go to bed, I close my eyes and . . . well, it sounds silly, but they come." She looked up, appealing at him not to laugh at her.

His breath stopped, the bottle in his hand felt heavy. "They come?"

268

"Yeah. And I know that you know exactly what I mean. To anyone else, it would sound stupid, crazy. But you know."

"They come," he whispered.

"Sometimes I can't even think about anything else. And they're sometimes so real. And they have—I can't describe it any other way—they have forms. Shapes. I don't know. It's . . . it's crazy."

"No," he said. "It's not crazy."

"I can't help it, but I'm not sure they're any good. But they come into my head and I write them down. I don't show them to anyone. I won't show them to you," she hurriedly injected. "I'm afraid you'll lie to me the same way you did to Mother. But when I read your work, when I studied it, saw that no matter how much I wanted to hate it, hate you, I somehow thought . . . ."

She looked out into the gathering night. His eyes, afraid to look elsewhere, followed hers. "Riders on the Storm," he thought. A good line. It described both of them perfectly. It defined what he always had been: a rider on poetry's storm. He had read it all, knew it all. The only problem was that he had believed what it said, what the poets themselves thought was true. And none of it was: not for him, not for anyone, probably not even for the poets themselves. And probably not for her, either. He was afraid.

"I don't know," she went on. "But after I get the degree, publish the book—I'm calling it *New Wine, Old Bottles*, by the way—after I'm established, then I want to write them for real."

"For real," he muttered and drank again. The bottle was almost empty, but there was another in the living quarters behind the office. He knew he would need it.

"Yeah," she said. "For real. You see, I want to be a poet. I can't be, not yet. I don't know enough. But I will. I'm starting with what you know. So I want your philosophy. And I want all of your poems." She paused, swallowed hard, then stared at him hard and continued in a voice so soft he saw rather than heard it. "That's what you owe me. Not just because I'm your daughter, but because I'm a woman. You owe me because I'm my mother's child, because every woman you've ever known is some mother's child. Because you, yourself are a mother's child."

He looked at her anxious, almost painful expression in the flickering light of the fireplace. He was hungry, suddenly, and he thought of a venison stew he had cooked and frozen a week before. She was beautiful, more lovely than any woman he had ever known, more anxious for what he had to say than any woman he had ever encountered. And, he admitted, she was right. She was more deserving. He owed her. He felt older than he ever had, more used up, but there was something else, some new resolve as well. He tossed the cigarette into the fireplace when he stood.

"You aren't going to like much of it," he said. "I won't tell you anything that isn't true."

"Truth is beauty," she smiled.

"Truth is a whore," he said. "It's for sale to the highest bidder, and in the morning you don't want to remember it."

"I'll want to."

He nodded, sighed. "Let's get some dinner started. I'll go light the heater in Cabin Eight." He started out, stopped. "This is going to take time."

"I've got time," she said. "I've got the rest of my life."

After he came back, he went to the office and watched through the flyspecked, dusty screen while she lugged her junk from the broken down car into the cabin. Her leggy figure struggled with the heavy boxes and cartons, but he made no move to go out and help her. For the first time in his life, no recollected verse came to his mind. He was frozen inside, dead, completely prosaic.

Rain splattered down now in quick, violent but indefinite spurts. It was cold. She blew into the office ahead of an icy blast, took a box of packaged toiletries from a dusty shelf and announced that she was frozen through. He hadn't moved and only looked at her with a cold, numb expression. She said she wanted to take a hot bath, so she would be a while, and since they had a while, it wouldn't matter. It was all right with him: A while was all he needed.

He took the sheaf of new poems from the drawer and every copy of his books from the for sale stacks, her copies as well from the stack next to her chair, and he fished around in her backpack for any copies that had escaped her notice when she unpacked it. Then he sat there and read them, read each poem quietly, allowing his lips to mouth the words in a barely audible whisper, his toe to tap out the metrical rhythms. Then he fed them, methodically, one by one, into the fire that crackled and burned as it sent his words, his life, his poetry up the rock chimney into the "lifeless sea" of the southwestern desert wind.

He then sat back, opened the fresh bottle and drank deeply. The whiskey burned going down, and he set the bottle aside, capped, this time for good. Somehow, he knew without shutting his eyes and checking for sure that they were now gone, finally exorcised, and they would never come back. And for the first time in as long as he could remember, he felt free: He didn't need anything at all.

XI

"That while you live, you live in love, and never get
favor for lacking skill of a sonnet, and when you die,
your memory dies from the earth for want of an epitaph."
— Sidney

*I always wanted to go to Europe. I think, in some ways, that's
my major regret among so many: that I never got across the Big
Pond. Not even to England. I always meant to go, to tramp around
Tintern Abby, to walk Yeats' wild western shore, visit Joyce's
Dublin, Hardy's Wales' greenswards. I wanted to visit Keats' house,
Johnson's house, Pope's house, Milton's grave, Stratford-on-Avon,
Scott's Edinburgh, Arnold's beach at Dover, the Lake District, all
those places in the Isles. And I wanted to see Rome, Florence,
Venice, Brittany, Nice, and Paris, where so many great poets flour-
ished. And I wanted to go to Greece, of course, and wherever they
think Troy was. I even had an idea, once, of calling on Sartre, maybe
spending some time just sitting on the Left Bank sipping wine and
wishing I could understand Harry Crosby and H.D. I wanted to sail
between Homer's Magic Islands, visit Byron and Shelley's and, of
course, Browning's Italy, go to Pushkin's Russia, Yevtishinko's
Moscow, Malamaré's France, Goethe's German forests. All of it.*

*But I never got there. I kept thinking I would. I kept thinking
that there would always be time to go: Maybe next year, maybe a
sabbatical, maybe a Fulbright, maybe—who knows?—a Prix de
Rome, even a Nobel Prize. Go on, laugh at my ambitious grasping,
but that's what heaven's for, Browning reminds us.*

*It doesn't matter. I never got to any of those places. I saw most
of the United States, though. Once even did a reading in
Guadalajara, and once in Ontario. Mexican women are better, I
think, than Canadians: warmer, somehow, less hung up in being
women. No, that's not right. They're more hung up in it, I guess:
Don't feel they have to keep apologizing for it.*

Overall, though, I think I prefer American women. I prefer America generally to anywhere else, even though I never went to much of anywhere else. I saw most of the country: the South, some New England, less California, more of the West—God, I saw the West!—and the Midwest, all of it, from Pennsylvania to Nebraska, from the Dakotas to northern Oklahoma and all that vapid emptiness in between. And there was the Southwest, exclusive of California: You know, Arizona, New Mexico, Texas, where I started from. A mother's son. And I wound up there, which would suggest that I liked it best. But that's not true. You see, I didn't have much real basis for comparison. Most of what I saw was from 20,000 feet or higher. Or lower, from the dirty windows of some—what is the line?—"one night, cheap hotels."

And the women, well . . . there's a kind of irony there. Wherever I was, it seemed that the women were always from somewhere else. I have no regional preferences when it comes to women.

Or when it comes to poetry. I think Wallace Stephens is no better or worse than John Crowe Ransom, Alan Tate in no way superior to Lawrence Ferlinghetti, James Dickey no more wonderful a versifier than Robert Frost. You see, it's not where a poet is from that counts. It's where his poems are from. That kind of difference creates preferences, differences in taste, but it hasn't anything to do with region, with place: It has to do with poetry.

And I got to New York. Twice. I also made LA, and Chicago, and St. Louis, and Dallas and Denver—or, actually, Boulder—Seattle and St. Paul, Fort Lauderdale and Washington D. C., Lexington, Concord, Van Nuys and Virginia Beach. I even got to Anchorage once. You name it, if there's a podunk college anywhere in the area, I did a reading there. Half the time—more than half—I got laid there, too.

But you know, in the whole country, in all those motels and bars, I don't think I ever did find out what I was after. I kept thinking it was poetry, and I kept thinking that poetry was between some comely young girl's legs. It wasn't. It never was. It was always between my own totally fucked-up ears, and if I'd figured out that, I'd have saved everybody a whole lot of heartache.

I don't know if I would have written any poetry. But in the end, what difference did that make, either?

So that's basically "what poetry means to me." You know, when I get into one of those "If I had it to do over again" moods I sometimes wonder if I would. I mean, there's been a shit load of pain: a shit load. And there've been precious few minutes that I could call something really good. And as I said, I never knew when I had it good. I mean, I took a lot of satisfaction when I was appreciated, when people—people I cared about—told me how good I was, but the truth of the matter was that when I was really good, I wasn't paying any attention. I just wanted to be better. I always had my eye on the fucking prize, on some kind of declaration of bona fides that wasn't possible. I just wasn't satisfied.

And there was that crazy connection. Which never really existed in the first place. I guess that was the hardest lesson to learn of all.

What I wanted wasn't any different from what most people want: I wanted to be adored. I wanted people—women especially—swooning around my feet, going all wet between their legs when I stood up in front of them. I guess most men want that. You see it happen to Elvis and the Beatles and Michael Jackson, and whoever's the Hollywood flavor of the month, and you want it, too. And when it does, even just a little, it goes to your head. Your manhood's head, anyway, and that's all the kick there is.

But there was still the poetry. And no matter how hard I tried, I couldn't get away from that. I kept thinking that I needed one to get the other, that one was caused by the other. But I was wrong. It wasn't the women, and it wasn't the sex: It was only the poetry. They were in me all along, and if I had known that, I might have done something worthwhile. I might leave something more than a slightly jizm-stained memory.

Listen, sitting there and talking about it into a microphone, watching it all going down on a little piece of brown tape, was astonishing. Getting it all out in front of me, honestly for once, not trying to hide anything, not trying to do anything but say it the way I thought it was an epiphany. There is no other word for it. But it wasn't for her. Not really. It was for me. I wanted to understand, to quit kidding myself and stop thinking I'm a bigger asshole than I usually felt like I was, an even bigger waste of time. I wanted to know me more than she did.

You see, the young always have advantages the old don't. But they have the same liabilities. And some have poetry. Not "in their souls" or anything of the kind. They just have it. And it's more of a burden than anything else, an obligation. Especially when they believe in it.

Hey, what're you going to do? Ignore your fate? Turn your back on your destiny? Run away from it? That's been tried, and it always turns out badly.

I wonder how my other daughter—you'll notice I didn't say

real—*would have taken it. I don't think she would have liked it. I don't think she would have understood. In fact, I think she would have hated me for it more than she probably already does anyway. You see, even though I've not seen her in years, have no idea how old her children are, really, I think I am kind of a presence in her life. The man who wasn't there, you know. A nobody. But who is she? Who, really? Alas, a nobody, too. And that's the living hell of it. That's the guilt. She never had poetry, and that was a blessing. But it meant, also, that she could never understand what a wonderful thing it is* not *to understand.*

It's best I've left her alone. It's best I didn't fuck up her life, too. I don't mind taking the blame for it. Because blame is a whole lot easier a thing to accept than guilt. Guilt is like a drug. It can kill, just as lies can. I know: I'd been lying to myself all along. What was worse, I let myself be lied to. I take the blame for that, as well.

But, when it was all over, when I was alone and all the poems but one were nothing but so much mesquite ash and the memories of them were just another golden whiskey haze, I had to admit that I was still lying. Not a little, but a lot. It's a hard habit to break. You see the new poems didn't have much to do with women. For once in my life I was trying to be as honest with my work as I could. And so if I showed them to anyone, they might take them, turn them over in their hands, and read them. And then just be really polite about them. Because, they might not be any good. They might not be any good at all. I don't think I could stand that.

It's harder to be dead long before you're gone than it is to die right in front of someone, especially in front of someone—especially a child of your own—who believes you'll live forever and do her some good in the bargain. I couldn't stand to see it in her eyes that they were bad. And I couldn't stand to see that famous mask that I've put on so often myself when I've looked over a rupturing of language someone handed me and called "their poems." I just couldn't stand it.

Burning them was easier. A kind of suicide, maybe, but more final, somehow, more painless. I told her what I did and why I did it, just like I've told you. And, guess what? She didn't understand.

Big surprise. She hadn't found out she was a poet herself. Yet. Not for sure. But she will. And after that, I think she'll understand. In the end, I don't think she'll care very much at all.

You see, most poets don't know that poetry is a lonely fucking business. There's you and there's the poem, and you can't share that with people. You can try. You can stand up and read to them. You can publish chapbooks by the goddamned ream and whole volumes by the ton. People can read them, silently or to each other, but they can't feel them. Not the way the poet feels them. Never that way. They can't feel the loneliness. Or the passion. Or the pain. They can't feel the art of it, or the love of it, either.

Every time I took some woman to bed, I think I was trying to share the poetry, trying to get past whatever it was that seemed to form a wall between me and my poems and those who said they understood. I wanted to make her understand that it was for the poems. But it didn't work. And, irony again: Every time I went through the motions—or almost every time—I came out with another poem or two, and the whole foolish, stupid thing started over again.

But what I didn't see myself was that it wasn't really for the poems at all: It was for the loneliness. I wanted a cure for that, a way out of myself. And that seemed to work. I guess luring them in with promises of making them what I was was both a lie and a trick. It was a lie because I couldn't do it. It was a trick because I wouldn't have if I could have. I've done a lot of shitty things in my life, but teaching somebody how to be that fucked up and lonely isn't one of them.

I never made anybody into a poet, not even somebody I should have loved. I'm proud of that.

I probably fucked up enough careers and prevented more people from becoming poets, too. I'm even prouder of that.

You know, the best time I ever had with a woman was an accident. No shit. Her name was Marlene, and she was tall and kind of horsey in the face, but she had a great body and legs that would wrap around me twice, even after I got my potbelly, didn't have two hairs to comb together. We worked together when I was teaching on some temporary gig or other, and we kept talking about having sex, but we never did anything.

Once, we went out for a couple of drinks, and we wound up in her apartment. It was the usual: reading a little verse, then groping around for a while, giggling, stripping off our clothes, and then climbing into bed like a couple of freshmen who just found a box of rubbers and couldn't wait to use them all up. I was just warming up good, you know, when she stops cold—just like a damned light went on in her head—and she tells me that she wants to know if I have the character to just lie there and hold her, just like that. No sex, no orgasm, no nothing: just lie there and hold her.

Character. Can you beat that?

Pope says that "most women have no character." But he never met Marlene. Hell, most of the women I've known—in fact, all of them—have forgotten more about character than that sawed-off little peckerwood ever learned. More than I ever learned, for sure.

You won't believe it, but I did it, just like she said. And we saw each other every night for about a month and then on a regular basis for another six months thereafter. And we never had sex: We slept together, talked about everything you can imagine, but we never did anything else. Not even so much as a hand-job. It was sort of incredible, because at that time in my life, I was bed-hopping all over the place.

Then, everyone began to start saying stuff. Nothing nasty, you know, just making sure that if we went anywhere, we were treated like a couple. That made her mad, and it made me nervous, since I was still thinking about saving my marriage at the time, so we quit.

It was then I realized what she needed—what I needed, too—wasn't the sex: It was the closeness of it, the feel of another human being who cared enough about you just to lie close and not want anything more. What it was was friendship. Corny, right? But that's what it was. We each needed a friend, and that's what we got. Character, right? I didn't understand what it meant, though, not then. I never claimed to be wise.

I'm not sure I really began to understand until I read through all my work all over again. Out loud, right there in the middle of the biggest wasteland in America, with the cold wind blowing outside, rattling the bones of memory and scuttling across the sandy rocks, and a more beautiful woman than I'd ever imagined being with planning to take them and make me into somebody once more. You see, the more I read, the more I really thought about it, the sadder I got. The more I realized that the whole thing was a huge mistake, and for once, I resolved not to make it.

I felt like some guy who had made a wrong turn somewhere. There he is, going down the road, congratulating himself for having such a smooth highway underneath him. And then, Wham! He realizes he's heading in the wrong goddamned direction, going the wrong way, and it's too late to turn back. So he stops, gets out, and shoots the fucking car. It doesn't do much good, but it makes him feel better, you know. Like it's the car's fault and not his that he's ruined the whole trip.

I don't expect anyone to understand that, let alone sympathize with it. How can you sympathize with a guy who's dedicated his life to being a fully realized son of a bitch? You can only read his work *and try to see what the connection really is. But you never will. I thought it was poetry and sex, you see. But it wasn't. It was poetry and loneliness.*

I once met this baseball player, a pitcher who couldn't go the distance, and he told me that he had just been sent down for the fourth and last time.

"Nobody understands," he said over a beer we were sharing in some motel bar in some town I can't remember the name of. "You stand out there on the mound, and it's just you and the fucking batter. And you may know the guy. You may even like the guy. Hell, he could be your brother. But it doesn't matter. You still have to strike him out, or throw trash at him until he pops up. You can't give him a break, because if you do, you fuck yourself. And that's on your mind, and the fans yelling at you are on your mind, and the score's on your mind, and so's your ERA and your shoulder, which hurts like hell because you're a year older now than you were a year before, and so's your contract, and so's your wife who's probably balling somebody in your own bed while she watches the game on TV, and so's your kid who's in Little League but who you've never seen play because you're on the road all the fucking time, and so's the catcher who said he'd whip your ass if you shake him off more than three times and don't get a strike-out—and he can do it, too, because he's five years younger and in a whole lot better shape— and so's the fact that you can't quit because you're earning six figures and everybody, from the fucking owners to the fucking Mercedes dealer to the fucking orthodontist to your fucking in- laws, is counting on you, and so's everything else in the world except that pitch you have to throw.

"That's loneliness," he said and drained his beer. "Nobody can understand that kind of loneliness."

But I could. Because I was a poet. But I didn't tell him that. Besides, there was a good chance I was the guy in bed with his wife.

So I took every poem and put them into the fire. Burned all of them. The old stuff and the new stuff. I burned the criticism, too, or what I had left of it. I just fucking burned them. And I burned the loneliness with it.

The only poem I kept was "Ode to Joy." It reminds me of something I need reminding of every now and then, every time I think I might have made some horrible mistake. So I framed it. And I hung it on the wall just over my desk, because, above all others, that one is worth hanging.

So, outside of moldy volumes in libraries and sun-crinkled books on the dashboards of tourists' mini-vans, I don't exist. It's a good feeling: I'm free, for the first time in years, maybe the first time in my life. I'm totally free.

It's nice not to be any more: It gives you a tremendous sense of responsibility.

Now, after all this time, I can get through the night alone and without a panic, without the poems. I can deal with my loneliness. They don't come anymore, and if they show up, I'll blow them away with an old shotgun I bought just for that purpose. The Hemingway Economy Plan: Buy Now and Avoid the Rush: two barrels, no waiting. They know that, you see, and they leave me alone. I don't need to drink or smoke myself to death any longer, either. In fact, I don't drink at all. The coughing has eased up, and the pain in my throat is gone. And I don't need a woman beside me to fulfill something in me that I thought was so goddamned important.

And, you know what? I discovered something: I like women. Not the way you probably think I mean that: I really like them, respect them, admire them. They've got it all over men, you know, and not for all the reasons I used to think were true. They're just more sure of themselves, have a better handle on who they really are, where they're going, where they want to be. I've been reading some work by some really good writers. And a lot of them are women. It doesn't seem to make any difference. But then, it never really did.

But I still see women—socially, I think is the proper expression—now and then. There's this lady named Carlotta, half-Mexican, half-Apache, she claims—who runs cattle just south of here. She has four sections of her own and leases two more. She's a hell of a shot with any weapon, but I think she's a better cook and bullshitter than anybody I've ever known. The only thing I can cook she'll eat is venison stew.

She's two years older than I am, and probably forty pounds heavier. But her health is better. She's stronger, too. On Wednesdays, she stops by to get me, and we let her hired man, Ramón, run the business for a while. We drive into El Paso, eat some really hot New Mexican-style enchiladas with salsa verde, and then we go dancing. Sometimes, we check into a room at the Holiday Inn, and we sleep together and don't get back until Friday afternoon.

But we don't always have sex. Some nights, we just lie in the dark and hold each other, and that's enough for both of us. Shades of the past? Not hardly. Not even character or friendship. This is something altogether new. For me, at least.

Tell you the truth, I think we're in love. We might even get married one of these days. She has one of the most important qualities I think anybody, man or woman, can have: She hates my poetry. In fact, she hates poetry in general. It's not that she doesn't know anything about it or that she "never was no good in English." She comes from money, and she's well-educated—Vassar, to satisfy her mother, and A&M for an MBA, to satisfy her father—it's just that unless it's got twin fiddles and a steel guitar backing it up, she wants no part of it. "Give me a western," she says, "maybe a Zane Grey. That's all the poetry I need, except, maybe, for an oldie by Marty Robbins."

Tell you another truth: That's about all the poetry I can stand these days, myself. I wonder why I never appreciated it before? Maybe it's because I was so totally fucked up, so totally committed to my own ideas of art that I couldn't see it when it was standing—or two-stepping—right in front of me.

In a way, I think it was always my destiny to be a poet. But in a much bigger way, it was my curse, too. I wanted to be somebody, something important, to have people respect me, because I knew, I guess, they never would like me, would never be my friends. I never gave them a chance, and that's my fault. But I made it on my own, without them, and I hurt a lot of people along the way, hurt myself, too. And in the end it really didn't amount to anything. The poetry, you see, doesn't really matter. It's the poet. And that, gentle auditor, was always the point after all.

Clay Reynolds has written six previous novels, including *The Vigil, Franklin's Crossing* (Pulitzer Prize entrant and Violet Crown winner) *Players* and *Monuments* (Spur finalist and also a Violet Crown winner). His most recent book is *The Tentmaker*. A professional editor and consultant, Reynolds is author of more than 700 publications ranging from nonfiction books to short fiction to book reviews and scholarly articles. An NEA Fellow, he is a member of the Texas Institute of Letters and presently serves as Professor and Associate Dean for Arts and Humanities at the University of Texas at Dallas.